Loyalty And Integrity.

W.L. (Stan) MARTIN

Loyalty & Integrity

Originally titled:-
"MY FRIEND, PATRICK O'REILLEY."
By: W.L.(Stan) Martin

Editors:- *John Lawrence Reynolds*
Neville L. Nunes.

Canadian Cataloguing in Publication Data

Martin, Stan, 1942-
Loyalty and Integrity

ISBN 0-9682646-0-3

I. Title.

PS8576.A.786L69 1996 C813'.54 C97-017470-5
PR9199.3.M37L69 1996

Photograph by:- *Stephanie Tula. Studio Times Photography.*
Cover drawing by:- *Garry Strong.*
Designed by:- *Stan Martin and Stephanie Tula.*
Printed in Canada: *International Print Brokers*

EAN # 978ISBN # 0-9682646-0-3

Second Edition

Published and Distributed in Canada By:-
Capricornus Enterprises.
Hamilton, Ontario.
Phone(905) 574-0043
Fax(905) 574-2404
E-Mail martinwl@netinc.ca

Preface

This book is about a span of my life and a Company of highly trained Commandos - one hundred and forty-five men plucked from different regiments, each trained as specialists and some of the people who had assisted me to get through it.

Most of the training related to jungle guerrilla warfare and terrorism, in preparation for dangerous assaults on enemies in Southeast Asia and served in Singapore, Malaya, Borneo, Aden, Kuwait, Kashmir, Cambodia, Vietnam and Cyprus. The Company, which was never publicly acknowledged or named by the military, enjoyed great freedom with little or no accountability to local commands, and occasionally was the official escort for the numerous military intelligence agents that operates throughout that region.

The Company was divided in two halves. One half commanded by a Captain Peter Cameron and the other by a Captain Mark Harrison. Each half was split into units of twelve, except for ours, which had thirteen. Everyone, it seemed, was willingly defying the age old army superstitions of three men on a match, walking under a ladder, the black cat and the unlucky thirteen adage, to retain friendships.

It is these thirteen Special Forces men to whom this book is dedicated, and to the three women in my life at that time, who helped me to learn about love and to cope with the aftermath of a devastating military experience. It is also dedicated to some of my respected relatives and life-long friends who maintained contact with me, even though I was negligent in corresponding with them.

I want to recognize Sergeant-Major Cyril (Tashie) Wickham, a very astute gentleman and humanitarian and a friend, who taught me the essence of truth, honesty and respect for my life and others.

But it is especially dedicated to Patrick

Monaghan O'Reilley–a decent dedicated honest person and teacher of my political awareness. He eventually became a very active IRA officer for the defence of his own country, and later became a victim of the same society in which he had served well. It is also dedicated to his family in Belfast Ireland.

In Memory of:-

Cornelius Zachariah Martin, Ethlyn Veronica Martin, Leonie Yvonne Martin.

In Respect to the Originals

Corporal	Patrick Monaghan O'Reilley
Private	Thomas Matheson
Private	Ian Mulligan
Private	Charley Green
Lance Corporal	Robert Muldoon
Private	Philip Hoyt
Lance Corporal	Jack O'Leary
Corporal	Stan Martin

In Respect to the Others

Private	Anthony (Skinny) Williams
Corporal	Rodney Langley
Private	Cecil Brown
Sergeant	Bill (Taffy) Llewellyn
Private	Peter Baron
Private	Dave Powell
Private	Derrick MacIntosh

"If I had to choose between betraying my country and betraying my friend, I hope I should have the guts to betray my country."

E.M. Forester;
(What I believe. Two cheers for democracy.)

NOTE:-

Some names in this book have been changed to protect people, living or dead. Any resemblance to others is strictly coincidental.

Mark Harrison

Died on the flight from Toronto to London two days after the events. A broken man, he could not subdue his hate for other people. "So he lived; So he died."

Catharine Harrison

We met by coincidence and became very good friends. She proved to me that love come in strange places and in different ways to some people. She died at age 63 at her family home in Somerset England.

Doctor-Major Helen Butterworth

A very dear friend and lover, who taught me how to have fun and to control my psyche, how not to become too endredged in military affairs. She died in 1979 from a stroke, after her ordeal with Mark Harrison and the military court.

Lloyd Compton

Now a very successful businessman in England. His real name was never told to him nor the relationship between his mother and I. That secret will stay forever.

Fiona McDougall

A wonderful woman to whom I owe a lot. She showed me love, affection and respect. Life with her could have been good, if I had been brave enough to try. I have no knowledge of her whereabouts, since her marriage and name change, but I say thanks and good luck to her for all that she had contributed to my life.

Sergeant-Major Wickham

Cyril (Tassie) Wickham died in 1965 in Chelsea London, England. I sincerely hope that his wife Mary and children did go to live in Jamaica as promised.

Patrick Monaghan O'Reilley

Shot dead in Toronto, Canada by the authorities, on the say so of Mark Harrison. True or false, he died attempting to change his country of birth to match his views of justice.

“I was born in Kingston Jamaica, January 6th 1942, to a loving and strong-willed mother, Ethlyn Veronica Martin and a very astute, politically involved father, Cornelius Zachariah Martin.

I would like to take this moment to thank Half-Way-Tree School in the 1956-7 era and Excelsior College, for the opportunity to have met and befriended many people who remained life-long friends to this date. To name a few:- Anne Stephanie Mathilda Golding, without whose advise, I wouldn’t have got this far. Theo and Fay Golding, George Walters, living in New York City. Armon White, who served in the Royal Engineers and is now owner of a successful security company in Jamaica. Johnnie Johnson, Neville Chung and Lloyd Campbell. To the teachers at Tulse Hill Secondary School in London, England.

I would like to thank my cousins Lorna Smith, Barbara and Shirley Gordon for their assistance throughout the hard times. To my children for being my therapy unbeknownst to them. Stephaney, Sonia, Suzanne and Sherwin. I would also like to thank my partner Amnah Small and great friend Vince Hall for their encouragement to complete this twenty plus years project.

Lastly, to the Military, where I received the most valuable education I could ever hope for. It gave me the opportunity to see many parts of our beautiful planet and to meet some very interesting people in so doing. Thus this story.”

The Author.

CONTENTS

Chapter One

THE END.

"A Death in Toronto."

I walked into the dimly lit room and heard the creek of the door as I pushed it open all the way. My knees were trembling as I gasped for breath from running up them damn stairs.

"Old age," I thought. "But how could I be so exhausted? I am only forty?" I yelled out aloud, trying to convince my mind of the feelings in my body. Oh how I remembered those six days' events, yet who could have forgotten them. I was shot at, beaten up twice and the scotch I was drinking caused my head to ache and my temples to pound.

"As they say, the legs are the first to go," I whispered.

It's been six days since all this shit began and I haven't had a minute of sleep.

I took a quick glance around the dimly lit, moldy-smelling room trying to get my eyes to adjust to the lighting. I tried hard to hold my breath without success, due to my exhausted physical state. Slowly I could make out the people present in amongst the smoke. It seemed like everybody from the old cloak and dagger spy school was there. I recognized Inspector Webster of the Metropolitan Toronto Police, leaning against the dirty window. The two RCMP officers, or whatever they were-I knew only as Melvin and Jack, with three others whom I had never seen before. In a corner, sitting reverse- straddle style on a rickety looking three-legged chair, was old Captain Mark Harrison, my regimental company commander of yester years. That son of a bitch.

Yes, the same son of a bitch who roped me into this bag of shit in the first place.

My focus and breathing were returning to normal, as I grew angrier. I started across the room pointing my finger at Harrison's face with a left-hook on my mind, but before I could reach him, my eyes caught the broken down bed and the body laying across it.

"Paddy!" I shouted in my mind and stopped dead in my tracks. The shock of seeing Paddy O'Reilley's body, started the pounding in my head again. I'm not even sure if that was his real name, but it was the only name I knew him by, since we met at training camp in Aldershot many years ago.

"What's going on?" I shouted in thoughts. "Paddy an IRA soldier? Paddy a spy and gunrunner, as they say?"

They asked me to identify this man who had served alongside me for four years and thirteen days, and whom have been my friend throughout those times. But the big question in my mind is still,

"Who the hell is this man? Is it really Patrick O'Reilley's body, but the face of Charley Leyland of Lethbridge, Alberta?" I asked myself.

As I stood there flabbergasted, my tired mind reflected on the past, drifting back to twenty odd years hence. My knees grew weaker as my body and mind became numb, stricken with the realization that I actually knew that person, or what was left of him laying across the bed, dead. The memory of long-ago days brought tears to my eyes. This was the end, the end of life for someone I once knew.

"Why was he killed?" I asked Captain Harrison. "Was it hate for his political ideology? Or just the way he combs his hair?"

He sat there with a smirk on his face. I looked around the room again, trying to get an answer from somebody, but I might as well have been talking to the wall because nobody offered any explanation. I stood in the same position for some time, just staring at the dead body. It seemed like a long span of time before I heard the voice behind me. It was that of Inspector Webster.

"Do you know this man?" he asked.

I tried to speak, but nothing came out. I could only nod my head. Then I heard him say to the others,

"That's affirmative. Make the record show that Mr Martin has made a positive I.D. of the deceased person in our custody."

He placed his hand on my shoulder.

"Thank you sir," he said as he turned in a very military fashion and walked towards the door.

"Take care of things here Peter, see you at the office," he shouted over his shoulder.

I was still in a daze, my mind unable to comprehend all that had happened in such a short space of time. I turned to look at Captain Harrison. I could feel that same sneer of hate on my face, but my thoughts of striking the SOB had subsided. I slowly approached and asked him to tell me the story of all this. He just nodded his head up and down, indicating that he would and felt a faint smile within my stomach as I watched his double chin bounce around his fat ugly face. After several nods, he finally detached himself from the old chair, shook his wrinkled pants straight then came over to me. He put his arm around my waist and in a whisper told me that we would have lunch the next day, at which time he would give me the entire tale. I took another look around the room, everybody stood there poker-faced. I didn't ever look at the body on the bed, I turned and walked towards the door pretending that none of this ever happened.

I headed for the streets, totally unconscious of the direction or how far I had parked, but I found my car and got in. I could still hear Mark Harrison's voice in my head shouting the same question over and over again,

"Is it him? Tell me Stan. Is the body Patrick's? I've got to know!"

Heading home to Hamilton, I kept thinking of those old days, the day we met at the Aldershot train station and the flamboyant attitude he projected on arrival.

I cannot remember how fast or how slow I drove, but all I knew was that a person I knew had been killed and I didn't really understand why. My mind kept going back to our first day in Aldershot and the subsequent friendship that developed throughout those years in the army, and the education I received by associating with him.

“Aldershot, England,” I silently laughed. “Now, there’s a place of history.”

I arrived home without any incidents, took a good long hot shower, poured myself a double shot of scotch and went to bed with my thoughts.

Chapter Two

"In the Beginning."

The morning seemed bright, although it had been raining all night and could smell the dew from the partially opened window.

"But when does it not rain in London?" I asked myself
Anyway, the days' weather really was unimportant because I was off to a new adventure, to somewhere unknown. I was on my way to a military induction centre in the south of England. I laid in bed and took a long look around my room, and the thought of not sleeping in that room for some time, gave me a chill. I wondered what was in store for me, but as a young adventurer, my mind kept telling me that it would be like all my previous adventures. I had tracked across Europe with my friends by hitch-hiking, stealing rides on trains, busses and boats. So this expedition was nothing. What could happen in the army? They said I would see the world and I had all intention of doing just that. It would be almost the same, except I would be doing it with a lot of other people.

"Yes sir," I thought, "those other blokes would be there too."

The feeling of knowing Alpine, who had joined a few months earlier, and myself would be reunited again, thrilled me immensely. Armon and I knew each other since boyhood, so I was ready for it and it would all be a reality in a matter of hours.

"Boy, do we have some plans!" I thought excitedly.

I sprung out of bed, rushed to the shower and was dressed in a short time. My suitcase, packed from the night before, were already sitting at the door. I quickly dashed downstairs to kiss my cousins and my brother farewell and although they weren't happy that I had signed on with the army and to see me leave, they wished me luck. They had tried to talk me out of it, thinking that I should have tried to dodge the draft notice because I was doing so well in school. But then again, they did not know that whenever the Queen wants you, you have to go.

"When one is drafted," I told them, "one doesn't have any recourse than to go where they tell you to go. And camp Bordon in Hampshire, seemed to be my go place."

I really didn't want to go there, but it's either that or directly to jail, and at age eighteen, I didn't think well of spending my days in a prison, especially the Scrubs or Brixton. So I decided that the best thing to do was to go where they sent me, and seeing that some of my friends were also drafted, I thought it might be fun. I grabbed my suitcase.

"Goodbye for now people," I said, yelling over my shoulder as I dashed for the door, thinking that I didn't want to miss the train.

At Goose Green, the corner of Lordship Lane and Peckham Rye, I paused to absorb the scenery. Trying to fix in my mind what the place looked like at this time until I return, whenever that will be. I wasn't too sure at the moment, but I was positive that I would see it again.

"Why me anyway?" I asked myself as I briskly walked along the street toward the bus stop. "I was doing well in school and with the girls, so why the hell me?"

I stopped to say hello to Mr Horowitz, the old newspaper man, who had been selling papers there for years. I told him of my expedition to the army and he wished me well. I never did find out what nationality he and his brother Herman was, although I had spoken to them on a daily basis for as long as I can remember.

Herman owns the green grocery where I worked after school delivering orders. He always praised me for working hard for the money to purchase my bicycle. I ran across the street to catch the bus to Elephant and Castle and then the Underground to Waterloo Railway station.

I had no difficulty in finding platform 23. I parked my suitcase at the gate and decided to walk around the station for a while. It was a thrill to walk through Waterloo station. To me, it's the largest and most attractive station in all of London, although I do enjoy Kings Cross-St.Pancras and Paddington also, but I liked Waterloo the best; and dared anyone to try to convince me differently. The architecture and art works within this station fascinates me and I felt proud to walk among the thousands of daily travellers, that used that station. I wanted to shout to all of them that I was going to serve the Queen's army.

"But then," I thought, shrugging my shoulders, "what would they care? Maybe they are doing the same thing also."

I got on the train and found, what I thought, was a very comfortable empty car and settled in. Since it was April and it does feel like spring, I opened a window to let in a breath of fresh air hoping that nobody would come in to complain of the cold.

I removed my overcoat and laid myself down on the seat to relax, feeling good knowing that I would be seeing the boys in a few hours. As the train started to pull away, I jumped up and looked out the window to watch the city slowly drift away from me.

"See ya, old smokes!" I shouted at the air, and repeated the statement a dozen times to make sure that it was heard.

I was so engrossed in my thoughts, that I didn't hear someone entering the car, and only came back to reality when I heard a voice say,

"Going to the services are you?"

Quickly I jerked my head back inside the window, banging it as I did, to notice a very attractively good-looking woman standing at the door. She wore a knee-length silky-looking, low cut navy blue and white dress, that seemed to know all of her curves personally. Her matching high-heeled shoe gave her the appearance of being taller than her five foot five frame. The pale orange ribbon on her blue broad-rimmed hat, seemed to be in contrast with her shoulder length honey blond hair and her dark pink complexion.

The glare from her baby-blue eyes seemed to dance their hypnotic powers, while her broad pearly-teeth smile mesmerised her prey.

"May I come in?" she asked whilst removing her coat. She had already placed her bags on the seat.

"Sure, sure," I said, "you can come in."

"Thank you. Can you please put my bags up top for me?" she asked.

I couldn't help but notice her shapely figure.

"Oh boy, this train ride could be very interesting," I thought.

But my excitement came to an abrupt end when I noticed that she was wearing a large diamond ring on her left third finger. I quickly carried out her request and sat myself down, quietly.

"So tell me young man," she said after settling into the seat. "what division and company will you be joining?" she asked as she tugged at the hem of her dress after crossing her long beautiful luscious legs.

"I know," she said without waiting for my reply, "Aldershot, right?. You're going to Aldershot, aren't you?"

"Yes I am," I replied. "Are you from Aldershot?" I asked.

"No, but I live there," she answered. "You see, my husband is an officer in the Service Corps and Paratrooper regiments, that's why I have to live there."

"Oh good!" I said excitedly. "That's where I'm going to be stationed, maybe I will see you there sometime."

"I would like that very much," she replied, "but it would almost be impossible seeing that you will be a private ranked soldier and all. And never will we cross paths with officers and their families."

I really didn't understood what she was talking about, but I nodded my head that I did. We talked for almost an hour as she told me everything she thought I should know about Aldershot and the surrounding areas. I felt I knew the whole damn place after she was finished. While the conversation was not boring, I was busy looking at her legs and getting hornier by the minute, wondering what it would be like to screw an older woman. I couldn't estimate her age but was afraid to ask.

Throughout our conversation, she kept pulling her dress and

deliberately crossing and uncrossing those luscious legs exposing her crotch, tantalizing me.

"How old are you?" she finally asked.

"Eighteen years and three months," I replied proudly.

"Mmmm, well the army think you're old enough for their purpose I suppose," she said in a matter-of-fact way.

"I presume so," I answered. "I have to do a compulsory two and a half years and I am not sure what I'm going to meet there."

"Do you have any friends currently serving?" she asked. "You'll need a friend or two to make life bearable in the army," she suggested smiling and quickly added. "But then again there are always the WRAC's."

"WRAC's? What are they?" I stupidly asked.

She lean forward and looked at me with her eyes squinting.

"You really mean that you're not aware of the Women's Royal Army Corps?"

"No," I admitted, "I've never heard of them."

"Ha, ha, ha." she laughed.

"What! What did I say wrong?" I asked nervously. "Are you one of them? Hope I didn't offend you."

"No, my sweet naive young man," she said. "But there are literally thousands of these horny women in Bordon and Aldershot. You're going to meet some of them and your two and a half years will quickly disappear. As a matter of fact you will not have to go looking for them, they will find YOU."

"Are you saying that they freely have sex there?" I asked.

My curiosity was aroused.

"Yes," she smiled, showing off those beautiful teeth again. "You are going to have enough to last you a life time."

I leaned back against the seat thinking of all the sex I was about to have with all those WRAC's in Aldershot.

"Have you any experience with women?" she asked. "I mean, have you ever had a bunkup?"

"Sure," I boasted, "with a couple of......."

"Your sister's friends in the bathroom I suppose," she said interrupting me.

"But I did screw with an older married woman once," I said trying to sound mature.

"Oh! So you're a wife seducer too, I see," she giggled.

"It wasn't like that," I tried to explain. "You see, this woman was a good friend of my older brother and she had asked me to repair something in her bedroom and secretly locked the door behind us. She took all her clothes off and we..., you know, did it."

"Was it good?" she asked.

"Excellent," I boasted, "she was excellent."

"Then where was her husband, when this IT was going on?" she asked.

"At work I suppose," I replied. "But we never done it again after that; although she tried on other occasions to get me into her room."

There was a long silence. Then she leaned forward, allowing me the sight of her firm rounded breasts.

"Okay, so what's the problem soldier?" she asked. "Afraid to make love on a train?"

There was a long pause again. I could feel the sweat on my brows and a strong nervous feeling in my groin.

"No, it's not that I'm afraid," I stuttered, "it's just that we don't know each other. I don't even know your name."

There was a look of disgust on her face.

"What I'm about to say might shock you, but..." she paused. "To tell you the truth, I have never made love to a black man before and I would like to take this opportunity to do so, because....." she said pointing her finger at my face, "when we reach Aldershot, this relationship would be over forever, like it never happened, so don't disappoint me now."

I sprung out of my seat and beside her in a flash. She smiled a wide smile.

"I think you should lock the door and pull the curtains first, don't you?" she instructed and began removing her clothing. "We don't want to be disturbed now, do we?"

I could see she had done this before by the way she did everything routinely.

For the hour we made love, she taught me things I never knew existed. I thought in my four years since I began having sex, I knew it all. I had experienced a few interesting women during that time and even the first girl I had sex with, was much older then I. But this lady was great.

"Are you not going to tell me your name?" I asked as the train pulled into the station.

"Catharine," she whispered while putting on her coat.

I got up to retrieve her bags from above for her.

"Catharine what?" I pushed.

"Catharine Harrison," she said. "But it won't matter because we will never do this again; not while we are both here in this town, right?"

She said a fast goodbye and left the train as soon as it came to a stop. I stood at the top of the steps observing her rear end, as she walked gracefully towards the car in the parking lot. I could feel a gleaming smile on my face.

"Oh what a wonderful day this has been," I thought.

I could hear a song in my head, but kept my mouth closed.

It was at this tranquil moment when a voice woke me up.

"Hey soldier! Get your arse off them steps and into this lorry," it said.

I looked to see a black Sergeant standing beside a green lorry where most of the new recruits had already loaded themselves into.
I was about to get in when I heard the Sergeant shout for another couple of stragglers. I looked to see three men who seemed slightly intoxicated, playing as they walked towards the truck. They were having fun.

One was a tall six foot plus medium built fellow with fox red hair. His square-jawed, sun-bleached face was clean shaven. The other was about five foot nine and muscularly built with a dark mustache and beard and the third one was much shorter with long shoulder length blond hair, that almost covered his freckled face.

The one with the fox coloured hair fell when he tried to climb into the truck. Everybody let out a roar of laughter. When he finally got himself up and into the truck, he said in his Irish brogue,

"Allow me to introduce myself gentlemen. I'll be Patrick Monaghan O'Reilley from County Cork, and for you English ignoramuses, that's in southern Ireland. And for all the other nig-nogs.... Well, I will take the time to teach you more about that beautiful country."

I noticed he looked at me when he used the word "Nig-Nog."

"Shut your fucking Irish mouth, shithead," said a voice from deep within the truck, "you couldn't recognize anything of beauty. And remember, you're now in the superior part of the Great Briton we've been educating you about."

The others applauded and jeered. O'Reilley replied that it wouldn't be long before changes take place in the north and hoped the English dogs would be ready for it. Until now, I never gave any thought to the Irish problem. As a matter of fact, I knew nothing of its existence. So hearing this kind of conversation only made me wonder why the white people were arguing amongst themselves.

But that intrigued me immensely. It was nice to see them argue and fight, which meant they would leave the blacks alone. I have had to literally fight the Teddy boys in my neighbourhood almost all my life. Many of whom were members of the Mosley brown shirts who liked to beat up on young black people, and since I was a young black person, I had to learn to defend myself from an early age and was very good at doing so. But I sincerely hoped these kinds of hatred wasn't very prevalent in the army. I had hoped that I wouldn't have to be confronted with it in the army, but if I did, then I would fight. I decided to wait and see. I could hear the continuing argument about who was superior and who was inferior to whom. It was only then I remembered I had not eaten anything all day.

"Hey Sarge," I shouted. "When do we eat?"

"When we get to the barracks, you have fifteen minutes to get washed and go to the mess hall," came the answer.

In the billets, all the new recruits were going from room to room introducing themselves to anyone they could find. People of all origins, sizes and colours, were trying to be friendly and to make new acquaintances as quickly as possible. Because I was hungry, I evaded the formalities and hurriedly washed and changed and went off to find the mess hall. As I passed the building of the Officers and NCO's, I met a soldier coming from the general direction and asked him the way, which he did without hesitation.

I got to the mess hall and stood in line. To my amazement, it was the largest dining room I had ever seen. I took as much food as possible. The mess Sergeant made a comment that I could return as many times as I wanted to.

"We have plenty here soldier," he told me, "you don't have to take it all at once."

After I had found a comfortable seat and settled down to eat, I, unsuccessfully, looked around the room to find any of my friends. I slowly eat my food, then went back for more.

After desert, I was about ready to leave when those Irish boys came in. An argument ensued when the mess-sergeant told them that they were late. Mr. O'Reilley promptly informed him that he must be fed because he was there on the request of the Queen, and against his will and wishes. They were both getting rather obnoxious and loud and O'Reilley told him to fuck off.

"Why didn't you stay home and join the IRA?" said the Sergeant.

O'Reilley got even hotter and louder as he became more enraged.

"Yes, you bastard," O'Reilley shouted in his Irish brogue, "some day I will."

He began beating himself on the chest with the palm of his hand. Just then a well-dressed officer entered the mess hall. The Sergeant and the other workers stood very erect and saluted him as the entire place went quiet. The officer spoke very softly to all parties involved and within minutes he had the Sergeant apologising to Patrick.

Patrick took his food and started to walk towards the tables. I watched with much surprise and amazement as the officer stuck out his leg and tripped him. There was Patrick laying sprawled on the floor with food all over him, even in his fox-red hair. The officer apologised for the accident and bent down to assist Patrick to his feet, everybody laughed. I kept my head straight, smiling to myself as I walked out the door.

"W " square, for a soldier in training is holy grounds, as I found out that evening after leaving the mess hall on my way back to the billets. I thought it would be shorter if I walked straight across the paved field. But as I got approximately two hundred yards on it, I heard a voice holler.

"Soldier," the voice said. It was a Scottish tone of voice.

I turned around not knowing who the voice was directed at, but there weren't anyone else around.

"Who me?" I asked, as the person came closer to me.

He was muscular medium-built man of about five foot ten, with closely trimmed blondish-brown hair. His tough unsmiling red Scottish face sported a large handle bar mustache that moved as he spoke. He was dressed in a tan coloured uniform, with many service medal ribbons and a large crown on the sleeve.

"Yes you nig-nog," the person said. "What do you think you are doing walking across this parade square?"

"I didn't know what this place was," I replied, "and what is a parade square?"

"You'll find out in a few weeks time," he shouted again.

"I really don't care for parades," I told him.

He began to laugh and quickly introduced himself.

I am Regimental Sergeant-Major Wickham and as long as you live, which might be a short time, never let me catch you walking on my parade square again. Unless you are in uniform and in regulation time."

"What's that?" I asked.

He promptly gave me a lecture on the required conduct of a soldier in training.

"Be at my office tomorrow afternoon, after your introduction and clothing issue, and I'll tell you," he said as he turned away.

I thought about all of this as I strolled to the billets. When I arrived, I found the noise level had risen ten decibels higher than when I had left. Everybody was trying to out do the other with their stories of home and I could clearly see that some were desperately trying to intimidate others. I walked over to the bed I was assigned on arrival, took my shirt off and stretched myself out. Now that I have had my food, nothing else really mattered, except to find my friends.

I laid there with my eyes closed meditating. I could sense a shadow standing over me and slowly opened one eye slightly to see it was the noisy red haired Irishman standing there. I closed my eyes again and asked him what he wanted. He explained that he felt a compulsion to talk to me.

"You seemed like a good sort," he said.

I reminded him of his rather derogatory statement at the train station about Nig-Nogs and he laughed.

"The term nig-nog dear fellow," he said, "refers to the new recruits not the colour of your skin. I'm a nig-nog, everyone of us here is a nig-nog, so don't feel offended."

I opened my eyes again and angrily asked him what he wanted. He first asked me if he could sit on my bed and I told him no. He stood there for a long moment, then with very selected words, he asked me to just listen to him for a moment and he would explain the reason he choose me.

"It's because you are not white and look like an intelligent person," he said.

I laughed at that statement, as I sat up to hear more.

"You may sit on the floor," I said, "because there are no chairs in this room."

He stared at me for a while, then he obeyed and sat as directed.

"Now," I said, "speak your mind and don't waste my fucking time."

He smiled and again introduced himself, then began his story. He told me about his place of birth and the beautiful scenery around it. He talked of his family's move to Belfast from Cork and of the people there.

"I'll have to take you there someday to meet my family," he said.

He talked about the things they had to do for a living and of his younger days in school, with him observing his parents and other relatives suffer discrimination in their own land. At this point I felt the urge to interrupt him.

"How could YOU proclaim yourself discriminated against, when your colour is white?" I asked.

He laughed heartily as he replied.

"Stan my boy, some people are not mistreated only because of their colour. I can see that I will have to re-educate you nig," he said with a smile.

I was about to get angry again, then something came to my mind.

"This man, which at first appeared to be an idiot, turned out to be a very educated and intelligent individual. Maybe I should at least listen to him," I thought.

He told me about the religious and political discrimination within his country and I again questioned his discrimination statement.

"Why would this be so, when you are all white?" I asked.

"I can see I will definitely have to re-educate you," he said. "You have been knowledge starved by the English."

"What!?" I exclaimed. "What the hell is knowledge starved?"

"It's like sex starve, but this is brain food," he replied tapping his head.

I felt like laughing but he was becoming interesting so I listened. He went on about the different political and religious policies of the English, as applied to Ireland, which they have used to divide his country.

"They took over the north by fraudulent means and had implemented laws that has prevented the Catholic Irish people from excelling in many areas within their birth place. I will definitely have to introduce you to some history books," he said. "But in time. We'll meet again to talk, okay?"

I in turn, when I got the opportunity to, spoke of the black struggle to have barriers broken down in England also. I was seeking to understand the Irish problem and drawing a parallel between my people and his. For the two hours that we chatted, I never found boredom within. As a matter of fact, I was fascinated.

When he was leaving he stretched out his hand for a shake. I hesitated for a moment, then took his.

"Friends?" he asked.

"Friends," I replied.

He left for his room and I went to bed with a lot of thoughts.

"Well he seemed to be a nice person," I said, "but I will have to tell him that I still don't like to be addressed as Nig and secondly I don't appreciate having my thought periods rudely interrupted. He want to be my friend, but I hope he's not queer."

On my second day in that camp, I discovered that a new Squady does not do anything to upset the Sergeant-Major, if he has intentions of living to a ripe old age. Mr Wickham had told me to make myself available at his office that morning, after collecting the clothing the army thought I needed to have for whatever they had planned for us. I discovered that nothing fits, so I had to visit the tailors to have then adjusted, for a fee of course. I am now beginning to understand that everything cost money in the Queen's army. I found my way to his office, but although the door was opened, I knocked anyway. I could clearly see him sitting at his desk engrossed in something in front of him. Without lifting his head he said,

"Come in private Martin, and don't sit," he said as if he had read my mind. "Now allow me to tell you that I'm the law in this camp. I don't stand for horse shit from anyone. When I tell a soldier to do something, he will do it and more. Any deviation from my instructions will mean, I shall have his guts for garters."

There was a pause because I wasn't sure if I was supposed to answer.

"Do you understand me soldier?" he shouted again.

"Yes sir," I stuttered.

To admit, he had me intimidated. But before I could piss my pants, he got up from the chair, stuck out his hand and said,

"Welcome to my camp soldier, if you keep your nose clean and your fingers dirty, we'll get along very good."

"Thank you sir," I replied through a forced smile.

We talked for almost an hour as he told me everything he thought I should know about the place. Then as I was about to leave, he again stuck out his hand for a shake.

"We will meet again in four weeks time only our return from camp Bordon," he said.

"Thank you sir," I replied.

As I was walking to the billets thinking about what Sergeant-major Wickham had said, I didn't see Sergeant Dawkins, the black sergeant at the train station, coming towards me.

"I see you've already met the Governor," he said smiling.

His emphasis on governor, was like describing the Duke of Edinburgh.

"Yes, and I think he's a fine gentleman," I replied.

"Oh, that he is young man, that he is. You will never regret meeting him and if you behave like a real person should, he would assist you to greater heights in the army. Remember now, in this man's army everybody needs some kind of assistance and or friendship for survival and for advancement."

We stood there talking for about fifteen minutes, then he shook my hand and told me that we would meet again when I returned from camp Bordon.

By the time I reached the billets, almost everyone knew that I was talking to the Sergeant-Major. Word got around like wild fire. Many came asking questions about what I perceived him to be. I felt like King Shit, having all these idiots around me trying to get information about the Sergeant-Major. This show went on until late that night, but during all that time Patrick sat in a corner without saying anything. After they left, he came over and asked if I really thought Mr Wickham meant what he said. I told him that I was not going to shut anybody out until I was able to make my own summary of their character, and that included himself. He didn't prolong the conversation, he said goodnight and left. That night I slept like a baby.

The next morning the siren sounded at five thirty.

"What the hell's that noise?" I shouted. "I've never heard anything like this in my civilian life," I said.

Then to answer my question, Sergeant Dawkins came in banging his pace stick against the metal lockers.

"Wakey, wakey;" he shouted, " time to be up boys. Come on, come on, time to be up."

We were up, washed and dressed by six forty five ready for breakfast and left for camp Bordon. The lorries were ready to roll by eight o'clock sharp. There was total silence as we got loaded in for the boring uneventful trip to this unknown destination.

Finally the lorries turned into the gates of camp Bordon, with a large sign above that said, 1st. Battalion REME. It didn't seem like a bad place and could see the hospital across the street with nurses walking about.

"Hey you arseholes, look!" I pointed towards the hospital. "Nurses and lots of them," I said.

"Lot's of bunk-ups now," someone shouted.

"Or a gobble," shouted another.

They all seemed to be awakened at this time.

"This could be a nice and interesting place to be," I thought, remembering what Catharine Harrison had told me about meeting the WRAC's.

We were directed to a set of billets at the far end of the camp and were told to secure our beds and kit then make our way to the mess-hall for dinner.

"How long are we staying in this camp?" I asked Patrick.

"About eight weeks, I am not sure. Why?" he replied.

"It will give me time to get to know some of them WRAC nurses," I said.

He sat there smiling.

"You randy little Bastard, you're going to kill yourself fucking," he said.

"I know," I said grinning. "But what a way to go."

We both laughed and continued having our meal.

Dinner was good. It seemed as though the army was trying desperately to please us. I felt impressed and proud to be a part of this establishment. As we were leaving the mess hall I spotted one of my friends and ran over to greet him. It was Charley Green, a Jamaican fellow who also attended Tulse Hill secondary school. We spoke as we walked back to the billets. He suggested we take a walk aroundthe camp later to find the others. It appeared that the army was on a large recruitment drive for some reason, because there were literally many thousands of us in that camp. When we did find the others it was like Christmas all over again.

We spent almost the entire afternoon talking about old days and planning for new adventures, with the help of the army of course. It was generally agreed that since we were there, we might as well take advantage of their generosity, without knowing what they had planned for us.

The following day was when the fun started. Firstly, we had to have a medical at the Hospital. Which was not too bad because we were now going to meet the nurses. The excitement started to build.

"Meeting all those lovely looking female-type WRAC nurses," I thought.

But on reaching the hospital, we were told to remove all of our clothing and wrap only with a towel and to form a line along the corridor wall. I cannot comprehend why hospitals always felt cold and smell funny. Anyway, I didn't care about that, my only thought were of those pretty nurses. We stood in that cold place for over an hour shivering and shouting obscenities at the nurses as they went about their duties mechanically. Patrick came beside me.

"I think they keep this damn place cold only to keep control our hormones," he said though chattering teeth.

"It sure seem so," I replied.

Then it was my turn to go in. I walked into the office and automatically turned to closed the door behind me. A kind of husky voice told me to drop the towel and turn around. I did and turned around to find standing before me, a female doctor. She was dressed in those green garbs that covered everything, with a cap to match. I tried to reach the towel, but she ordered me to stand straight.

"Now young man," she said, "you are in the army now and things are done differently here than in civvy street. If you're shy, you'll learn to get over it and to get used to female doctors fondling your balls."

She wasn't smiling, only a plastic look on her face. After checking every other part of my body, she finally reached down and took hold of my nuts and told me to cough. She looked in my face and smiled.

"Very good," she said, "I can see some randy young nurse is going to have a pleasurable time with you."

I didn't make any comments or even try to change my facial expression, as I wasn't sure of her thoughts.

"Now, get your towel and leave," she ordered.

But as I bent to retrieve the towel, she stuck her finger in my arse hole. That was a shocker within itself. After a brief moment, she withdrew her finger and told me to leave. This time I faced her when I did reached for the towel.

"You know something lady?" I said angrily. "You've seen and fondled enough peckers that you couldn't enjoy a good bunkup."

She stood there smiling. Then she reminded me that I could be charged for insubordination. I questioned her reasoning and she softly explain.

"A private soldier should speak to an officer in uniform with respect at all times, immaterial of the circumstances, otherwise he could be charged."

"What would happen if the officer was in civvies and not on camp?" I asked.

"That would depend on how the soldier acted and what he said," she answered.

I nodded my head and she winked at me as I passed close to her.

"We will meet again Mr Martin," she said.

"I'm sure we will meet again sir...ma'am, but I hope it will not be under the same circumstances," I replied and left.

I waited until Patrick and Charley got their examination and we were on our way back to camp before asking,

"What do you think of that Doctor in there?" I said. "Imagine she stuck her finger up my arse hole."

"Oh yes, me too!" said Charley. "It really surprised me."

In the mean time Patrick was plainly white and dumbfounded.

"What about you Paddy?" I asked. "What do you think of that?"

A long moment later he replied.

"When the army said it was giving us a complete physical, they meant complete. It's the first time I've ever had anything up there, other than shit," he said.

We all laughed.

"And them damn vaccinations sure hurts," said Charley.

"Yes," I agreed, "four all at once."

"Maybe they brought us here as guinea pigs," said Patrick. "You know, for experimental reasons. They use to do that to soldiers in the Second World War too."

"Shut your mouth," said Charley. "That can't be true."

"Yes," I concurred.

Patrick was serious and very insistent in his statement.

"Believe me friends," he said, "it happens to be true. My father told me so and whenever I can find the books, I'll prove it to you."

With that we walked in silence, to the billets.

For the next four days, I was very sick due to the vaccinations. Finally, Patrick and Charley persuaded the sergeant to send me to the hospital to have my fever checked. They walked me across the street and to the desk to sign in. As I was about to do so, I felt a hand on my shoulder and looked around to see major Butterworth, my favourite female type doctor standing there.

"What's the matter soldier?" she asked in that sing song tone of voice.

"I feel sick ma'am, I'm having a fever," I replied.

Without hesitation she motioned for me to follow her to the examination room.

"Okay fellow," she said, "take your clothes off."

I stood there for a moment, wondering if she was about to put her finger in my arse hole again, but I was too sick to disobey her command. She did a thorough examination of my entire body including the finger bit. Then she had a nurse take my blood and urine for analysis. Finally she called another nurse and instructed her to get me admitted.

"You will be kept in for observation for a few days," she told me.

Immediately another nurse came and I was given something to reduce the fever. All I remembered of that evening is that I sweated like a pig the entire night.

The next morning when I awoke, I was surprised to find that I had slept until past noon. A nurse came in and took my temperature and pulse rate, then someone else brought my dinner. I ate well and felt good, but was told that I couldn't leave until Dr. Butterworth saw me, about seven thirty that evening. So the entire day was spent socializing with the nurses, which I liked very much. I also got some sleep and tea. Finally it was seven thirty. She just barged into the room and seeing that I was the only patient there, she came directly to me.

"Okay soldier, what's your complaint today?" she asked in a perky sing song tone of voice.

I told her that I felt good and wanted to know when I could leave.

"You will leave when I say so," she said smiling.

In the mean time, she had stuck her hand between my legs feeling around my balls again.

"The fever has gone," she said, "you either had a touch of a virus or a reaction to one of the vaccinations. It will be gone in a couple days. Get some rest now and I will be in to check on you tomorrow."

Before I could answer, she rushed out the door.

That night some of my friends came to visit, using me as their excuse. But their intention was only to check out the nurses and the nurses were willing to come by on the minute, to attend me.

"We're making sure the patient is resting well," one of the nurses told me.

But everyone present knew what the game was. The boys chatted with the girls most of the time, not to me. But then I didn't care either, because a cute little Scottish lass took a liking to me and occupied my attention for most of the time. I was in good hands for the rest of the evening. Eventually, my friends were tossed out by the matron at about eight p.m. leaving me alone with Fiona McDougall. We talked about many things that night and arranged to meet another evening, after training.

Doctor Butterworth came bright and early, singing a cheery good morning. She took my chart and sat on my bed beside me.

"Now to enlighten your mind young man," she said grinning, "everything seems to be fine, but I would rather like to keep you in for another day, Just to be sure, mind you."

I took the liberty and placed my hand on her thigh.

"I too am hoping that things will be fine eventually," I said.

She didn't waver or attempt to remove my hand from her thigh, only to remind me that she was an officer and could have me on a 252 sheet, which I found out later, was a charge sheet. But in any case she seemed to be liking it.

"Butterworth!" I said. "What kind of a name is that?" I asked.

"It's just like Martin, a very proper English name," she replied tossing her head back smiling.

"It sounds like saying expensive curdled milk," I joked.

She laughed and we talked for some time about the stupid sound of our names, until a nurse came in to tell her that somebody was waiting for her.

"I'll see you tomorrow," she said as she sprung to her feet, "in the mean time, rest."

She patted my face, waved and breezed out of the room. I laid there watching her leave.

"She likes me," I thought, smiling.

I was released from the hospital at about ten thirty that morning. I strolled across to the barracks as if I were back home in London. Immediately, a Corporal reminded me that I was in the army and for me to take my hands out of my pockets and to look sharp. I went to the office to make sure that they knew I was back. That was a mistake, which I swore never to let happen again, because as soon as they saw me I was given a job washing dishes in the mess, not as punishment mind you, but as a duty. It turned out to be a punishment for being stupid.

When my friends came to tea and saw me washing dishes, I was the laughing stock for the evening. Charley, Ian, Tom, Jack and Patrick came to enquire of my health, and after I assured them that I was feeling good, Patrick commented that Irishmen and Jamaicans are proven stronger than black Englishmen, which was a reference to me. I jokingly waved my fist at them and continued to do my job.

After tea, we decided to walk across the park in hope of seeing the nurses. It seemed that they too were waiting for us. It was nice to see Fiona McDougall again. She had been very attentive to me in the hospital. We had a nice chat in there about herself and her parents. Fiona, at five foot six, appeared taller than the average nurse. Her curly-brunette hair seemed to match her greyish brown eyes and high-lighted her pale tan-like complexion.

"My father was born in Barbados, to a black mother and a Scottish father," she explained. "The family moved to Scotland where he schooled, met and marry my mother. Which means I have some degree of colour within me," she jokingly said.

She talked about being born in Edinburgh on January seventh, one day after me, and joined the army to get away from her parents and her two older brothers.

"I wanted a little independence of my own," she said, "and I would not get that freedom under their wings. So I came here for that purpose."

All that evening I behaved as a gentleman would.

"That is a very lovely name," I told her. "I have never heard of anyone named Fiona before. Is there some significance to it?"

She seemed happy to be with me, constantly holding my hand and smiling.

"Yes, I was named after an eighteenth century Scottish lady," she said, "who had helped young Prince Willy to escape custody and in turn had to serve time in prison for doing so. This showed her love for him, and in the process changed the lives of many women in Scotland at the time. This, I think, inspired my mother to name me after her."

"That's nice to know," I replied, "that your parents found inspiration in someone else's deeds and to name their child in honour of that person. Would you Fiona, have done the same for me?" I asked.

She didn't answer.

When I walked her back to the hospital, she gave me a little kiss.

"After I get to know you some more," she said, " I will let you know how far I would go with you."

We said goodnight and made arrangements to meet the next evening at another part of the park. I stood there and watched as she disappeared within the hospital doors.

I returned to the billets to find it empty. It seemed the others got lucky, except Patrick. I found him sitting on the steps looking dejected and joined him. I enquired of his loneliness and he explained that he was starting to feel home sick, because he didn't have any friends there and he did not feel like drinking. I asked him about his two friends Ian and Jack and he became angry.

"Look Stan," he said angrily. "Although they are southern Irish and are white Catholics, they sometimes behave as ignorant as those Protestants in Londonderry."

"Hey!" I shouted. "There you go again using that racial slur. You're a very bitter man you know? And you talked about the English people who discriminates?"

"Wait a minute!" he said, waving his hand. "Just hold on a fucking minute. I told you of the different kinds of discrimination that exist within us. People hate people for different reasons. I don't hate Ian and Jack personally, I am talking about their attitude. And I bet you have some kind of hate deep inside of you also, and if given the chance, you would kill whomever to defend your feelings."

"Right you are," I agreed. "But I had never denied that fact. I recognize that it's within me, but I would not deliberately do it to anyone."

"But if you think of it," he said, "you might see that I am right."

"Yes, you're right," I replied, "but you're sitting here feeling sorry for yourself when everybody else is out looking for women."

"Yes," he said, "maybe I should be doing that too, but I intend on staying loyal to my lovely girlfriend back home."

"Suit yourself my friend," I said, "but please don't blame anybody else for your inadequacies when it comes to dealing with women or your loneliness. It's your problem, your concern. Or maybe you're queer?"

He did not dignify my remark with any comment. He held his head low as he spoke.

"Friend, when the army conscripted me I wanted to run and hide, but my father said I could meet new friends and broaden my scope of education in the military."

"And he's right," I offered back. "You and I have become friends, right? Also Charley, Jack, Ian and Tom. We are going to be together for a long time. Matter of fact, I am going to sign on as a regular for six or nine years."

"Hey!" he said. "Jack and Ian were talking about the same thing last night. Well, if you lot are going to do it, so would I."

He was now sounding a little more enthusiastic about life.

We sat there for a good hour expressing our thoughts towards the army, religion and politics. Finally some of the boys came home, so we got up and went into the room where the discussions continued. I discovered that like myself, many of them were oblivious to the world's problems and hadn't a clue about anything outside of the community from which they came, and would be arguing wrongfully on a point.

"I can see I will definitely have to take you all under my wings for educational purposes," Patrick told the group. Everybody laughed at his suggestion.

"Go ahead teacher, we are at your disposal," Bob Muldoon said.

The laughs continued until late. Even some of the others from other billets came to hear Patrick speak and found it amusing. Some out right objected to his philosophy, and stayed anyway.

The next couple of weeks were very tiring. We were introduced to the drill parade, which started from after breakfast to lunch and to tea. My friends and I worked our butts off, learning to bull boots and caring for our uniforms, also dressing the army's way. Most of us got our hair cut, whether it was needed or not, which made some of us look strange. The army was making sure we learnt the meaning of "hard labour" the hard way. We didn't even have time to see the girls as regularly as desired, although most of us were hoping to see them on the weekends. In the meantime, we were being prepared for whatever was to come. Drill parade three times daily.

One Friday evening right after tea, I quickly got showered, dressed and headed for the hospital gate to meet my lovely Fiona. I found out that she was on duty for the night. I was furious and was ready to kill the officer or whomever that was responsible for this infringement on my sex life. Anyway all was not lost, because my little Scottish lass ran out to apologise and we made another date for the Saturday night. We talked for a long time until she had to return to the wards. I also spent some time talking to some of the others before they ran off to catch the bus to Aldershot, and to their dates in the NAAFI centre.

My friends tried to convince me to come with them, but I refused their offer. I told them that I was returning to the billets and would see them the next day. When they left, I decided to take a lone walk around the park. I must have walked about twenty minutes before I saw the person coming towards me.

"Hey! what is Major-Doctor Helen Butterworth doing here walking alone in the park?" I asked myself.

As she came closer, I could see her dark shoulder length hair that surround her pear-shaped face. This time it wasn't hidden by the green hospital hat she always wore. Her yellow sweater, although loose, still showed the couture of her large breasts. Her well shaped legs protruded from the baggy, light tan shorts, although it hid her lower body parts well. I made sure that I walked directly at her, but as we came face to face, she pretended not to see me.

"Good evening Doctor Butterworth," I said.

She acted surprised.

"Hello Mister Martin," she replied smiling. "What are you doing walking alone in the park this lovely evening?"

"Well ma'am I...." I began.

"Your girlfriend is on duty, right?" she interrupted. "And please don't call me ma'am. I hate being addressed as ma'am," she said. "My name is Helen."

"But your rank is a...."

"Major," she said. "But you can call me Helen. I gave you permission to call me Helen whenever we are in private, okay?"

"But what if there are other officers around?" I asked.

"Then I am expecting you to salute my rank and call me Major or Doctor, but never ma'am," she said smiling.

We queried each other's reasons for not having a date that evening, and on my suggestion we took another direction across the park to a rather remote and secluded area, which is unseen by anyone walking on the street or even in the park. We sat on one of the benches and continued the conversation. I could see that she was very comfortably relaxed in my company. Finally I reached over and kissed her, and without hesitation, she put her arms around my neck and returned my kiss very passionately. She offered no resistance to my advances and we made love there on that park bench.

That evening meant something special to Major-Doctor Helen Butterworth. After making love on the park bench, we sat and talked until about nine forty five. We decided for me to walk her home. When we got within a hundred yards of her home, she told me to turn back, because if the MPs saw me leaving the area I might get charged and it might be very embarrassing for the both of us to try explaining our presence there. With a quick kiss, we said goodnight and parted company. My stroll back to the billets felt delightful, probably because I was not thinking about anything unpleasant. I did not speak to anyone, I went straight to bed to savour the thoughts of Helen.

That Saturday night, I dressed early and went to the hospital gate to await Fiona's arrival. She was very neatly dressed in shorts and a tight blouse that expressed the firmness of her breasts. Her long brunette hair were braided as one reaching down to her back. She looked sexy and smiling as she approached me. I could feel a warm sensation growing within me. As before, she gave me a kiss and we left to catch the bus to Aldershot. We went to the NAAFI for a few drinks and a couple of dances then we left early without even telling our friends, except for Patrick, who was standing at the door.

"Sneaking off eh?" he said. "I promise not to tell anyone."

Fiona and I laughed as she kissed him on the cheek.

"Except for matron, I don't really care who the hell you tell," she replied.

He bade us good night.

Fiona and I went back to Bordon and to the park bench, where I had spent the previous evening with the horny Major-Doctor Helen Butterworth. We began to kiss and fondle.

"Look, Fiona," I said. "Are you sure this is the right thing to do?" I asked.

" My sweet little cocker spaniel," she said smiling, "from the very first time I saw you in the hospital, my panties got wet. So what I want now is to wet what's inside my panties," she replied in a very stern kind of voice.

"But," I said, "I don't have a safe with me, aren't you afraid of getting pregnant?"

She gave me another surprise when she reached into her purse and produced one.

"I wasn't sure if you would bring, so I did," she said smiling."

"It looks like you were prepared for this evening," I said as she began to remove her shorts and panty.

"Yes," she replied, "and I wasn't going to be disappointed either."

We enjoyed a wonderful screw on the bench, although not very comfortable.

On reaching the hospital, Fiona gave me another surprise.

"Stan," she said, "if we both weren't so young and just joined the army, I would've loved to marry you and have your babies. I've had sex with a fellow back home, which I didn't enjoy very much and lost my virginity in the process. But tonight I made love to someone I really cared for. In fact, you're the first man I ever wanted to make love to, willingly. I enjoyed it immensely."

There was a gleeful smile on her face as she continued.

"I would like to do it as often as possible with you, and for a long time into the future."

"Does this mean we're in love?" I asked.

"Certainly we are, and I would do for you what Fiona the first did for Prince Willy, without reservation."

With that, she kissed me and ran through the gates, smiling and waving as she went.

The six weeks in camp Bordon were very interesting and I was never short on sex. I was kept busy by both Doctor-Major Helen Butterworth and Fiona McDougall. We took trips around the country side, separately of course, and did things I had never done in London, like making love in the open fields of Lands-end, then on the sands of Littlehampton's beach. First with Helen and then with Fiona.

I knew that although I would be in Aldershot, we were going to meet as often as possible for the purpose, there wouldn't be any drastic changes in our relationship because we seemed to enjoy each other's company very well. Çatharine was right about my encounter with these WRAC's, I was beginning to enjoy my army time very well.

Helen had a car and would pick me up on my time off for long drives to places like Southampton and Portsmouth, while Fiona and I would take the bus to closer places. We delighted each other and became very good friends and even exchanged some of our deepest thoughts of our past lives.

Patrick in the meantime kept me very busy talking politics. He would engage me in these conversations whenever possible and I was never bored with them. On the contrary, I found these sessions very stimulating and educational. He would be precise in his facts, and sometimes brought the relevant books as proof and at times cross referenced them with the bible. The word got around camp that we were forming an army of our own. A few of the sixteen other room mates became reluctant to be part of our little brain food evenings, and said so, and had to be moved in order to prevent any arguments. One room had Paddy, Jack, Ian, Tom and Charley. Bob and I were in another with Rod, Philip and Derrick. Then it was back to Aldershot.

In Aldershot, the orientation went well for those who knew that they would be leaving for various reasons. But for those of us who would be staying, it promised to be hell. One day I caught up to Paddy as we were walking from the parade square.

"Hey Paddy!" I said. "I'm going to the office now to sign up for the six to nine years we talked about. Want to came along?"

"Sure," he said, "but let's get the others, they have also been talking about it."

"Okay, they are up ahead," I said. "Hey fellows, stop for a minute," I shouted as we approached them. "We're going to the office now to sign up as regulars, anybody else want to?"

They looked at each other.

"Yeah," said Jack. "Why not."

"Come on then, let's go do it," added Charley.

The signing-up took all of half hour. It seems that the army knew we would be doing so at this time, the papers were in the hand of the secretary almost instantly. We walked away from the office talking about the amount of extra money we would get and the places we would go.

"Now, you stupid Irishman," I said to Paddy. "You're fully in the Queen's army now and you will have to behave accordingly."

"Sure," he replied, "that will give me enough time to educate myself, to apply the pressure back to them, whenever I return home."

"That's right, and they would not have any excuse to prevent us at that time," agreed Ian.

"And we could still be Irish, right here," said Jack.

"What am I seeing here, a revolt?" asked Charley. "Stan you have just opened the tiger's cage. These Irish boys and this Scotty here might just be revolutionaries in disguise, and are amongst us as their cover."

We all found this amusing and went directly to Paddy's room to continue the conversation.

"Look at us," said Bob getting to his feet. "Six white boys and three black ones have become friends. If I had stayed in Aberdeen, I would never be a part of this union."

"Well," I said, "you'll all be known as nigger lovers from now on boys."

"So what!?" shouted Patrick. "Whom ever don't like it, will have to defend it physically."

He stretched out his hand for a shake.

"Friends?" he asked.

Everybody placed their hand on his and replied.

"Friends forever."

That night, I decided to write the names of my army friends and my thoughts of them, in my note book.

Patrick Monaghan O'Reilley:- Irish nut. Tall with darkish complexion like a farmer. Highly educated and wants to be a politician in Ireland. Love to talk about the family and his hard working father. Only speaks in his brogue whenever he is upset and beats his chest with the palm of his hand. I have never seen anyone with fox-red coloured hair like his before.

Thomas Matterson:- Irish, good man. Big bushy eye brows with a scar he obtained in a street fight. He is about my height and weight and is a great dancer.

Although he considers himself subordinate to the English, he is quite aware of the politics in his country. He very seldomly talk about his family at home, although he sends most of his pay to them. He lives in the same neighbourhood and went to the same school with Paddy and Ian. He looks weird without his beard and moustache now.

Jack O'Leary:- Born in Dublin. He's about six foot three in stocking feet and is the tallest of us all. About an inch taller than Bob and Rod. He has dark brown hair to match his darkish complexion and is very muscularly built. He's strong and loves to wrestle. Jack enjoy telling stories about his father who is an accountant in Dublin, and whom he refers to as "The Juggler."

Charley Green:- Jamaican born. I met Charley at Tulse Hill Secondary school in London through playing soccer, and became friends. He too is tall and strong and loved weightlifting and wrestling, and at six foot, is an even match for Jack. Charley likes girls, beers and playing practical jokes on his friends.

Bob Muldoon:- Is from Aberdeen in Scotland, with reddish complexion and sandy hair. He is a very quiet person and a neat dresser, and eat's like a horse to support his two hundred and thirty pound, six foot two frame. Likes to talk about the many girls he left crying in his home town of Aberdeen, and knows the name of every beer produced. Bob never starts a fight, but loves to finish them.

Philip Hoyt:- A born Barbadian and is the oldest of us all. Phil is an all round nice person and sports enthusiast, and would do anything for his friends. He is about my height and size, likes women and scotch. He likes drill parades and is usually up before everybody else in the mornings. He plans on making the army his life's career.

Derrick MacIntosh:- Scot from Glasgow. Although tall at six foot he's slimly built. He's an excellent soccer player and could drink a dozen beers in the time I drank two. Derrick loves to dance and got caught many times in the WRAC camp. The army removed all of his unruly blond hair, leaving him with a brush cut.

Ian Mulligan:- Irish from Belfast. He lived with his parents about two streets from Paddy's home and attended the same school as Paddy and Tom. Although he is the shortest of us all, he makes up with his bravery. He loves to start fights in the NAAFI and spent a few days in jail for it. Ian has brownish blond hair and a freckled face. His nose is larger than that of Rod and has taken some razzing from us about it.

Rodney Langley:- English from Newcastle and is known as the beak. A very educated, quiet but tough person. Said he joined the army to get away from his father, who owns a law firm in Newcastle.

"I needed to grow up and stop being sheltered by him," he told us. He loves to converse with Patrick about politics, and smokes a Sherlock Holmes pipe.

Major-Doctor Helen Butterworth:- English. She has shoulder length brunette hair, hazel eyes and a pear shaped face. Helen exercises regularly and is a muscular woman of about five foot seven and weighs one hundred and thirty five pounds. Although she is an officer and is twice my age, she choose to be a lover and a very good friend to me. I admire her courage to even attempt such, defying the rules of the military. Helen's a fine person.

Fiona McDougall:- A mixed breed, sexy woman born in Scotland. We're both the same age and shared many nice evenings together, enjoying sex. We seemed to appreciate each other's political and religious points-of-view. We have shared some of the most intimate details of our desire for a family and our life's expectancy for the present and future. We care for each other and I do believe she loves me.

I read the list aloud as though it was a roster and smiled to myself.

Although we were given the scare speech by Sergeant-Major Wickham, some of the fellows spoke of not being able to be broken and talked of their plans to beat him at his game. That evening, Patrick came to my room just before tea and asked if I would meet him at the library.

"I've found a couple of interesting books on discrimination that you should know about," he said.

I agree to meet him. After tea, I found him in the history section and sat across the table from him.

"What have you found?" I asked.

He pointed to a pile of books on the table in front of him.

"Go ahead," he said enthusiastically, "feast your eyes on those. Take a look and see for yourself how these fucking English people have been practising this form of oppression for years," he paused for a moment then added, "and so they have become proficient at it."

I leafed through the books. Some were history of the African slaves and their subsequent placements in North America and many parts of the Caribbean. When I found that I was reading pieces all over the place, I decided that for me to get the proper gist of the books, I should take one at a time to read more completely.

"I say old chap," I said. "I think you are onto a gold mine of information here. I think you'll have me as a reading partner from now on. Tuesday evenings would be fine," I promised.

Quickly he jumped out of his seat, grabbed my hand and shook hard.

"That it is my boy," he said. "That it is. You will learn how the Anglo-Saxons have used psychology to brainwash the rest of the world."

I nodded my head in approval as we parted company for the evening. I smiled inwardly as I walked away.

"Patrick only speaks in that Irish brogue whenever he becomes excited or mad about something," I thought, "and I must also be getting like him, to understand it."

As I was returning to the billets, I ran smack into our Sergeant Major going home for the evening.

"Hello sir," I said without breaking stride. He was almost past me when he stopped.

"Oh, Mr Martin," he said, "starting tomorrow I would like you to go to the gym more regularly. I think you could become a good athlete in your own rights."

"If you say so sir," I replied with some reservation and I am sure he detected that in my tone of voice, because he just bowed his head.

"We'll see," he said.

He whirled and in one motion he was in stride and gone. I realized that people have a tendency to evaluate and want you to do things they think you should do, for whatever reason. I decided right there and then not to let anyone crowd my lifestyle or influence me into things I don't want to do, although I was willing to attempt anything, as a self test.

The training was very intense. They spent enough time on our physical and psychological development and our personal well-being as a parent would. They made absolutely sure that any questions you might have are answered, maybe not always to your satisfaction, but an answer anyway. They also made sure you got the best medical and dental care. Food was in abundance, there was no excuses for going hungry. They even taught us how to live off the land in case of isolation, and how to survive in any condition no matter what the weather. I was introduced to a rifle and firing range for the first time in my life.

"An S.L.R could be a soldier's best friend, if you treat it like one," the instructor said and emphasized the importance of keeping it clean. I got to understand that a self-loading rifle could kill effectively at a distance of six hundred yards and was capable for use in sniping and grenade launching.

"Get to know this weapon," he said.

I squeezed the trigger and felt a jolt in my shoulder, not even knowing where the bullet went although the smell of the powder lingered in my nostrils. I fired again and this time I saw the target shook.

I fired three more times and the magazine was empty. The instructor told us to go up to inspect our targets. Although I had hit the target, only two was within a five inch circle of the bulls-eye. I noticed that Patrick and Charley had theirs about two inches to the centre. This practice was an every day occurrence thereafter as was our mile run in the mornings before breakfast and the PT. games in the gym. The obstacle course and the occasional route marches, became fun.

Occasionally we would be dropped off in the woods and told to find our way back to camp. The boys liked this exercise, because we enjoyed finding ourselves and to deduct our position and the challenge of finding our way home. I was beginning to like the life. Thanks to the Sergeant Major for some early advice, I was more able to adapt than some of the others. He had told me the formula to accepting discipline in the army and how to deal with some people.

"One should never lie to oneself," he told me. "Own up to responsibilities, even though you could be punished for doing so. Have confidence in your ability. Be proud of your colour and cultural heritage and it will assist you in developing character."

He had me believing in myself, to the point that at times I found myself getting too cocky. But whenever I got into some tight spots, I was able to get out of them by applying his methods of diplomacy.

It started when he first suggested that I get more involved in physical training, because in his opinion I looked like a boxer. It turned out that I was much better than I realized and it helped in my obtaining recognition and respect from the others in the camp.

"The army is a good institution, my boy," he told me, "only if you learn to follow the rules; but never become dormant and too dependant on it, or you could end up dejected and despondent."

With those words from Tashie, I became my very own person, and it never prevented me from having good friends of all colours and creeds. But his reason for befriending me kept a hold of my mind, and whenever I asked him, he would not answer and sometimes just simply changed the subject. Every Tuesday evening, Patrick, Rod and I would be in the Library reading the political materials that he could find. At times he would say,

"Nig, someday you will be able to teach your children these same things, assured of the history and facts as written here and know that it was an Irishman who brought it to your attention."

I silently agreed with him, although my objective was for my own development, and to watch the white people's reaction towards me in conversations. I felt I was gaining an education from all angles. From Patrick, Rod, Wickham and Dawkins. Dawkins, himself being black and Jamaican, was better able to confer with Charley, Dave and I, and whenever we showed tendencies to step out of line, he was always there to guide us back to the reality of the army.

I began to evaluate and compare some of the people to many of the characters in the books I had been reading. I visualized Patrick as Don Quixote, fighting a solo war of an insane person, against imaginary foes. I saw Tashie Wickham somewhat as Ghengis Kahn or Julius Caesar. He was a strategist who motivates people, who I think could be a sneaky fighter if meed be, using all available weapons to his advantage. I saw Helen as Joan of Arc, devotedly willing to apply herself against the odds for love. Fiona appeared to me like Mary Magdalene, a very caring dedicated person.

I was having fun visualizing these people in the various scenes and the knowledge I was gaining through them. I was not losing anything in my sex life either, due to Helen and Fiona. I could say that I was maintaining a full life in the army because, Monday and Wednesday evenings were spent with Helen, while my Fridays and Saturdays were for Fiona. Thursdays was my boxing training nights with Tashie Wickham and Tuesdays with Patrick and Rod in the library.

Helen and I had been meeting secretly twice per week at a pre-arranged locations. She would come to the camp in Aldershot, then ask one of the NCO's to get me. I would go to the medical room office and there a meeting place would be chosen for the evening. But on this occasion she came directly to the Sergeant-Major's office. As I entered, she spoke freely not caring if anyone overheard her.

"Oh there you are," she said, "I have to see you urgently."

I wondered why here and not at one of our meeting spots. My mind was running wild with thoughts. She was smartly dressed in a very tight-fitting dress for the first time, instead of those baggy military type things she normally wore. I quickly hustled her out the door.

"What are you doing here?" I angrily whispered.

"I came to get you," she replied with a wide grin. "This is very important to both of us sweetheart."

Seeing that it was a Friday evening when Fiona had to work, I had no objection in accompanying her to wherever she wanted. I felt happy and ready for the evening with her, although my curiosity was still running wild as to her reason. As soon as I got into the car, she informed me she had already made us tea back in Bordon, and that we will go directly to her house for the entire weekend. Although I was delighted, I questioned her logic remembering the danger of us getting discovered. She told me she was getting posted to Singapore and would be leaving in four days time, so it wouldn't matter now if anyone saw us together.

"Tonight is going to be very special for us, darling," she said. "We'll make love in a bed, totally naked."

She was happy and without objection.

"Totally naked?" I thought with a smile. "Now I will see her nude and in the light."

She spoke at length about Singapore and the excitement of performing her craft in the fields and of her hope that I would get a posting there also. I, in turn, spoke of missing her and my hope of continued communications with her, even if I didn't get the posting there. We agreed to that. On reaching her house, she parked the car and we both walked briskly to the door. I was a little afraid to look in any particular direction in case somebody recognized me. In my mind I was still apprehensive about it.

"Here I am about to be imprisoned for having sex with an officer at her quarters. What would the judge say?" I wondered.

But she walked with a "I don't really care now," attitude. I couldn't help but notice that her arse did look good in that dress from behind.

We entered the house and she explained that the army always supplied the officers with good accommodations and hoped it would be the same in Singapore. We washed and hurriedly ate because she was getting excited and horny. When she got undressed, I was astonished to see that the lady had a nicely shaped body. I knew that she exercised regularly, but was surprised any way.

Unlike the times we made love on the park bench or in her car, laying in bed was much more interesting and controlled. We were able to caress and foreplay a lot longer and do things to each other that we couldn't have done in a car. Her breasts looked much larger in the lights than in the dark, and her nipples stood out very strongly for a woman her age. This was the best of our times. She was much more vocal than ever before. After about an hour and a lot of sweat, we laid having a cigarette when she said,

"Darling, I wish that we could have stayed together forever, but the army won't permit it. This weekend will always be for our remembrance, but It would be fun to deceive them."

"Sure it would," I agreed. "And it will be a lasting memory. I am now fully understanding the ways of the army."

"You're the first man to come to my house in three years," she said. "I don't know what it is, why I felt compelled and a willingness to make love to you anytime, any place. My God! Stan, you make me feel so good, like a young teenage girl again."

"Oh?" I said. "How old are you? Not that it really matter."

"I'm thirty six years old," she answered without hesitation. "And yes, I've made it with many men in medical school and at the military hospitals, strictly for sexual satisfaction mind you. But you're somewhat different and it's making me a believer in an old adage."

"Yes?" I said. "A believer in what old adage?" I asked.

"You know what they say. Once you go black you never go back?" she said.

I laughed loudly.

"I never heard that saying before," I said. "I must say that you people always come up with some kind of slogan for everything."

She laughed and repeated it.

"You know," I said, "for a woman your age, you have a very nice body?"

"Sure I do know," she replied proudly. "I keep it in good shape so that you young men can look at it and wish, and is temptation for the older ones."

"Oh! So that's your game? Entice the young soldiers then put a needle into them, unexpectedly eh?" I teased.

"No my darling," she replied, "only the special ones get this far and you're very special to me. From the first day I saw you at the examination, I had this urge to be with you."

"Why didn't you pick one of the white boys?" I asked curiously.

She paused for a moment in thoughts then replied.

"It's a long story, but someday if you ever get posted to Singapore, I will tell you everything."

I didn't want to argue the issue or to force her to talk, so I returned my mind to our love-making, which was much more enjoyable than previously, and to watch her having a pleasurable time with me. That night we slept very soundly.

The next morning I heard her cheerily singing in the bathroom, I smiled as I remembered her slogan and felt proud that I was the black man she chose to feel good with. I used the bathroom to get showered and readied for breakfast and some more screwing, which we did almost all day Saturday. Then in the evening she made us tea and we listened to some music and talked about our family life and us meeting in Singapore. The entire weekend was very nice, it felt good to make love to a woman twice my age and have her enjoy me.

Periodically my mind flashed back to Catharine and our day on the train to Aldershot, but Helen was for this moment. We exchanged corresponding addresses and promised not to lose contact no matter what. Then on Sunday afternoon she took me back to the camp in

Aldershot and departed with a strong goodbye kiss. I learned a lot about Helen and her family that weekend. She told me about how she wanted to follow in her father's foot steps and how she wanted to break the military male dominance, in the field of medicine. She wanted to be a liberationist as her mother and getting married would hinder her plans. She wanted to be a strong woman within the military system, and to be able to correct many of the wrongs there. She talked about the life of her unhappy sister, who got married and is now living in Australia and her retired parents.

"Stan," she said, "I want to be able to function and to do the things I want to without having to explain my reasons to anyone."

I understood and felt the loyalty within her soul to be right.

"Her purpose for being with me probably will never be clear, but I will enjoy her for as long as I can," I thought.

She came to see me on the Tuesday evening, with tears in her eyes. She was departing to Singapore and wanted to say goodbye again. Patrick told her that he would take good care of me, until we meet in Singapore. I realized then that I was something special to her, but what, I couldn't say.

"I'm going to make him a good citizen of this planet, even if it kills me," Paddy promised her and she thanked him.

We departed his company to spend a few quiet moments alone together, not knowing if we would ever see each other again.

The following week, seeing that Helen was gone I spent most of my evenings, either in the gym with Tashie or the library with Patrick, Rod and Tom. I was able to sneak a phone call to Fiona and she was happy to hear from me, but because neither of us had any form of transportation, our meeting during the week was out of the question, so a date was made for that Friday evening. The gymnasium held most of my attention, which pleased the Sergeant-Major, because he got to spar more rounds with me.

Patrick received some letters from home, which made him very happy and I for him. It was the first time in a while that I had seen him so cheerful. He read them to me and explained some of the Irish jargon.

"Now hear this nig-nog," he said reading from a letter. "My younger sister Teresa, just celebrated her seventeenth birthday and they had a party for her. Look at this picture of her, pretty eh."

I looked at the photograph.

"Yes sir," I said, "she sure is pretty."

"Don't get any ideas," he said laughing. "You're not going to get your hands on her. I won't let any sex crazy fiend near her. Only if I let you."

He laughed out loud, tilted his head to the sky and said,

"God knows, I wouldn't know what to do, if she ever fall in love with a black person, especially you."

"Now, you see who the real bigots are?" I said angrily. "Remember how you try to convince me that the English was the perpetrators of such demeaning acts? Well listen to yourself."

"Hey, arse hole," he said, "don't get yourself in a knot. We, you and I, are going to see them in two weeks time, if you want to."

He was standing there with his eyes open anxiously awaiting my reply.

"We're going to Ireland in two weeks time?" I asked. "Did I tell you I wanted to see that fucking place?"

"No," he replied, "but since we're getting a ten day pass, I thought you might want to see somewhere different other than just grubby old London for a change."

"Okay!" I said. "What about the other guys? Are they coming along too?" I asked, getting my blood pressure back under control again.

"Yes," he said. "With you, there will be nine of us."

I thought about it for a moment then said,

"In that case, don't worry if I make your sister fall for me."

He only shook his shoulders and said,

"If she's stupid enough to fall for you, then it's not my fault. Is it?"

We left the library and went to make plans with the other fellows. They were enthusiastic about the trip and Patrick never stopped telling us of the great times we were about to have. He named almost all the pubs in the city of Belfast.

"Fellows," I said, "you know you are not going to have a moment's rest from now on. This bastard is going to remind us on the hour of this little exercise."

They all laughed and shook hands and retired for the night.

That Friday evening I went for Fiona as soon as the Sergeant said we could leave. The bus ride to Bordon was slow. I had not seen her for two whole weeks and I was getting excited and horny for her. We planned to ride down to Bournemouth to stay for the weekend, where we could go to the Isle of Wight for a day, but when I arrived at the hospital, she ran to me crying.

"Hey girl, what's the matter?" I asked.

"I'm on duty again," she cried, "because one of the nurses is sick."

She was crying hard and the tears were running down her pretty face.

"And I know the bitch isn't sick!" she said.

She laid her head on my chest sobbing. Beverly, a Trinidadian girl who was dating big Mac, suggested we stay in the hospital for the weekend. It meant I would have to sneak in and hide from the floor matron at all times.

"That sounds exciting and daring," I said, "just like Robin Hood."

Fiona began to smile as the conniving thought hits her mind.

"You know something?" she said. "That idea is very devious and conniving and I like it! Darling, we could get some of the girls to smuggle food up to you while the others could keep matron busy. She wouldn't know a thing. Come on!"

She held my hand, leading me to the hospital door.

"Firstly we'll have to smuggle you in," she said.

I pretended I was visiting somebody and signed in. Then when the coast was clear, I made a dash for the nurses' quarters. Sure enough, they had left the door opened for me, so all I had to do was to keep as quiet as a mouse. Since Fiona was on duty, she had to pop in and out almost the same as I had to do going in, until her break time. Finally she was finished around mid-night. I was asleep at that time, but she had a quick shower and came to bed. The feel of her naked body next to mine awakened me and right away she wanted to have sex.

"Fiona," I said, "let me get a safe from my pocket, I don't want you to get pregnant."

"Hey! That wouldn't be a bad idea, but let's take the precaution anyway," she teased.

When we were through making love, she laid there laughing.

"You know something?" she said. "This was the best idea any of those girls ever had. Tonight, I think I've exerted the most energy and expelled more fluid than I ever done in my whole life!"

"Good," I replied.

I was feeling too good to even remember where I was. I had forgotten that the matron could enter the room at any time, and if she did, we both would be in jail... or maybe just me. The thought quickly vanished and the sleep took over.

I hid in that hospital all weekend, bobbing and weaving every time the matron made her rounds. Fiona and the other girls were enjoying themselves sneaking in food to me. It was fun to be breaking the rules, to be daring. I felt like Robin Hood or even Sir Lancelot, sneaking around in the woods or the castles, stealing from or fucking the masters wives, then heading back to the hide-out to tell their friends of their escapades. Anyway, it was really a lovely and exciting weekend for Fiona and I, even though she had to work.

When I was leaving that Sunday evening, Fiona expressed her fascination with our time and announced her love for me. I also told her of my feelings, which made her even more happy. We made another date for the next weekend and told her that I had volunteered for the Paratroopers and would be going to Farnham for some more training. She became quiet. I could see that she wasn't thrilled with that idea.

"Darling," she said, "that part of the army is very dangerous. Most time they are the first ones sent into action somewhere. I don't want to lose you, not just yet anyway, but go ahead and try it."

On the bus back to camp, I gave thoughts to the danger of being in the Paras and had to agree that it was dangerous, but then I realized that for some unknown reason, some women are fascinated by men who are daring. They seemed to get sexually excited whenever a men talks of danger and I am very much interested in those types of women.

The Monday morning as we were about to go on parade, Sergeant-Major Wickham came over to me.

"Mr Martin," he said, as he gestured with his pace stick like a sword-fighter, "I see you have volunteered for the Paras."

When I did not offer any explanation, he continued.

"I hope you intend on giving it your best? I know that you'll prove them wrong."

My curiosity to his statement got my attention.

"Whom must I prove wrong?" I quickly asked.

"Don't worry about it," Tashie said. "I have confidence in you. I'm one who believe some of you nig-nogs can be good soldiers. Just earn those wings, then come back here to show them off."

I knew he meant well for me and the others, but his interest seemed to be more focussed on my welfare, and I didn't really understand why.

"Maybe someday I will find out why he wanted to be my friend," I thought, and I let him hear my views.

"Sir," I said. "I've been listening to some of the derogatory remarks expressed by some of your white NCO's, saying that we blacks cannot be good soldiers. So when they asked for volunteers, I decided to show the bastards that I was not afraid. And furthermore, I hate parades and taking commands from people who couldn't beat my sister in a street fight."

He looked into my eyes and said,

"By Jove, I think you're angry. You're really upset. That's the kind of sprit this regiment is looking for. Good luck to you, and you can miss parade today."

He whirled around in that strict military fashion I had seen so many times, and was gone in a flash.

I could sense the smile on his face as he walked away from me. By the time I reached the billets, I could hear the noise of the drill pig shouting the commands on the parade square. I smiled at the thoughts that I won't have to do any more of that guff. I was surprised on entering the room, to see all my friends sitting there.

"What are you all doing here?" I asked.

"We also volunteered for the Paras," said Jack.

Each one had their own reasons for joining. But the most interesting of all was Patrick's. He told us of his intention to learn as much military tactics, so as to return to his homeland to assist in getting rid of the "protestant oppressors." We all laughed at that idea, but in my mind, I wasn't too sure that he didn't mean it. We sat around talking a while about making the para regiment and getting the girls.

"Stan my boy," said Charley. "When I heard that you had gone and volunteered, I told the rest. So we went and signed up also. You thought you were going to get rid of us eh? Well, not on your Nelly my friend."

"Let's face it," I said, "you were all afraid of being alone."

"Yeah!" said Tom, "That plus we couldn't bear to think that you alone would be getting the girls."

"Do you realize what we're doing?" Ian pointed out. "We're becoming a team within ourselves. We're formulating our own little army."

"We certainly are," replied Rod. "And maybe that should be so, because friends should always protect one another."

I could see where this discussion was leading, but before I could respond, Jack read my mind by saying,

"Gentlemen, maybe we should think of our friendship as a unit and develop some kind of a code in talking to each another, something positive that only we can understand."

I could see the wheels turning in their heads, that idea was embedding itself within them and silent, it was agreed with a hand shake and a smile.

"Stan," said Patrick grinning proudly, "you and I will get the books from which we could use some words to formulate our codes."

"Yes," said Bob, "but we should make them simple ones, so as not to make others suspicious."

That conversation went on for some time. It was agreed that Jack, Ian, Rod and Charley would be responsible for formulating the codes.

"Maybe we should make a pact to personally inform each other's families in case of an accident to any of us," said Bob.

The room was silent. Then it was agreed with a hand shake.

"Friends?" asked Rod.

"Friends forever," came the reply in unison as we dispersed.

I decided to write a letter to my good friend Armon who was in the Royal Engineers in Yorkshire. I wanted to tell him of all the things that had happened in Aldershot since I came. I ended up writing to my mother, to my brother in Canada, my friends George Walters, Rudolph Scarlett, to three of my cousins and a couple of girlfriends in London, explaining my reason for going to Ireland rather than coming to see them. I was surprised to know that I had written nine in all and left for the post office to get stamps. I walked along a path that led from the camp through the park to town.

Although the walk was long, I didn't mind because the solitude was relaxing. I reached and was in the process of purchasing the stamps when I saw her. She looked the same as when I had met her on the train.

She wore an orange coloured knee-length, skin-tight dress that showed her curves, with matching shoes and purse. Her wide brimmed hat seemed to cover a portion of her tanned face and the pale blue polka dot scarf, was identical to the colour of her eyes. I looked at her very shapely legs and envied the skin-toned stocking that clung to them.

"Catharine!" I whispered to my self and wondered if it would be appropriate to approach her there in the post office. I remembered what she had told me on the train.

"In Aldershot! we'll never cross paths!!"

With that in mind, I decided to mail my letters and leave. As I was doing so, she turned to look at me.

"Don't you speak to friends?" she asked in that sexy tone of hers.

I was shocked at her approach and at the same time, very elated to hear her voice again.

"Hello Mrs. Harrison," I said nervously, my voice slightly trembling, "fancy seeing you here."

I gestured awkwardly with one hand and at the same time trying to avoid her beautiful eyes.

She told me to wait, as she went over to post her letters. I started to get a hard-on just watching her arse as she walked.

We left together, but as we reached outside, she began to query me on my time in Aldershot.

"And how are you doing with those WRAC nurses?" she asked smiling.

I told her that it was a long story, but if we could go across the street for a tea, I would be delighted to tell her. She agreed and we did. Catharine seemed quite comfortable in my company. We must have talked for an hour, with her telling of her life in Aldershot since returning and I describing my military activities so far. It wasn't until I mentioned that I had volunteered for the Paras, that she got upset and quickly wanted to leave.

She grabbed her purse and dashed out the door and I followed her. But as I stopped to pay the bill, she disappeared down the street. I caught up to her almost a block away.

"What's the matter?" I asked.

"I am not going to explain anything to you at this minute," she said, "but if you meet me this evening at the park, we could talk about it."

"Okay," I said, and as an afterthought I shouted back, "which side?"

"At the east side idiot," she hollered back. "At seven thirty sharp."

I hurriedly walked back to camp and to my room to rest, with Catharine on my mind. Luckily Big Mac came in to awaken me. I asked and he told me it was six thirty.

"Oh my god!" I exclaimed. "She told me seven thirty sharp."

I quickly ran to the showers, hurriedly got dressed and ran out the door. I was ecstatic about my date with Catharine and all the time recalling our encounter on the train to Aldershot. I ran down to the mess hall for a quick nosh and left. Luckily, I met a Corporal driving home and he gave me a lift to the park. When I got there, she was already sitting on a bench, madder than hell. She was just fuming. I tried desperately to explain my dilemma and could not get the chance.

"If you're going to keep on with this perpetual babbling about my tardiness, I'm going back to camp," I said finally.

I don't know if it was the sternness in my voice, my attitude or because she didn't want me to leave, but her perpetual talking came to an abrupt end.

"That's better," I said. "Now, can we begin what we came here for?" I asked.

"Yes," she replied, "if that's the way you want it. But we're only going to talk and nothing else."

"That's fine by me," I said.

We talked for about an hour and a half, then I reminded her of our day on the train to this city. She smiled.

"You know something," she said. "I really enjoyed that day. Do you think we could recreate it again?"

"We'el," I said. "It would be a pleasure to try."

I put my arm around her waist, pulled her towards me and kissed her. She responded by wrapping hers around my neck. I began to rub my hand on her thighs, but as I almost I reached her crotch, she pushed it away.

"What was that in aid of?" I asked.

"Not here my sweet man," she said mimicking a Jamaican like accent, "it will have to be another day and another place."

"Why? Afraid to make love on a park bench?" I said playing back her words on the train.

"No my darling," she replied. "I'm having my period, that's why."

She got up to leave, then re-sat and kissed me hard again.

"The weekend would be good if you could get away," she said. "We could go to Portsmouth on Saturday, then spend the night at one of my friend's place there."

I told her of my relationship with Fiona and that I had a date with her for Saturday night. She told me that if something should happen to break it, I could meet her in front of the NAAFI about seven o'clock in the morning. Although I didn't like to do it to Fiona, I really wanted to spend the time with Catharine. We parted company without she being told of her earlier tantrum at the cafe.

I returned to the barracks to see Bob Muldoon and Patrick sitting at the table reading.

"What are you two criminals doing here tonight?" I asked. "Couldn't find a date?"

"My girlfriend is working this evening," said Bob.

I nodded then looked at Patrick.

"Are you queer? Why don't you have a girlfriend?" I asked him.

"That's the problem with you people," he sneered. "You fuck anything. As long as there's a hole in it, you'll fuck it."

I realized that he was angry, but I decided to prolong the aggravation anyway.

"And what's so wrong with that?" I asked.

"Nothing," he replied, "but all I'm saying is, don't categorize me because I don't indulge. I do have a nice girl back in Galway Bay and I love her. So I have no desire to find any here."

Quickly I grabbed him in the ribs with both hands. He almost jumped out of the chair.

"Then show me her picture?" I said. "Come on, where is her picture?" I insisted.

"Okay, okay," he said, "I'll show you what a real goodlooking Irish woman looks like."

He reached for one of the books, opened it to a page and took out a mid size photograph.

"Take a good look, then give it back," he said.

I had to admit that she was pretty and I was not lying either.

"Well," I said teasingly, "when we go to your home-town and she lay eyes on me, you'll be finished boyo."

He laughed hard.

"I've already written letters home, telling everybody that a pack of wolves are coming, so they should lockup their valuables and their daughters. We all had a chuckle at that, then sat down to discuss some real life army politics.

We talked about the policies of Edward Heath, Harold Macmillan, Harold Wilson and Anthony Eden and how their policies favour the industrialists in England and penalized the poor. Patrick carefully described its effect on the Irish people and that of the ruling party in his country, who take advantage of its powers.

"They will differ, deviate and deceive the people at all cost," he said, "we should have a system that penalizes dysfunctional politicians, who are suspected of carrying out criminal acts against the population's wishes, as these men have done to the people, yet they are allowed to continue being politicians, immune from any such prosecution."

"And if the people revolt against these policies, they will undoubtedly be classified as communists or socialists," Bob added.

The discussion took us back into history, searching for a honest, truthful politician but couldn't find one. We talked about Mr Mosley and his ideology for cleansing England and comparing him to Adolf Hitler.

"Imagine," I interjected, "he proposed to remove every and all immigrants from the soil of England. And when they kick out the blacks, who would be next?"

Patrick sat in thoughts as he mumbled,

"I guess it will be the Irish Catholic's or some other poor bastards."

"Like the Jews?" asked Charley.

"Maybe," said Paddy. "It's been done before."

"Is that what it meant to be integrated under this new multi-culturalism?" asked Big Mac, "or is it to keep us from getting together, organized and becoming a power within yourselves?"

"Yes," said Patrick, "look at what they've done to my people over the years, it's the Roman policies all over again."

"And what is that?" I enquired.

Paddy got out of his chair and began pacing the floor.

"My friends," he began. "Pontius Pilot had Christ crucified for questioning his policy while he was feeding the Christians to the lions. Julius Caesar came along and did almost the same and wanted to either conquer or destroy everybody in the world that he personally disliked.

He almost conquer all of Europe and Asia, until he ran into Atilla the Hun. He, Julius, is the designer of our existing policy and these pigs are still doing it to us. The idea of divide and control, was his. But I know that someday I will get my chance to repay some of them for those actions, you wait and see."

I also agreed that I might have a vendetta against the English too for the things they had done to the African people. This discussion carried on for quite some time. We seemed to agree and disagree on many points throughout the evening, with each stating their personal ideas on communism, socialism, capitalism and religion. It was very enlightening and educational, and in some respect, we were now starting to understand each other. We could disagree on subject matters without animosity and all seemed to like the idea.

"Friends?" hollered Big Mac.

"Friends forever," all repeated.

Charley reminded us that we must start to formulate our code soon.

"I have been doing some wording for that purpose, want to hear?" Charley said, sounding excited about his achievement. But Rod stopped him.

"Not now Charley," he said, "leave it until we meet again on Tuesday evening."

We all shook hands and parted company.

The feeling of being part of our little army was delightful. I had made some friends and was now very capable of mixing and discussing politics with anybody. My family would be very proud to know this and would be happy for me. Although, I was not ready to tell them of the many things I had already done and the type of people I had done them with.

"Maybe," I thought, "I will write a letter to inform them of my newly acquired skills or should I say, my newly developed mind."

It was a surprise to myself, that in such a short space of time
I have been successful in changing my attitude and began to trust people around me. I began to recognize the inner thoughts of others and had

concern for their welfare. I discovered that they, like myself, had some emotions that they wanted to encounter, and the idea of us doing it together, thrilled me.

"Maybe the army isn't that bad after all," I thought.

I pondered these things within the confines of my room. The solitude was very relaxing and gave my mind the latitude necessary for those thoughts to flow. I was never a loner, because growing up in an household of three plus two cousins, nobody could be alone. It was an atmosphere of sharing, although at times, I enjoyed being alone. I've come to realize that I worked better alone, but here I am forced to do things with others, and I'm liking it.

The army, it seemed, is not a place to isolate oneself or to be isolated. People here quickly develop some kind of friendship for various reasons. If it wasn't for fear, it was for the security of not to be categorized by the authorities, but mostly not to die alone. I discovered that, some came to the services to escape the pressures of parental control, or because they were not very functional in the required school work, which translate into dysfunctional in civilian life.

The army does not care to understand what your deficiencies are, their only objective is to weave you into something usable. Then there were those, like myself, who didn't want to be there in the first place, who had a good rapport with their parents and very good marks in school. But for the threat of being imprisoned, I would gladly stay a civilian and be whatever I wanted. An Engineer to be, was my soul desire.

"Maybe this was my destination in life," I thought. "Maybe this is where I am supposed to die. How the hell should I know what's in store for me? And then again, I could be lucky and live a long and full life. But one thing I know, this could be a great education for me personally and I intend on accepting that challenge."

I fell to sleep thinking of all these things....and more.

Some time during that week, I met and asked one of the dispatch riders to deliver a message to Fiona at the hospital. He did, and brought back a letter from her, apologizing that she had to work on the weekend. Although I felt sad not being able to see her, I was happy to know that I was free to meet Catharine that weekend.

Saturday morning, and I was up early. I got dressed, had my breakfast and went to the NAAFI and waited. She arrived on time and as usual, Catharine was very neatly dressed in a floral summer dress and a white hat to match.

"Hello mister soldier," she said in that Jamaican tone as she stopped the car in front of me, "would you like to go for a ride?" she asked.

Quickly I got into the car and she sped away. I commented on how well her clothes seemed to highlight her features and wondered if it was deliberate, and she assured me that it was.

"Do you have any duties this weekend?" she asked.

"No, none at all," I replied.

"Good," she said. "We can go to Portsmouth for the day, then to a friend's house for the evening and all day tomorrow."

"And where will your friend be?" I asked.

"She's meeting her lover in London this weekend and won't be coming home until late Sunday evening," she said smiling. "Are you afraid?"

"Not really," I replied. "But remember that you're a married woman and an officer's wife and I am a lowly private."

"How can I forget," she replied. "But I can assure you there is nothing to fear for this weekend, or any other weekends hereafter."

Catharine drove hard and we made Portsmouth in less than record time. She quickly found the place she wanted us to spend the day, upon a hill over-looking the sea and parked. While I removed the baskets of food and drinks from the booth while she was busy spreading the blankets under a large tree. We ate and talked for most of the day, occasionally tracking down the hill to the sea to play in the water and socialize with some of the many people, who were doing the same as us. Catharine seemed happy to be with me and to be talking about her family and herself and at times and behaving like a little girl.

Finally the sun began its decent, so the decision to leave was made. We packed the picnic items in the car and she once again sped to our destination. She parked the car in the driveway of a rather typically English looking country house and opened the door with a key she had. It seemed it was well arranged, because the drinks, the ice and glasses were properly placed for our convenience. She turned on the record player and Sinatra's "Paper Moon," filled the room.

"Relax," she said. "We're alone here and nobody else will be coming here."

I took my tunic and tie off and we began to dance. By the time the record was over, Catharine was dragging me to the bedroom. She wasted no time removing her clothes and was helping me with mine. We dove into bed and began our weekend long reunion of our meeting on the train to Aldershot.

In between our steamy lovemaking, we talked about the army and her fears of losing me to it; which was her reason for being upset the day at the post office. We talked about my relationship with Fiona. I asked her about her husband, but she rigidly refused to talk about him and their relationship, although she talked about her parents and their differences towards him. She told me about her feelings for me since returning to Aldershot, and I told her how I didn't want to be in the army in the first place and my desire to be an auto engineer. I told her about my father who was an ex military man from W.W.2. She was very understanding of my thoughts.

"I can't do anything to change that now," I said, "so while I am here, I might as well indulge and enjoy myself and the paras can offer me some excitement."

Somehow that seemed to satisfy her and we enjoyed a very wonderful weekend together. She let me out of the car near the camp gate and with a long kiss, we made another date to meet after I returned from Ireland.

Chapter Three

" Ireland: My First Time."

The day we were waiting for, came. It was the day to leave for Ireland and to see the beauty that Patrick spent so much time convincing us, existed only in that part of the world. It was a long train ride to Gatwick Airport, but the plane ride was even worst. It seemed that they had saved the most rickety aircraft for us.

During the journey, we had to listen to Patrick's descriptions of his home for what seemed like the ten millionth time. But we weren't bored, because we were happy to be away from the army and also looking forward to seeing the Irish girls. Our excitement rose in anticipation of the events to follow.

Seeing Belfast from the sky, was beautiful. Except for the few burnt out and destroyed buildings, nobody could suspect any form of violence there. The landing was a little shaky, but we were safely on the ground. We got our kit bags and headed out to the streets where we took a bus for his parent's home. Paddy was right. In a way the place was really pretty, and seeing it from a local bus was ideal and sharing the experience with the local people, was more fun. I was getting a first hand lesson in their language and found most of the people were friendly and the kind hearted type who were willing to talk to me. Patrick was in his glory being a tour guide, describing the historical buildings as the bus passed them.

"Yes," I thought, "Belfast was a very beautiful city."

The idea of people wanting to destroy such beauty annoyed me.

"It's the people," I said aloud to Patrick. "It's the damn stupid people that destroy places. God made this world very pretty, but he made the mistake of letting mankind run it."

Patrick didn't reply, only nodded his head and mumbled.

"Mmmmmmm."

On reaching the house, we were greeted by his younger brother Eric, then his mother Ella and sister Teresa. Eric was sent somewhere to get his father Shaun. I noticed that although they too had red hair, it wasn't as bright as Patrick's. When Shaun and Eric came, the introductions started all over again. Shaun got out the drinks and his best visitor's drinking glasses. He told us that he had already heard about us from Patrick, but wanted to hear the stories personally, one at a time. I realized that it was Shaun who had the fox-red hair.

Father O'Reilley, as we all referred to him, stood about six feet tall and weighed about two hundred plus pounds. He had a little grey amongst his full head of hair. I assessed his age to be in his late forties. He was a handsome man with his own teeth and smiled a lot to show them off. We took turns telling stories of Patrick, from his attitude in the army, to his politics and his fears of the women. Ella decided it was time to eat, so between her and Teresa the table was set with a lot of food. Some extra chairs were borrowed from the neighbour's to accommodate us.

At the table, the stories were told by Shaun. We heard about his family's move from Cork to Belfast for a better job and how later the management quickly dismissed him, after finding out that he was a southerner. He talked about Patrick's life from birth, until they kicked him out to join the army. Everybody laughed at that. After tea, Shaun O'Reilley suggested we visit a local pub for a few pints. Everybody agreed to that, so we left the house to invade their favourite one.

At the pub, I was leaning against the bar doing the vacation drinking we had planned, when Teresa came in. She asked to be told about the politics of Jamaica. I had to explain that although I was born there, I really didn't know much about the country's politics, but I could tell her about the beauty of some places there. I did and she found my description of Jamaica fascinating.

"The only things I know about Jamaica," she said, "is what I read from the books at school. Why don't you learn more about your country?" she asked.

I really didn't have an explanation for my ignorance.

"I promise you," I said, " I will study more about my place of birth someday, whenever I can find the time. And that would fascinate my father very much, he always wanted me to do so."

"And why so?" she asked.

"Because of our cultural heritage, he has always prompted us to do so. But..."

"Is your mother and father Jamaican born also?" she enquired.

"Certainly," I replied. "My father was born in Jamaica but his parents are of African descent."

"You mean your grandparents were direct descendants from Africa? How did they get there? Were they slaves?" she asked excitedly."

"Well I don't know, but according to my father they are from Ghana in West Africa. They went there to live," I answered.

"Charming!" she said. "Have you ever been to Africa?"

"No I haven't been there as yet, but I will some day," I said.

"How did your grand parents get to Jamaica?" she asked.

"I couldn't tell you that either," I replied. "I really don't know how they got to Jamaica, but...."

"Then how come you have that kind of pigmentation and features are you mixed with something?" she interrupted.

I realize that she didn't really know anything of the multiracial and cultural make up of Jamaicans, so I explained.

"My dear mother is a Cuban of Spanish descent, that's why I look like this," I said, "African and Spaniard, a very weird combination eh?"

"And a very handsome one at that too," she said with a grin.

Finally she asked me to dance. I quickly asked Patrick if it was alright to dance with her and he reminded me of what he had told me in Aldershot.

"If she's stupid enough to fall for you, then I wouldn't object," he said.

I noticed neither mother or father objected to her hanging on to me all evening. She led me away to a seat in a corner, where we talked endlessly about her educational expectations and her love- life's desires. She talked about meeting a man that she wanted to spend the rest of her living days with and the number of children she wanted. When the evening ended at the pub, Patrick quickly announced that he had booked some digs for the boys, seeing that it was nine of us and all couldn't stay at their house. Before leaving mother O'Reilley made us promise to have breakfast with them the next morning, we agreed and they went home, including Teresa.

"Now that they're gone," Patrick chimed up, "you're in my town now and it's Saturday night, so let's go."

"Take us to the girls fearless leader," said Phil.

"Don't let your hearts be troubled boys," he said jovially, "just follow me."

We all slapped our hands on each others shoulder and started singing a filthy rugby song as we walked out the door. It was a short walk to the dance palace. We paid the required five shillings entrance fee and quickly found the bar. There were girls everywhere and I could see the happiness on the boys faces.

At the bar, Paddy began ordering drinks. He waved to some friends across the room and in a little while, three nice looking ladies came over. He kissed one of them and proceeded to introduce her to me. I recognized her from the picture he had shown me in camp. Ian, Jack and Tom hugged and kissed the other girls, then Paddy's girlfriend left and brought back four more. It seemed that he had paired off everybody.

"Shoo, shoo," he said, "go and dance or something."

When they left, I noticed that I was standing alone.

"Hey twit!" I said. "What about me!?"

He looked menacingly at me, then said,

"You're already taken, and furthermore you can't cheat on my sister."

I looked around to see if she was in the place, but no luck. I swore under my breath, then relaxed to enjoying myself alone for the evening. I must've spent an hour talking to different girls around the place, but whenever he thought I was getting settled with any one of them, he would interrupt the conversation.

Suddenly I felt someone's fingers holding my biceps. It was Teresa.

"Ah, here she is," I silently said. "Hello Teresa," I said aloud. "I wasn't expecting you back here."

I had to step back slightly to look at her. She was very smartly dressed in a pink and white knee length dress. Her hair, although red, was much darker than that of Patrick's and was combed differently from when I first saw her. It made her appear older than seventeen. I was astonished at her new looks. The perfume she wore, although aromatic, was subtle and matched her demeanour.

"I seemed to be taken in by red heads also," I thought.

I was now discovering something else about myself that I didn't know existed.

"You look very nice my dear," I offered in a mimicked Kentish tone.

"Thank you sir," she replied, "I had a feeling that you would like it."

She patted her hair and batted her eyes alluringly at me. We both laughed and walked to a table in the back while all my friends whistled and jeered, as we passed them. I was trying desperately to keep from saying anything or to appear eager for her, but I guessed she already sensed that I was. I liked her. She told me that Patrick had already told her everything about me in a letter, and her parents didn't mind her coming to meet me there. We talked and danced almost all night, then I walked her home.

On reaching the house, I lightly kissed her on the lips. She quickly wrapped her arms around my neck and returned the kiss passionately. I took that opportunity to try a little petting but she pushed away my hand.

"You'll have to wait my dear," she whispered.

We said goodnight and I left for the digs.

The next day was planned to take us all to Galway Bay in Southern Ireland. Paddy had arranged with a friend with a bus for the long trip. Seeing that I had read so much about the place, through Patrick of course, I was familiar with some of the places. Our first stop was in the town of Cavan, then on to Virginia and Ceanannus Mor. I was actually telling the others about landmarks we saw going there. But during all this time Teresa was hanging on to me as though we were married. She would not allow any of the other girls to get close to me, even for a short conversation.

Patrick sometimes stop the bus for us to see some special sights in places such as Mullinger, Moate and Athlone. We went into a lot of places and parks and climbed a lot of stairs into abandoned houses and a castle. It was a good and enjoyable day. That evening Patrick decided for us to overnight in a little town near Lough Ree, named Kiltoom, at some nameless friends of his, farm.

"We shall stay here tonight," he said, "then tomorrow go on through some lovely country."

He was demonstrating confidence and pride in his country and he was right, and as far as I was concerned it was beautiful. I had seen some nice places in England, but such great hospitality, scenery and historical spots, I had never encountered before. I was delighted to be invited to see it. Indeed, an enjoyable day. That evening, we drank the beers and stout that was provided by Harry, the bus driver and had supper with the nameless owners of the farm. Some stories were told, then to bed.

Although Teresa and I slept together in the same bed, she wouldn't make love to me.

"You'll have to wait sweetheart," she said while kissing me, "just be patient."

I could hear the others making love, but for some reason I liked this woman and wasn't angry. I let her cuddle up in my arms and we both fell asleep.

The next morning we were up at five o'clock with the chickens. Everybody was running around getting themselves ready for the trip, while the lady of the house was busy making breakfast for us. Here again Patrick and Ian were playing the tour guide, by describing the next scenes of the places we would pass. This time we only made two stops, first at Ballinastoe and then Craughwell. Seeing Galway Bay from the hill top seemed like standing in a painting, a picture dotted with many little white cottages. I admitted to him that it was a spectacular view.

"Look you bunch of idiots," Patrick shouted. "This is what we call beauty. Take a good look, so when you go back to dirty old England you can tell them that you've seen this."

Patrick was overjoyed and proud to show it off and emphasized details of its history and its meaning to the Irish people.

"The Vikings came here first, as well as the Normans and the Saxons. Some of them still live in its natural setting on the Aran islands, just out there," he stated.

There was total silence.

"And would you believe," he continued, "it's almost all owned by the English upper crust? And the Royal family owns the most," he said in a sad tone.

We stayed there for a day and saw everything that Patrick could find to show us. I was very impressed with the place and was comfortable with having lovely Teresa hanging on to me all the time; although I would've rather make love to her. During this time, the boys were having fun with their girls. I could hear their conversations which were mostly about the army and their places of birth.

The next morning we left Galway Bay and made a stop in Limerick, again it was with some relatives of his and left later that afternoon for the city of Cork. It was late night when we pulled into the city and to the pub owned by his uncle.

"This town is mine," Paddy shouted as we parked in front of his uncle's guest house. I was happy Patrick had invited me along to see

Ireland, and his home town friends seemed delighted to be with us also. Although, they did not talk much about themselves or anything political, we all seemed to enjoy their company. I noticed that during the entire trip, Patrick kept his comments of dislike for the English to a minimum. Maybe because he was having a wonderful time with his lady, whose parents I learned, are English and Norwegian.

"Hey Paddy," I said. "I must admit that Ireland is really a pretty place, but tell me, why are some of you trying to destroy it?" I asked.

He thought for some time then in a soft controlled tone he replied,

"In some societies, like the Chinese for instance, they don't condone stealing, fornication or adultery, which in sone cases are punishable by death. Where some times the family's house is burnt to discredit the guilty in the public's view. That is to discourage any others from indulging in this form of immoral existence."

I knew that if I had asked a question relating to morality or the breaking down of the fibres of our society, I could get him to respond in terms of other country then compare that to the new problems facing Ireland.

"As everyone can see," he continued, "King James had the bible rewritten especially for himself, to satisfy his selfish desires and to defy the Pope, like his grandfather had done. So he set out to destroy Catholicism by any means, which was also attempted by other kings in other times. He didn't spare the use of force against the common people of any country he felt the urge to attack, and it's now Ireland's turn."

"Yes, and the rest of the so-called commonwealth too," said Charley.

"What about lady Scotland Bob?" I asked. "How did she survive the wrath of the English throughout history?"

Bob Muldoon, who was busy with his girl and had been quiet during this conversation, responded almost instantly.

"We had to learn how to circumvent the English rules after being defeated in many wars and Ireland will have to do the same, soon."

I was expecting Paddy to get angry, but nothing came. After a long pause he said,

"Maybe the Scottish people didn't fight hard enough, but we will."

Nobody responded and the conversation ended.

We stayed in Cork that night and most of the next day and left in the afternoon. The trip back took the rest of the night and part of the next day, with only two stops. One in Dublin where we met Jack's parents and had a late supper and some drinks with them, then at a small town north of Dublin. We stayed at some digs for the night and left the next morning for Belfast with Jack doing most of the driving.

On returning to their house, Shaun O'Reilley insisted we have tea with them. Everybody was happy to be together again for the evening because we talked and joked for most of the night. We were kept entertained by young Eric and Shaun, who took turns telling tales about their family and their escapades. Finally a story was told about an uncle in England, who was fired from a job for no apparent reason, then was arrested, tried and imprisoned as an accomplice in a robbery, he didn't know about.

"He was unfortunate enough, as things go," said Shaun, "he happened to walk down a street at the wrong time and couldn't prove his innocence, so he got five years in prison."

"What happened after that?" Rod asked.

"He went insane waiting for the appeal hearing," said Shaun, "and never recovered from that experience. He's still walking around Liverpool talking to himself.

That story seemed to spark something in Patrick, he became enraged instantly.

"Now that's classic of the Brits for you. To them it doesn't matter if it was only circumstantial evidence, you're guilty for being Irish," he shouted.

"According to the laws," said Rod, "one should be innocent until proven guilty; shouldn't they?"

"That's right!" replied Patrick. "That's how it should be, in accordance to their democratic process of law. But...."

"I don't think it was because he was Irish, but one never knows what judges will think at the time," said Rod.

"In this society," Tom said, "as an Irishman, it's the opposite. One is guilty for being alive."

This discussion took on a strong political tone and went on for sometime, until Ella reminded them that we were guests in their home. Patrick told her that we are friends and understood each other's point-of-view in these kinds of things.

"You see mother," he said with a grin, "this is why I want to learn all there is about explosives, so that I can blow them up when I return home."

"Patrick!" shouted Ella. "I don't want that kind of talk in my house. Stop this instant. You shouldn't be talking like that while in the British military."

"Patrick," said Charley, "do you honestly believe that your action would solve the problem?"

"Maybe not," he replied, "but it would drive some fear up their arse and many of my friends would be delighted to assist in the bomb making also."

Again Ella shouted for him to stop.

Shaun quickly reminded him that he was now in the British army and talks like that could get him into serious trouble. Patrick just smiled and said,

"These fellows have all suffered their wrath in Aldershot, in more ways than one, so I'm not afraid of them telling on me. I know they can be trusted."

"As a Jamaican," said Charley. "I can tell you some stories that would curl your hair, about the Englishmen in my country."

Everyone sat quietly while Charley told his stories.

Then Bob expressed his displeasure for the government, who have an history for mistreatment of his people also.

"Even though we have the industries in Scotland," said Bob. "they're all owned by the English."

I was learning something new about people and their inner selves and the effect of historical exploitation. It's amazing how an innocent conversation on a topic could trigger a memory of incidents. I was learning something about how the mind functions, believe me. Maybe Freud could explain it.

All during dinner and throughout the lengthy discussion, I noticed Teresa made sure she sat beside me, often holding my hand. But because I was so engrossed in the intense conversation, I didn't bother with her until Bob reminded them about his date with the girl he had met at the dance. I was about to get up when she pulled my hand towards her chest.

"I don't feel like going out tonight," she said, "let's stay here for awhile."

"Oh, oh, this looks like marriage, eh father?" said Ella.

Shaun just looked at us with a smile and said,

"Well let's leave them alone, it's time for our bed anyway. Come on woman."

Eric started to tease her, but she flashed her hand at him, and he ran out to join the boys. By the time they left, she was all over me with kisses. This time when I put my hand on her firm breasts, she didn't remove it as before. I opened her blouse to expose them. There was no objection, so I knew that she was ready to make love to me. Which we did on the sofa. I don't recall at what time I left the house, but it was nearly morning light. I walked to the digs, to find the boys already up and chatting.

"I say old chap," Bob Muldoon joshes me, "lovely night the last, what? Care to tell us about it?"

"A gentleman should never tell of his love affairs, especially when it involves a wonderful lady. And a friend should only observe and not ask questions," I said as I walked away.

Everybody laughed. Then Patrick came over and said,

"You know something? I had a feeling she was ready for you last night. But then again, from the time I wrote telling her about you, she made it quite clear that if you looked as good as I had described, she was willing to make love to you."

"What?" I exclaimed. "You mean to tell me you told her to make it with me?" I was really surprised that he had done this.

"No my friend," he said, "I didn't. But as I had told you, if she was stupid enough to fall for you, then I won't stand in the way."

We stood there looking at each other for a long moment. We shook hands, then I went for a shower.

As we were leaving the digs, two of Patrick's friends came. He stopped and introduced us to them. When that was over, he advised us to carry on because he had some things to discuss with his two friends. The rest of us left to walk around town. He caught up to us about an hour later and announced that we would be leaving the next morning for Dublin.

"Will we be going to Dublin by the same bus we went to Galway in?" enquired Philip Hoyt, who like Tom, very seldom spoke.

"Yes," replied Paddy.

"Why should we leave town now," said Phil, "when we only just got here and are now established with the girls?"

Jack opened his mouth to reply, but Tom was much quicker.

"Gentlemen please, you came to see Ireland and I intend on showing you Ireland," he said, "at least some of it anyway. The good and bad of it. So please relax and see the place, and to Dublin we shall go tomorrow."

"Yes," said Charley, "and we're going to meet some more pretty Colleens there too, right?"

I stood looking at Tom, because for all the times we'd been together, this was the first time Thomas Matterson ever spoke of Ireland in an emotional tone. His outburst had me dumbfounded for a moment.

"What did Patrick stick up your arse last night?" I asked him. "Tom you have never talked about Ireland."

"Stan my boy," he said seriously, "unlike Paddy here, I don't like to discuss or publicly demonstrate my emotions about anything political. But I am very proud of my country and my people. It's true that the politics need to be revamped somewhat, but I love this land anyway."

"All of us here are friends, and each of us loves our respective place of birth, but we're also receptive to other places and things, that's why we're here in Ireland,"said Bob. "Maybe I will get the chance to show you all of Edinburgh and Glasgow some day also. So come on idiots, stop all this bickering and lead the way to the food, I'm getting hungry."

While we were eating, the conversation returned to Dublin again.

"What time did you say we're leaving?" I asked.

Charley who was busy stuffing his face, answered.

"Tomorrow morning by bus and just when I was getting to know that lovely little girl, we have to leave."

"Don't worry about that," said Patrick. "We'll be coming back here Thursday."

"Oh yeah?" said Charley grinning and sat up straight in his chair. "That's okay by me."

"Well Paddy mi lad," I teased in a mimicked Irish brogue, "by what means are we travelling?"

"Remember that friend who drove us to Galway? He will be coming to pick us up with the same bus."

"Good," said Bob, "with food and beers, I hope."

"Yes Bob," replied Jack, "with plenty of beers and food."

"We'll be riding in style, eh?" said Phil. "Good, it's better than those rickety street buses or trains."

Everybody laughed.

Harry, our ever-smiling but nameless bus driver, arrived on time. I wondered why he didn't want to tell us his name or never offered any comments or opinion throughout the entire trip last time. He never spoke to any of us about anything at all. He very seldom showed any emotions whenever somebody criticized the Country's politics or commented on any of the violence there. Everybody called him "Harry the Irish. Man without a tongue." We loaded ourselves into the bus and was on our way.

As we travelled along Patrick pointed-out places and referred to them as "Our stronghold," or "Our position." Nobody questioned him on this. All the discussions were either about women or money. Once when Harry and Patrick were talking about something unknown to the rest of us, the word "Sinn Fein" was used. Rod asked him what or who he meant was Sinn Fein. Patrick just smiled and said that we would find out some day.

The rest of the trip was fine until we reached Dublin. The driver quickly found a pub and let us off, saying that Paddy, Jack, Ian, Tom and himself had some business to attend to and some relatives in the area to see. They promised to meet us back at the pub later. Charley, Bob, Phil, Rod and I were left to fend for ourselves. We didn't really care, because all we intended on doing was drink and seek out girls, if we could.

In the pub, we questioned the owner and some others about the women of Dublin.

"Come back later," said the publican, "the ladies will be here then."

We decided to find a good restaurant to have something to eat, then seek out the town.

"Dublin is such a large city," the publican told us, "be careful where you go."

A warning we didn't pay much attention to. We hit everywhere we could find opened to us. We did the town from one pub to another via a taxi. When we finally reached back at the first pub, we learnt that Paddy and the boys had been there and left again. Since the night was at an end, we decided to find digs, but that was impossible due to the lateness of the night, so we walked the downtown streets until morning. As we were walking along the street of the first pub, we saw the bus parked. They were asleep inside it.

"Hey, you bunch of bastards!" Phil shouted angrily as he opened the door. "Leave us out in the cold will you. Imagine we had to walk the streets all night. It's a damn good thing that Bob had this bottle of rum."

He waved the empty bottle at them as proof of our night's drinking. Nobody offered an explanation so the quarrel got more intense. Finally Patrick got up and said,

"Gentlemen, allow me to apologise for our action last evening, but we had some business to attend to, which took more time than anticipated."

There was dead silence for about two minutes.

"Is that all?" asked Charley.

Still more silence.

"Then take us back to Belfast so we might go home," Rod shouted. "I think this fucking holiday here is ended."

"Come on fellows," Paddy pleaded, "try to understand."

"Yes," shouted Bob, "we do understand. You didn't want us outsiders to know what the hell's going on so we were left in the cold. I agree with Philip, Rod and Charley. Take us back to Belfast, then we can go home."

"Yes, we will go home boys but....." said Tom.

"But nothing," shouted Rod.

There was a blanket of silence again.

Only this time it lasted for almost half of the trip back to Belfast, where we arrived later that evening.

The four Irish men left us alone again so we went to the rooming house and after getting cleaned up and a change of clothes, the five outsiders entered another pub in the Protestant area. There was a loud explosion and a fire. We ran to the area to see that it was a large factory ablaze. The fire-fighters were busy and there was a large gathering of people cheering. I was rather shocked to see this, and stated my question to some of the people close by. Rod grabbed my arm and told me to mind my own business, so we left and walked around some more. I was still upset about the fire and the people's attitude, but said nothing about it.

"They were actually cheering a destruction," I thought.

We reached back to our original pub and began discussing my feelings again, when Ella and Shaun walked in. They joined us for a beer.

"Where is Teresa?" I asked.

"She's at home waiting for you," Shaun replied.

"Is it alright for me to go there?" I asked.

"Sure my boy," he said with a grin.

I left them all at the pub for the house and to Teresa.

About noon the next day I left the house in the direction of the digs, when I saw the others coming towards me.

"Hi boys, what's going on?" I asked.

"Absolutely nothing," replied Charley. "We took the girls out last night. Bob and I was with those two sisters at their place until midnight. Phil was with that teacher and stayed at her place all night. And we found Rod standing in front of the pub later."

"Why?" I asked.

"The girl wouldn't let me stay at her place," said Rod, "it was late when I got back to the digs and was locked out. Paddy and his friends didn't come back with the bus, so I walked the streets until the boys found me at the pub door."

"Yeah," said Phil, "and we're still walking."

We walked to the pub and enquired of the owner for Patrick and and the boys.

"They're all asleep in the back room," he said.

I opened the door slightly and peeked in to see the four of them on a bed sleeping. Softly I closed it again and told the others. We began banging things, making a lot of noise. Eventually they came out to join us.

"What's all the commotion out here?" asked Jack. "A man can't even get some kip."

"You want some kip?" shouted Bob. "What about us poor bastards? We haven't slept a fucking wink all night. We have been walking the fucking streets again, just like in Dublin."

Before I could say anything, Rod described that we went to investigate a fire and how the people reacted. None of them seem concerned.

"Oh, by the way Paddy," I said looking around the room "where's Harry?"

Everything was silent for a while.

"Harry had to go to work," he replied.

"When are we going back to England?" Bob asked.

Patrick directed that we would be going to Londonderry the next day to see some other friends. Then we would be coming back to Belfast to see his family and the girls, before taking the ferry to Liverpool and then to London for the rest of our holidays.

For all the times we spent in Belfast, I never once asked or questioned their activities. I did not consider any of their movement devious, although some were surely questionable. I never pressed any of them about their political feelings about their country, although I had already formulated an opinion on that matter. But I couldn't resist the thought that the three blacks, one English and one Scot, were always left alone, whenever they went to see their "friends."

I decided not to air my point-of-view until the time was right, even though I was a little perturbed by this. We were still having fun and I must admit that I had thoroughly enjoyed myself on my first visit to Ireland. But I could not overcome the attitude and joyful reactions of the people, whenever we heard of some destruction befalling the people or property in that city, and the radio news was full of those devastations hourly.

We left Londonderry with the same quarrel as we had gone there with. We hurriedly got back to Belfast, collected our things and left for England.

Leaving that city on the ferry to Liverpool was somewhat satisfying. In a way, for some unexplained reason, I was glad to be back in England. I was getting annoyed by all the violence in such a nice city, and to people who seemed quite hospitable. I was angry for numerous reasons but said nothing. As a matter of fact, I had accused Patrick of diverting me away from his sister and he apologised for screwing that up, explaining that it was not his intention to stop us from being together and promised to make it up to Teresa and I in a letter. We stayed in Liverpool for a day, mostly in Merseyside. The night-life there was fantastic and there we visited a club to see a new band named the Beetles.

That was what we wanted to cheer things up a bit, and it did. Most of the time, we took cheap shots at Patrick for taking us away without saying goodbye to his parents. At one point I said,

"You know something? I think it was you four that burnt down that place in Belfast."

Right away Jack became very defensive and told us that our friendship was based on trust and if any of us thought they had anything to do with it, we might as well abolish our relationship now. Patrick intervened with a wave of his hand.

"Gentlemen," he said, "what kind of shit is all this? What am I hearing? We shouldn't be quarrelling over trivial things as this."

He paused for a moment then added,

"We four are Irishmen," he said indicating to Ian, Jack and Tom, "and anything that happens in our country is our concern and I don't expect any of you to feel the same way we do."

Everybody stood there looking at him, as he continued.

"I wish you will take some time to read and try to understand some of the problems that exist there; not only as they are reported by the authorities, but by listening to the people. Try to visualize their point of view, hear their voices, which sometimes could tell you more about what's going on."

We conceded our thoughts and agreed that the accusations were confounded. I stretched out my hand for a shake without saying anything else. He quickly took it.

"Friends?" he asked.

"Friends forever," everybody repeated in unison.

We left on the eleven twenty-five train to London and since I had journeyed in this direction before, I was planning to point out some of the interesting places to them, but because it was night and everybody was tired, the couch seats were a welcomed sight. We were all asleep by the time the train left the station.

When I woke up the next morning and checked the time, it was past eight o'clock and we were almost in London.

"Now," I said yawning and stretching my body, "when we get to my city, I am going to show you arseholes how to have fun."

I didn't let any of them speak.

"This city has everything you can think of. I am going to take you to the West-End, you know, Soho? And maybe even to a strip show. You will all see from Buckingham Palace to the Borough of Brixton," I said boastfully.

"Remember now, we only have three more days and it's back to Aldershot," said Jack, breaking into my speech.

"So we'll all be drunk when we get back, who cares," said Charley.

"Wasn't that the purpose of our holidays?" asked Bob.

The conversation once again took on a women and money tone, and went on until the train pulled into Paddington station.

Everybody quickly grabbed their bags and rushed off to the streets. First I took them to the Union Jack club in Waterloo to secure some rooms for later. We bathed and changed clothes, then it was up to Crystal Palace to see my relatives. We spent two hours with my cousins in Clapham Common, who were pleased to meet my new friends. Charley and I went to Forestgate in northeast London to get two old friends, while the others went to the Union Jack to await us. Rudolph Scarlet, George Walters and I, had been close friends since boyhood days in Jamaica. Maxfield Avenue in Kingston held some very exciting memories for us. They too were pleased to meet my army friends. We sat in the lobby of the Union Jack and talked until about ten-thirty that evening.

"Come on boys I have some womanizing to do," shouted Ruddux, "and tonight seemed to be a good time to begin."

Everybody agreed to that.

"It's the boys night out," I said, "and I am sure some passengers will be lodging their complaints to the London Transport Office about our noise on the Underground train tonight."

"I'm sure they will," replied Rod. "But I'm also sure that other squadies have done the same before."

In the West-End, they were in seventh heaven. It was like letting children loose in a candy factory. They couldn't make up their minds what to do first. We agreed to eat first, then a strip show and then it was one pub to another. Bob and Jack decided to try out a prostitute in the Strand and were gone somewhere. Rod, Ruddux, Charley, Philip, George, Patrick, Ian and I headed for the Roaring Twenties club. Tom found a girl in a pub at Trafalgar Square and stayed there. Later we all met at Piccadilly Circus and just walked the streets aimlessly, sight seeing.

Around six forty a.m. my friend's George and Ruddux, left for home.

I made a phone call to Faye Macleod to let her know that I was in London, but couldn't meet her. We decided to return to the Union Jack club to get cleaned up and then off to see some more of London.

"Okay then," I said boastfully, "where do you fools want to see first? The Palace is in that direction, Hyde park is not far from the Palace or maybe you would prefer to see Leicester Square? How about you Rod?" I asked.

Rod, although English born, lived in Newcastle all his life and had never been to London before.

"I would like to see the Palace," he said. "I have seen many pictures of it, but never saw it real."

Patrick was also very affirmative about his preference.

"Yes!" he said. "Let's see the Palace. I want to see the Castle in which the Irish people got shafted from."

"You mean," said Bob in a questioning tone, "the house of Kings and Queens? The house that Adolf Hitler wanted to have tea after the war?"

"Yes," he replied, "that same house. The house that should be blown up, and maybe stop the corruption that is overtaking our world today. Did you know that this is where all discrimination is rooted? Where political exploitation is practised? And that's an historical fact," he concluded.

There was a long silence.

"Paddy my boy," I said, "maybe you should wait until you get to

Hyde Park, you know the speakers corner, before making those statements."

"Maybe so," he replied, "but did you know that the Windsor family is related to the Czars of Russia and their mixed up brothers and sisters in Germany, Holland and Denmark? Yes sir, they are all one of the same. They wanted to control the world since the second century and are still trying to do so today."

To that, nobody argued, so Patrick continued.

"They wanted everybody to abide by their rules, unquestioned. Just the same as what Julius Caesar wanted and used his armies to try to implement it. Also other rulers had done it previously. Don't forget Napoleon and the many others like him, and now the English intend on using the same military to enforce this ideology, at all cost also."

We got off the underground train at St.James park and walked to the Palace. I found that although they were very enthusiastic about seeing the Palace, and willing to be familiar with its history, as told by Patrick of course, they all seemed to be unsettled. I was mostly intrigued to watch Patrick's and Jack's reactions throughout our tour around the grounds. I could sense the anger within them, although they kept it subdued and at times were very silent. I showed them the balcony from which the Queen addressed the loyal subjects.

"It's magnificent!" exclaimed Rod. "Seeing it in real life, is better than in the usual photographs. I did the history in school but, this is great. Have you been here before Stan?" he asked.

"Yes, many times," I replied. "Remember I lived near Crystal Palace, which is a stone's throw from here."

Although Phil and Charley lived in London, they had never been to the Palace either. Sometime later one of the others would josh the Irish boys about coming to see the Great house of democracy and they in turn would josh back about King Willy and the troubles he caused in Ireland's history. As a matter of fact, this was the topic for most of the afternoon.

They were impressed with the changing of the guards. I took them across to St.James park to see the horse guards station.

"These aren't the only people who guard the Queen," I told them, "there are more elite military personnel around."

We went to the Westminster Abbey, then walked all the way to Leicester Square. Then along Charing Cross road to the Strand. Suddenly Tom stopped.

"Look fellows," he shouted, "a tattoo artist. Let's get one done."

I wondered what would I be doing with a tattoo.

"No thank you," I said, "I don't need one."

All of them went in except Charley and myself. We went for a walk and returned when we thought they were done.

Bob had the Scottish flag with love and a girl name written under it, also Aberdeen his home-town. But the Irish boys had some funny looking design and some Gaelic words within it.

"Hey!" I said. "What's the significance of that?"

They were silent and wouldn't say. Patrick said that he would explain it to me someday. I continued to prompt him until he became very angry and adamant at my insistence.

"It's not for your knowledge," he said. "You not knowing about it won't make any difference to your life."

Nothing more was said about them for the duration of the holiday.

On the train to Aldershot, the conversation was on everything we did to the places we had been. The subjects ranged from money, politics and women and the controversy over their significant value to mankind. I got on to Patrick again about leaving his sister the way we did, without even saying goodbye, and once again he apologised and promised to write an explanation to her on my behalf, when we reach camp.

When we got into camp, I asked him again about the tattoo. He just stared at me menacingly without words, never answering my question. I let him know that staring would not frighten me off, and we dispersed to our respective rooms and to attend the things we had to do in preparation for the Sergeant-Major's parade the next morning.

Getting back into the swing of things felt awkward. It felt as if we were coming to camp for the first time. But we knew the routine.

Because if you didn't know it after five months, then you won't know it again. The Lorries were waiting to take us to Farnham and to Sixty Three Para Regiment, and ten more weeks of training.

"This is where one try to prove their manhood," the Sergeant Major told us. As a matter of fact, the two sergeants who interviewed us, tried in some degree to intimidate us by emphasizing how tough it was going to be, although there's a pride that goes with having that wing on your shoulder and the badge on your maroon red beret. I decided that I was willing to give it a good try. That's all I could think of doing, was my best.

I also realized that I wouldn't be seeing Fiona for another couple of weeks. One of her friends told me that she had gone back to Scotland, on a well deserved holiday to see her parents. I wasn't sure about Catharine at this point in time either, so with Fiona and Helen gone, I am high and dry sex wise for a while. Anyway, my thoughts were only on being in the new regiment and their expectations of me.

Tashie Wickham, was in a good mood this morning. He had been making a few jokes, which he rarely does, about his children leaving home.

"Now listen you nig-nogs," he shouted, "if for some reason any of you don't make it with the Paras, you can still come back here. I have every bit of confidence that all of you are good solders that would fit well into my regiment."

"Thank you sir," everybody replied.

"Now here is your new commander and training officer, Captain Mark Harrison."

When I heard the name Mark Harrison, my mind flashed back to the day on a train with Catharine Harrison and hoped he was her brother and not her husband.

I guess he was standing behind us, because it took a while before he appeared. He was a very large burly red haired man of about six foot two and 250 pounds. His reddish pigmentation indicated that he was from the midlands of England.

"I am your commander and will be for the duration of your time in this regiment," he said, as he paused for a moment to look on our faces, "For those who don't make it in the Airborne, your records will show that you had duly participated in the training programme, and the rest will receive their wings."

I wondered why such a large person spoke so softly. He went on to show the SAS (Special Air Service) insignias on his tunic. He told us a story of an incident involving himself as a young officer in Hong Kong. When he was through talking, Tashie came forward again to wish us luck and took turns shaking everybody's hand. When he reached in front of me he said,

"Mr Martin, remember as a black man, a high calibre of respect is expected from you. You will be subjected to a lot of degrading tactics, but don't let them deter you. That doesn't mean you must subdue your character for anyone, be strong here," he pointed to my head with his pace stick, "and you will get admiration and respect from here."

Again he pointed, this time to my heart.

I stood there staring into Tashie's eyes and realized that he meant every word he just said.

"Thank you sir," I said. "I promise to do my best."

He opened his mouth to begin another speech, but opted to say instead,

"Look after those Irish boys for me, it seem they only obey your commands."

"Do you really think so sir?" I asked. I was very curious to his statement.

"Oh, I know so young man, I know so. See you in a couple of months," he said and turned to dismiss the parade.

We loaded ourselves into the trucks along with our kitbags. We were on our way to Farnham. Captain Mark Harrison also rode in the back of the truck I was in and I wondered if Catharine ever told him what we did on the train from London. I kept a curious look on him from the corner of my eyes all the way. We arrived at the camp and were billeted separately away from the regulars already there.

"Gentlemen," said Harrison, "please make yourselves at home and do try to familiarize yourselves with every corner of this camp, because you will be required to use it."

He paused long enough for us to digest what he had just said.

"If you have any problems," he continued, "my office is always open every minute of the day or night. Any question? Then I will see you tomorrow."

That night was spent in the NAAFI for a few brews, then bed.

The next morning, Mark Harrison came right after breakfast. He took us through a camp familiarization tour and constantly spoke of the discipline that it takes to become a paratrooper.

"One has to be strong," he said, "psychologically prepared to perform the physical things requested of you. Decisions here are made at a split second and one must be equipped to do so. Our training is designed purposely to achieve that objective, as you will see in the days ahead."

The silence was thick.

"You're going to encounter many different training officers who will teach you many things, some of which you could not apply to civilian life later, but will help you to survive if you're ever sent into action. Any question?"

I knew that somebody would, and Patrick was the first.

"Do you think we could be called upon, sir? And where do you think it would be?" Paddy asked.

The Captain replied that he does not know for certain, but it might be in the Far East. He assured us that we would have the opportunity to hear the facts, when that time came.

That night was our induction into the regiment. It seemed the entire regiment came to our billet. They ordered us out and into a truck, which took us to a swamp pond somewhere in a wooded area. We were ordered to remove all our clothing and get to the other side. I discovered that it was hard to walk in mud and swimming wasn't any better either. I took about forty five minutes to reach across, but it was done. Then we had to run back to camp naked. One hour of soap and water wasn't enough to remove the stench that seemed to cling to my body.

For the first six weeks they made our lives very miserable as promised, although there wasn't any kind of parade as in Aldershot.

We were required to do a five mile run before breakfast every morning. The obstacle course began with a set of twenty five steps leading to a platform, from which you leap from to a set of ropes that is used to slide back to the ground. The ropes were also used to swing over a mud pond, the same one we had on initiation, before climbing over the five foot fence. The three hundred yards run along a path led to a twenty foot concrete wall, with short ropes. There were some barbed wire, about two feet off the ground, that you crawled under. The set of seventy five steps led to a thirty five foot long steel bar, which you walk along to a platform, then another set of ropes to climb to the thousand foot steel cable that is used to slide across another mud pond, to the ground.

The PT was every day and sometimes at nights, and seemed never-ending. We had to jump from the back of a lorry, moving at thirty miles per hour, to learn the roll and to familiarize ourselves with the feeling of landing on the ground at that speed. The swaying of the practice jump platform gave the sensation of being in a plane.

Learning to fold your own chute, was to develop your ability to concentrate on your personal safety, because we were required to climb up the thousand foot ladder to the platform to test them. The ripcord, which is hooked up to a line, ensure that your chute would open almost instantly on your jump.

Most of our exercises were done on Salisbury planes and some times included other troops. The night jumps are the most dangerous ones, because of the unexpected obstacles and swamps in that area.

We learned hand to hand combat, both in the gym and in the field, to perfect our techniques and how to read a map, even in the dark. They spent a lot of time teaching us of the conduct required in any given situation and how to survive in the wilderness. The nine of us worked hard on our physical, even doing extra time in the gym and on the obstacle course, to ensure passing the test.

Mark did everything with us, even the gas tent, and although we were around him everyday, nobody seemed to get to know him well. He had taken us under his wings as his personal property and I noticed that he would spend an enormous amount of time explaining things in detail to us. We became his special interest platoon and Patrick, Jack and Ian seemed to be his most valuable ones, although Charley, Phil, Rod, Tom and I were also treated well.

At the end of the seventh week, there was a parade called to announce the names of those who would be released to other regiments, and those who would go on to earn their wings. The list was long, but included only one of our friends. Phillip Hoyt didn't mind going to another regiment, but promised to keep our friendship intact. Some were given the opportunity to go to the Air Dispatch, REME, RASC or the Royal Engineers.

By the end of the ten weeks, we were assured of passing our final test and to become fully trained paratroopers. Although I was spending most of my time off with Fiona in Bordon and the one weekend in London with Faye, there wasn't much to my midweek sex life. I was afraid to go into town in case I ran into Catharine and then have him kill me. Most of the time, I was either reading books that Patrick would bring over or at the gym in Aldershot, boxing with Tashie Wickham. Patrick did write the letter to Teresa on my behalf and she did reply to me telling of her plans to come for our passing out jump. The rest of the family from Ireland were also coming. I also invited some of my relations from London to be there.

I felt very proud knowing that I had endured the ten weeks of tough rigorous training, which included a lot of degrading racial abuse from the training sergeants, and the many fights in the NAAFI. But due to the advise of Tashie Wickham and the constant encouragement of Patrick, I was about to earn my wings.

We were given that weekend off to do whatever we wanted, on a promise to Mark Harrison that we would refrain from any fights. The boys agreed to hangout in Aldershot with the girls that Friday night. We reached down town very early to start the drinking and womanizing and by about eight thirty, we had swallowed quite a lot of beers at the NAAFI Centre. I was on my way from the bar to the gents room to relieve myself of some excess beer, when I saw her standing outside. I had to decide to either go to the men's room first and risk missing her, or to go see her and hope not to piss myself. I choose the latter. As soon as she saw me, she became excited, flashing those beautiful evenly-matched set of teeth as if she was specifically waiting for me.

She was well dressed as usual, in a beautiful green floral dress, which clung to her braless bosom like a glove. Her shoes and purse matched her orange coloured broad-rimmed hat and scarf. I got a stiff on just smelling her perfume.

"Well, hello Mrs. Harrison," I said in a sexy tone of voice. "Waiting for a bus?" I asked.

"Hello mister soldier," she replied. "No I wasn't, although I was hoping you would come along."

I assured myself that she was telling the truth.

"Would you like to go into the NAAFI for a drink?" I asked her.

She declined, but suggested we go for a drive instead. Catharine was that kind of a woman, very much assertive in whatever her desires were. I was elated for her offer and told her to wait for me a minute. I ran quickly bach inside to the men's room, then hurriedly returned. By that time, she had already walked across the street and stood beside her car waiting. I got into the car and we left almost instantly for the drive into the countryside. She found a nice quiet spot overlooking the city and parked. She got a blanket and spread it on the ground.

"Well soldier," she said, in that mimicked Jamaican accent, "it's a very beautiful summer's evening and this is your opportunity to make love to me on the green grass."

Her suggestion took me by surprise. I stuttered and for a moment forgetting what I was to do, but that was only a small lapse in a fragment of time. I returned her affection and we began removing our clothing and made love on that hill in the most enjoyable fashion. In between, we just laid there naked under the stars, talking about life for the both of us. It was getting late, so she wished me luck in the rest of my training and possible posting to the Far East.

"Stan I am going to miss you immensely," she said.

In the dark, I could feel a trace of tears from her eyes trickling down her face.

"Life for me has changed drastically since I met you," she continued, "and I am a little reluctant now in letting go."

I took my finger to wipe the tears away and knew that she meant every word.

"I will miss you too," I said.

We made plans to see each other often before I left, as she drove back to camp in the early morning. I was relaxed from the smell of the fresh air and happy to have spent the night with Catharine and making love on the grass.

As I was about to get out of the car, there was a shadow standing beside the door. I looked up to see the goodly Captain there. He did not try to stop me from getting out, but I was being cautious anyway.

"Good morning Mr. Martin," he said. "I see you know my wife."

I didn't know what to say, so I kept quiet.

"Where and when did you meet?" he asked.

I was just about to tell him when something came over me and I felt the urge to stand up.

"Sir," I said very affirmed, "I didn't know she was your wife and as you might know, when two people meet under the influence of alcohol, anything is possible."

I wasn't sure what his reaction would be, or if my statement made any sense to him, but I took a defensive stance just in case. Nothing happened. He stared at me for awhile, then asked me kindly to leave.

"I would like to have a private conversation with my wife, if you don't mind," he said.

I looked at her and she nodded her head in agreement.

"I will be fine darling," she said. "Go ahead."

I took her advice and was on my way, but all the time I was wondering what will become of Catharine. I headed for the billets, and there I was confronted by Patrick.

"You should've told me where you were going," he said. "We would have blocked him from finding you."

"Thanks for the offer," I said, "but this had to happen some time anyway. Better now than later," I replied in a matter of fact way.

Patrick insisted that I should have told them what was going on, because brothers must protect each other at all cost.

I told them the story, except some of the intricate details about us on the train. They all laughed at the episode and expressed their fascination of how quickly I was able to pick up such a beautiful woman.

"That's expected from someone like you," he said, "and that woman should have been hung for deceiving her husband."

"What can I say, I am very charming and they can't resist my advances," I boasted. Everybody laughed at that also.

For the next week I tried desperately to keep out of Captain Harrison's way, but to no avail. Although he never said anything, the disgusted looks on his face told me of his disapproval of my relationship with his wife, and the boys never mentioned it either.

The day we were all waiting for, was nigh. I received a letter from Teresa saying that none of the family would be coming, due to the politics. I spoke to Patrick about it and although he was disappointed, he expressed that we must stand strong and do what we came there for. That Friday evening, Captain Harrison announced the names of those who would be jumping in the first group the next morning and I was in the unlucky number thirteenth spot. To make matters worst, he also said he would be behind me.

"Oh my god!" I thought. "He'll have the pleasure of checking my pack. All he has to do is to fasten the strap so my pack wouldn't open and I would be dead."

My thoughts had me in a vice all night.

"I was caught fucking the man's wife and now he's going to kill me and it would be legal. Nobody would suspect him of murder and even if they did, it would be considered justifiable homicide."

I didn't sleep a wink all that night, worrying about what was to come. My imagination ran wild.

"My body will be splattered all over Farnborough air field," I thought.

It was Saturday morning and we were supposed to have a good breakfast but I couldn't eat anything, only coffee and toast . Maybe it was my last meal. I was shaking like a leaf, trembling in fact,. and got even worst when my name was called.

"Ok Martin," Mark's voice sounded from behind me, "what's your problem then?"

"Just a little nervous sir, that's all," I replied.

But anyone could hear the shakiness in my voice.

"Don't worry," he said, putting his hand on my shoulder. "If I was going to kill you for fucking my wife, I would've done it last week Friday night. Today you're here to earn your wings, so prepare to do your job soldier."

I couldn't answer and didn't offer any kind of conversation to my commander.

We got our gear on and was trucked to the airfield and into the transporter.

By the time we were loaded, I was starting to overcome the fear of him killing me to the natural fear of jumping.

I felt my body left the plane and into open space. I began my count. I could see the ground twirling around and rushing towards me. All the weeks of training returned to my mind. The times before on Salisbury planes, the chute was opened by direct hook-up, but this time it was a free-fall.

"Ten." I said aloud and pulled the ripcord. I felt the jolt of a pull on my body and looked up. I sighed a sigh of relief when I saw the canopy opened above my head.

I looked down to see the markings for the drop zone and all the people and other planes. It was a beautiful sight to see and I was enjoying myself. I steered my chute towards it and in a few minutes I hit the ground and heard the people applauding.

Quickly I recovered my chute and ran over to my friends to boast about my experience. I felt a hand on my arm and turned to see Captain Harrison standing there, I quickly introduced him to my cousins and he shook hands with them then he told me that someone else wanted to talk to me, and escorted me to her. She was sitting with some of their friends in the stands. He introduced us to satisfy their friend's eyes, then he excused himself and left us alone.

"Well Catharine," I whispered, "what happened last Saturday morning? And why didn't you tell me he was your husband?"

She slowly looked at her friends sitting behind us, then whispered back.

"Let's not talk about it here, please," she said.

I agreed and we talked about my jump for a while. She softly told me that she would be going to London the next weekend, the same time as I was on my seventy two hour pass and for me to meet her there. I was a little reluctant, but I agreed to her suggestion.

"And where will he be?" I asked about the Captain.

"Oh, he'll be in Yorkshire, where you will be in two weeks time," she replied. "He'll be visiting his family in Sheffield, then to meet you all in Ripon."

I was surprised to learn that she knew almost everything about the troops movement. She told me that since I was only going to be there in Yorkshire for two weeks, she would stay in London and wait and I should meet her there again. I told her we would talk about it when we meet in London the next week. We parted company for the day and didn't see each other for the rest of that week.

I phoned her when I got into London.

"Hello sweetheart," I said into the phone. "I'm here now, where do we meet?" I asked her.

"There's a little jazz club named Gigi on Grosvenor Road," she said. "It's right across from Normans of Westminster, meet me there at eight o'clock."

"Right-o," I replied. "See you."

Gigi's was a quaint, but seductive little jazz club used by many of the upper crust party goers, and which I found out even Princess Margaret sometimes frequented. Catharine was already there waiting. We got seated and ordered our drinks. I began to question her on Mark's reason for not being up-set about our Saturday morning confrontation.

"Look," she said. "Mark and I never had a cohesive relationship from the beginning and have been apart for the last three years. We stayed together because of the Officer's corps as agreed. That morning, Mark and I had a reasonable discussion on the matter, and I told him that I was in love with you and wanted out of our pathetic marriage. Although he admitted that it has been over for the last three years, he still refused to give me the divorce; but agreed for me to see you whenever I so desire."

"Why would he make such an agreement?" I asked.

"Because my darling," she replied, "he has no other recourse. About a year ago I made that request and he's now recognizing that our marriage is really over."

"I'm hearing what you're saying," I said, "but I still don't understand why."

"My sweet darling," she said holding my hand, "when you understand how the army works, you'll understand what I am talking about."

After a few drinks at Gigi's, we visited Ronny Scot's jazz club for an hour of dancing, then we did the town as much as possible for the night. We took a taxi to her rather upper-class apartment in Marble Arch and she opened the door. As soon as we entered, she began removing her clothes.

"Come sweetheart, you're home now, so relax, okay?" she said.

By the time we got into bed, she was ready for intercourse. We made love for almost the rest of the night. She waited until I lit cigarettes for both of us, then told me the rest of her story.

"You see my dear young soldier," she said in a scornful tone. "the British army officers corps is considered the elite of all military personnel, or so they think. And it is considered shameful if an officer becomes divorced. But if his wife is having an affair, discreetly of course, nothing is wrong with that."

I listened very intently to her explanation and wondered what life would be like in the days of King Arthur. Was Sir Lancelot really fucking Guenevere? Did the King know of their affair, but refrained from doing anything about it?

"Typically British, what?" I thought.

"You know something?" she said with a sneer, "I can see it now, he would be the talk of Sandhurst military college if this ever got out that Captain Mark Harrison's wife is having an affair with a young Negro soldier. It would kill some of them."

"Do you think that's right?" I asked curiously.

There was silence. I turned my head to look at her face and saw that she was in deep thought.

"Some time ago, I probably would think so," she replied, "but now I really don't care."

She paused and there was silence again.

"Okay," I said, "spill it. What's on your mind?"

She turned to face me, propping her head on her palms.

"Darling," she said, "when I met you on the train to Aldershot, I didn't have a clue that I would fall in love with you. It was supposed to be my black experience, my sexual expedition to real openness. I thought it would be a solo screw and that would be the end of it. But when I got to Aldershot, I felt an emptiness, a want, a desire I had never felt before. I was the most miserable person alive, so after a couple of weeks, I decided to find you."

She got out of bed and stood naked at the window in deep thought, not caring if anyone saw her from the streets.

"So what did you do?" I asked.

"I decided to hang around the NAAFI centre, hoping to see you. Then we met at the post office. I was so anxious to speak to you, to hold and kiss you and to tell you my feelings," she said.

She came towards the bed and stood looking down on me laying there.

"Stan," she said. "I am in love with you and yet... I know it will have to end some time."

"Why does it have to end?" I enquired.

"For one thing," she said, "look at our age difference. And that's not all, there are other things that cannot be explained right at this moment, but hopefully someday."

I gave thought to her statement and realised that it wouldn't make any sense to force her to talk.

"Who own's this apartment?" I asked.

"I do. This is mine," she replied, "but that's not the problem. My parents are...."

"Oh! Are they racists?" I asked.

"Not really, but...yes in a way they are. Look I will have to explain these little problems at a later time, okay?" she replied.

"Why not discuss it now? It's going to come up again you know?" I said hoping that she would take the prompting, but she flatly refused to.

Catharine and I spent a beautiful weekend making love and partying at some of the very nicest clubs in Soho.

"What would my relatives think of me, if they knew that I was here in London and never came to see them?" I thought.

"Anyway, I will write a letter promising to see them after I return from Yorkshire."

If Catharine was acting out a lie to me, she was successful, because I believed every word she told me. I bid her goodbye at the train station, I could see the tears from her eyes running down her rosy cheeks. I felt sad leaving her there. The picture of Humphrey Bogart and Ingrid Bergman in Casablanca crossed to mind.

I turned back.

"Would it be alright to kiss you in public?" I asked her.

Without a second thought, she wrapped her arms around my neck and pressed her lips to mine. Her tongue began searching for a path to mine. I guess we kissed for some time, because it was only when the conductor shouted for all on board, that we pulled apart.

"I will write to you," I shouted as I ran to the platform.

"I'll be waiting," she replied and watched me as I boarded the train to Yorkshire.

The ride to Yorkshire was lazy and quiet. I tried desperately, most of the time successfully, to avoid any conversation with anyone. The boys were already gone three days ago. I found myself alone in my car, so I kicked my shoe off and laid back on the seat hoping nobody would come in to interrupt me. All I wanted was to recall making love to Catharine and to vegetate. I wasn't even worried about what was awaiting me up there.

"Here I am just eighteen years and ten months old, fucking a woman who is now thirty six, a married one at that. She's in love with me and I don't know why. What if her husband decide to take revenge on me, somehow? I grew fearful, but fell asleep with those horrible thoughts.

The train stopped at Sheffield, then Leeds. A while later it pulled into the Ripon station. I felt relaxed and lazy, so all my actions were slow. I got my bags and walked outside to see if anyone was there to collect me. There wasn't, so I went back inside to enquire on the procedure and was told that the army usually sent a truck every hour. I had fifty minutes to wait. I sat on my bags for awhile, then got tired of that too. I saw a pub across the street and decided to go in for a drink or two or whatever I had.

I remembered somebody pulling me out of the pub and helped me into the truck. The ride to camp was rough, but I didn't care because I couldn't feel too much of anything and slept through the entire trip. The truck turned in through what I felt was a gate and stopped somewhere.

"Get up soldier, you're home," a voice shouted. I slowly got out of the vehicle and looked to see I was standing in front of the guardroom. A provo sergeant came to look at my papers and directed me to a set of billets further along the same side of the walkway. As soon as I get to the billets, I was greeted by Jack and Patrick coming from somewhere.

"Fancy seeing you here," Patrick said, putting his arms around me in a hug. "We couldn't live without our favourite nig- nog."

I punched him on the shoulder.

"I'm only here to keep you two alive, so get my bags boys," I said, waving at them as I started towards the steps.

"Yes master," said Jack, bending like the Hunchback of Notre Dame. "Us white slaves are willing to do our chores sir."

We spent some time talking about the things we did on our pass and they briefed me with detail of every nook and cranny of the place. We went to the mess hall for something to eat, then to the NAAFI for a couple of drinks and some more talk.

"Remember the codes we had agreed to?" said Jack. "Well Ian, Rod and Charley have completed writing them out. I'll get them now to explain it to the rest of us."

He quickly ran out and in maybe twenty minutes he returned with them. They all greeted me and sat.

"Here we all are, so let's begin," said Ian.

He pulled some papers from his pockets and handed everybody a copy. He began to read.

"Red," is for danger. "White," is quiet. "Blue," is guns. "Orange," is to be careful. "Green," is to go. "River," is bullets. "Sunrise," is east. "Sunset," is west. "Ice," is north. "Snow," is south. "Behave," is to be alert. "Fools," are enemies. "Moon," means caution, but it also means one two and many enemies like in, "Quarter moon fool," is one enemy, "Half moon fool," is two enemy, "Full moon," means more than... many. "Bed," is location. "Clean up," means kill all. "Neck tie," mean to use a knife. "Hat," means to take prisoner. "Pimple," is officers. "Grub," is NCO's. "Tchaikovsky," is to fight and "Beethoven," is peaceful.

"We will add more as time goes on," he said. "What do you think?"

Everybody sat quietly listening intently, so Ian carried on.

"Take Tchaikovsky for instance," he said. "He's a Russian, right?"

"Right," came the reply.

"He plays nice music, right?"

"Right," everybody said.

"But we know that Russians love to fight, right? So the word Tchaikovsky would mean to fight."

Right!" they replied.

"Let's say that some people decided to punch up Patrick in the NAAFI here. So on passing any one of us, he would simply say, "I like Beethoven rhapsody, but not Tchaikovsky's Eighteen Twelve overture. Get it?"

The group sat quietly thinking. So Ian explained.

"The word Tchaikovsky, would alert us about the fight."

"Hey! Then those idiots would not know that he had friends to back him up, right!" I said excitedly.

"That's right," agreed Patrick.

"Let's say we were on a night mission," said Rod, "and you heard this on your radio. `I'm at Sunrise Ice Zero. It's red. Use your green oranges. Don't be fools.' What then?"

"I got it!" shouted Tom. "It means you're at northeast of the zone and it's dangerous. There are many enemies here, come with caution."

"By Jove, I think he's got it," teased Bob.

"Okay, let's try this one," I said. "I'm at sunset snow. It's a full moon with white fools. Clean up the bed."

"That's easy," said Paddy. "You're at southwest of location and saw some enemies sitting around. We must kill all of them in the area."

"Very good Paddy," said Charley.

"Just listen for the telling words," said Rod. "A whistle like this, Tweet or tweet, tweet. mean to be silent. Or the word Behave and tweet, tweet. means quiet but alert."

They seemed happy about being together and to have devised a code of our very own.

"And what will we call our platoon?" Rod asked. "We'll have to get a code name for ourselves, you know."

"What about Robin Hood and the Merry men," I suggested.

"Naaah," replied Ian. "It has to have a personal meaning to all of us."

"Hey!" shouted Bob. "We could call ourselves the Nig-Nogs, the Nig-Nog platoon."

"Nig-Nogs!! said Charley. "That's for new recruits and the idiots."

"Absolutely my point," replied Bob. "Nobody would know who or what we were referring to and for those who understood what Nig-Nog meant would think we were calling each other idiots. But to us it means action."

"That's right," agreed Paddy. "We could be Nig #1 and two and three and......"

"We could draw numbers from a hat," Charley suggested.

Quickly some paper was torn and numbers written and was drawn from the hat. Rod #1, Ian #2, Jack #3, Charley #4, Patrick #5, Bob #6, Stan #7 and Tom #8.

When we left, it was closing time and everybody had a copy of our codes to study in bed.

The next morning we were up very early, from the noise being made with a siren.

"What a fucking place," I thought, "using a noise-maker like that for reveille. If they had used a bugler, then somebody would have the opportunity to kill him."

I laughed at that joke, which I had seen in a movie some time ago, and kept on smiling within to think that it's probably what had happened to the last one.

I got showered, shaved, dressed and went for breakfast. It tasted good, so I knew that I had not lost my appetite after all that drinking. I didn't even remember my headache from the night before.

The parade was to introduce the regimental commander to us. Colonel Trinkwan of the Royal Engineers, was a tall gangly man with a large moustache that occupied most of his face. He also wore a SAS insignia on his tunic. He introduced Captain Mark Harrison as the commander of our newly formed company of commandos and that we were there for some special weapons training.

"You'll be doing some tactical exercises," he said, "with real ammunition and other explosives."

Trinkwan also made it quite clear that the paras were guests of the regiment and should be treated that way. I was surprised to hear Captain Harrison telling them not to treat us with kid gloves, because we were trained tough and wished to be treated that way. Certainly we were trained tough and very disciplined, but I would rather like to be treated with more gentle respect.

That evening I met a young Sapper named Anthony "Skinny" Williams, who had just been transferred along with four others to our unit. I asked him for my friend Armon White, and was told that my friend had been posted somewhere in Germany. I was very disappointed not seeing Armon, I would've liked to exchange some boy days talk with him. But I promised to write him whenever I got the address from the company commander.

Skinny also told me that a Barbadian named Phil Hoyt, had been posted in. That excited me, so I walked to his billet to find him and our reunion was lovely. When I told him that the rest of the boys were also there, he got excited and invited all of us for a piss-up in the NAAFI the following evening, at his expense.

Two of the new boys, being black, clung mostly to me and Charley; although the white boys did accept them in our group. The others were happy to be with us also. We decided to teach them our codes, after we were satisfied that they were loyal to our friendship.

A meeting was called to select numbers for them. The list are:- Rodney Langley #1, Ian Mulligan #2, Jack O'Leary #3, Charley Green #4, Patrick O'Reilley #5, Bob Muldoon #6, Anthony Williams #7, Thomas Matterson #8, Peter Baron #9, Taffy Llewellyn #10, Cecil Brown #11, Dave Powell #12, Stan Martin # 13.

Because of his superstitious beliefs, I exchanged my #7 with Skinny Williams for #13. Both Derrick MacIntosh and Philip Hoyt were now with the Royal Engineers, although they spent most of their spare time with us. They were often overheard telling others about "Those Para boys," advising against getting tangled with us.

The two weeks turned out to be four and a half and the exercises were more intense than anticipated. For the first time I felt I was about to be killed, either by accident or wilfully and wondered if dear old Captain Harrison wasn't the one plotting to kill me, for screwing his wife. Everything was combat readiness. I was a little afraid for my life, but somehow survived the entire ordeal.

The obstacle course was almost like that in Farnham, except for the two hundred yards of barbed wire to crawl under while the gunners fired live ammo over our heads. There were two extra walls to climb over, much larger unavoidable swamps and rivers and pop- up target figures to kill or not, either with a gun or knife. We learned how to make, handle and use many different kinds of explosives. Some we had to devise for ourselves from different commodities and used live grenades. We learned to attack a building to retrieve things from inside or to rescue hostages.

We learned hand to hand combat for killing, which was an every day part of the training. We practised on dummies mostly, but in some cases we used each other, with fake weapons for demonstration. We were being taught the many ways to kill with our bare hands. I didn't realize that the human anatomy was so vulnerable in so many areas. Mark Harrison was making us into his own killing machines.

I learnt the many ways to kill a human and spent an enormous amount of time practising this art with my friends. We even developed our own techniques and some times pretended we were in situations like being taken prisoner and to counteract them. We installed secret compartments in our clothing and developed more ways to use our codes. We could send a message, in what appeared as a normal conversation, without alerting anybody who might overhear us. We practised to leave messages on a trail by bending twigs and branches in certain ways and marking trees that only we could understand.

During all of this confusion in Yorkshire, although we were always together; there were things we didn't talk about as openly as we used to. We became more protective of each other and the friendship was more like a brotherhood with a silent understanding bond between us. Often others, including Mark Harrison, would make comments on our little army. The use of our codes became more prevalent amongst ourselves. We could carry out an operation on an exercise without talking to each other, and our commander saw this in us. Mark was always praising us, for the way we handled ourselves and to know where each of us were in the fields at all times.

One morning on parade, Harrison made a bet with Colonel Trinkwan, that the thirteen of us could infiltrate and capture a whole company of his Engineers in five days and bring back the officer in charge as proof. It was agreed for us to do a jump almost twenty miles away, then locate the company by map and radio only. We were told to infiltrate their position using red paint, our only weapon, to mark our presence.

That morning while we made our drop twenty five miles away, the company moved out by vehicles to their unknown destination. We used our radio to locate each other, then regroup to plan out our strategy for locating them. It took two days to find their camp, then another day for planning. We placed ourselves around it strategically and plan the silent infiltration for that night. Their sentry passed us in the woods many times, in the process of their patrol, without seeing us. That night I gave the orders by radio.

"Nig thirteen, sunset ice, behave in bed," I said. "It's a white green-cheese moon tonight. I'll have pimples under my hat. Tweet, tweet, tweet."

Our movement in their camp was swift and silent. Somebody even painted a Lieutenant having a shower. I entered Colonel Bailey's command tent, covered his mouth and silently escorted him out. He was surprised that I could enter his tent passed his guards, unnoticed.

When this was done, Mark forced Colonel Trinkwan to praise us publicly on the parade square.

"I listened to the radio transmission throughout the exercise," said Trinkwan, "and couldn't understand a damn word of what was being said. I would like to know what codes you were using," he asked Mark.

"I really couldn't tell you sir," Mark replied. "It's their own and I am not privy to it's meaning."

Colonel Bailey told the parade that he would be afraid to meet any of us on a road after dark.

Thereafter our platoon was always the invading enemy to be caught. The thirteen of us never let each other out of sight or alone and in the fields after a drop, we always located and secured each other's position. It became natural for each of us and was noticed by Harrison, Trinkwan and Colonel Bailey. So when the training was over and we were told that the company was being posted to the Far East, I was excited but not surprised. But that was our agreement anyway, mainly to Singapore strictly because of Major-Doctor Helen Butterworth.

During that time also, I had kept up communications with Fiona, Teresa and Catharine, but never received any replies from any of them. Although I was upset, I knew that letters would be awaiting me in Aldershot, and that made me happy. At the end of it all, the bastards threw a party in our honour. They had invited some WRAC's from a close by camp, which I didn't know existed until that night. We were told that nobody could leave the camp for any reason. In my opinion, it was a form of torture. Cruelty by decree. It's been over five weeks without sex and now we're told, "here's the women, but you can't make out with them." I could only exchange addresses with a couple of West Indian ones, strictly for future reference of course, because the Commanders watched our every move like a hawk.

Two days before leaving Ripon, Mark informed us that we were granted a pass to London for seventy two hours, but he was willing to send us off a day earlier "because you deserved it." I was hurrying to get packed to catch the six fifteen to get the hell out of there, when I saw the boys talking to the Captain. I rushed back to their midst in time to hear them asking to go to Ireland instead.

"There goes my plans for Faye in London," I thought.

This time it was Ian, Tom, Jack, Patrick and I to Ireland. Rod, Bob and Phil decided on Newcastle to see Rod's family while Charley and

Williams went to London. Taffy, Powell and Baron stayed in Liverpool.

The train to Liverpool was a little late getting there, so we had to rush to catch the ferry to Belfast. It was almost midnight when we reached. The O'Reilley's didn't expect us, so it was a total surprise for everybody when we showed up at their door. Ella was in tears of joy and so was Teresa, hugging and kissing me. I too, was happy to be there on my second visit.

Mother quickly arranged some sandwiches for us. Shaun told us to drop the bags anywhere we felt like sleeping that night and we left for the pub. I was tired from all the activities and drinking on the train and ferry, but knew I wasn't going to sleep at this time. Teresa wouldn't let me any way. Patrick's parents behaved as though we were long lost relatives. I really felt like a relative. The colour of my skin did not seem like a hindrance to anybody present.

The next morning we all got up late, Ella made breakfast and we spent a lot of time talking again. About four in the afternoon, we left to visit Ian's home and again we were treated to food. Later we stopped at Tommy's home and then to the pub. Shaun and some of Paddy's friends came and a dart tournament began, with Jack the eventual winner. When Teresa came into the pub, everybody cheered and started to sing a song about sex. At first I was a little embarrassed, but saw the humour after a while, so it became fun. She seemed to be liking every minute of it also.

We returned to the house and sat around talking for quite a while, then Jack left to see a girl he had met on our first visit, Ian and Tom decided to spend the night with their parents. Patrick announced that he was going to see his girlfriend, so I was left with lovely Teresa. She tugged on my arm to follow her up to her room, leaving both mother and father watching telly. It was as though she had something unfinished to attend to. We made love and I fell to sleep.

I was awakened with a kiss, as she announced that breakfast was ready. After a wash, we were sitting at the table alone.

"By the way," I said. "why didn't you want me to use a safe last night?"

"No reason darling," she replied. "I just wanted to make love to you in a hurry, that's all."

"I know that you're trying to get pregnant," I said. "I can see it in your eyes. Why?" I asked.

"Because I want to and I am selfish," she said smiling.

I couldn't find anything to contradict her with, so I kept silent. It must have been around noon before I discovered that nobody else was in the house. We went back to bed.

"You just lay right there in bed," she instructed. "The last time you disappeared on me without saying goodbye. So this time I am not going to take the chance. I'm gonna hold on until you have to leave."

I obeyed and stayed in bed, reflecting on some things I wanted to do in London and some of the people I would've liked to see, but I was here with a lovely woman and was really enjoying every minute of it.

We ate and talked about many things. She, unlike Patrick, although bitter with the British political ideology and its application to the Catholics in Ireland, thinks everyone should learn to live together for the betterment of their country. I pointed out that, sometimes it is necessary to apply some kind of force to attract the attention of the government to the problems. She agreed that force can be a good tool, only that the innocent people get caught between and some get killed.

"I, for one, cannot comprehend why the government don't want to face the problems and rectify the injustices," she said. "In my mind it's very easy."

"I can agree with that," I replied. "They have imposed the same thing on other people around the world over hundreds of years, and they will not easily change. They have always used force and that's the only thing they understand."

"It's always the very ordinary people who are left to carry out the dirty deeds," she said, "whilst the real culprits, namely the rich industrialists and upper classes, sit on their backsides or hide out in other countries and wait until it's all over, then they return to reap the benefits, later."

That conversation lasted for almost the rest of the day. It was the first time she ever spoke about her inner feelings to me, and I was ecstatic for her to do so. We also talked about marriage and joked about our black Irish children.

"Stan darling," she said, "you would be most welcome amongst our people, although we probably would have to live in the south, because here in the north, we wouldn't get a moment's rest from the racism."

I pondered her suggestion for a moment, then I reminded her that the British Government had just passed the multicultural laws, and the people would have to respect our wishes. I believed in this new social legislation, that the government say would break down the colour bar and bring unity to the population. She insisted we made love again.

"Are you deliberately trying to get pregnant?" I asked her as if I didn't know.

"Yes sir," she answered, "this baby would be all I have to remind me of you. I am not taking any chances of you coming back to me."

Leaving was sorrowful, although we really meant well for each other. We made promises to keep in touch by mail as often as possible. I was a little concerned that she might even be pregnant and end up with more social problems than anticipated in my absence.

"What?" I thought. "Me a father at this age? I sincerely hope not; but if that's imminent, then so be it."

The entire family came to the ferry station to see us off. Teresa was making sure that every minute was spent with her this time.

"Please hurry back Stan," she said and jokingly patted her stomach, indicating the possible child she might be bearing.

The five of us boarded the ferry to Liverpool and made ourselves comfortable. I noticed Patrick was not being himself.

"Hey Paddy," I said, putting my arm around his waist, "what's all this then? What's your game?" I said in my cockney accent. He kind of looked sidelong at me.

"Stanley me lad," he said, "there's some trouble in my camp."

He was now starting to sound like Patrick of old.

"First, the girl told me she don't want to get married to me. She said her father requested that she marry another fellow, who is Norwegian. Then I found out that she had been screwing with him for some time now, and that's giving me a complex feeling of rejection. Then the problem of dad. I hope you all realized that he has cancer," he said.

None of us knew of his father's problem, he didn't show any sign of a troubled person. I felt a heavy feeling creep into my chest and a tear in my eye. I felt as though I was losing my own father. I told him not to worry, because we were all going to be right beside
him, always.

"Friends?" I said as we shook hands.

"Friends forever," he replied.

We went to Powell's parent's house to get the boys as agreed. Some had met us at the station. We caught our train to London. The train ride was very different this time, because the conversation was different. We chose to discuss some of the political problems that were confronting the people of Ireland. Patrick was at his best in these discussions. He just loved to talk about the fallacy of their religious teachings, the lies and deceptions of the controllers of our society. He quoted from many books, including the Bible, and from the scripts of many politicians such as Karl Marx, Winston Churchill, Eisenhower, Lenin and others. He was giving us a lesson in politics.

Although I learnt about the Magna Carta in school, Patrick could quote it verbatim. There were articles in it I did not totally understand, but with Patrick, I had it explained thoroughly, in detail. My attention for the subject was in focus all the way on this trip and I wasn't bored.

For the first time when the word money was brought into the conversation, it was about the stock market and the world wide manipulation of the peasants through labour. He pointed out how people like us are forced to leave school early to enter the labour market, so as to earn money to assist our families.

"That way," he said, "none of us will ever become a threat to
their stranglehold on society. None of us would be educated enough to

oppose them."

I sat there thinking about the life of the elite and their attitude towards the less fortunate, like me. The thoughts of rich Catharine Harrison and her reasons for wanting to be with me, a young black man, engulfed my mind.

"Was I being used and for what reason?" I wondered.

Maybe so, but for reasons I still don't fully understand. Anyway, I am learning about the ways of the White Anglo-Saxon Protestants. Just before the train reached London, I said to them.

"I am going to write a story about all of you arseholes some day. So what I would like to do starting now, is to get some background material on all of you."

They all sat quietly for a moment in thoughts.

"You know something," Tommy said, "I think he would, and it mightn't be too bad an idea."

I looked at Paddy.

"And you'll be my first victim, I've been making notes about you already. Want to hear them?" I offered.

"Yes, yes," shouted Tom, pointing his thumb at Patrick, "let's hear the shit you have on this old bastard."

I pulled out a piece of paper from my bag and read.

"Patrick Monaghan O'Reilley, born June 15th 1940 to mother Ella and father Shaun in Cork Ireland. His parents moved to Belfast after brother Eric was born and where lovely sister Teresa was later conceived. A beautiful girl, if I might say so. But young Patrick was not a backwards little Irish boy, he was very much interested in politics, even at that early stage in life.

At age seven, he began to read books about Marx, Lenin and other political figures. He was not very popular with his teachers, after he wrote an essay about these people. He's a man of integrity and decency, who believed that all people can live on planet earth in peace and harmony. I think he is a very humanistic person."

I stopped to let them know that it will not be a sugar and spice book, because I intend on saying things about their bad side also. We all laughed at it.

"He felt rejection when his teacher rejected a piece he had written on the monetary system, and the evil it had bestowed upon mankind since inception. He had expressed the wickedness that had befallen mankind because of the love for money. He also felt rejected, when he was told that he sounded like a communist."

I do believe that at age fifteen one is very impressionable and this was very devastating to a young Catholic Irish boy, who thought he had the freedom of speech.

"I remember the teacher saying," he told me, mimicking the teacher, "If the king believed in using money as the basis for bargaining, then so should you."

I could envision the hurt in his expression then and the anger today, as his people still suffer from the prejudices designed by that same King. He has his mind set on running for a parliamentary seat, after the army; against his parents' wishes. He woefully believe he could make changes to the society, by making changes to some existing laws.

"He once told me, that his parents could not afford to pay the tuition for him to obtained the higher education necessary, at any of the few recognized institutions. So he decided to join the army to get as much as he can. And if they refuse to assist him, then he has other alternative plans. Whatever those are."

They all laughed and made suggestions for my book and I made notes. I closed my book and sat back to enjoy the ride, but in my mind I was thinking.

"Patrick is quite capable and very keen on carrying out his orders. He never deviate or bluff his way through anything. If there was something he didn't know, he was never afraid to admit to that fact. Instead, he would enquire on ways to find out more about the subject matter and proceed from there. At times he would get angry when someone would mention that we were only soldiers and not politicians. He would remind us that we were there to protect lives and to portray good humanistic qualities, to whomever confronted us."

"And that's political." he would say.

"All in all, the man Patrick Monaghan O'Reilley was a real person in my view, who could become violent, if the need arose. He seemed to have no fear of anything, not even death."

Chapter Four

"My First Posting."

Returning to Aldershot was very delightful for me, because there were so many unfinished things to catch up on. There were two ladies to deal with, if they were in fact still interested in me. I was home and ready to confront any eventualities. I was proud of the man I had been transformed into. I am now grown up.

That afternoon the Sergeant-Major came to the rooms welcoming everybody individually, and was behaving like a "Mother hen," telling everybody how important they were to him and the army. He told us that some will be posted soon, while others will be going on special courses, before going to Singapore.

"You will be hearing more about this in the next couple of weeks." Tashie said. "Mr. Martin, you'll be going to Farnham for two weeks, then to Yeovil in Somerset for another four, whilst three others will be going back to Yorkshire for three weeks."

I was pleased to know that I would be around the area for at least six more weeks.

"Lovely," I thought. "I might as well get started tonight in Bordon, with lovely Fiona."

All the time I was in Yorkshire and writing letters to her, I never once got a reply. The army had told us that our mail would be sent to Aldershot and not there in Yorkshire. All my letters were late and outdated. I heard from a friend that Fiona had gone back to Scotland due to her mother's death and there was the possibility that she might leave the services for good. I spent the evening talking to two of her friends at the NAAFI, over a couple of beers. They told me of the good things she had said about me and advised me to speak to the matron for her address.

As I left the Park walking towards the Hospital, I heard a whispering voice behind me.

"Well, now that she's gone, may I take her place?" the voice said.

I turned to see the Matron almost beside me.

"Oh! Hello Matron," I said in a surprised tone, looking hard under her bonnet to see her face.

"I was on my way to see you," I said. "I would like Fiona's address please."

She pushed her bonnet back so that I could better see her.

"Yes," she replied. "I knew you would be coming. I'vc been expecting you. Before Fiona left for home, she told me all about you."

Once again I peered at her face.

"And what, pray tell, was the bad news?" I asked.

She smiled and gestured for us to cross the street.

"You see young-man," she began, "there isn't much that eludes my attention within my Hospital, and when you both spent that weekend together in the dormitory, I deliberately ignored it. I didn't want to spoil it for you both."

"You knew about that?" I exclaimed.

"Yes," she replied, "and a lot more. As you can see, I am not the old hag I am made out to be."

We reached her office and she sat behind her desk.

"Now," she said reaching for the pen and paper, "you would like the address of Fiona McDougall, right? And while I am at it, do you want that of Doctor Butterworth's as well?"

I sat there flabbergasted, wondering what else this woman would come up with next. I could only bow my head answering,

"Yes ma'am."

She smiled and told me that those women should consider themselves lucky, to have fallen in love with someone as nice I. Sister matron was a very attractive woman herself and I wondered why she had become a nun. I questioned her for the reason she hadn't fallen in love herself.

"Did you not meet any man you could fall in love with?" I asked.

"Oh sure," she said, "but it was a case of conflicting religious beliefs. So I made my decision to be a nun instead," she assured me. "The health of others were more important to me than my personal satisfaction."

I believed her. I realizes that to some people, a career can be used to fill a void, and she was a prime example.

I reached back to Aldershot about nine o'clock that evening and since it was early, I decided to hit the NAAFI for a quick beer and to find my friends. I found two at the bar and joined them. We were in the middle of the drink, when Jack remembered and told me that a good looking woman was there earlier asking for me; but she had left. I realized it was Catharine.

"Well, I missed her," I thought, "maybe tomorrow she will come back."

I finished my beer and started to leave when she came in.

"Hello soldier," she said beaming that wide familiar smile that almost filled the room, "need some company?"

I was so happy to see her, I just stood there. She motioned for me to follow her. I had no intention of objecting to the offer. She guided her car to a very secluded place we used previously and carefully parked the car and shut the engine off.

"Did you miss me as I missed you?" she asked, as she began pulling the buttons of her blouse.

"Yes," I responded and reached for her breasts, "and I had written three letters to you without any replies," I concluded.

"I did reply," she said assuring me of her effort, "but I cannot comprehend them not arriving to you."

"It's not important now my darling, this moment is more special to us."

That seemed to strike a note, because she took all her clothes off in a hurry and sat beside me totally naked. I realized that I too must get naked. We made love in the Jag as though it was our last time, like two condemned people trying to enjoy our last request. The windows were steamed up from our hot breath and overheated bodies as she screamed in delight. I could feel her finger nails biting into my body, as her teeth gripped my lips.

"You seem to be very hungry my dear," I asked.

"Oh yes!" she exclaimed. "I love you, I missed you, I love you," she repeated over and over.

"Couldn't we have gone to your house?" I asked.

"No darling," she replied, "it mightn't have been the same, and furthermore, Mark came home with some of his friends earlier this evening."

I didn't question her any further. We got dressed and talked for almost an hour, then she drove me back to the camp. We made arrangements to meet again the next evening in Farnham, as we kissed goodnight.

I made my way to my room. The boys joshed each other on our evening out, until about two o'clock in the morning. Just as we were about to break it up, Patrick piped up.

"Now that everybody had their rocks off, maybe we could redirect some of our energies to some of the political issues that are in our presence."

Everybody told him to shut the fuck up and started to leave when Jack announced that Paddy was out with a girl last evening.

"Surprise, surprise!" said Tommy. "Wonders never cease. And here I am thinking that the boy was queer."

We all stared at him with interest.

"Come on then! Let's hear it," I prompted.

He had no excuse for holding back now.

"Well, you see," he began, "tonight at the NAAFI, I met a cute little Irish girl named Greta Paisley. She's a new WRAC in Bordon. We talked and danced then when I took her back to her camp, she sneaked me into her room and we eh...."

"Screwed?" asked Bob.

"Yes, we screwed," Paddy replied. "This is the first time I've ever screwed anyone other than my girlfriend."

I crossed the room to face him.

"Paddy me lad," I said, "welcome to the real world of sex."

He smiled as though he had won the Pulitzer prize.

"And," he continued, "she's pure Irish, who incidently is very active in the movement."

Nobody asked any question or changed expression, so he continued to talk about this girl for another half hour. Tommy suggested we leave some for the next day and we dispersed. Since it was almost morning, I had a shower and sat in the window chair to watch the sunrise. I thought about Fiona, Helen, Catharine and me.

The trip to Farnham was quick. Because I had already spent time there, I felt good to be back on familiar grounds although all my friends were gone. I went around to see some of the people I knew and by the end of the day, I was tired. I showered and laid on the bed to get some sleep. I woke up about six that evening late for my date with Catharine.

"Oh my god," I whispered to myself, "I'm late again and she'll be mad."

I quickly got dressed and left for the town and sure enough she was there waiting for me, this time she was not angry. Matter of fact she seemed anxious to see me. We drove to one of her friend's house in Aldershot and opened the door with the key she had. We entered.

"Okay soldier," she said after closing the door behind us, "here we are in a house with a bed, what are you going to do about it?"

"Is there anything to drink in here?" I asked.

"Yes my darling," she replied, "look in that cabinet over there," she pointed to the liquor cabinet as she walked towards the sofa. I found the glasses, ice and the scotch. I fixed the drinks and went to join her on the sofa.

As soon as we sat she placed both her feet in my lap and laid back.

I slowly removed her shoes and began to rub my hand along her very smooth legs. She laid there allowing me to do whatever I wanted to her. I got up and turned out the lights.

By the time I rejoined her, she had already removed her clothing and was laying there naked. I know Catharine was sexually attracted to me and sometimes liked to pretend that we were other people making love in different scenes. She sprung awake and wrapped her arms around my neck. The glasses fell to the floor as she did and I could feel the heat from her face on mine.

"Take me to bed now, please," she demanded.

I carried her into the bedroom.

"This is the kind of woman I always dreamed of," I thought as I rose to meet her excitement.

Catharine was always able to do that to me. Since our first encounter on the train, I have always thought of her as the most unusual and thrilling of all the women I had made love to. She was no comparison to the others. We both fell to sleep after our interlude.

"Hey soldier!" she said, "it's time to leave. Although I don't want you to."

I sprang awake and looked at my watch.

"Oh shit!" I said. "It's six o'clock in the morning and you know what that means."

I hurriedly put on my clothes. My thoughts of spending time in the nick again for the neglect of duties, flashed across my mind. Disobeying a direct order of the CO. is very dangerous. My first time in jail, was for knocking out an officer who had assaulted me. But although I was within my rights, I was sentenced to twenty one days in the nick.

"A soldier never touches an officer on the parade square. Next time any officer touches you, you invite him to the gym, after you salute of course, then you beat the living shit out of him legally." Sergeant-Major Wickham told me afterwards.

I did twenty one days for that. But for this, I am not sure if they would throw away the key. She hurriedly drove back to camp and with a quick kiss, she left. I started for the mess hall to have breakfast instead of going to the billets and ran smack into Captain Harrison.

"Good morning Mr Martin," he said. "Did you have a good time last evening?"

"Yes sir, a very good evening," I replied.

He stood looking at me for a moment.

"When she didn't come home, I realized you both must be having a good time somewhere. Anyway, that's not very important at this time, is it?" he said.

I was about to leave when he indicated that he would be joining me for breakfast. We walked to the mess together and got our nosh and sat at a single table away from everybody. He continued with his previous conversation.

"You know something?" he began. "She could have fallen in love with many other men and I can tell you that many have tried, but she choose you. Why? I don't know, but it's you, and I have no recourse."

He paused to stuff some food into his mouth, while I sat there watching him.

"I've been very curious of her choice and thought it was an infatuation that would be over after the novelty wears off. Now I'm convinced that she's in love with you and I'm not upset. As a matter of fact, I'm delighted to know that she's capable of loving someone."

Once again he buried his face into the food and I too began to eat mine without saying a word. We were almost finished when he said,

"Tell me about our friend. Is she a good screw?"

I looked at him quizzically, because I was puzzled by his question.

"Yes, that she is. Why? Didn't you ever screw her?" I said earnestly.

It seemed unbelievable that a man of his stature would have a woman as beautiful as her and didn't fuck her. He didn't answer, only a slight smile and told me that someday he might explain. We left the mess.

"Your team worked well together, and it's my intention to recommend keeping you intact for a Far East posting," he said.

I had nothing to say to that. He didn't even want to know my opinion. He kept on talking as though I wasn't present. He talked at length about the Far East and the Chinese problem in Hong Kong, Malaya, Cambodia, Vietnam and any other country in that Region he could think of. He expressed his displeasure of their political beliefs and the various formulas required to rectify the problems there. To me, he sounded like a person who needed to vent his frustrations. But I remained silent throughout his monologue.

"You know something?" he said. "Patrick O'Reilley is one man I would like to turn loose on them bastards. He hates everybody, and if he should kill some of them, he might forget about killing the English Protestants."

I became slightly angry at this point.

"What do you mean? Paddy is a very good person? Certainly he has suffered some strong discrimination in his country in a short space of time. But his ideology of rectifying it is his own. Nobody has the right to deny him his thoughts." I said this in defence of my friend. realizing that I was sounding angry, but continued nevertheless.

"Why is it you Anglo Saxons always think everybody else is wrong? You can always find a reason to fault others," I said.

He grinned and told me that in due time I would understand. Maybe I would, but it was evident that they always stir up people purposely; and I wasn't any different. I only realized this, after he had left me wondering about my friends and their politics. I didn't go to the billets, I went straight to the parade square to await the arrival of the others. The Sergeant-Major saw me and approached me.

"Good morning private Martin," he said, "and what brought you out so early?"

"Well sir," I said in a kind of sorrowful tone, "I was out last evening and I am now feeling the effects of my sins."

He raised his head to the sky and laughed out loud.

"This is the first time a soldier ever told me a story like this one. I've never heard it put like that before, and you know what? I am going to let you off with it."

"Do you mean I could go back to bed sir?" I asked, surprised at his words.

"Right you are," he replied, "but you must be up by ten thirty for a fiver with me."

I quickly agreed and ran to the billets for some much needed sleep. Ten thirty seemed to come in double-quick time, but I was ready. This was a serious moment, just me and the Sergeant-Major on a five mile run. This was my big moment to show him all that I had done since he advised me to attend the gym. I was now a fully trained Paratrooper. We took the regular route, but after about three miles he stopped. He made some feeble excuse that he was tired.

"What do you think of the army now," he asked.

"It's not too bad after all," I replied. "At first I hated it and wanted to leave. But now..."

"Good," he said, tweaking his handlebar moustache, "I have plans for you. My intentions are to recommend promoting you."

"Promoting me sir?" I asked in a shocked tone. "You must be joking, sir!!"

"Look young-man," he said. "I don't joke about things of this nature. I have a lot of confidence in your ability, so I've recommended for you to be promoted to Lance Corporal."

"Who, me?" I said, "an NCO?"

I was getting excited and afraid at the same time. Being an NCO is a lot of responsibility and I wasn't ready for that as yet. He was watching my reaction very keenly.

"Tashie," I said, "why do you want to do this to me? I.. I'm not sure that I can handle it."

I was trying desperately to find an excuse.

"I have confidence in you my boy," he said proudly. "And furthermore, you'll learn to do so. Sergeant Dawkins and I think you're capable and I feel you are ready to be proven."

I could see a glitter in his eyes as a father might have for a son.

"Yes," I thought. "that's it, he's making me into his son."

"You know something?" he went on, "I met Lance corporal Dawkins in Jamaica, when I was in the Royal Fusiliers stationed there, as a drill instructor. He's a fine upstanding man. So eight years ago, when I was offered this posting here as Regimental Sergeant- Major, I requested him to accompany me as my right hand man and he has now excelled to the respectable rank of Sergeant."

"Well sir," I said honestly, "he has always spoken highly of you too. But me, I am very new to the army and am not too sure if I could live up to your expectations."

"Thank you for the exercise lance corporal Martin," he replied, totally ignoring my negativity, "you will have to come over for tea one evening and to meet my family."

He told me to be well dressed for the CO.'s orders the next morning.

"Okay sir," I said, "but I'm still not at all certain that you're making the right move promoting me, there are others who could fit the roll much better."

He remained silent for a little while as we ran back towards camp.

"Maybe so, but I have never been wrong yet in assessing any of my men. I won't tell you my method used in analysing you and the others, but I believe that your friends have a lot of respect for you. By promoting you, they will be more receptive to the requirements of this man's army," he said.

I couldn't find anything else with which to contradict him, so he continued.

"I am absolutely positive that you are a leader and by doing this, the likes of Patrick, Ian, Charley, Jack, Philip and the others will eventually learn how to grow as men."

He sounded earnest.

"Sir, am I being used?" I questioned.

He stopped in his tracks and looked at me in a strange manner.

"In a way, yes. I should think so," he replied.

The next morning I was looking my best, due to the fact that I had spent almost all night cleaning my kits.

"Here I am, only a soldier for such a short time and now been given an NCO's ranking," I thought. "What will my friends think of me now? Will I be accepted as before? They all seemed delighted last night when I told them."

Anyway, I felt good and proud walking to the office. For some reason I turned to see them in the windows watching me. They waved and I returned the pleasantries.

Although I felt a little nervous, I felt proud to be standing in front of the commanding officer. Brigadier Langstaff was one of the regular type officers, who always said hello to everybody and on many occasions he would stop to talk to me. I walked into his office and saluted his rank while at attention.

"Corporal Martin," he began without wasting time, "you have been given this commission because you showed that you can be a leader of men, and that you're not afraid to do a job when asked to."

I tried desperately to keep my head straight, almost afraid to look him in the face. He talked for some time about being a good soldier, and I listened. Only after he had completed his speech, did I thank him for the confidence he had entrusted in me and promised to live up to that trust. I was dismissed, so in my best military fashion, I about-turned and marched out. Wickham shook my hand and told me to get the stripes on my uniform quickly. I wasted no time getting to the tailor to have my Lance Corporal stripe sewn on. The tailor advised me to bring all my other uniforms to be done at once.

I reach the billets and back to the tailor shop, with a promise to meet my friends at dinner. At the mess, all of us sat at a table where they took turns mouthing off congratulating me and making jokes of what things they intend getting away with. I in turn made remarks on how I am going to put them all in the nick, for anything and everything. We stayed there laughing and talking for a couple of hours, until the mess Sergeant came to remind us that we aren't on duty and should leave his kitchen. He too took time to congratulate me and joked about me being the smartest of them all.

"Don't let them others drag you down with them," he told me.

We left the mess and decided to make a short visit to the NAAFI for a few brews and was late getting back to the billets.

The next day was very busy. It seemed that Wickham was waiting for me purposely. My first embarrassment came when he announced that I would be taking the parade.

"Who me?" I asked shakily. "You must be joking sir," I said.

He stood at attention and shouted.

"Corporal Martin! I do not joke on my parade square; get yourself out here and direct this parade, NOW."

I hesitated but obeyed. I marched out in front trying hard to remember the drills, which we had done so often. After the first two commands, I saw that the troops had carried them out precisely and realized that I was in command and starting to like it. I drilled them for about fifteen minutes then halted them. I then marched over to him, saluted, then handed them over to him. After the parade he called me to his office, where he told me that I did very well.

"Except young man," he said smiling, "you don't salute an NCO, not even me."

We both laughed about it, then he handed me an orders sheet of my day's duties. I left his office still smiling until I saw the number of things on that sheet, then I wasn't smiling. All my friends were delighted that I had survived the first day and took turns razzing me.

"Oh Corporal, can we do this, can we do that?" or "Corporal, I'm having a problem can you help me?"

It was all in fun and I took it that way.

On returning to my room, I felt relieved when they left.

I wanted to get some sleep, but couldn't immediately. I laid there thinking of what I would tell my relatives and the ladies about my promotion.

"I must write to Fiona," I thought. "She would be delighted to hear the good news, and also a long one to Helen in Singapore and to Faye in London."

I intended on telling everyone about it. I shuddered at the thoughts of what Catharine's reaction would be.

"What if she thought I had sold out to the army? What if she thought I was becoming too much of a friend to her husband and stopped loving me?"

Those thoughts gave me a nervous chill inside. Anyway, the sleep crept upon me and the next thing was hearing the alarm waking me the next morning.

The next few days were very interesting, because Mr. Wickham kept on my arse as much as possible. When he saw that I might be getting a little agitated, he called me to his office.

"Okay Corporal Martin," he said in his Scottish drawl, "this evening I'm challenging you to a couple of rounds of boxing. Are you game?"

I realized that he was only trying to cheer me up and to find some time to talk. I agreed to fight him, but assured him that I had a date so we should start early. He smiled and shook my hand. I returned to the billets and told the boys about the fight, but they all refused my invitation to see it, because it was a fight with my friend.

I reached the gym about three minutes before him.

"So you came early and got warmed up eh?" he said as he entered.

"This is a very serious matter," I said jokingly. "It's not often I get to beat up the Sergeant-Major legally. And I hope you'll take all precautions in defending yourself."

We sparred around for what seemed like ten minutes, then he decided that it would be better for us to hit the bags and skip ropes instead.

"Don't want to get killed, eh?" I teased.

"You're so right., he replied. "I saw what you did to Harvey Pratkowsky a few weeks ago and he still doesn't seem right since. Anyway my purpose here this evening is to talk to you."

"Oh yes, I forget that you have to keep me in line as of now." I said sarcastically.

"No," he replied looking into my eyes, "not to keep you in line, only to give you some directives."

He became very serious at this point.

"As you may notice, there isn't many coloured officers or NCO's in this part of the services."

I shook my head in acknowledgement.

"And I intend on proving that there are some of you people who are smart and can do the job as well as any of the whites."

He didn't have to say too much more, for the point was well taken. I sat quietly as he spoke of the discrimination I will be facing in the years to come.

"You'll have to develop a mental crust so as to overlook that problem," he told me.

He assured me that he has spotted something within me and was willing to put his career on the line to prove it. I felt elated that he chose me to be his prodigy. He went on to tell of his intentions to promote Patrick and a couple others.

"Maybe Jack O'Leary and Bob Muldoon," he said.

I was delighted and relieved to know there were others on his agenda also.

"Well sir," I said, "I am not going to promise you anything, because as you've said, things can happen to change people's lives. But I intend on giving it a damn good try, and no matter what, I will always remember what you've done for me. And will maintain a strong degree of respect for you as a gentleman, forever."

He sat there silent just staring at me. I didn't wait for him to respond.

"Sir,"I said, "I have learnt a lot since joining the army. There are things here that I would like to see changed, but since I cannot change them myself, I will try to influence those who can do. And I am absolutely sure that my pigmentation will not change, no matter what."

He got up smiling.

"You know something Martin?" he said. "I am positive that you're going to be alright. You have the discipline and disposition to do it. Nobody will be able to push you around, and you do have enough diplomacy to get along in this man's army."

We got out of the gym and headed towards the square. I watched him silently to see if he would cross the sacred grounds, but he didn't; he walked around. I smiled inwardly when I realized that I was the son he wants to be proud of.

"Tell me, do you think Patrick and Jack are serious in their political threats against the English?" he asked without breaking stride.

"Sir," I said, "those boys are friends of mine, all I care about is their well-being not their political ideology. I think they're good decent human beings in themselves, and I will never be judgmental. You would have to find that out for yourself."

We continued walking without a word.

"Sir," I continued, "both Patrick and Jack could be very good politicians if they get the opportunity. As I see it, they're willing to learn the proper way to present their ideas to the people, but they will need assistance from the influential few who are in control of their country's politics."

He nodded his head in agreement.

"See you in the morning," he said.

We parted company at his office.

I reached the billets and quickly checked the clock, it was getting late but I got dressed anyway and headed for the NAAFI.

"Why not?" I thought. "It's Friday night after all and being a newly appointed NCO, shouldn't stop me from associating with my friends."

I found them in the usual corner and as soon as I reached them, Jack was the first to call for a drink, for me.

"Here's your brew sir, and whenever you are ready I will shine your shoes sir," he said teasingly.

I felt good to be with my friends.

"Don't get too cosy with me you bunch of layabouts," I said, "or I'll have you all in the nick, but keep the beers coming in the meanwhile and I might reconsider it."

We all laughed and began chatting about our usual things. The topic of women and money lasted a while. We staggered back to the billets and to more discussions about the women, money and politics, until we all seemed weary and dispersed to our beds.

Patrick sat quietly at breakfast. He had a distant glare in his eyes.

"Okay O'Reilley!" I said, "what's your problem?"

My question seemed to have caught him off guard or maybe it was the sound of my voice, because the only thing he said was,

"Mmmmm? What were you saying now?"

I looked at him for awhile in a wondrous thought. He seemed to be in a different galaxy, but I decided to tell him what the Sergeant Major said about promoting him. I knew he heard what I said, but his response was negative.

"Did you hear and understand what I said?" I barked at him. I was firm in my statement, as though I was giving him a command. He finally looked me in the eyes and told me of his brother Eric's death.

"And the bastards shot him after beating him," he said through clinched teeth. I could see that he was really hurt, although distraught would be a closer description.

"What!" I asked excitedly. "When did this happen?"

He realised that I was very concerned and began to tell me as though I was a brother. I listened intensely and we both began to cry.

"Why do things like this happen to nice people?" I said. "Eric of all people, he was such a nice quiet person."

"Yeah!" said Patrick. "If it was someone else, I wouldn't be too upset because they would be working for the cause, but he wasn't."

My mind jumped to attention instantly and I became curious, my eyes pierced into his.

"What cause?" I asked. "Do you mean working for the IRA?" I asked in a demanding tone. I didn't wait for any reply. "And tell me the truth," I said.

He looked me right back in the eyes as he replied.

"Believe me Stan," he said. "My brother Eric wasn't involved in any part of Ireland's politics, not in any way shape or form, but those protestant pigs killed him anyway."

It seemed like hours that we sat there at the breakfast table. Nobody else came near us, so we were assured nobody could have overheard our conversation or seen us crying. We didn't bother to finish our food, we left for the billets and to talk more about it.

"It's the Ulster group that done it," he began, "and I intend on finding some of them and avenge that act."

I didn't rightly know what to say, but to console him, I said, "Yes you should, but after we leave the army."

Finally, I told him that I had some duties to carry-out for the Sergeant-Major and would see him later. I reached the office and got my orders from the duty Sergeant and was about to leave, when his voice stopped me in my tracks.

"Corporal Martin, my office," Tashie shouted.

I didn't hesitate, it was a one motion act. And as soon as we entered the office and the door was closed, he asked.

"Is there something wrong with O'Reilley?"

"No sir," I replied. "Not to my knowledge."

As soon as the words left my mouth, I realized that I could be making a mistake and quickly changed my mind and apologised for saying so.

"Yes sir," I stuttered. "I think something is drastically wrong with him. You see, his brother was killed a few days ago in Belfast by a rival group."

Tashie stood there for a moment watching me.

"And what do you propose to do about it?" he asked. "You're his NCO or did you forget?"

I almost jumped to attention when I realized what he was insinuating.

"Well sir," I said. "If I could recommend that Patrick, I mean Private O'Reilley, be given a compassionate leave to visit his family in Ireland....."

He smiled and quickly called in his secretary. He instructed him to make out a pass for Private O'Reilley.

"And a pass for Corporal Martin also, who will escort him to ensure that he doesn't go AWOL."

As he was leaving the office, he turned and said,

"You're only to take four days and be back for parade. And another thing, would you come to have tea with my family this evening?"

"Yes sir!" I answered. "What time?"

"At 1830 hours sharp," he said winking as he left.

I felt chuffed to know that I was able to get my friend a pass for home, and me alongside him.

I gave Patrick the good news about the passes to Belfast that evening in the presence of our friends. Everybody was delighted at my action and teased us about going there to get drunk and to screw the women. They were sympathetic towards Patrick's loss and asked us to convey their condolences to his parents after he told then of the incident with Eric and the details of me getting the passes.

When I told them of my having tea with Tashie's family that evening, the joking began again.

"Oh! oh! oh! Brown nosing eh, Corporal?" Bob teased. "First the Sergeant-Major, then it will be the General."

Everybody laughed at that statement.

"Or maybe he's trying to get you to marry his daughter?" asked Charley.

"No, no, no fellows," Ian chimed in. "You've all got it wrong. Don't you know that Wickham has adopted him and is now going to introduce him to his family?"

I smiled, because that sounded more logical than the other suggestions.

The walk to Tashie's house was rather refreshing, because I had time to think about going to Ireland again. Except this time it's a rather depressing circumstance. I knocked on the door and he opened it.

"Come on in Stan, and for this evening don't call me sir," he said.

"Then how do I refer to you?" I asked.

"You can call me what you all do behind my back, Tashie, or by my real name, Cyril."

I began to smile and he noticed that I was.

"Okay! What's so funny about my name?" he asked.

"You don't look like a Cyril to me," I said. "You're more like a Tashie."

He smiled and beckon for me to enter the room.

"Then Tashie it will be. What would you like to drink?" he asked.

"A Scotch and water please," I said and followed him to the cupboard.

"How could anyone drink such a vile tasting drink? You should try Brandy sometime," he suggested.

I was about to argue the issue, when she came down the stairs. She was a very beautiful woman of about five foot five and one hundred and twenty pounds. She was very properly dressed in a suede brown white trimmed dress with matching shoes. Followed by her two lovely teenage daughters both wearing white dresses.

"Welcome to our home Stan," she said descending the stairs and approaching me.

I kissed her cheeks.

"I've heard so many good things about you," she continued. "I am Mary Wickham and these are our daughters Elizabeth, who is sixteen and Carol, fourteen."

"It's nice to meet you also although I never did hear anything about you," I replied.

She wasted no time in directing us to the table to sample her cooking. I pulled the chair for her then the two girls. We talked about the army as we consumed the lovely meal, which I thought she had worked on all day. Roast beef with mini potatoes, Yorkshire pudding and a green salad and trifle, my favourite dessert. Finally, she spoke.

"I see that you're not surprised that I am black," she said while scrutinizing my face for some kind of reaction.

"Why should I?" I asked. "Was I supposed to be surprised?"

Everybody laughed at that statement as I continued.

"That's between you and this man here," I said pointing to Tashie. "You're a very beautiful, charming and gracious lady and I am delighted for your invitation to tea. If I may say, you do look lovely and please don't believe all the stories you've heard about me."

"Hey, hey!" Tashie shouted. "Are you making eyes at my wife?" he offered in a jovial tone.

"Not at all, Cyril old boy," I joshed. "I'm only stating a fact, and so are the girls," I concluded.

Mary brushed her hair back in a pleasing way and the girls giggled.

"Go on Stan," she said, "tell me more, flatter me. It's not often that I get these compliments, you know."

Tashie talked of his posting in Jamaica, where he had met and marry Mary and also where the children were born. She also talked about her parents' home in Bog Walk and of their farming background.

"Someday," said Mary, "I wish for us to return to Jamaica to live forever. Then the children could excel and have the better of both countries."

She sounded home sick for the island, but was willing to go wherever Tashie went. She seem to be very comfortable talking about her desires to me.

Tashie assured them that I will be a frequent visitor to the house, for the duration of my training period and they seemed happy to hear that.

"Stan could you take us to the movies one evening? Father won't allow us to go alone," said Elizabeth.

"Sure I will," I replied. "As soon as I return from Ireland."

"I will be looking forward to that promise," she said.

I left after thanking them both for a rather lovely evening.

Our trip into Ireland was very interesting, because we were there to see his family and to pay our respect to his slain brother, who had already been buried. We visited the grave site for almost all of the first day. I could see that he was very annoyed and agitated about not being able to do anything about it. He kept repeating to himself, and occasionally directly at me.

"The Ulster boys done this," he said. "I know it's that group and I am declaring personal war against them."

He was shouting and sometimes jumping around, beating his chest with the palm of his hand. I realized that I had to do something to calm him down, for him to get his head into a more comfortable and relaxed mode. I wanted for him to realize that I was truly his friend.

"You know Pat," I said in a soft voice, "we can't do anything personally at this time, but that doesn't prevent somebody else from doing it," I suggested.

That seemed to strike a chord in him, because he just grabbed and hugged me.

"Let's go home now," he said excitedly, "I have some thinking to do."

I could sense the happiness within him.

We reached the house and he quickly told his family that it was I who arranged the passes and how proud he was to be my friend. We spent that night and most of the following day with the family and the visiting friends. Then on the third day Teresa and I decided to stay home to make love while the others went to the pub. She was anxious to get into bed and I was willing to oblige. We talked about the days we had spent together previously and the things we had discussed in our letters after. When they returned about two thirty that night, we got out of bed to join then for a cup of tea.

We talked about many things, until the subject of Eric and the IRA came up again, that's when I realized that Patrick had not returned with them. Shaun explained that Patrick was visiting with some friends.

"Who am I to pry," I thought, "my only concern was for us to leave the next morning. I knew from the time we stepped on the train that something was drastically wrong, but my friend was not saying.

He stayed quiet for almost an hour whilst I enjoyed a talk with an old geezer, who had joined us in our car. The old man told me of his political aspirations when he was younger and his plans to change the world, but he never achieved any of this because time ran out on him.

"That's one thing young-man," said the old man, who spoke with a tremble in his voice, "do what you must do while you're of the age to accomplish it."

I could see the disappointment in his eyes, that kind of blank stare as he continued.

"Nobody is going to listen to you, when you become old and feeble like me."

I agreed with him on most points.

Occasionally I glanced over to Patrick to see his reaction, but it was negative. He just laid there with his eyes closed, I could almost hear him thinking.

When the train came to a stop and the old man left, Patrick sat up straight and said,

"You know something Stan? That old bastard had the right idea. One must throw a fuck into them, before they can fuck you."

I sat quietly listening to him for two reasons. One, I was talked out by the old man and two, I wanted to hear his thoughts. I felt if I interrupted him, he might just shut me out. He went from his boyhood days to the birth of Christ, through to the Roman Empire to the life of Napoleon. He spoke of the evils of the Anglo Saxons and their version of Christianity, to the enslavement of the Africans, and the politics that will prevent them from excelling in the present society of their own country, if changes are not made now.

I was intrigued and interested in learning to something that was new to me. I was observing Patrick in another light. I wondered what he would be like under pressures in a Parliamentary atmosphere. I felt happy to know he was my friend and not an enemy. We slept and talked some, all the way to London. We got a few more beers there to accompany us to Aldershot. Luckily a couple of WRAC's joined us for the trip to Aldershot, so Patrick's political talks was kept to a minimum. Neither one wanted to screw, but during our conversation I found out that they were lesbians. Anyway, we enjoyed their company and better yet, I didn't have to listen to Patrick talk any-more.

In Aldershot, we made a date to see the girls on the weekend and went straight for the barracks. There was a lot of catching up to do, but firstly I needed some quality sleep, to be able to deal with all the rest.

The morning sun shone brightly into my room and I felt relaxed. Suddenly I remembered that I had to report to the boss this morning.

"Shit!" I thought, "Tashie will be waiting for me, I had better get the hell out of bed."

The thought of being late got my adrenalin flowing, I rushed to get myself together and hurried over to his office.

"Come in Corporal Martin," he greeted me. "Sit down and tell me about it."

I was surprised to hear those words, Sit down. I gave him the whole story from the time we landed in Belfast, omitting any IRA talk or my love-making to Teresa. He expressed his confidence in my ability to control a situation of delicacy and promised to speak personally to Patrick. He told me to place O'Reilley on orders for that purpose, the next morning.

That evening, I decided to walk around the park and through the beautiful gardens there alone, which I always enjoyed doing occasionally, strictly for some brain exercise. I was so engrossed in my solitude, that I was startled by the tap on shoulder. It was Catharine. I was surprised that she was able to walk up on me unnoticed.

"There you are," said Catharine, mimicking a Jamaican accent, something I noticed she has been doing more often of late. "Come with me you sexy man, I want to rape you."

I was ever so happy to hear her voice. We kissed for a long moment, then I suggested we go somewhere to make love. It seemed that's what she wanted to hear and quickly we ran to her car and to our usual parking spot, overlooking the city of Aldershot.

Being with Catharine, always seemed to take away all the other concerns of life's adversities. All the tiredness of the trip to Ireland seemed to vanish. Her lovely smile had a way of making me relaxed and to forget my woes.

"You know something Stan?" she said while taking off her clothes. "Every time you leave, I feel an emptiness within me, but whenever you return I am very happy to see you again."

I thanked her for loving me and her patience of always waiting for my return. She talked about all the things she did in my absence.

"I went to visit my parents in Somerset for a few days," she said. "I stayed very busy doing many other things, except for sex. I deliberately refrained from contact with anyone that could be construed as sexual," she said to assure me.

And for some reason, I believed her.

"Anyway Mark will tell me if she did," I thought.

He told me that she wouldn't go with anyone else, because he had introduced her to many men in the past, but without response. Ever since that night at the car, he made it his duty to tell me of everything she did and where she went. He seemed to be keeping a watchful eye on her all the time. Maybe to assure me that she had been good throughout my absence. I often wondered why.

"Is it especially for me? Or are there other ulterior motives?" I wondered.

Lately, I found myself being a little suspicious of their odd relationship. He tells her a lot about the troops movements, especially mine and I am wondering what she tells him about me.

Although she never asked me anything about anyone, I often wondered if she was screwing with me for information on the boys or setting me up for something else. Occasionally I would test her, but she had always came across clean and honest. If she was a spy for Mark, she would be a very convincing one in my view. I had no reason to suspect or doubt her actions towards me, or my friends. She made me a believer in her.

We laid there quiet after making love on top of the hill.

"Mark told me that you'll be going to Somerset, is that true?" she asked.

"Yes," I replied. "I am going for some special training in Yeovil and I am not sure what the schedule will be, or when I will be back here."

"Darling!" she said excitedly. "Somerset is where my family lives.

Remember? There's the large family house. Maybe we could meet, I would love to introduce you to my parents."

She spoke with a little glitter in her voice.

"My father built it for mother. It's a very large house with a lot of property attached to it with a river running through it. I think it's the largest house in that area and when I come to visit you in Yeovil, we would have a place to stay. I would love to show it to you."

I too, was delighted to know that this kind of convenience would be at our disposal and looked forward to meeting her parents, whom she talked about for another hour.

Suddenly she became silent.

"Stan," she said. "What would you do if I ever got pregnant? Don't get nervous now," she said waving her hand in my face, "because I am not at this time. But, should I ever get knocked up, what would be your reaction?"

I was not nervous, but my curiosity was certainly drawn to attention.

"That might not be a bad idea," I replied. "Just think, Mark would have to give you that divorce, then we would be free to get married and have another couple more of our own. We could be very happy together, don't you think?"

She hugged and kissed me and began to cry.

"Darling," she said. "I love you very much and being with you and having your children would be the only thing I wanted in my life. Every day I dreamed of such a time, but I know Mark would not grant me the divorce easily and I wouldn't be able to explain having a black child to some of my family and friends."

We both laughed at that scenario, but within my mind the question of her falling in love with me still remained."

"Why wouldn't he give her the divorce?" I thought. "What evil thing could he be holding over her?"

"If he doesn't want to give you the divorce, then we could always live common law," I told her.

Catharine gave thoughts to my suggestion than said,

"That would have to wait until the day come darling," she said, "and whenever that happened, we would deal with all the repercussions. In the meanwhile, we must keep enjoying each other for as long it can last."

It was early morning and I had to return to camp. We kissed goodnight or should I say good morning and promised to see each other as much as possible when I was in Somerset.

I had a shower and laid down, making sure not to close my eyes in fear of falling asleep. My thoughts ran from Helen and what had become of her, to my family and friends in London. I thought about Fiona and me not knowing where she was, to Catharine and what we had discussed last evening and the consequences there of. My mind flashed to Patrick.

"Oh yes, Patrick," I thought as my mind became alert again. "I will have to address him to the CO this morning. Wonder what will be his reaction? One never knew with O'Reilley. One minute he could be cool and calm or he could be very arrogant and obnoxious, if he feels like it. I am hoping that he will be in a good mood this morning, against all wishes."

I fell asleep, but fortunately someone came into my room to awaken me in time to get organized. I dashed over to Patrick's room to get him. He was ready and looking spiffy.

"Sergeant-Major Wickham will be proud of us," I whispered to him as we strolled towards the offices.

When we were almost there, he only smiled and said,

"You know something Nig? I feel very nervous about this. I'm excited and angry at the same time, because I know that I will not get the same respect as would a protestant."

"There you go again," I shouted. "That's pure negativity."

I tried to calm him and myself by telling him how the army are showing their confidence in his ability.

"And that in itself should tell you that there are still some good in people in this world, immaterial of their religion," I said.

We reached the office and entered. I ordered him to stand at attention until I returned. After conferring with the Sergeant-Major, I opened the door and drilled him into the Brigadier's office.

Langstaff at times, could be a very unpleasant person to talk to. He seemed slightly eccentric or in layman's language, nuts. He gave Patrick the usual military lecture on being an officer representing the crown, then bestowed on him the promotion and quickly rushed us out. During all of this, I noticed that Patrick kept very quiet, which I thought was very irregular of him, but decided to listen to him later. The Sergeant-Major congratulated him afterwards.

"By proving that you can be good soldiers," said Wickham, again behaving like a mother hen, "you're making me a genius."

We went to the mess hall for a late breakfast and a talk. He almost talked my head off. Finally he left for the tailors shop and I walked alone to the billets reflecting on the first day we had met and the progress we have made in ten months.

Tom and Jack was sitting on their beds when I got there.

"Okay Nig," said Jack. "What've you done with our favourite Paddy? You've been acting cagey lately and we're afraid for his life."

"Yeah!" said Tommy, "and we want to know where you hid the body and his money."

I told them that the Irishman was enjoying his promotion and had gone to get his clothes adjusted.

"What surprises me though," I said, "is how quiet and adaptable the son of a bitch took it all."

They sat there staring at me in disbelief.

"You're serious!" said Tom, shaking his head. "Do you mean that he stood there without any of his political sarcasms about the English people?"

"Yes," I said. "I stood there shocked, as that cunt behaved like a real cunt."

Jack jumped to his feet and shouted.

"Oh my god! Do you realize what this means? It means we're going to be subjected to more of his mouth later."

"Yes gentlemen, Patrick O'Reilley is now a full-fledged soldier in the British army," I said and meant it.

We sat there in silence for some long time, lost for words.

"Yes," I thought, "he has grown up, I hope."

That evening when Lance Corporal O'Reilley returned to the billets, he gathered everybody to tell of his reasons for accepting the promotion. So as to distract him, I promptly reminded him of our date on Saturday night, with the two lesbians we had met on the train to Aldershot. He told me that although he hadn't forgotten, he would prefer to see Greta Paisley, the new girl he had met a week ago. I also preferred to see Catharine, so it was agreed to send Jack and Ian as our replacements, without telling them of the girls sexual preferences.

We spoke about not seeing each other for awhile, but made arrangements to have a bash whenever I returned from Yeovil.

The posting to Somerset was just before Christmas, so I asked the CO for and was given a vacation pass, for three weeks to London. The few days in that camp was very interesting, because I wasn't required to do anything and in the interim, I had met some new people. It was nice to see big Johnnie MacIntosh again, we had met in Bordon. He took me to a local pub for a mug of scrumpy and told me all about the places around, that he went for fun. He introduced me to a couple of girls from the WRAC camp which was situated almost across from our camp and we had a few pints together.

"So Johnnie my boy," I said, "where's the fun?"

"Dorchester and Weymouth," he said. "That's where the WRAC girls go on the weekends. You'll have the pick of your life there, but when you come back from your holidays, I'll take you there."

"The stay here might not be too boring after all," I thought.

Johnnie, the girls and I would meet at the pub in the evenings for the pleasure of each others company and a few pints.

Two days later, I received a phone call from Catharine asking of my plans for Christmas. I told her about my pass to London and she quickly gave me the phone number to her apartment in Marble Arch. We made arrangements to spend the second week of my holidays together.

Chapter Five

" Christmas in London."

The Christmas in London was exciting. I was able to spend some time with my family and friends, who I had not seen since I went to the army. On the third day of my holidays, Faye Macleod came to visit.

"Somebody told me of your arrival and I am here to get my share," she said.

"Your share of what?" I asked.

She did not reply only walked around the house checking every room as if she had left something there. I wondered what she was looking for, but did not ask. It wasn't until she started to remove her clothing, that I realized she had sex on her mind.

Faye was always a willing participant when it came to sex with me. She never resisted and our long absence apart made it more pleasurable.

She was a very attractive Jamaican born woman, one and a half years younger than I. Her parents came to England when she was only a year old, and being the only child, was a spoilt brat. She used her beauty to demand her desires from people who might have an interest in her. She enjoys hitting people and at five foot five and one hundred and three pounds, everybody was timid to even shout at her much less to physically retaliate. Especially me. Her parents belongs to one of those churches that hates, and believes everybody else's religion is wrong. They hated me because I refused to convert, but still hoped that I would, if I marry their daughter.

After sex, we laid there naked talking for some time.

"You know something?" she said. "When you left for the army, I was very mad at you for leaving me alone. Every time I looked at your picture I swore that whenever we meet again, I was going to kill you." Her tone of voice had that seriousness I knew so well and realized that she meant it.

"So mister soldier," she continued, "it's my intention to kill you with fucking today, so prepare to meet your doom."

Faye and I spent the entire day making love until we were certain that somebody would come home soon. We got dressed and went to a pub for tea and spent most of the evening catching up on things. We talked about our life together, although we both knew it was impossible.

"Stan," she said as we entered her parents' home, "I want to have a baby."

I stood there staring in disbelief.

"Yes," she continued, "a baby would be the answer. I feel that if I was to have your child my parents would not be able to stop us from getting married, immaterial of our religious differences."

This time I felt I should answer her.

"Girl, you must be crazy!" I said angrily. "Firstly, you would be sacrificing your education and secondly life for a woman alone with a child could be hard. Think about it. Do you think it would be easy for a woman to maintain a child on her lonesome and work at the same time?"

I felt I was getting through to her. I continued speaking not even caring for an answer. She didn't reply.

"No, I am not going to let you spoil your life. You will just have to wait until I return from the service, then I can deal with your parents. We could get married and have children legitimately then," I said.

We entered the house on her insistence and spend some time together. Seeing that her parents were already in bed, she demanded for us to make love again. So we did on the couch. It was only when I had been to the bathroom, that I discovered the broken condom.

"Oh my god!" I exclaimed in mind. "She might even get pregnant.

Could this be a plot by her? Why was she asking about babies and things?"

I returned to the room and informed her of the broken condom, she just lay there giggling.

"Stan," she said. "When it's born, we'll have something to admire and love and if my parents still objected to our marriage, then they will still be looking at your face, through their grand child."

I realized it was hopeless to argue with Faye, so I angrily left the house. But in some way I was pleased that I was the man she wanted to have a child with. Or was it to get even with her parents?

The next day I tried to avoid her as much as possible, but to no avail. She caught me at my cousin Barbara's house in Clapham Commons and made me promise to return to see her that evening. Reluctantly I went to see her and entered the house as I had done so many times in the past. I said hello to her parents and as usual, her father wanted me to talk about politics with him. Her mother decided to question me about my future plans and my intentions towards her daughter.

"I assume you will be changing your religion and your worldly ways?" Mrs Macleod asked, looking at me as though I was a piece of rag sitting there.

In my mind, I thought that it should be a crime to let some black people become wealthy, because they could be obnoxious towards others. Her father had won a lot of money on the football pools and ever since, they became snobs. I really wanted to tell them to kiss my arse, but my parents taught me to respect my elders.

Hypocritically, as always, I restrain my feelings just so that I could screw their daughter. Finally her father said with a scornful facial expression.

"Get yourself upstairs, she is waiting for you."

I ran up the stairs, all the time angry at Faye for her little trick she played the day before. I had everything I wanted to say to her, planned; but as soon as I bust through her bedroom door, there she was laying across the bed stark naked.

"What the.....?" I said and stopped in my tracks.

I slowly advanced towards her bed, after closing the door.

"You're a bitch," I said softly. "First you tricked me so as to get pregnant, then I don't know what lies you've told your parents about me and my religion, now here you are naked ready to screw again."

She slowly rolled over on her back and spread her legs.

"And what's your objection?" She said teasing and tempting me. "Sex with me was never a problem before. Was it?"

I anxiously began to remove my clothes and tossed them on the floor. I dove into bed beside her. Somehow I couldn't stay angry at Faye for long, she had her ways to attract my attention. I began to reflect on a time before, when she did the same thing to me.

I was about twelve when her cousin Hyacinth, who was then twenty, lured me into having sex with her. Faye saw us from the clothes closet, but never told anyone about it. A year later she told me what she saw and wanted the same from me. It took another year of arguing the issue and many objections by myself, until I gave in.

She had invited me to her home when her parents were away on holidays.

"I have some new comic books in my bedroom," she told me. " Do you want to see them?"

I agreed and went to her house. I laid cross her bed, as I had done many times before, scanning through one of them. I didn't notice that she was busy removing her clothing.

"Hey Stan, look at this," she said.

I couldn't believe my eyes. She was standing there stark naked showing off her young body. She then threw herself on top of me.

"I want to be a woman today and I want you to be the man to do it," she said demandingly.

"Come on Faye," I protested. "You're only twelve years old and a virgin and furthermore, you could get pregnant."

"Yes I know all of that," she said waving her hands in the air. "mother already told me all about the evil things of sex and I want to have it now," she insisted.

I was still trying to fight her off, but she was very persistent and I became weaker.

"Someday we'll get married," I told her. "It could wait until then, you know?"

"No sir," she insisted. "I want it now, I want to be a woman today. What if one of us died and we never got to do it?" she asked.

Faye knew that I was already convinced, so when I agreed, she jumped from the bed, ran into her parents' room and brought back a French safe.

"I stole this from my father's pocket one night," she happily said. "I think he has another woman somewhere."

We screwed many times that day, with the same safe.

This time was no different, she knows exactly how to capture my weak mind.

"Stan," she said. "From ever since we were young, I've always believed that we were destined for each other and there's nothing that will prevent us from being together. We might not ever get married due to the circumstances surrounding us, but if I had a child for you, then we will be together, always."

We made love and I fell asleep. It was only when I heard her mother's voice asking if I was still there, that I realize what she had done. She deliberately let me fall asleep, so I could be blamed for her pregnancy. I hurriedly got dressed and left. I was feeling disappointed in Faye for her deception of me.

"What a bitch," I thought as I made my way to Brixton.

I got into the Atlantic pub for a few brews and a conversation with a fellow I knew some time now. He didn't know that I was conscripted.

"Stan Martin!" said the voice from behind me. "What are you doing here?"

It was the voice of George Walters, a long time school friend from Maxfield Avenue in Jamaica.

"Somebody told me that you were in town and I had hope to see you, but finding you in this pub is a bonus," he said.

"Mr Walters," I said, surprised to see Georgie. "What the holy hell are you doing in Brixton this time of night?"

He explained about taking a friend home and accidentally came to this pub. We talked about politics, money, women and life in the military. I obliged them with my thoughts in all categories. I surprised myself by being conversant on all the subjects, including military operations and silently thanked Patrick for his encouragement in reading those books. I was very confident in my ability.

We staggered out of the pub just before closing time and stood at the corner of Atlantic road and Acre lane making arrangements to visit another friend in Forestgate the next day. Finally we said our goodnight.

I got to Lloyd Campbell's house about noon, with a hangover from the night before. He was surprised and happy to see me.I flopped in his bed and went to sleep.

About two hours later, I was awakened to eat and since I was up, we began drinking again. Later that evening George suggested we go to Plastow hospital to meet three girls he had met the previous week. Strictly for therapeutic reasons. They were receptive to our suggestion for a movie and a party, so they quickly got dressed and we all left.

Georgie was with Beverly and Lloyd with Norma. The girl I was stuck with was Yvonne Carpenter. She was tall and skinny, like in the song "Boney Marony." Yvonne turned out to be a very versatile, learned enjoyable person. We danced and talked for most of the night then we took them back to the hospital. I thanked Georgie for the introduction, because Yvonne and I became good friends and saw a lot of each other after that. She got very emotional at the Friday-night party when I told her that I was returning to the army. We agreed to keep corresponding with each other after I returned to duties.

All that week, Georgie, Ruddux, Lloyd and I spent a lot of time together and talked about solidifying our friendship. We even went to the gym to watch Ruddux train. He was a very good boxer.

Saturday morning I left Lloyd's house and took the Under- ground train on my way to my cousin's home in Clapham Common. I got off the train in Angel and found a card shop. I searched and found a card, one with the appropriate verses I wanted, signed it and posted it to my Irish family in Belfast, wishing them a Merry Christmas. I spent the rest of the day visiting friends in the Elephant and Castle, Peckham, Dulwich and Battasea.

As I was approaching Barbara's house that evening, I saw another cousin and her friend leaving. Madlyn Morgan and I knew each other for many years but had not seen each other since I went to the army.

"Hello Stan," said Maddy, "I am so glad to see you. Could you escort me to the hospital? I am working the midnight shift and the Teddy boys are out looking for trubble."

I decided to walk her to the Clapham North hospital where she was a resident nurse. She expressed her desire to have sex with me and I agreed.

"How do I get into the nurses residence?" I asked her.

She directed me down the side road, saying that she would open the gate for me but the gate was locked.

"What shit luck," she said. "Somebody locked it and I don't know where to locate the key."

"Do you want me in there tonight?" I asked her, laughing.

"Sure I do," she replied, "I need to hear more about your army life and a good screw."

I checked for prying eyes and climbed over the fence like any good soldier would. Maddy and I screwed before she went on duty and I had a good sleep until she came in the next morning. Luckily the authorities do not check on the nurses' rooms like they do in the military, so we were able to make love and talk all Sunday. She brought in food for me after she went on duty again.

"Aren't you going home? It's Monday morning you know?" she said standing at the door with her hands on her hips. "This is not an old age retirement home you know."

I sprung to my feet.

"All I need is a shower and I'll be on my way," I said.

She handed me a towel and soap and directed me to the bath.

When I got back to the room feeling refreshed, although I had on the same drawers from the day before, she began removing her clothes and insisted we have sex again.

"I might never see you again," she said, "and I probably won't get a screw like this for a long time to come. How do you feel about it?"

"Good," I said. "I haven't had a nice screw like you for a long time either," I lied.

On reaching the house again, Barbara informed me that a very attractive white woman had come to see me.

"It's Catharine," I said. "Did you talk to her?"

"Not really," Barbie replied. "She asked for you and I told her that you weren't here and she left. Who is she?"

I could see she was curious about Catharine, so I told her everything, because we've always been honest with each other. She gave me a lecture and a warning about screwing around with white married women. When Catharine returned, I introduced them and they exchanged pleasantries. Barbara's inquisition into Catharine's life seemed embarrassing to her, so I quickly put a stoppage to it and we left.

"Why did you stop her?" Catharine asked.

"To prevent you from any embarrassing answers," I said.

She sat quietly for a minute.

"I liked her," she said. "She was only looking out for your welfare. She was protecting her loving cousin. And if I was her, I would probably do the same for my cousin also."

I didn't reply, but was surprised at her thoughts.

"Next time," I said.

As soon as we reached the apartment, she began to rip her clothing off. I could see that she was horny.

"Hey! Can't you wait?" I asked.

"No sir," she replied. "I am hungry and in heat, I have been waiting for two whole weeks to be with you, so hurry."

"Okay!" I said. "If it's just a quick bang you want, I'll oblige, although I missed you also."

We were laying, laughing about our short but enjoyable screw and comparing it to some we've had in the past.

"You know something?" I said. "We've had some good sex in the past, but I still remember the first time on the train to Aldershot as the best."

She thought for a moment then said,

"Come to think of it, that encounter was thrilling because I wasn't sure how I would feel about you afterwards."

"Maybe," I said, "I was fulfilling your curiosity about black men?"

She simply nodded.

"Yes sir," she said, "and I was right. You're the first black man I ever looked at in a sexual way and fell in love instantly."

She kissed me lightly and continued.

"If my mother ever find out about us, she would be shocked to death, although she's not a prude," she said and paused again. "I will definitely take you to meet my parents when you're in Somerset."

She talked about her wealthy family, telling stories of her younger days with her brother and sisters. She told me things which were family secrets within their house.

"You know something Catharine? You're a spoilt rich girl and I think you are playing a game between Mark and I."

She didn't reply, so I continued.

"I cannot comprehend why a man as he would have a lovely looking woman as you and allow another man to be screwing her and a black one at that."

She thought hard about my words, and when she felt she had the answer, it came in a flurry.

"Stan, tell me," she said. "What would I have to gain by deceiving you? I could've had any white man I desired and God knows, I was approached or introduced to many. But I met you and have been sexually and mentally satisfied. I will admit there are some obstacles to over come; obstacles that will need addressing later, but not at this very moment, okay?" I laid there silently listening to her and feeling badly for mentioning it.

"And furthermore," she said. "I want to enjoy your young body now, because you could be gone to some faraway land in a few weeks time and I mightn't see you for a long, long time thereafter."

"Tell me something Catharine?" I asked. "Does Mark always tell you about the troops movements and activities?"

I was curious and wanted to formulate an opinion of them.

"No," she replied. "Only if I asked him about yours."

"Then what does he ask you about me?" I asked.

She smiled.

"I know what you're getting at. You want to know if he questioned me about our sex life. If I find you attractive in bed? Yes he does and the answer is yes, and I am in love with you," she said happily.

"No, not that, I mean about my personal self. Questions about my family and type of friends."

"No," she replied, "he seldom asks questions of that nature, but he sometimes make statements about you hanging around with those Irish boys. I don't think he likes them very much."

"Oh? What doesn't he like about them?" I asked.

"Well he talks about them being terrorists who hate the English, especially Patrick O'Reilley and would rather see them out of the service," she said. "I really don't care what he does with them. My only concern is for your well-being, and furthermore I haven't a clue about the Irish problem. I don't really understand any of the politics surrounding them and I won't ask."

"Didn't your family ever discuss it?" I asked curiously.

"No," she replied. "I was too busy enjoying myself to care. And with Mark, I often believed he was a racist, so I never listen to him talk about them either."

I was now confident that she was honest with me.

"You know something?" I said. "Until I met Patrick, I too really didn't know anything about Ireland's problems. But now I am very much concerned for their well-being."

I realized that I shouldn't question her loyalty to me any more, she probably was telling me the truth. What would she have to gain from all this, other than our hot passionate sexcapades?

She went to the kitchen and returned with two brandies.

"Do you want something to eat?" she asked.

"Okay," I said. "Maybe just a sandwich of a kind."

She rushed off back to the kitchen and I could hear the rumbling of pots being moved around. Finally she emerged with sandwiches for the both of us.

"In the morning," she said, "I am going to make you a great breakfast. I am a good cook, I'll have you know. Just because I grew up with maids and a butler, doesn't mean I don't know how to do those things?" She bragged.

I laughed at the way she said it in a Jamaican accent.

"If I were in your financial shoe," I said, "I wouldn't do any of those things either. I would be snapping my fingers for service."

"That day might come," she replied. "You'll get that chance."

We finished the sandwiches and she washed the dishes and we returned to bed.

"Darling, I would like to have some more," she said. "How do you feel?"

"Catharine," I said. "For you, I am always in the mood for love."

She let out a loud roaring laugh.

"That's a song! Maybe it was written specially for us!! That's what I like about you, you can make me laugh at all times."

She cuddled up into my arms and began to fondle again.

The morning light came through the window to awaken me, I laid there relaxed reflecting on my life and wondered what would William Shakespeare write if he was in my place now.

"What light through yonder window breaks?" I said.

I laughed at the quotation. She must have heard me chuckling and laughed also.

"Hey!" I said. "I thought you were still asleep."

"No darling," she said. "You were so relaxed, I didn't want to disturb your thoughts."

I could hear that sincerity in her tone of voice again.

"It's so nice to lay beside someone I love and care for," she said. "My only wish is for it to last forever."

I didn't react, so she continued.

"Maybe it was some sort of faith that brought us together. Look at the age difference between us and we are enjoying very good sex. For all my life I never dreamt of falling in love with a young black man and wanting to spend the rest of my life with him."

"Catharine," I said. "I too was very surprised at myself for wanting to be with you for the same reason. I've been wondering why and can't find the answer either. So I'm willing to let things take their course and see what the end results will be."

We laid there in silence. I could see the sunray's dancing shadows off the curtains onto her breasts. She cuddled into my arms again and we fell asleep.

I awoke to the sound of music from the radio. It was Matt Monroe singing "Walk away." She had been up making the promised breakfast.

"Good morning," she said, "hungry?"

"Sure I am. What's cooking?" I asked.

"I made an omelette, plus bacon, toast and sausage. Do you want coffee or tea?"

"Tea please," I responded as I entered the bathroom.

We talked as we consumed the food and made plans to meet in Somerset.

I was happy to have spent the five days alone with Catharine, as I assumed she did with me. She took me back to Clapham on Christmas eve, where she spoke with Barbie for an hour. From the next room, I could hear Barbara telling her about my parents and my younger life. We kissed goodbye as she left for Somerset and to her parent's home for the family Christmas dinner.

Christmas morning, I laid in bed thinking of what I would be doing in the coming months.

"I might not see London again for a long time," I thought. "Sergeant-Major Wickham had said we might be gone for a year, maybe more. Oh well, that's all part of being in the army."

My solitude was broken, when cousin Lorna called me for breakfast. I was happy to be spending the holidays with them. I knew that whenever I left, I wouldn't be seeing Barbie, Lorna, Kirk, Cherry and Geddies for a long time to come. I wondered what George and Lloyd was feeling after last night's drinking spree, It seemed we had tried to finish all the booze in the pubs and the after hours club in Soho.

Some friends, who had gone to the Commons church service, came to visit. We wished each other well for the joyous occasion. Barbie told them about Catharine and they all wanted to know more and I told them a very concise story.

"Hey Stan," shouted Barbara, "aren't you going to open her present? I would like to see what it is."

Quickly I ripped the paper off and opened the box. There was a dinner jacket, a shirt and a tie.

"Ha, ha!" exclaimed Barbie. "See I told you that she loves him!" Everybody laughed.

"If Faye ever find out about this," said Lorna, "she would kill him."

"Why?" chimed in Kirk. "Her mother hates him."

They quizzed me about Catharine and I told them what I wanted them to hear. I know that if I wasn't with them for Christmas it would be a miserable time for me. Except with Catharine.

On Boxing day, I decided to visit some old friends of the family. I knew they would have liked to see me in uniform, so I got dressed because I wanted to impress them. I was now feeling proud of the uniform, although I didn't want to be in the army at first. I looked at the regimental crest on my tunic and the Para wings on the shoulder and my maroon red beret with the airborne insignia on it and smiled.

Some wanted to hear about life in the places I had been in the north and south of England. They wanted to know how the white people reacted to me. I was delighted to tell them about the politics, most of which Patrick had encouraged me to read up on, with confidence in my ability to express my own political ideology.

I was now a learned man, expressing the education I had obtained in the last ten months.

"Coming into my own," I thought, "and proud of it."

By the end of the day, many of them were happy to have talked to me and wanted me to stay longer.

Although I was enjoying my visit with my family and friends, I found my mind constantly reflecting on the boys. I felt as though I was missing some other families. Yes they were in a sense, a family away from the family. I was delighted to be here with mine and thoroughly enjoyed myself, knowing that I might not see them again for whatever reason. My cousin's showed their love for me, while George, Ruddux, Lloyd and I talked about our friendship and our reason to maintain communications. It's a Christmas I will never forget.

Catharine and I agreed to spend the last two days of my holidays together. She had made arrangements for us to visit her youngest sister Doreen and her family in Hammersmith. During the drive there I asked her.

"I presume you've told your sister about us?"

"Yes I did," she replied.

"How does she feel about our relationship?" I asked. "Our colour differences I mean?"

"I really don't know, and I really don't care what anybody thinks of me," she said. "I am going to live my life strictly according to my feelings."

I got the answer as soon as we reached the door. Her sister rushed to us and threw her arms around my neck and kissed me, then Catharine.

Doreen was a medium height, slightly plumpish brunet haired woman of thirty. She appeared quite comfortable with her family life with her husband John and her three children. John, a tall seemingly educated man and who is five years her senior, managed one of their father's many businesses.

"Come on in you two," said Doreen, " I've been slaving over a hot stove to make this breakfast, so let's eat it!"

Doreen and John Heatherington's house sat on a very large piece of suburban land near Hammersmith, with a rather well kept attractively designed garden. After the introduction and the meal, John took me on a tour of the house and garden, then we visited his next door neighbour, a Captain Gretcham, who was a retired RAF world war two fighter pilot.

Gretcham, whose hobby it was to refurbish vintage planes, welcomed us into his house and offered us a Scotch and water.

"So you're a jumper eh?" the old man asked, twiddling his pipe in the corner of his mouth. "I am delighted to know that there are young people, as yourself, willing to defend this country," he said and went on to tell us of his war exploits. Finally John excused us and we returned to the house for tea. Doreen introduced me to her three children who were out somewhere on our arrival. Robert, Catharine and John junior. Young Catharine was proud to tell me that she was born on the same date as her aunt, with emphasis on the fact that she was just as pretty.

"I am only eleven years old now, but whenever I grow up I would like to be just like auntie Catharine," she said. "Do you think so Mr. Martin? Am I as pretty as her?" she asked.

"Yes my dear," I agreed, "and you will grow up to be even lovelier than you are now," I assured her.

Young Catharine was happy to hear this and spent the major part of the evening sitting beside me, until it was bed time. Doreen, John, Catharine and I sat and talked about many things that night. But I noticed they never once asked any questions relating to my personal self. We slept overnight there and spent the entire day playing with the children in the garden. Catharine seemed to be happy that they had welcomed me openly and even requested me maintaining contact with them, from abroad. It was a very enjoyable two days with them.

That afternoon while we were sitting on the porch relaxing, Doreen came to sit on my lap, hugged and kissed me and said what I thought should've been said from the outset.

"Catharine when you first told me of finding the man of your dreams, I never thought he would be black, and now that I've met him, I am not surprised. When you said he was handsome, you weren't lying, because he is. Sometimes I wished I had the guts to do adventurous things as you. It makes me very jealous of you, but I am still happy that you've made the move from Mark." Doreen paused for a moment looking into my eyes. "Has she told you about Mark's father and our father as yet?"

"No, not yet," I replied. "But she promised to do so at a more convenient time and I can wait."

John, who had been quiet during all this, jumped in saying,

"Stan, don't let anything prevent you two from being to gether. It's the first for a long time I have seen her so relaxed and happy."

Catharine sat there smiling without a word and I in turn was listening. I could see that there was something else to be said, but nobody was saying it.

Finally Catharine got up.

"Well thank you very much children, we have to return to Marble Arch now. We have a lot more loving to do before the holiday's ended. Be assured my darlings that I am going to live my life from here on, as I deem fit. I hope it will always be with Stan, no matter what the outcome may be."

We left their home with a hearty goodbye and thanks.
Catharine began to speak as I drove back to Marble Arch. She told me of her wealthy parents and of her father's bigoted thoughts.

"He either owns or controls a lot of businesses throughout England and some in Scotland," she said, "and is now venturing into parts of Europe. He would like to have total control over me, as he dose with his businesses and I am not going to let it happen, even though I might lose their financial support and family privileges."

"Then why do it?" I asked her.

"Because my darling, I am a person with a mind of my very own and my father don't want to recognize that. He wants me to adhere to all his requests to live a life of misery without questions and I am not going to succumb to that," she answered.

"Then what about your husband? What does he think of your defiance?" I asked.

She gave thought to my question then replied in an abrupt tone.

"We were married under protest. I don't care for him, never did and never will. But my father insisted on a wedding for his business purposes and now I want out of it," she answered.

"Well then, maybe you should just leave him," I responded.

"That my dear, is the dilemma at this moment. I have been requesting a divorce for two years and he won't grant it. But some day I will get away from him to be with you, forever."

I didn't reply, I kept driving with my thought until we reached Marble Arch. We spent the night making love and talking about our lives for the future.

The next morning we parted company at the train station. I to catch the train to Yeovil and she to drive back to Aldershot.

Chapter Six

" *Posting Number Two.*"

My arrival back in Yeovil, Somerset, was a little disappointing and depressing. My birthday was coming up in a few days and I didn't have anyone to spend it with. I was a very agitated and as grouchy a human anybody could encounter.

"Imagine my birthday will be Sunday and nobody to celebrate it with," I thought angrily.

I decided I would take a trip somewhere on Friday, maybe to Weymouth, as suggested by Johnnie "Scrumpy"MacIntosh and maybe there I would find a WRAC to get drunk with.

On the Friday afternoon, as I was about to leave the camp, MacIntosh, a big burly six foot four Guyanese man, caught me at the bus stop. He told me there was a phone call in the Guardroom for me. I got the phone and it was Catharine.

"Darling," she said, "I am so happy to have caught you. I would like for you to come to my house, so that we could celebrate your birthday together. Remember I had promised to show the house to you?" She sounded excited about it.

"That's a rather lovely thought," I said, "where's the house and how do I get there?"

She gave me the directions and I caught the bus to Shepton Mallet, then a taxi to the house. When the driver let me out, I stood there absorbing the architecture of the magnificent house. It looked like something out of a mystery movie. It was a thing of beauty, a mini castle and I was about to enter through its doors. I knocked and she opened it. She was radiant as usual, although she was dressed only in a negligee with absolutely nothing underneath. I entered and we walked through the large foyer to the extra large drawing-room. I could see that the furnishings were antiques, although I didn't have a clue of what era, but they seemed to fit well in their places.

Catharine watched my reactions as I perused the rooms looking at all the paintings and artifacts there in. The eight by four foot painting of her father, over-looked the entire room. His eyes seemed to watch every movement of the people entering his domain. There was a smaller painting of her mother beside his and of the children, all at age twelve.

"That's a nice painting of you," I said. "But why are your fists clinched?" I asked.

She looked at the picture for a moment smiling.

"I didn't want to sit there all afternoon," she answered.

"You're a very rich woman," I commented.

"Well yes," she replied. "But it's my father's. He worked hard to get it and struggled for many years to keep it. Although someday it will be for my brother, sisters and myself. Are you disappointed?" she asked.

"Not really," I said, "but you might've told me earlier so that I could prepare my mind for all of this."

"Darling Stan, forgive me," she said apologetically, "but I thought that if I had told you of my family's wealth before, you might've shunned me, seeing our differences. I couldn't bear that happening. I just didn't want to lose your love, because of this,"
she said pointing around the room.

I didn't know what to say, so I signalled for her to proceed with the tour. When she thought I had seen enough of her drawing- room, she said,

"Ever since as a little girl, I promised myself that whenever I met the man I fell in love with, I would make love to him everywhere in this house and it seemed the time is now and you're here," she stated, "are you game?"

She kissed me and at the same time loosening the buttons on my tunic and shirt and removing them. I was down to my underwear when she quickly removed her negligee leaving herself naked.

Although it was January, the weather felt more like spring.

"Where's everybody?" I asked.

"My parents are in Australia on holidays and the maids and butler are off. We're alone in this house and nobody else will come here for the entire weekend, so don't be afraid."

I completed the removal of my clothing and we made love on the drawing-room floor, then on the large oak desk.

"You know something?" she said. "Mother would just love you. She would adore and spoil you rotten. But someday I will have to introduce you to her, after they return."

"Then what about your father?" I asked.

"Oh he would hate you," she replied. "Firstly because he doesn't like black people and secondly because he would blame you for my attitude. You see dear, I am breaking his traditional family policy."

"So I could be easily killed for being with you?" I asked.

"Yes," she giggled, "but I would be there to fight to the bitter end for you. But for now, come let me show you the rest of the house," she said dragging my hand.

She led me to the stairs into the cellar.

"I've got to show you this," she said. "Come and see the wine cellar."

We rushed down to the dark stairs to the cellar. She showed me the leavers to open the doors and the switches for the dim lights. It appears like a dungeon from an old Sherlock Holmes novel, except there weren't any torture equipment. I was expecting a skeleton to jump out at anytime. She took me through the passages of
barrels, as she explained how the grapes are crushed and the juices are fermented into making this palatable commodity for the rich and a novelty for the poor ones, like me.

The caretaker of the wine, seemed to know that people often came down there for a taste, so he deliberately left the paraphernalia accessible for that purpose, which Catharine and I did as we walked.

"Here Stan!" she exclaimed, "I would like it right here please."

She quickly laid on her stomach over a barrel and spread her legs.

"I've always wanted to do it this way down here," she said.

She made noises that could awaken the dead and she really didn't care what would happen, if there really was any ghosts there. She took me through the rest of their dungeon, and even the secret passages that led to other parts of the house.

"This family must be some weird one," I thought, "to own a house like this."

I was trying hard to restrain myself from voicing it.

"I would really like to meet your parents. Where are they now?" I asked.

"In Australia at this time," she replied, "but you'll meet them someday darling, I promise you. As a matter of fact my mother would love you."

"What about Mark," I asked curiously. "How does she feel about him?"

"She was against the marriage from the start, but my father insisted for his own selfish reasons. You see, both my father and Mark's father decided on a business venture, so to complete the transaction, I had to marry Mark."

"Oh, oh, so there's some friction within the family I see?" I said to antagonize her.

"Yes my darling, there has," she said in a slightly perturbed tone. "But let's not talk about that now please. I am having a good time with you at this moment and don't want to spoil it, okay?"

I agreed with her and that was the end of my inquision. For the rest of that weekend, we must have had sex a dozen times in various parts of that house, down by the river and carving our initials in the oak tree there. Even out in the gardener's shack, with her pretending to be the Lady Chatterley. We talked about many things regarding our parents and younger life. She told me of the mischiefs they got into in that house and how she perceived her parents would react to our affair. She explained the entire scenario of her relationship with Mark and her reason for wanting a divorce from him. Catharine proved that she was a very good cook, as she had done in London, so we ate well without leaving the house. She even baked and decorated a cake and we both celebrated my nineteen years on planet earth.

"Yes, I did enjoy my birthday, immensely," I thought.

Sunday evening, when we were leaving after locking up everything, she made me promise to write every day and that I would see her when I returned to Farnham. We parted company at the camp gate in Yeovil with a kiss that lasted for about ten minutes. I stood watching as she drove away.

"Goodbye for now my love, see you in Farnham," I whispered to myself. I wonder what it would be like to meet her parents and how would they react to me, a black man. These thoughts and more occupied my mind as I prepared myself for the education the army wanted me to have.

The training course was on procedures for certain rescue and mechanical repairs in the field during a battle. It was very intense and compact so there was no time for anything else, except for the occasional evenings at the pub for a few mugs of scrumpy. MacIntosh had introduced me to a couple of WRAC friends of his, but although we spent most of our spare time together, I found they weren't as enjoyable as Catharine or Fiona. Nevertheless, our conversations were good. The course went well and was over fast. Before I knew it, I was on my way to Farnham again. On my arrival there, I found out that all of my friends had already been posted to Singapore, bound for Malaya.

"Hello sir," I greeted him, "I'm here again. I've heard that the boys are all posted."

"Hello Corporal Martin, I am glad to see you again." Sergeant Major Wickham said. "Yes they are and you'll be joining them in Singapore in a short while. Both Bob and Jack were made up to Lance Corporal before posting."

"Good for them!" I said excitedly. "Maybe now they will understand what I had endured as a new NCO."

He laughed and invited me to tea at his house.

"Mary and the girls want to see you," he said. "How about Wednesday evening?"

"That's fine with me sir," I replied.

"Okay then, I'll tell them to expect you on Wednesday."

Wickham made sure to speak to me every day as a reminder, even on the Wednesday morning. That evening, I got dressed and casually walked to his home.

"Come in Stan," said Mary on opening the door to me. She was delighted to see me again as was the children.

"I want to hear all about the last few months and Catharine," said Mary.

While we had tea, I told them all about the things that went on in Yeovil and my Christmas holiday in London and my birthday with Catharine. In the mean time Elizabeth was desperately trying to keep me for herself, from Carol. She wanted to confer with me about some thing privately but Carol kept interrupting. Finally I promised her Thursday evening alone to talk. Later as we sat in his study having a few brandies, he made me promise to take care of his boys in the field and for me to write him with details about them every day. Although he was still trying to get the ugly one, meaning the commander, to assign him to our new regiment.

He told me that he was sure that Patrick and Jack do have IRA revolutionary tendencies.

"Stan," he said, "those boys really scare me. I would be very cautious when dealing with them out in the field, especially if you are sent into action. But as long as they are pointing their weapons elsewhere, it might be okay."

"Well sir, they are good soldiers who have unquestionable respect for you. They are my friends and I trust them with my life," I replied.

"That I know my boy, that I know," he replied.

I left Tashie's house late that evening.

The weeks in Aldershot and Farnham went by very quickly.
I was slated to leave at the end of February. Although I was spending a

lot of time with Catharine she was demanding more and crying every time we met.

"You'll be leaving me shortly," she said, "and I want to get as much to last me until we're together again."

She says things like this while crying and sometimes reminded me that she wanted a baby, then promptly tell me she was joking. Wickham was also making certain to see me every day to give me instructions. I felt like James Bond going off to a foreign country to carry-out some espionage act. Catharine and I spent a lot of evenings together with the Wickham family for teas and talks. I became the older brother and confidante to the girls, who is filled with wisdom and information. Both Mary and Tashie were fussing over me and worried for my safety in Singapore as was Catharine. She was also happy to meet and talked to Mary and spent a lot of time discussing me with her. Especially on the night before I left.

The morning of March eight came and it was time for us to leave. It was a kind of happy-sad day for me. I wanted to and did give thoughts to the fact that I might never return here again, so I absorbed the place mentally for that purpose.

"If you have to go, you have to go," Catharine said while seeing me off at Farnborough airfield.

"This is my destiny darling," I told her. "What ever is to be will be."

Catharine and I kissed in public for friends of hers and Mark to see for the first time. There were fifty of us with full equipment being loaded on a transporter bounded for Gibraltar. I smiled within and willingly got on the plane for a place of uncertainty.

We landed and stayed in Gibraltar for two whole days doing absolutely nothing, then on the third day we loaded up again to leave.

It was a long but rough flight to Singapore and riding in a transporter was not as ideal like flying in a commercial airline. At times we were flying high and other times we were very low. The captain sometimes opened the cargo bay door so that we could see the ground and sea below. I could see the many Naval ships, of all descriptions, out there.

We landed in Singapore at dawn the next morning. It seemed that half the place was the airbase. The city itself was not a large place and seemed most of the natives worked on the base. There were umpteen thousands of army, navy and of course the air force people there. Some are stationed there and some, like me, only pass through or are on rest, for one reason or another.

I was directed to a set of billets on the other side of the air field by a Major McTavish, who told me that I would be going on to Malaka in a few days to join my unit. Hearing that I would be seeing my friends again, delighted me.

"Tell me sir," I asked Major McTavish, "where is the base hospital? I have a friend there that I would like to see."

"Oh! A hometown nurse eh?" he said with a grin. "It's right over there soldier, on the other side of the airfield, you'll need a Land Rover to get there."

I thanked him and spent the next day sorting out my gear and observe the place as much as possible. Nobody seemed to care or question my presence in many of the areas I wondered into, so I just drift around. I sought out Major-Doctor Helen Butterworth and found her at the Hospital, after three days of searching.

She was ecstatic to see me. We greeted each other with a hug, after I saluted her in the proper military fashion. She whispered her residence address and told me to be there that evening.

"And don't to be late," she told me.

As soon as I could, I went to speak to Major McTavish to get a pass and he was very receptive to my request. I didn't waste any time getting dressed and to her place, which was almost in town. She was excited to see me and quickly invited me into the house and made us both a drink. That evening the renewal of a lovely friendship began again.

"Welcome to my home Corporal Martin," said Helen holding the glass above her head and smiling. "Welcome to Singapore and to the beginning of our life, love and longevity."

"Well thank you ma'am," I mimicked an American tone, "it's always nice to see old acquaintances, especially in a new country."

"Cheers," she said. "Do you know that this is my first drink since I got here? I am so happy to see you again. Since I got here, I have engrossed myself in the job so as not to be bored. Singapore is not what I thought it would be."

I studied her expression very keenly.

"Why did you take it on, if you felt it was not what you wanted?" I asked her.

"Well darling," she said, "one never knows what the future holds until you get there and the grass always look greener on the other side of the fence."

We both found that funny and laughed.

She told me that she was promised a promotion to Colonel and to become the second in command of the hospital, but that has been cancelled.

"And the fact that you would be posted here too," she added.

"Well two out of three isn't bad, here I am," I said jokingly.

We talked for almost an hour about many things in our lives, since we last saw each other. She motioned for me to come sit beside her as she laid on the sofa and I did.

"I want to make love right here," she said. "It's been a long wait."

We hurriedly did, then she got up and led me to the bedroom where we talked and made love almost all that night until three a.m. It was indeed a beautiful reunion. I announced returning to camp and she quickly informed me that I didn't have to.

"You don't have to leave sweetheart," she said proudly. "This is not like in Bordon. We don't have to hide anymore, you can stay here for as long as your pass allows. Furthermore, I don't care who knows about us."

Seeing Helen naked again was a thrill, she was looking real nice for her age, since she had lost weight and had toned up her muscles.

"I saw Patrick and Charley when they came in a few weeks ago, on their way to Malaka," she said. "We had lunch together and talked about you."

"Good!" I said, remembering my friends. " How are they and what did those reprobates say about me?" I enquired.

"They looked fine," she said,"and they told me about all the women you had been screwing back home. We had tea and talked again before they left for Malaka, but you'll see them whenever you get there."

"You're going to be tired on the job tomorrow, if you don't get some sleep now," I suggested. "What time do you go in?"

"Don't worry about that, I'll sleep some other time. I usually leave at six thirty in the mornings, but we'll see what tomorrow brings," she advised.

"So shall we get some sleep now?" I foolishly asked.

"Not on your Nelly! I have been waiting to do this for a long time and now that you're here, I would like it all night please."

And so we did for the two whole days.

We drove into camp the morning in her Land Rover and made arrangements for that afternoon.

"I am going now to change my schedule, so that I can be with you every evening for the rest of the time," she said smiling, "because I know that you're not leaving here for another two weeks. Officers privileges you know."

Helen was grinning from ear to ear.

"Remember," I said, "I am a mere Lance Corporal and I don't want to spend the rest of my life in a prison, for a little twat."

"Don't worry about it sweetheart. Singapore is much different than in Bordon," she assured me.

I realized that she didn't have to hide her feelings for me anymore. She was not afraid of anyone seeing us together, so I saw and enjoyed all of Helen and beautiful Singapore for the two weeks. I had to admit, she was looking really nice now.

"Maybe it was the tropical weather," I thought.

The morning I was leaving for Malaka, she made me promise to see her every time I got off duty and in Singapore.

Our camp was located about twenty five miles north of the city of Malaka. As soon as I got out of the lorry, lo and behold Captain Mark Harrison was coming towards us, all two hundred plus pounds of him. We stood at attention and saluted. He faced each of the men and said some private words. I waited until he came face to face with me, then I accorded him the respect.

"You big redheaded Yorkie git," I whispered, "nice to see you again. Where are the boys?"

He smiled then said loudly.

"Good afternoon Corporal Martin, it's so nice to see you again." Then he muttered in a low tone of voice and pointed in a general direction.

"Your colleagues are waiting to see you. You'll find them in that billet over there."

He then turned his attention to the others.

"As you can see, I am your Commander here and I demand and expect a high calibre of respect from all of you, where your duties and your encounter with the local people are concerned. Corporal Martin here will attest to my rules and regulations."

I looked at the faces of the men standing there and saw that they didn't want to be there either.

"You should pay attention to what the commander is saying," I said. "your life might depend on it later."

There was a sound of "Puuutttt" from somebody and a "fuck off nigger," from another.

"If anyone here think I'm an easy pushover nigger, come and try whenever you see fit. But I'll have news for you," I said.

He stood there smiling as though I had just given him a present.

"There will be a regimental meeting at 0900 hours tomorrow morning and for the NCO's; be in my office in two hours. Okay Corporal Martin, dismiss the men."

I waited until everybody left before asking him if he had spoken to Catharine before coming to this land. He assured me that he had. We walked together to his office talking about her and life in Malaya and he told me about the new Company and the operations that we will be involved in. He even confided in me the date and time they would begin.

"We won't be staying in this camp always," he said in a matter of fact way. "Our company will be based near Taiping close to two other para regiments stationed at Baling and Kuala Kral."

"Are there any other troops in the area?" I asked.

"Yes," he said smiling. "the full contingent is here. Engineers, Fusiliers, Service Corps and...."

"Okay," I said. "I get the picture. It's a war zone isn't it?"

"Yes," he replied without looking at me.

Mark also expressed his concern for Patrick and some of the others, but it was his intention to keep our unit together, for reasons known only to himself .

That part I didn't mind, because we knew each other's moves and we had our special codes. I left him for the billets to see my friends. I sneaked quietly into the room to see him laying on his bed reading. I pounced on him and in a flash my arm was around his neck, my knee in his back and the other arm holding him so that he could not move. He surrendered very quickly. I released him and he sprung to his feet and hugged me.

"You black arse hole," he screeched at me rubbing his neck,. "you could've killed me with that hold you know."

"That's what I wanted to do," I replied while laughing at his reaction. "Then there would be one less Irishman to worry about."

All the boys were happy to see me. We sat and talked until it was time to go to the office. The few weeks there, hadn't changed Patrick's political ideology any. Jack and Tom were now NCO's so they too were at the meeting.

"This promotion," said Jack, "entitles me to see and hear some things that would otherwise be restricted to me, but I will do the job anyway even if it's only to please Tashie Wickham."

In the meeting, Paddy questioned everything he could think of. Mark, it seemed, found his inquisition very intriguing and spent a lot of time explaining to him about the operations in that country, yet some other questions were brushed aside. I could understand his reason for being nice to me, but to Paddy? I was a little suspicious. Anyway, I realized that none of us knew him well. I sat there thinking and studying and analysing his demeanour, trying to visualize what he might be in certain situations. He appeared to be a very compassionate person who would do anything for his men, but could be cruel if the need arose. I got the jitters just thinking that there was more to Mark Harrison than was apparent to my eyes. I knew that he came from a fairly wealthy family, as Catharine had told me, and spoke seven languages fluently. Right there I promised myself to start learning some too. I believed him when he said that he would do anything at all cost, to protect and defend us.

Catharine had told me that the males of his relations were all career officers in the military at sometime or another and him being an SAS also told me he was a trained military intelligence officer. I was not sure about his politics as yet, but he appeared to hate everything about the Chinese, Indians and even the Irish; maybe the blacks too.

I couldn't visualize to what extent is his desire to liberate the world, but looking at him sitting at the table briefing the men made me realize that we didn't know him at all. I listened very intently to the words of Mark, as he expressed the importance of this newly formed Company that will serve as an assault unit, totally independent of all commands, except his.

"We will have the freedom to carryout the actions as deemed necessary by me, without interference," he said, "and I am expecting full cooperation from everyone, within their specialities of course. Your personal safety is dependent on your actions in the field, so due attention to my commands must be adhered to."

Everybody was silent, so he continued.

"These people here," he said pointing to a picture of a Chinese person, " must be made to conform to the real world of democracy, so do your jobs correctly and we will achieve the ultimate goal. We simply cannot allow communism to rule."

In sorting out the units, Mark told the meeting the animal names of everyone and that one unit would consist of thirteen men, all the others would be twelve. He called the code names of the units and those people who belonged to them. Mongoose, Cobras, Tigers, Rats........He stopped and asked the thirteen of us to stand.

"Gentlemen," he said proudly, "these men you're looking at are skilled in some special techniques that are very vital to all of our operations in this region. I would dearly appreciate if nobody, I mean nobody, questioned their actions in the fields or in this camp," he paused to look at the faces, then continued.

"They are the Pythons, but will be using the name Nig-Nogs in the field; if you should hear reference to these names please be cautious and don't accidentally shoot them. They will be reporting directly to me. Everyone here will be given an identity code that they will be using whenever we are in the zones and as I have said before, it's vital to our operations here."

The place was quiet. If a pin fell you could've heard it. Nobody questioned any thing that was said. The map briefing was intense and detailed. It was a good thing I had a very large breakfast that morning, because we walked out of that place at twenty after two for dinner. I felt sure that I knew the terrains of northern Malaya well, thereafter and could exist there for any length of time.

The thirteen of us went for dinner together and talked about many things relating to Malaya. As usual we expressed our brotherhood and talked about how we intended on protecting one another and not being too dependent on the others.

"Listen you Nig-Nogs," said Jack in a serious tone. "Them fucking chinks won't have any sympathy for any of us if we are caught, so don't take any unnecessary chances."

"Unless you are covered," added Patrick.

"And furthermore," Jack went on, "we could learn something here."

"My friend," I said looking at him. "I don't want to be taught anything. I'm here to do a job, then get the fuck out."

Ian, who had been quiet all along stated that we would be making

Mark Harrison a hero.

"We'll be making him look good to the upper brasses. He would be getting the glory, not us," he said.

The conversation took on a political tone and as usual we differed in beliefs. Patrick got pissed off because we decided to change the subject to women.

"Look you arseholes," he said angrily, "these fuckers only want us here to carry out their dirty work for them, so we must be realistic about our position and take care out there. It's called self- preservation."

We all sat quietly listening to him. When it was realized that he had made his point, Rod softly chipped in.

"Remember to use our codes boys, matter of fact, let's go over them tonight, okay?" he said.

We discussed the drop for the next day.

"Seventeen miles from the border," I thought. "It doesn't sound like much, but in the jungle, a half mile could be a week."

I could feel the excitement level rose within me, a sort of nervousness of the impending danger.

"Kill or be killed, that's how Wickham had expressed it," I thought.

Everyone was busy packing their gears and checking their weapons, ammo and their first aid equipment. I looked at Patrick and saw that he was shaking.

"Hey Irish pecker!" I shouted, "what is there to be afraid of? You can only die once?"

He only smiled and said one word, "Chinks."

Jack who appeared to be calm, reminded us of a slogan we had heard before.

"As Wickham told us, death is only a bullet away if you let it."

We all laughed at that, then once again resumed the packing.

We were armed to the teeth. We even had plastic weapons in secret compartments in our clothing for certain types of situations. We had places on our person that only us knew about.

That night Mark gathered us all to a meeting. As we followed him into the woods, I started singing the pied-piper song and everybody joined in. When he was satisfied that our attention was drawn, he began, and with a flashlight he showed us on a map what buildings we must take and what kind of documents we should look for.

"Anything that looks important," he said. "Blow any safe and retrieve any and all documents," he instructed.

To me it sounded very exciting.

"Hey Captain!" Jack shouted. "What if the chinks outnumber us? What if they knew we are coming and we get captured?"

Everybody laughed, then Mark spoke in that familiar stern tone of voice we all came to know so well.

"Men," he said, "if by some chance that you are captured, remember the rules, name, rank and serial number only. But if you think you cannot withstand any possible torture, then remember the little pill in your kit."

At that moment, I could see everyone searching themselves for it, as an air of tense seriousness surrounded the area instantly. Some people began to realize that we were going to war. In the very dim light, I could see my friends getting anxious about the mission we were about to embark on. Mark went through a check list and all replied to each check.

"Patrick O'Reilley, Tom Matterson, Bob Muldoon, Stan Martin, Charley Green, Rod Langley, Ian Mulligan, Jack O'Leary, Anthony Williams, Bill Llewellyn, Peter Baron, Cecil Brown and Dave Powell," he said and went on, "we will be operating with a Ghurkha unit up there. I really don't like them, but we'll have to work closely because they are familiar with the enemies."

I could almost hear the rattling of their brains, but nobody questioned him. Then as it was suddenly called, the meeting came to an abrupt end and everybody dispersed to await our call to action.

The call came at four a.m. that morning and just like routine, we all walked silently to our transporter and everybody took up their position without question. Our plane was the last of the two to take off. I don't think anybody cared to know how long the flight took, the atmosphere was very tense. All eyes were on the ready light and like robots, when it did came on, we carried out the operation very smoothly. There were also four other officers, whom I had not seen before. During the flight Mark introduced them and told us that they were accompanying us for observation only.

The jumps felt good. I heard the swish of my chute as it opened above me and the heavy pull on my body when it happened. I could barely make out anything on the ground, only the silhouette of things. I was a little apprehensive about a jungle drop, because I was unsure of what to expect and wanted to reach the ground as fast as possible. On landing, I quickly got my equipment under control, then preceded to find my men. Imagine me thinking of them as "my men." But, in an operation one does not have the luxury of much time to think, you must act instinctively and instantly.

"Tweet, tweet," I whistled and waited. Then one at a time the sound of tweet, tweet resounded to my ears.

"Nig thirteen sunset snow bed. It's a green and white orange," I shouted.

Their voices returned their location. Taffy was the only person at the zero zone, so I went to his location to find them. I hurriedly went over their duties. When all seemed to understand what we were about, we took up positions. Captain Harrison found us a short while later and repeated exactly what I had done. One of the boys told him that they had already been briefed by me.

"Well done Corporal Martin," he said and rushed into his position. In a flash he whirled and waved us to the attack. Two of the new officers came with our platoon.

"Take good care of yourself thirteen," Patrick said shaking my hand.

"And you keep your foolish Irish head down," I replied.

Instantly the rest of the boys gathered.

"Friends?" Rod shouted.

"Forever," replied the others.

Shooting at unseen enemies wasn't too bad. We did this for five days, with the help of the artillery who were only a few miles behind us. I could see the lights as the shells exploded in front of my eyes. At times, I thought I could see soldiers ahead, but that might have been my imagination. The bombardment ended late into the fifth day and when it stopped, we got the word to advance. As we did, the enemies were apparently retreating, so we did not made contact for another two days. When we did, it seemed like eternity as the shooting intensified. I was running towards a building when I came face front with an enemy. I don't know what it was, but I squeezed the trigger of my SMG and watched as the body in front of me danced a little jig, then laid lifeless on the ground. Suddenly, I felt sick to my stomach and vomited on my boots. I turned to see Patrick standing almost beside me.

"My friend," he said, "it's your first kill, so it's alright to feel sick. You did the right thing, never hesitate."

He patted my shoulder and we dodged our way towards the assigned building. Once inside, it seemed that all the training came back and I began to flash orders to the men, directing them to find things. We found two safes and blew them. All the papers and things that looked official, were taken and handed over to me. I wondered why, but then I remembered the commander telling them that I was the "officer in charge of documents." Our platoon was operating like real professionals, some stood on guard while the others were behaving as veterans would and being very efficient about their duties.

Some of the prisoners that were captured, were interrogated by the new officers and released, while others were tied hand and feet to be taken back.

"Clean up, clean up now," I shouted, " and leave a timer."

Which means to blow up the building. I took the grenades from my waist band, wrapped the elastic band around the hammers of each, then pulled the pins. I broke a cigarette in half and lit them. I placed the lighted cigarettes under the elastic band and carefully left them beside some petrol cans. One of the officers asked me what I was doing and I told him to watch. We withdrew an hour after the beginning as agreed and hurriedly ran to the designated safe area.

"Bang, bang, boom."

The explosive packs and grenades, which were planted around the ammo and petrol storage, began to go off. I stood there watching the lights and fire brightened up the sky. It seemed that our Company of 145 and the 30 Ghurkhas had completed their assignment.

For the duration of the next four days there, Captain Harrison and his four new officers were busy searching through every piece of document. Mark got Patrick and I to assist in the sorting of these documents, although I didn't understand anything written in them. Mark would translate some of their contents to us and did not hide anything from us. Sometimes, whenever we weren't present or close to him, he would call us to witness the documents.

"Stan, I find this very strange," Patrick told me. "He has been trying to get close to me ever since I got here, and it's making me nervous."

I could see the curiosity in Patrick's face, so I called Jack and Ian over to hear the conversation.

"I was just telling Stan here," said Paddy, "that I am very suspicious of Mark's sudden liking to me and it's making me very edgy."

"Well," replied Ian,"it's ironic that you said that. Yesterday Charley was saying the same thing about him. Hey Charley!" shouted Ian,"come here, tell these boys what you told me about Mark."

Charley hesitated and thought for a moment.

"Oh yes. Just last week, I overheard a conversation between Mark and Captain Cameron. Mark told him that he has to keep close to his men for two reasons, one so that they would carry out the orders precisely and two, so that he could know what they were thinking."

The silence was thick. I could see the clocks working in their heads.

"Boys," said Jack, "from here on in we should keep a closer watch on him, agreed? But never mention this to anyone else."

We shook hands in agreement. I was still in shock from that news but I muster up enough to say.

"I know what the problem is. He's mad at me and is using that to get at you all. I am his adversary. Rest assured that it's me he is after. Yes, he may also have you Irish boys in thought, but it will be me."

Everybody shook their heads then Bob who had joined the meeting late said,

"Never mind who he's after. We must all keep a very watchful eye on our commander from here, okay?"

Ian stuck out his hand. "Friends?" He asked

Everybody placed theirs on his and in unison replied.

"Friends, forever."

The withdrawal process was a slow struggle. It took two weeks to reach the zone. We were fighting the jungle and resistance fighters all the way. Mark referred to them as gorillas. At one stage I remarked to Patrick,

"Paddy mi lad, this is the longest seventeen miles I have ever walked."

"Yes," he replied, "but it's even longer if you're over the border seventeen miles plus the twelve miles to the enemy town."

"What?" I exclaimed. "Are they trying to kill us? I will have to talk to Mark about this."

"No my friend," he said firmly, "save your breath, and next time check your maps to be certain. See this? look. Here we are and here we were. From now on keep your eyes open for false information, that's all."

We stayed on patrol in the border area for about two more weeks, fighting off any attacks and assisting in the setting up and briefing of the engineers and other troops who would be taking over from us. To get their position established, some of them had to patrol with us. I noticed the four officers had disappeared. We were later transported back to Malaka.

I was laying on the floor of the truck thinking when Patrick's voice brought me back to reality.

"Still concerned about the fellow back there?" he asked.

"No," I said, "not really. I come to realize that if I wasn't quick enough, then it would be me laying there."

"That's the spirit," he said, "it's them or you."

I could see that he was pleased that I hadn't allowed it to become an hindrance or an obsession to my mind.

Going back to quiet beautiful Singapore for two lovely weeks, was my kind of living. People there are so polite and peaceful. I didn't mind at all, because I was able to spend a lot of time with Doctor-Major Helen Butterworth and when I was not, I could visit one of the lovely parks to write many letters to all the people I had promised to correspond with, or to one of the local bars. The things I did find a little strange were, they told us to use an address in Germany and not to divulge any of our activities of where we have been. So my letters to friends and family were very basic and about my health. I decided to bring it to my friend's attention.

"Look Paddy," I said. "We're not allowed to write the address here, do you think they are censoring our mail?"

After a long pause he replied.

"Come on Nig, use your noggin," he said. "This is the army and they are going to reduce your activities and contact to a bare minimum, and if you think for one moment that your life is yours, you're wrong."

I realized that he was right and concluded the conversation forthwith. Three days prior to our leaving for Malaka again, Helen came to pick me up. When I got into her land rover she quickly informed me that she had obtained a pass for me to spend all that time with her. I was delighted because I wasn't sure when I would see her again, if ever. It was a pleasure to make love to her. She always made me feel special like our first time in Bordon.

That night, after I had returned from my most wonderful weekend with Helen, I was walking towards the transporter that was Malaka bound when the goodly Captain approached me. He had one of those "you're in trouble now," look in his eyes.

"Mr Martin," he said in a harsh tone, "may I have a word with you?"

"Oh, certainly sir," I replied sarcastically.

We strolled together to an area where we could not be overheard by anyone.

"I am going to tell you something that might affect my life later," he said, "but it's very important that you know."

I was ready to listen with interest.

"You see Stan," he began. "I know that you've been wondering about me and Catharine's life together, so here it is in a nut shell."

He paused, lit a cigarette and scratched his balls before continuing. Something he has always done whenever there was something important to be said. My curiosity was aroused and my eyes were glued to his face. Then in a sombre tone of voice he said,

"Sometime ago, after Catharine and I got married, I, as a young officer just graduated out of Sandhurst, was sent on a special mission in Hong Kong. My duties took me to a place near the city of Canton, where a Chinese terrorist made bomb exploded close to me. After I awoke in an Hospital, I was told how lucky I was and that a piece of shrapnel had severed a nerve or something somewhere in my lower spine. A year later and a lot of begging, I was allowed to stay in the military. Although all other parts of my body worked, it prevented me from getting a hard on."

He paused again, looked at me for a long moment, then continued without any response from me.

"Since then, I have tried to get Catharine to entertain other men friends of mine, but she flatly refused."

Still I didn't respond.

"I asked her to have a child by one of those men, which I would care for as my own, but she refused that proposal also. I don't want to loose her, but I know she is in love with you. I am not sure what her reaction would be if I tried to stop it, so I am not going to attempt it. The only thing I will ask of you is, please write to her as often as possible. Better yet, tonight when we reach Malaka, put in an official request for a phone call to her, okay?"

I stood there with my mouth open, after hearing his story. I realized that he didn't know Catharine had already told me about their dysfunctional marriage. I wanted to laugh and at the same time to sympathise with him. As a matter of fact, I was shocked at his offer of a phone call to her, because he's the one I would have to make the request to.

"Are you sure we can do this sir?" I asked him.

He gave me one of his patented sneers.

"Yes I can. I can do a lot of things for any of my boys," he replied, as he walked away, leaving me standing with my mouth open.

After reaching Malaka and making the phone call to Catharine, I went to his office to thank him.

"You're welcome soldier," he said without raising his head and added. "Do you want her to meet you somewhere? On a vacation that is," he offered.

"Yes sir, if it's possible," I happily replied, again surprised at his offer.

He told me that I would have to make an official request and to do it soon, because it would take about six weeks to process. He gave me the forms and I signed them and he did also. I thanked him again and left.

I went straight to talk to Patrick and told him of the entire conversation with Mark and of the promise he made to get Catharine to meet me for a vacation. Although I was still a little sceptical about his offered deed.

"I'm certain that he was lying about his accident," I said to Paddy, "because the army would have discharged him with such a serious injury."

"Yes they would," said Paddy. "Furthermore, what the hell was he doing in Canton anyway? Maybe he was spying."

"Maybe so," I replied. "But which ever way, we're here to avenge his dilemma against the Chinese people. Catharine and her sister told me that their arranged marriage was only for their father's business convenience. She didn't want to marry him in the first place and her mother was totally against it also."

Patrick sat there in silence listening to me.

"I think he's lying and he's doing to us as he's doing to the people here, getting his revenge. I'm almost certain that he told me that story to disrupt my thoughts of her and to be sympathetic towards him. I hoped someday I will be able to take her away from him completely," I said.

"And how do you propose doing that?" he asked.

"I don't know that as yet, but I will think of something, and when we meet again, I will talk to her about it," I replied.

"I am sure you will. But if you do need my assistance, I will be there to help like a brother would," he promised.

We talked about the problem for the greater part of the night, then Patrick got up shook my hand saying,

"Maybe we should keep this between just you and I for now, but we'll have to make plans, later."

We were awakened at five in the morning without warning to move out and back to the zone. Everybody was rushing around gathering their things in surprise, unaware of the length of stay or the mission. When the boys were all gathered, there were total silence. Somehow we seemed to understand the army's requirements between us, so there weren't any questions. I watched Patrick as he went about his preparation silently and with the deliberate tenacity and precision I understood so well.

We reached the zone and were again engaged in the nightly attacks just as before. It felt as though we hadn't left. The weeks up there went by slowly and during that time I was able to talk a lot more to Mark and Patrick on many different subjects.

It appeared to me, that they both were suffering from some sort of psychological injuries obtained at a young age and the army seemed to be the place for them to release these inner anxieties. In the case of the Irishman, he seemed to be enjoying himself in these fights. At times he appeared to be anxious to get into action but got defensive whenever I asked him about the tattoo. He would get angry, telling me to mind my own business or that it's his secret. The same went for Tom and Jack.

It made me feel that something was not totally right about them. I was now getting to believe my own thought that it was an insignia for some white voodoo sect. I almost gave up asking, but for the fact that it intrigued me and they were my friends.

Whenever I found a quiet moment, I would go off somewhere to write my thoughts in my notebook.

"Last week whilst on patrol," I wrote. "Ian, Charley and I were confronted by a platoon of those commies. We killed seven and imprisoned five." Or it would read. "Today Patrick and Jack killed four more." Or "Today I spoke to Mark Harrison again without any satisfaction." Making these notes seemed to satisfy my curiosity regarding our duties more often than I realized. I still couldn't comprehend who and where these so called guerilla's were coming from. Mark told us that they were Thai soldiers mixed with Burmese and Malayan communist rebels.

At the same time, I was having some rather interesting conversations with Mark on the subject of his inability to screw. We talked about Catharine a lot and my question of him stepping aside for us. Sometimes he would be very negative and on other occasions he would agree to leaving us alone. But out here we're in the jungle and our business is that of killing, so one's thoughts can run wild. He would continually remind us of the importance of our presence and doing our job correctly, and so we did. We obeyed his orders and carried them out precisely, although my suspicions of him made me very cautious in my dealings with him and knowing that he had a distinct hate for Patrick, Jack, Tom and Ian, made the feelings even more so.

Yet he would always praise us for doing a good job, sometimes being very specific about it and with commendations.

Our tour of duty took us to places like North Borneo, Sarawak, Thailand and Hong Kong on the border of China. On each operation, we were given specific jobs, either to plant or to find documents, maps and any kind of information we could lay our hands on. Who we had to kill to get them was not important. The company, with it's four quiet nameless intelligence officers, seemed to enjoy destroying the opposition's military installations and whomever therein. Blowing up their ammo or petrol storage to cause chaos in their operations was deemed excellent, for the preservation of British sovereignty of course.

Watching my friends in action frightened me somewhat, because they seemed to be liking it and I felt some were becoming callous towards the ordinary souls of the land, and in conversation, some of them admitted to their negligence to care.

On one operation in south Thailand, as we were returning to our zero under heavy enemy fire, I came upon Taffy and Peter Baron bending over a body. It was that of a fellow from the Cobra platoon with two bamboo arrows protruding from his midsection. He was screaming at such a high level the boys had to stuff a bandana into his mouth. I remembered the medics telling us, at an instructional meeting, not to pull them out because they are made like fish hooks and would rip the inside of the person to shreds. Peter and Taffy carried him for about a mile to where he could be picked up by the medical chopper. I never did saw Bernard Christie again, although both Peter and Taffy have always asked about him.

Our platoon of thirteen were dubbed the "The cut throat platoon." because most of our jobs were done with either a razor, machette or knife, an art learned from the Ghurkhas. We even sneaked into enemy camps to plant explosives, using only our code and a compass, things other members of the company refused to do without the full coverage.

Our reputation was getting around the other troops and the rumours had it that we were working directly for MI. Six. At times, I would question Mark on the validity of these accusations and came away with mixed feelings. Sometimes he would brush it off jokingly, but there were the other times when he would say,

"Consider it as doing a service for your country."

I wasn't too sure it was a service to England, but I realized that politics was very nasty in any arena. I was now seeing and living some of the things Patrick and I had rationalized since training camp in

Aldershot. I became very intrigued at some of the operations and where we were sent and what we did. I decided to start keeping a more precise diary of our activities as well, and remembering that I had promised to write a book on the boys, I thought this would be a good period to include in it and to expound on it later in conjunction to what I had started on the train to London. But I often wondered if I would be able to complete it, due to the circumstances surrounding us then and what would be the contents.

I confronted Mark after one such operation in Kari Khan in south Thailand.

"Sir," I said angrily, "explain to me why we're here killing these people for their land?"

He stared at me for a long moment and when he felt he could not avoid my question, he angrily replied.

"Corporal Martin! This world is made up of many different kinds of people, there are the dominant and dominated. Some do not want to conform to progress and must be dominated and forced to comply. You and I are the dominant and progressive ones, so we must conquer and direct their future lives for them."

I listened for a while, deep in thought at his crap.

"Then what about our stealing from and killing of the innocent ones? You know, the villagers?" I asked.

"Don't worry your head about them," he replied. "They are gorillas who want to implement communism here and our job is to preserve the freedom of democracy for the people."

"Whether they want it or not?" I questioned.

He seemed a little agitated by my last remark and began to turn red in the face.

"There you go again!" he shouted. "I am sure that it's that fucking Irish twat, who's been telling you this shit. That arse hole should be spending more time killing the fucking enemy than telling you these things. Maybe he is the enemy."

At this point he was furious.

"Don't blame anyone else for my thoughts," I said. "I have a mind of my own. When's the next assignment?" I asked.

"You'll hear about it soon," he replied angrily, as he hurriedly walked away.

One evening, Taffy called a meeting of the platoon to discuss his thoughts of what has been happening up in northern Malaya. The consensus was that, although we knew it is wrong, we should not question it, just carry-out our assignments as designed by Mark and to protect each other as usual. Patrick was quick to point out that most of the industries here were British owned.

"None of the damn gold mines or rubber companies are locally owned," said Paddy. "And the amount of drugs that has passed through this area, should tell you the story of their business. Remember what they told us? Kill the carriers, but bring the drugs back as evidence."

Just then Jack piped in.

"I am sure it's being sent to England somehow and by somebody."

"Hey!" Rod shouted. "Last week a convoy of the confiscated drugs was sent to Kuala Lumpur. Maybe we should question some of the RASC boys, to find out where it was destined for."

There were silence for a long while.

"Then is Mark Harrison lying to us?" asked Charley. "He keeps telling us lies that he doesn't know what's going on."

Everybody looked at each other in silence.

Being a little naive of the politics of the area, I asked Patrick,

"Are we really here protecting the industrialists in Malaya?" He let out a roaring laugh as he replied,

"Yes old man," he said jovially, "these people are stealing the natural resources of the land and using us to destroy the natives, who are fighting for their rights to retain it. We are destroying the real people of the land with our guns, who are classified as communist gorillas by some authorities."

"Then what can we do about it?" I asked.

Ian who was also in deep thoughts replied in a matter of fact way,

"Fucking nothing my friend, absolutely nothing. Remember we're solders and could be court-martialled for any unsubstantiated accusations against any officer."

Somehow he made sense and everyone agreed with him. Again, we agreed to look out for each other on all future assignments and to just keep a careful watch of our suspicious commander.

"Friends?" somebody shouted.

"Friends forever," came the reply.

I kept asking my friends about their tattoos, but got the same negative response every time. At one encounter with Ian, I asked him about it and he became angry.

"It's better for you not to know my friend, trust me," Ian told me.

I reminded him that I might develop my own opinion which might not be very close to the truth. He only shrugged his shoulders saying,

"If that's what it comes down to my friend, so be it."

I reminded him of the possibility of his name being etched into my book.

"And you'll go down as uncooperative," I said jokingly.

He laughed and began to tell me about himself and I wrote:- Ian Mulligan. Born September 16th 1942 in Belfast, Ireland. Not very educated, but is well aware of the politics of his country. He is the third of five children born to a very religious Catholic family and joined the army to get away from the poverty to try making a different life for himself. He believed the people he has met in the services so far, are the best friends in his entire life. I completed my writing and was now studying his face when Bob approached us.

"Tell me mister reporter, is this an interview for that book you intend on writing?" he asked.

Before I could reply Ian said,

"Yes, and I hope he will tell the truth about you too, you Scots haggis bashing bastard."

He then turned his attention to me.

"Are you going to tell about him too?"

"Yes," I replied, nodding my head to Bob. "But I promise not to mention your sheep shagging days back there in Aberdeen or the twenty five charges of rape against you."

Bob laughed as though it meant something to him.

"Oh great," he said, "just fucking great. I will be famous in my own home town and I will have you to thank for it. Whenever you're ready for me, I will be available. Have any of you two seen Charley? Mark Harrison needs to see him, urgently."

I looked and saw Charley walking in the opposite direction.

"There he is," I pointed and Bob dashed off to catch him.

We were dispatched to Aden, Saudi Arabia a few weeks later. I discovered that it was also a deadly place to be. The operations were the same there as the other places we had been. We were told that there were some problems with the Yemenese, who wanted to take over Aden and the British Petroleum Industries. We did a night drop over their border to sabotage two of their military installations. We had to maintain silence, no radios or voices except our whistles. The whole operation was so fast it was over before they realized that we were there. Those Champs were very good vehicles for the desert, they made our retreat very quick and smooth.

Although there were other troops there, the company was the contact unit in the encounter with the Yemenese and my platoon was directed to retrieve properties and documents along with the two M.I.6 officers as usual. It seemed that we were always meeting the elite troops of the opposition at all times, which meant killing in either hand to hand mode or at close range.

I made notes of my friends and the things we had talked about. I made notes about Captain Mark Harrison's actions, who seemed delighted to direct his men in all phases.

At some intervals, I would drift off into my brain food time to think. I was becoming concerned for myself.

"Am I becoming like the others?" I wrote in my notebook.

One quiet evening as we were enjoying a little solitude in our base camp, with some members of another platoon on guard, it happened. We were relaxing when suddenly three young Arabs approached the area dressed as Wogs. For some reason the outer guards had allow them to pass as they kept repeating in English.

"Don't shoot, don't shoot," as they walked towards us and the command post. Patrick quickly opened fire on them and I watched in bewilderment as the three bodies blew up in front of me. I couldn't tell what his thoughts were, but his action seemed to save our lives.

"They were walking kamikazes sent to blow up our camp and whomever else," he said.

" Well done Paddy," I said, patting him on the head. "I wouldn't have suspected them."

He only nodded, then as an afterthought said,

"They were only children. What is happening to us? Is our purpose here to kill young children too? Why are they using these little ones to carry out this kind of task?"

He was very visibly upset. I could see the tears in his eyes.

"What?" I thought. "Paddy going soft? Is this his hidden emotional side?"

I put my arm around his shoulder and said,

"Remember in Cambodia when I shot that fellow? You told me it was either him or me, right? Well view this in the same light. They came here to kill us and due to your quick response, we're still alive."

"But they were only children," he said. " I am here killing nippers."

"Yes," I said to console him. "Who were willing to kill you."

A few moments later, Mark Harrison appeared shouting his congratulations and approval of Patrick's actions. He promised to get us a commendation for it and we both looked at him in silence. When he saw we weren't about to respond, he walked away. Later as I sat in my solitude of my brain time, I wrote in my book.

"Neither Mark Harrison nor any of the upper brasses would ever comprehend, the psychological anguish that encumbered a soldier who has to do this sort of thing, and I feel Patrick is now having a sense of guilt for being the one to kill hem. But this is the hazards of our presence in these people's country. My friends and I are changing into heartless monsters, or are we? Can this ever be reversed? I have my doubts."

Chapter Seven

" Patrick in Action."

After two years of active service, my platoon was considered to be veterans and was treated with respect by all the other troops around. "The Mark Harrison's gang," was becoming a very proud and conceited bunch, some even began thinking they were invincible in the field. I watched as my friends began to transform into hypocrites, sometimes sitting around bragging about killing the chinks and behaving like the unconcerned others in the company. Some were given medals for bravery, which also assisted in bringing about this conceit. I was getting concerned for myself and the changes I was experiencing.

"How long can I maintain this?" I wrote in my book. " It's disturbing to my mind to be killing people I don't know, people who haven't done anything to me. But I was brought here to do a job and I am forced to protect myself. It's kill or be killed."

Mark was always busy handing out personal praises to his men on a regular basis. Charley, Rod, Ian and Tom and I were the main recipients of these daily praises, although the others would receive theirs too. Although I knew of his hate for Mark, O'Reilley, at times, would remain silent whenever Mark came to dish out these honours, but sometimes he would vocalize it to the boys. Everybody was changing, even Paddy, who would brag of cutting an enemy's throat as though he was cutting a steak. I continued to monitor the actions of my friends in and out of the jungle.

Once while having dinner, I decided to confront Paddy about his feelings.

"Paddy," I said, "do you realize that we're becoming callous towards the people here?"

He sat up straight in his chair staring me in the eyes as he replied,

"Certainly my boy, certainly. But this is good practice for me because whenever I return to Ireland, it will be natural to perform on some of them there."

"But you will be performing on your own people. Wouldn't that be like murder or genocide?" I asked.

"Not really," he replied. "I will be avenging my brother Eric's murder. Don't forget how they killed him, unmercifully," he reminded me.

"Are you still going to join the IRA?" I asked curiously.

"Stan mi lad," he said smiling. "I don't have to join."

We concluded the conversation, knowing that I was more confused now than ever before, but still understanding his cause.

Somewhere about here we were sent on a rest period to Australia. We were told that "Thirteen of Briton's best" were going there to give special instructions to some of their army personnels, for a month. I was happy to be away from the killing business for a while and so were the boys. Australia and the people, was the main topic of our conversation every day in anticipation of the enjoyable times we intended having there.

In Aldershot, I had read a lot of books about Australia and the diminishing aboriginal population and wondered why. So, I asked Patrick.

"Nig," he said, "them damn Englishmen have systematically been killing them off."

"How?" I asked.

"They have poisoned their waters, destroyed their fertile land with chemicals, then chase them into the desert where they cannot grow food. Then there's the VD thing," he replied.

"What VD thing?" I asked.

"They give them VD and they die," he answered.

"How did they do that?" I asked curiously.

"Through inoculations and prostitutes. They would capture a few men and inject them with the virus, telling them it was a vaccine against some form of disease then turn them loose within their community and then watch them infect the others and eventually die. And some would be introduced to prostitutes with the same results," he replied.

"Then that would be like genocide, would it not?" I asked.

"Technically yes," he said, "but they are English doctors, so the rest of the world never questioned their actions or believe that they would do it."

I couldn't believe what Paddy was telling me and asked the same questions of everyone I came into contact with. Some were very negative without care, while others stated that the problem is with the government. Even when I was with Helen I was thinking about it and said so. She told me to forget it and just go there and enjoy my rest period.

She also told me about her sister living in Brisbane and if I got the chance to, I should go to see her. But we were going to Sydney which is miles away and I was not cognisant of the agenda for our visit, so I could not promise to meet her sister. But she gave me her phone number anyway, just in case I got the opportunity to call. I couldn't really understand why we were going to Australia to teach their army anything. The Aussies were well trained men too and could probably teach us some things about jungle fighting.

"But who cares," I thought. "We were going to Australia for a rest and some good female interaction."

Although we were separated and residing at different area camps, my platoon kept in contact regularly. I noticed that myself, Charley and Skinny Williams, the three blacks were billeted in a rather remote area away from the whites, but only used it as an observation.

At times we would be transported to the main camp for

discussions and meetings, then back to our cage. On the fourth day I saw my boys getting off a truck with their bags.

"What the hell happened over there?" I asked as if I didn't know.

"We told the fucking commander that if our personal nigs cannot stay in our billets, then we are moving in with them. So here we are," Rod replied.

Everybody unloaded their gear and began to make themselves comfortable. Patrick informed me that Mark Harrison said he will ensure we get beds the next day.

I was now sure of the depth of racism within Australia, English style. During one of the briefings, the Australian Commander made mention of Vietnam and what would be needed to rectify the problem there. I had heard the same suggestions from Mark in previous conversations. I got up and requested permission to question, he granted it and I stated.

"So the rumours were right," I began. "It's quite evident now what our purpose here is, it's to prepare the men for some kind of operation in that country, right?"

"Corporal Martin," the commander replied nervously. "Your assumption is incorrect. This is only a training session to familiarize each other's regiment, of the kind of action needed in those places to conform them to our way of life."

I thought about it for a minute.

"Is it to conform them to the Queen's fashion of democracy and religion, for their good? If so, then tell me why Christ did not need a gun to preach his form of life's conformity?"

I could clearly see I was aggravating him.

"I don't want to discuss it any further Corporal," he shouted abrasively.

There were redness and beads of perspiration on his face when he could not answer my questions. I could hear many other voices begin to throw similar questions at him. The commander quickly dismissed the meeting. As we got outside, the boys gathered.

"Stanley my boy, you sure caused a commotion within the commander," said Tom. "He was shocked out of his rotten little racist mind."

"Yes," added Ian, "and O'Reilley didn't even speak. Mark Harrison is going to think that it was him who instigated it."

Patrick, who at this time was smiling from ear to ear, replied.

"Let him think what he wants. He'll now realize that there are many other disgruntled people amongst us, than he anticipated."

The conversation continued to the mess hall. On the way there Bob Muldoon called a halt.

"Listen fellows," he said, "there's something bothering me for sometime now and I want to express it. As a Scotsman, I have never encountered this blatant kind of racism as I have seen here in Australia and it's a cause to fight for. I am proposing that we should all agree to go to Ireland after our service and assist with their problems there."

There were absolute silence.

"I'm in agreement to that," said Rod and stuck out his hand.

Everybody quickly placed their hands on the top of his, except for Patrick.

"Gentlemen," he said, "it's quite noble of you to want to assist us in our struggle, and I for one would be delighted to have you all. But it's an Irish problem that have to be resolved between our people, only the Irish people can make that decision, politically or physically. But I thank you for the offer anyway my friends."

He stuck out his hand and everyone placed theirs on top.

"Friends forever," they replied.

I was a little disappointed in him for refusing our gesture, but at the same time I could understand his motive for not involving us.

"Then while we are here," said Charley, "maybe we should agree not to go into Ireland as British soldiers ever, for any reasons."

"Do you mean to refuse being sent there for service?" asked Bob.

"Right," replied Charley.

Everybody looked at each other then held out their hands saying,

"Agreed."

It was off to dinner and more talk about the women each of us was involved with back in Singapore.

Occasionally, we would be taken to one of the beautiful beaches of that area for swimming and barbecue and some good old- fashioned womanizing, Australian military style of course. I could clearly see that they didn't appreciate us talking to any of the white women, who approached us and seeing that there weren't any black ones around, our attention were on them. Some of the women seemed petrified to be seen talking to us, but did anyway, although from a distance.

At times there were arguments. It was either Patrick, Jack and sometimes Bob or Taffy, who were also good talkers, would be arguing with the Aussies about their racist attitudes. Then it would either be me or Charley that would prevent any fighting from breaking out. We, the black ones, were never allowed to see the city at nights so my friends deprived themselves the privilege just to be with us.

During the third week, Charley met a Filipino girl who worked in the kitchen and made a date to see her after work. She took us to a club where most of the few Indians, Africans and Filipinos went and introduced Williams and myself to two others

Somehow, the commander heard about it and created another argument, with him threatening to release the girl from her job, but we threatened to get Mark Harrison involved and he quickly dissolved his charges, instantly.

At the next meeting, one of their Generals came to address us. He emphasized that our presence there were an exercise for recreational purposes only and not for military purposes, although we did more military than recreational.

Nevertheless, we did get to see something of their very beautiful modern city's offering, other than just the camps. I was very happy and grateful to have met those lovely women and enjoyed the rest of our time in Sydney, Australia.

Then it was on to Wellington, NewZealand, also a very pretty city, for a month of supposedly total rest. Each of the boys took time to reflect on their personal perspectives of life and discussed it amongst ourselves. Our camp was located about thirty miles from the city, so most of our time was spent on the compound and in their NAAFI. Two days after arriving there, the powers that be arranged a party for us, and like in Australia, the women were also brought in. The boys discussed this indignant method of recreation and agreed to take it up with Mark back in Malaya.

The conversations took on the same political connotation as always, but I observed that Patrick had subdued his ideology about the politics in Ireland and asked him why.

"My boy, one has to rethink ones position and convictions under certain circumstances," he told me, "because one never knows when you might need their assistance."

"Ah, ah," I replied. "You mean that you might want to come back here after service, right?"

"Something like that," he said smiling. "I might need to do some business here and will need to make contact with someone."

"What kind of business?" I asked.

"You know, some kind of Irish and NewZeland business," he replied.

I didn't take his words seriously then, although I realized that there were something sinister in his thoughts, even though I couldn't pinpoint it.

I also observed that their racial policies in NewZeland were identical to that of Australia. We the black ones, were restricted from cohabitation with the native aboriginal and were asked to stay within the confines of the camp. Even the bus refused us a ride into town. One night during the second week, Charley and I sneaked out and were given a lift to town by a sympathetic Sergeant. We had a lovely time with some girls we found in a club, then took a taxi back the next morning and got into a disagreement with the brasses for doing so.

Their commander tried desperately to show authority over us, by demanding that we do not leave base again. But when it was discovered that we were not normal minded soldiers, the entire charade was dropped.

"Boys this is my camp and whatever I say goes," said Colonel Pellick. "Whenever I give an order it must be obeyed to the letter, and I say nobody leaves this camp."

"Yes sir," I replied, "but whenever my mind asked my body for sex, I am going to find a woman, not you. And if I have to disobey your ignorant racist orders, I am going to. If you would like to court martial me, feel free to try."

He was plainly embarrassed for his inability to control us.All the boys laughed so hard and scornfully at the discussion, that he decided to consult Mark Harrison for the action he should take against us. After two days of consultation with Mark Harrison, in a phone call to Singapore, he decided to allow us the freedom of movement throughout Wellington for the duration of our stay there.

"Stan mi lad," said Paddy, "I hope you're making notes of their subtle presentation of racism, both here and in Australia."

Paddy was smiling with the satisfaction of proof and I in turn acknowledged his point of view.

"My friend I am making notes." I assured him. "It's quite evident that even though I am an NCO in the British Airborne Army, I'm not accorded the same respect as the white ones."

"Ah, ah," he said, "you're learning friend. Think of how the Irish Catholics felt in their own country."

I thought about his words. Then it struck me to say,

"You know something Paddy? All the boys are geared up to come to Ireland to assist you with the fight, maybe you should re- think."

He looked at me for a long moment then said in a rather distinct tone.

"I know that they are willing, but I want all of you boys to understand that this is an Irish struggle and I don't desire any of you to be implicated in any way shape or form. Just maintain a prayer for a decent conclusion to it. And I will say the same to the others."

We shook hands and concluded the conversation. The rest of our stay in NewZeland was peaceful and relaxing, because we were allowed to go wherever and to do whenever we wanted.

Back in Singapore, we were bombarded with instructional briefings in a two weeks long span of meetings, in preparation for a peacekeeping roll in Kashmir. The purpose was to stop those already there from being killed, due to the ongoing war between Indian and Pakistani rebels. We were told that a regiment of Paras and our company was going there. I didn't get enough time with Helen as I used to. Most of our spare time was with each other discussing the methods presented by the General on "public relations," there.

"Now this is fucking ridiculous," said Bob Muldoon. "We're combat troops and what do we know about this kind of diplomatic business? Do you realize that we will have to turn ourselves totally around? Adopt a whole new attitude strictly to accommodate this kind of operation?"

Nobody replied to Bob's questions. I looked at the faces of my twelve friends, hoping to decipher their personal thoughts, so I said in response to Bob.

"I know that there's more to this than is presented and Mark Harrison knows it. I am very suspicious of these orders."

"No fellows," shouted Charley, "nothing will change. We will be doing exactly what we are accustomed to do."

Charley wore a face of deep seriousness as he continued. "If things were cushy there like they said, they would've sent some other people, not us. We're going there to clean up things, see?"

Jack got up speaking as he did.

"I agree with Chuck. The fuckers want us there for another reason other than so-called peace keeping, what do you think Paddy?"

I noticed Patrick was a little slow to reply and could sense the concerns of his mind.

"Yes," he replied, "we're being used, and it's for the protection of the rich ones as usual. But when we get there we'll surely find out."

We discussed this for hours that night without conclusion. I promised that in the morning I would confront Mark with our theory, but I already knew that he would deny that fact.

On our arrival in Kashmir, the Company was dispatched into position around the city guarding some very important buildings, which indicated that exactly what we had theorized prior to getting there, was true. My platoon's job was to protect a church, mosque, synagogue or whatever it was. That very first evening we were attacked. Rod and I had taken our position near a door with a small wall. I heard the tweet, tweet of a platoon member. Then a voice hollered.

"Nig 1, 13, behave Red Orange. Fools moon sunset Ice Zero."

It was Taffy's voice.

Quickly we checked our bearings to realize that the four enemies were directly behind us. We both fell to the ground and crawled behind the wall and as we did, suddenly a volley of shots breezed through the spot we had just vacated. Rod and I fired back and saw the four bodies hit the ground. Taffy's voice shouted again that two more were coming on the right side also. Quickly, I changed magazine in preparation.

"Rattttt," the sound of a Sterling. Then the voice of Skinny Williams announced his neutralization of them.

"Nig seven, it's a clean white river and a green Orange. He said.

"Nig ten, nine behave under," Taffy shouted again. "Red full moon green cheese."

Both Taffy and Peter Baron were under attack and pinned down. Rod and I quickly ran to their location and began firing.

Williams, who had worked his way to a ledge above us, threw a couple of grenades in the enemy's location, some ran and got shot in the process.

We were under attack daily thereafter and the fighting lasted for about three weeks. The job of preventing any terrorists from getting inside to do any kind of damage or to kill any of the rich politicians residing there, was hard. I wasn't sure who they were, but I was told that they were both Pakistanis and Indians. We followed orders and killed anyone who tried to enter that building. Things became quiet after a while and I discovered that we were protecting the politicians from both sides, who were using that city as a "safe haven." to enjoy themselves in luxury while the ordinary people were busy killing each other, with the blessing of the Queen's army of course.

Paddy and I had discussed these findings and agreed that politics stinks everywhere and it was a futile effort to ask Mark Harrison, because he did not care.

One night after eight weeks in Kashmir, which seemed long, a fresh regiment of peacekeepers came, we were summoned to a quick move in full armed equipment back to Aden.

"Now that Kashmir is secured," Mark told us, "these people can take care of things here, our expertise is needed elsewhere."

It seemed that all the plans were already in place. We only had time long enough to piss, shit and have a quick meal then board a transporter for a drop somewhere in the desert. We were briefed during the flight, on the specifications of this operation. We were dispatched in the desert early the next morning to join up with another regiment that was already there and had to fight for the next four days to establish our authority.

"It's them fucking Yemenese again," said Mark. "They want Aden badly and the control of the oil shipping port."

"Then whose is it?" asked Charley.

"It belongs to Briton," Mark replied angrily. "We captured it and it will remain that way. I don't want to discuss the political ramifications here, so let's get on with the job at hand, shall we?"

During the fourth day was when it happened. Being one of the Company's four mechanics, we were sent out to rescue an ammo vehicle that had been pinned down. Any repairs had to be done out there in the desert. Which was hard because it was totally manual power and this one had a damaged transmission. While we worked under the vehicle, my twelve platoon members were acting as scouts. We were told that the truck's contents was very important to our operational needs and we must be brought back, at all cost. While we worked, I heard a pinging whizzing noise and realized that a bullet had ricochet off something above me. We continued to work, thinking it was the propshaft that got hit and because it didn't hurt anything, we paid less attention to it's significance.

In the meanwhile, some of our boys had taken care of whomever that was shooting at us. In a couple of hours when things were completed and we were regrouping, I removed my helmet only to find a crease along the top. It was only then I realized that the bullet had hit my helmet. I became very nervous instantly. My knees started to tremble and cold sweat ran down my face.

"Oh my god! That was close," I thought, when I realized that three inches lower and my head would've been blown off. Many things came to mind, but I felt a little relieved when they all came around me. Jack, Bob, Charley and Patrick had just returned from cleaning up. They all patted my head. Then Ian sounded off.

"I think you're blessed my boy, you have the luck of the Irish. It was not meant to be," he said.

Paddy stood there grinning.

"Yeah, that's true. But we don't want to loose our favourite nig-nog yet, so keep your helmet on, okay?" he said.

"You can all laugh," I shouted, "but do you realize how close that was? I could've been killed. On my birthday too!" I said.

They all looked at each other, patted my head again and laughed even louder.

"Happy Birthday thirteen," shouted Charley.

"Happy Birthday," said the rest.

I realized later, they were happy that I didn't get shot. That night I laid awake thinking about it, still shaking from the experience. I could visualize the inscription on my tombstone. "Here lies number thirteen Nig."

The following four months in Aden, I took as much precaution as possible and there weren't any more close calls to speak of. But on every occasion, the boys would talk about the incident and about losing one of us.

"Here Nig-Nogs, listen up," Bob shouted. "Remember the group's commitment to inform the other's relatives personally of any demise. And to make sure that a proper burial takes place."

He emphasized these unwritten agreements. We talked about the closeness of our Brotherhood and agreed that it should never be broken. We felt it was very important to our lives forever. We returned to Singapore for some much needed R and R. and like wild fire, the news got around that we were back. I was promptly greeted at the air field by Doctor-Major Helen Butterworth. She was making sure that I did not go anywhere else and even helped me to load my things into her Land Rover.

After taking them to the equipment hangar, we left to her place, with her behaving like a neglected wife again. She had already prepared dinner for us, so a bath, food and to bed it was. She gave me a naked massage while in the nude herself. She was now slim, unlike when I first met her in Bordon. My thoughts drifted back to those times and to know she wanted to make love to me from the first day we had met.

"Happy belated birthday Helen," I said. "I'm sorry for being away for your fortieth birthday my love. That's a very important age for a person, you know?"

"I missed you so much," she replied. "I just hate it when you're sent away for such a long time and to places where I am not sure that you'll return from. The uncertainty is like torture."

She kept talking as she was doing sexual things to my body. I could see that Helen was excited for my return.

"I've waited all these weeks for this," she said. "Thank you for this belated birthday present."

And repeated it to make sure that I had heard her. Our love making lasted all that night.

The next morning she was still lying in bed.

"Aren't you going to work today?" I asked.

"No my darling," she replied. "Today we are going to eat, drink and screw to make up for some lost times. Then tomorrow we can return to normal routine, okay?"

That was fine by me, because all I wanted to do was chat, rest and make love to her also.

"Helen," I said, "do you know what my job is for the army? I mean what I do and where I do it and to whom?"

"Stan darling," she replied. "allow me to explain something to you, as an officer, I am allowed some information about the troops movements, but that's very limited in some instancies. Our goodly Commanding Officer advised against asking too many questions, especially about you lot. Mark Harrison keeps everything about you boys, private."

I believed her, although I was still curious to know why she was always waiting for me and having knowledge of my times of arrival.

"Don't worry your head," she said. "Mark watches over you all like a mother hawk. He protects everything about his men, with extreme rigidity. My sole purpose of enquires is to being with you. I enjoy having sex with you and if you don't know it as yet, I will tell you that I'm in love with you. Have been since I met you in Bordon."

I laid there observing her actions and realized that she was being honest, but I am sure she's keeping a watch on me for Mark.

"And I love you too," I said, "for some crazy reason and yes, Bordon was an interesting place for us."

Three whole week of being in Singapore with Helen had gone by. We were informed that we would be going to North Borneo again, for a short stay drop. The last time in Borneo, I shot more animals than people. I chuckled within, remembering how Sergeant Kito, my Ghurkha friend, showed me how to kill a wild boor and throw it into the river for the Pirana, before crossing and to cook snakes for dinner. As usual we began to prepare with the briefings and map studying sessions. It wasn't long until we were there. It was a night drop, which is always dangerous and for some weird reason, all that day I had a bad feeling about this operation. We came down under heavy fire and I could see the red hot bullets coming up at us. I felt like a cardboard duck at a shooting gallery. I removed two grenades from my belt, pulled the pins and dropped them. I saw them explode but couldn't tell if they had exploded before or after they hit the ground.

By the time we reached the ground we were already engaged. The fighting was intense for about four hours. Then as it started, the same it ended abruptly and the mind boggling silence there after. It was beginning to be first light.

"Tweet, tweet, tweet," Then silence. "Nig 10 5 8."

It was Taffy, Paddy and Tom to the left of me.

"Tweet, tweet, Nig 13." I replied.

The sounds of whistles continued to allow everyone to know where we were I joined Taffy and he told me that Brownie was dead and Charley was shot in the leg. I realized that Jack was missing and quickly gave instruction to the rest of the platoon to take up our positions. I called Patrick to accompany me to find him.

Although it was quiet, everybody knew that the danger were still there, because in the jungle at night everything is on the alert for danger, including the animals. So care is very necessary. The animals are just as dangerous as the people, even at dawn.

We must have walked for twenty minutes through those bushes using our ID codes to pass through the other platoons.

"Orange Pythons, Nig 5 13. I'm a lost sheep, Rembrandt loves green beds," Paddy kept repeating as we went.

Then we heard his mourning and a weak voice said,

"Nig 3. Green oranges are as nice as apple seeds. Are you Irish?"

"No," I replied, "but I'm related to one."

After checking for enemies and animals, we found him under a tree. He was shot and it looked bad. I picked him up on my shoulder while Patrick took his and some of my gear and started back for the camp. We tried to hurry as quickly and silently as possible, but his mourning was getting louder and I sensed his pain getting worst. I had to stuff an handkerchief in his mouth to keep him quiet. In the mean time Patrick was doing the scouts movements that we used out there. I never saw him so nervous in all these years. He was fidgety and jumpy, but alert to any sounds around us. Because our progress was so slow, we had to change position a couple of times to rest. Although the journey took only about half an hour, it seemed like six.

On reaching the camp area, I laid Jack in a dry and what looked like a secure spot, on a ground sheet. By the time I looked around to send Patrick for the medics, he had already left. Jack was moaning in pain. I took my razor and cut away his clothing to see the wound and it looked bad. I reached into my kit for a pain pill they had given us and forced it into his mouth. He swallowed it. I was very anxious for it to work and when it seemed that it wouldn't, I got out

a syringe, but the medics arrived just about then and did what I was about to do. They patched him up the best they could and radioed for a chopper to pick him up in the morning. All that night both Patrick and I took turns laying beside him, to keep him warm.

Sometime during the night, he started mumbling things, things presumably influenced by the drugs. I leaned over to ask him if he was okay.

"Thirteen," he said, "please remember that if I should die, you must go to Ireland to tell my parents personally."

"That, dear fellow, will be done,"I assured him.

"Stan, I know that you want to know about my tattoo, so I am going to tell you," he said.

"Yes, but not now," I replied. "Rest and when you're better we'll talk about it."

"No sir," he said, "there's no time like the present."

He told me it was his identity as an officer in the IRA just like Patrick, Ian and Tom. I was shocked but not totally, because I had suspected it's relevance to that organization from the start. He talked about being in the British army to learn some techniques to take back to teach his people. Somehow I was finding it hard to believe that last statement, but he was my friend and my only thought was to keep him alive. Jack and I talked for quite a while until he fell asleep.

The chopper came early the next morning and took him, Charley and the body of Brownie to Singapore. I told the rest that it was not a bad wound and he would be fine. I wondered off alone to have some brain exercise time. I sat under a tree and say a prayer for my three friends and began to write in my note book about this North Borneo operation.

"The first night, Cecil Brown was shot dead during his descent and we will have to get words to his parents. Charley Green is injured, shot in the leg but not too serious. Jack O'Leary shot in the abdomen and it seemed bad. Although the fighting didn't last very long, our company lost eleven men and our platoon is short by three. My thoughts wondered why Mark was not on this mission with us and why so little details. This is the first time I have had to deal with this kind of a problem, having someone this close to me dead or injured was a shocker. They are three of my closest friends," I thought. "Who's next?"

We were told to take and hold the position until an infantry regiment could be sent to replace us. For some reason, unknown to us we had to hold that position for the next two weeks. It seemed they were reluctant to replace us and the messages read the same every time. "Soon."

While we were there I kept asking Ian, Tom or Patrick about the IRA thing, but still the same answers. Then a couple of days prior to us returning to base in Singapore, Paddy came to my tent.

"Hey Thirteen," he said, "lets go for a walk."

I excitedly sprung to my feet and we left the camp and went into the jungle. We must have walked about a half a mile then he said,

"Here," and pointed to a large tree.

We checked the area thoroughly for springe, then sat down.

"You know something," he began, "ever since I met you in Aldershot, and the Lord knows that was a mistake, I have had a kind of love, a brotherly feeling towards you. I realize how much you mean to me and I must admit that you have made a lot of changes within me also."

He paused long enough to light two cigarettes and handed one to me.

"One should never," he emphasized and repeated the word, "never deceive, lie to or conjure up anything harmful or false to a brother, so I am going to tell you the truth about some things and only some things mind you, because I do not know everything myself. I'm going to confide some things to you truthfully."

I nodded my head in understanding.

"In Northern Ireland," he began, "the Irish Republican army was formed for the defence of the Catholic people's existence there. Then a few years ago they formed a political party named Sinn Fein, that will try to serve and represent the common people's needs and for the preservation and unification of our country. We believed that we could run for parliament and have representatives within the house to debate the necessary changes for this unification. I'm hoping that I will be able to serve in this intricate part of that party for the better-ment of the struggle."

He told me stories of his father's and uncle's plight in Northern Ireland and of the blatant acts of discrimination they had suffered in England. He talked about the restrictions they faced in their efforts to change some laws, through the Irish parliament and in England.

"Those obstacles were deliberately placed in front of the Catholics, to create costly legalities, that would encumber their efforts and push them into obscurity," he said.

He talked about some who were imprisoned, falsely accused of being a part of that movement.

"The Protestants have changed some of the political processes, which forced some parts of the activities underground," he said.

Just then I remembered the story that was told about his uncle on my first visit to Ireland. He spoke at length about the Protestants control over everything in his country, with the help of England.

"In my observation, it has created a demeaning existence for my family," he said. "They, the Protestants, are doing everything to annihilate us. They have no intention of sharing any part of the power with us. They want to control and dictate our total existence, like the Romans did to the rest of the world."

At this point he was becoming very perturbed and angry. He

sprung to his feet with his SMG in hand to show me how he intended to mutilate the oppressors. I sat there quietly until he calmed himself down. When he realized what he had been doing, he apologised and sat down again beside me. He put his arm around my shoulder and said,

"Brother Stan, I'm asking you to trust what I'm saying and please don't despise me for my beliefs. I know that you respect and understand my politics but I am not asking you to appreciate how I intend on doing it," he paused for a moment, then continued, "I have always respected your opinion on any matter and I trust you with my life. All I'm asking is if anything should happen to me, please go to Ireland and give the news directly to my parents."

"That I will do friend," I said, "although I would prefer that you were there when I get there."

"I would very much like that too," he said, "but bear in mind that the movement will not cease with or without me. And then again I might be too deeply involved, to be a close friend to you."

"That my friend, would be your choice," I said. "But I would not be coming there to see your political organization, I would be coming to see my friends and his family."

There were a long moment of silence. I sat thinking about all the things he had said and knew he was waiting for my reply.

"Nig Five," I said," I don't really know anything about the problems of the IRA, the Catholics or the Protestants and their politics in Ireland, except that which I have learned from you. But what I do know about is you. I know that you're a very concerned and caring person who has encountered some bad times in your place of birth and will defend that to the end. I have no intention to try and change or criticize your political ideology or to judge it in any way. Paddy, whatever you choose to do, as long as you believe it is absolutely necessary to change your country, so be it."

He looked at me for a long time before replying.

"Thank you my friend for the understanding," he said. "Ireland needs the chances and I'm willing to try. Now, If I don't get into that Sinn Fein circle, I will still be available for other areas to do things as necessary to convince the British government to allow the people to decide their own fate."

He was now talking to his friend, his brother or whomever I appeared to be to him. I could see the pride in his eyes when he spoke of the political wing of his army.

"Then, why do you find it hard to tell me about your tattoo?" I nudged.

"Oh, it's not hard to tell, but I'm deliberately avoiding doing so for your neutrality. If Mark or anybody else should question you, then you wouldn't know and thus would not be a suspect or be subjected to anything derogatory. You really would not know," he said.

I smiled knowing that I really did understood. I assured him that none of this will be voiced to anyone else, although Helen had told me that Mark had been keeping a dossier on him and the others and maybe even myself.

"I'll wait until I write my book, then I will tell about you," I said.

He laughed heartily then placed his hand on my shoulder again.

"You know something 13?" he said, "I have no doubt that you will write that fucking book. But if you ever spell my name wrong I will somehow find you and cut your throat. It's spelt with two "L's." O'Reilley. But if I should die before the publication, I will come back to haunt you."

He was now smiling as we walked back to the camp.

"You know something five?" I said. "When we get back to Singapore, we must visit that Nig-Nog Jack O'Leary in Hospital and make life miserable for him. Don't you agree?"

"Yes sir we should," he replied, "that skiving gubshite sitting there enjoying life with the nurses, while we sweat our balls off in this place."

In camp there were people sitting around playing cards, since things were quiet in the jungle. The mission Commander, a young Captain named Weyberton, found and summoned me to the command tent for a meeting.

"Corporal," he said, "when we return to Singapore I want a full report done and delivered to Mark Harrison."

I felt he was talking about Patrick, but realized it was the injury of Jack and Charley and the death of Brownie, I was to make the report on.

"Consider it done sir," I said and left him standing.

He knew how I felt about the death of my friend and the injury to the others, so there weren't any reason to prolong the conversation with him.

"We'll be going home in a few days time, so tell the men," he said as I walked out of his tent. During the next two days, Patrick and I talked a lot more about himself and his involvement in the IRA. Although I completely understood his reasons, I still felt it wasn't the right way to do things, yet he never rebuked me for my opinion on the matter.

In Singapore, I made the report and left it on Mark's desk on my way to the hospital to see Jack, I met Mark coming from that direction and saluted as we came face to face.

"Cut the bullshit Stan," he said, not even acknowledging my respect. "We're alone now, and furthermore there are more important things to worry about."

"Like what?" I asked.

"Well," he said, "I just left O'Leary and he doesn't seem to be doing good and we'll have to think of his future."

"I'm going to see him now, maybe I will learn something from him. I mean what he would want," I said.

"Well then," he said, "come to see me after, let's discuss an easy posting for him or even a discharge."

"Yes sir," I interjected, "that's one of the things I wanted to talk to you about also."

"Good, but not now; okay?" he said, giving me one of his patented sardonic like grins.

"Oh! I almost forgot," he said. "Here is a letter for you, it's from Catharine," he smiled as he handed it to me.

I looked at him and then the letter and noticed that it was not opened this time. The army had this habit of opening personal letters, but this one for some unexplained reason, wasn't. Anyway, when he realized that I wasn't going to open it in front of him, he handed me the rest of my censored mail and left.

The entire platoon was at Jack's bedside when I walked in.

"Hey Stan!" shouted Bob in that weird Scottish accent of his. "I heard that you're about to be made full screw."

"Oh yeah?" I said, "I just saw Mark and he didn't say anything of the sort."

"Well that's what we've heard, and I think it would be good for us boys to have someone else to blame for the general's fuck-ups. Congratulations," said Ian as he grabbed my hand and shook it.

"Well," I said, "the Captain hasn't mentioned anything to me, but if it is true, I will find out tomorrow."

"Yeah," said Peter Baron. "Now we'll have two of them. Him and the taffy nosed Welshman."

The laughter was loud enough to bring a nurse in to request quiet. We listened as Jack explained that he would be up and about in a few days. Nobody disputed anything he was saying, but I could sense the doubts in their minds.

"Hey Charley, how do you feel?" I enquired.

"Not too bad Stan boy," Charley replied, "the bullet went right through my leg muscles and not the bone, lucky what? Anyway, Mark told me today that I would be getting a posting to Germany after I recovered."

"That sounds good Charlie boy, but we must keep in touch, okay?"

"Do you think for one moment I would ever forget you lousy bunch of bastards? Anywhere you all are, I'll find you," he said with a grin.

When we left the Hospital, Bob told me that Jack had lost a kidney, some intestines and probably spinal damages.

"But the Doctors asked us not to tell him. If he lives he may never walk again," said Bob and was getting a little emotional in describing Jack's injury.

I guided him to the billets and gathered the rest of the boys, where the conversation was only about Jack. I mentioned that I had spoken to Mark about a posting for him and everybody agreed. They were happy at my initiative. I went to bed and couldn't sleep but said a prayer for all my friends.

After breakfast the next morning, I went to the office to get the forms for Jack's posting, only to be told that Captain Harrison had already filled them out and they were there for me to sign. I read them through and it was done as though I had done them myself. They were Jack's discharge request. Mark was waiting outside for me.

"Did you see the papers?" he asked.

I nodded my head that I did. He waited a while then asked,

"Then what about Catharine, what did she say?"

"I don't know as yet," I replied, "because I was so busy with Jack's affairs, I didn't even read her letter as yet. But as soon as I do I will let you know."

He seemed a little disappointed, but agreed to wait. We talked about many things relating to the boys and what's to be done.

"Corporal Martin," he said grinning, "take your uniforms to the tailor to have your stripes sewn on, your new promotion has come through, congratulations."

He was awaiting a reply and I obliged him by saying,

"Thank you, sir."

He didn't move for a long minute. Then as though something penetrated his brains, he said,

"Stan, this unit is very important to our Company's job out here, and whatever it takes to keep the morale high, I will do. I know that even the General is questioning my reasons for using you all in every critical operation, but I have my reasons. As long as you all want to work under my command."

I assured him that all of us wanted to and will, as long as we can.

"Good," he said, "I'll be sending three others to join you, so prepare to accept them, okay?"

We parted company with me promising to tell him what Catharine said in the letter.

As soon as I was alone, I sat under a tree to read my letters. It was a delight to read Catharine's. She told me everything that she felt was important to our well being and also told me that Mark had set things into place for the two of us to meet in Nairobi Kenya, a week from then.

I got all excited and rushed over to his office to chew him out for not telling me. He must have seen me coming, because he was already at the door waiting for me.

"I know what you're thinking," he said, "but she asked me to get her a trip and that's the best I could do."

I stood there speechless.

"Look," he continued, "I've decided that all of you boys needed some R and R, so the whole damn platoon will go to Nairobi."

"Then what about you?" I asked, hoping that he would not be with us. Then acted dejected after he told me that he would not be there. All the boy's wives and or girlfriends from England, would meet us there. I dashed over to the billets to bear the good tidings which everyone was happy to hear. I made a point to let them know that it was Mark who did it.

All that week I spent time with Helen at her house, but always in the back of my mind, I was thinking of Catharine and the lovely time that was planned for us, and at every free moment the boys would gather in the rooms to discuss the upcoming event. Everybody had their clothes cleaned and packed ready for the day.

The evening prior to leaving, I went to see Helen. I told her that I would be away for a week on a secret mission, which I'm not allowed to talk about. That's what Mark had told us to tell everybody who asked. She told me that Mark had already informed the officers meeting of our movement. Unfortunately, some injuries came in and she couldn't leave the hospital, so we said a hurried goodbye at the air field.

The flight into Nairobi, Kenya, was long but very smooth.

We were treated well by the airport people. I was happy to see some of my people being in charge rather than the labourers. The bus driver took us through the city, showing off some of the new modern buildings in the African country. He advised us to take a trip to Mount Kenya to see how the others lived as he rushed us to the hotel.

The only rules we were asked not to break, were our camp location and not to wear uniforms while there. This was due to the Mau-Mau uprising. As soon as we got to the hotel, everybody rushed away to find their woman. The desk clerk told me my room number and handed me a slip of paper, which said all meals and drinks were free.

That delighted me immensely.

I did not wait for the bellman, I grabbed my kitbag and ran up the stairs two at a time. I entered the door and she was waiting for me, dressed only in her panties. She ran across the room and jumped into my arms. The excitement in her welcoming voice was enough to tell me what she wanted immediately. We kissed for a long moment as she held me tightly and I knew she was crying, because I could feel the tears between our faces. Her body felt warm as she forced it against mine. I picked her up in my arms, headed for the bedroom and laid her on the bed. I was getting excited for her as well and began removing my clothes, but she couldn't wait. Her anxiety was getting the better of her so she got up and helped me to take them off."

"Talk can wait," I thought, as we plunged into each other with a forceful lust of passion.

It was the beginning of two days continuous lovemaking.

Catharine was more anxious to make love than anything else and wanted to wherever we were. We were always rushing back to the hotel because she wanted to make out, which we did sometimes in a secluded part of a park or even sneakily in the back seat of a bus

I met a Kenyan police officer, who took us on a tour to Mount Kenya on my request. I wanted to see where the Mau-Mau lived and to get a view of the city from there. It was a lovely breath-taking sight, which I will never forget for the rest of my life. Although it was spicy hot, we had some of their authentic food in a village and was blessed by their elder priest, Catharine really enjoyed the days outing.

That night after making love I asked her if she was deliberately trying to get pregnant. She assured me that she was.

"Darling," she said, "I am thirty eight years old and I must have this child now, if I am ever going to have one. Time is running out on me and I really want to have a child."

"But Catharine," I protested, "it could make life very difficult for you, I mean with your parents and with Mark."

She paused to look me in the eyes.

"Darling," she said, "I am a woman now and at this stage, I really don't care who gets upset. I intend on having this child and that will be that."

"Then what about the divorce?" I asked.

"Mark is behaving like an immature person," she said, "he's being very irrational and I cannot wait for him to proceed so I have already initiated it myself."

"You did?" I asked surprisingly. "Mark never mentioned it to me."

She giggled as she said,

"That's because I haven't told him as yet."

The vacation was nice; we spent a lot of our time talking about us and what we should do for the possible baby. I told her that when my tour was over I would apply for a posting to either Germany or to Honduras, then we could be together without interference from anyone. She was happy and behaved in that little girl's character she liked to, and mimicked that Jamaican accent.

"What about Mark?" I asked. "How does he feel about you wanting to have my child?"

"I don't know," she replied. "At this time, I don't really care what he thinks any more. I have to look about my own welfare now," she said in a very stern tone of voice.

At the restaurant, Patrick and Greta came to join us at the table.

"Hello people!" he said grinning widely. "Catharine you do look lovely, it's no wonder I haven't seen this bloke for four whole days."

"I wanted to be alone with him, because I don't know when we will see each other again," she said, holding my hand tightly.

"And so you should my dear," he replied. "Out here, nothing is certain and the army has a way of telling us at the last minute."

I seized the opportunity to request his assurance to see to her welfare in case anything should happen to me and he agreed.

"Stan my brother," he said, "whatever you ask and I'm empowered to do, you can rest assure that it will be done."

I thanked him and so did Catharine. It was good to be with

Catharine again and happy that she felt the same way also.

"Patrick," she said, "you're the best friend to Stan and I hope you both will always be friends."

"I can agree to that my dear," I said, "and if anything should ever happen to me, please find a way to make contact with Patrick personally and he will give you assistance on my behalf, okay?"

She was happy to hear that and squeezed my hand in acknowledgment.

"Better yet," I continued, "he will get in touch with you. Just remember the Somerset house wine cellar. I will give him the details of how to use it, to get to you."

Greta Paisley left us and was having a conversation with Bob Muldoon and his girl Brenda at the next table, so I continued with the instructions. Patrick gave her his uncle's address in London.

"All you have to do is go there and say the word "Help," and I'll get the message. Then I will meet you in the wine cellar, okay?" he told her.

She nodded understandingly and shook his hand.

I was now feeling assured of her safety for the future. So for the rest of the breakfast the conversation changed to our time in Nairobi. I held up the coffee cup and said,

"I would like to propose a toast to Captain Mark Harrison for allowing this moment of togetherness to happening for all of us."

Catharine, Greta and I held up our cups and said. "Here, here." But Patrick kept quiet.

We talked about our visits to Australia and NewZeland and the many other places we had been, without mentioning any military operations. The ladies didn't want to talk about the army, their sole interest was strictly on sex. So when Catharine announced our departure back to the hotel room, Patrick and Greta agreed and left also. We saw a lot of Nairobi in the next two days and as usual always, we were rushing back to the hotel for more sex.

The morning came for the ladies to leave. We were awakened by the voice of the bellman shouting in broken English, the names of the people who were leaving.

"Com on now, yu all hab to reach de aport soon, de plane won't wait fi yu," Catharine said mimicking what the man had said. We quickly got out of bed and had sex in the shower and was almost late for the airport. All the time she cried.

"Darling," she said between sobs, "I don't want to leave, but I will have to. I am going to cherish these few days in Nairobi Kenya with all my heart while I await your return to England or Germany."

"Yes," I said, "Nairobi will always be ours forever my dear. A beautiful African city for a beautiful English woman.

We got the bags and ran downstairs to the bus. At the airport we didn't have time for a long goodbye, she had to rush to the plane, which was already out on the tarmac. We kissed and I could feel the tears running down her face again.

"I love you," she cried as she ran towards the door.

"I love you too," I shouted back at her.

I stood there waving as the plane started to taxi. I could relate to the feeling Bogart did in "Casablanca." I tried desperately to fight back the tears and to subdue the lump in my throat. When the plane was airborne, I was surprised to find Patrick standing beside me.

"Parting is such sweet sorrow," he said quoting Shakespeare.

"Oh yes it is," I said as we turned to leave the airport.

"Catharine and I hate goodbyes. I hope the next time we meet, we'll never part again," I said.

"Maybe you won't have to then," he replied.

I reminded him that we are also leaving the next morning so we should get our things packed today.

"Don't worry about that, I've already done so," he responded.

We walked to a little restaurant near the hotel and had a couple of beers.

"Now Nig," he said. "I do like the way you two are. You and Catharine. I really think you're truly in love with each other. There are many guys who would give their right arm to have such a beautiful woman love them."

He paused for a moment to light a cigarette.

"It's admirable, but how do you feel about it? Can it last forever?"

he asked. "I would rather like to see you with my sister, but if she's more your type, then I would not object."

"Thanks for your understanding friend," I replied.

He began to laugh.

"What so funny?" I asked.

"Mark Harrison is being such a gentleman about your affair with his wife. Some men in Ireland would kill both of you. Or maybe you have something to blackmail him with?"

For some reason I felt a reply was in order.

"Maybe the English are more civilized than the Irish," I said sarcastically.

He sat there dragging on the cigarette and studying my face.

"You know something nig? I think you're holding some sort of secret for him, but I don't want to hear about it. All I will say is, be very cautious with him, I think that after all is said and done he will try to eliminate us."

"I think so too," I replied. "But how."

There was a long period of silence as we both gave thoughts to his last statement.

"Anyway," he said proudly, awakening us from that trance, "I had a very good time with Greta, although she wasn't the woman of my choice."

I knew right away that he was talking about the girl in Ireland and knew that the British government wouldn't have brought her out here.

"So you had to settle for second best eh?" I said.

"Yes," he said, "but Greta was very enjoyable and maybe I will marry her, when I return to England."

"Maybe you should," I replied.

We left the restaurant for the hotel to finish the packing.

That evening was spent in the ballroom at a party arranged especially for us by the hotel management, who seemed delighted that some British soldiers stayed in his hotel without breaking a glass. We drank enough to last for a long time.

In bed, I laid awake thinking about Catharine and our baby until six a.m. It was the voice of the bellman that awakened me, he was shouting the same instructions as he did the morning before. There was no need to rush because my things were packed and getting to the airport was a cinch, because we were well organized.

When we were airborne about twenty minutes, I said to Patrick.

"Paddy, if anything should ever happen to me, please find Catharine and take her to a safe place away from him, okay?"

As if he already read my mind, he patted my knee smiling.

"I know that mi boy," he said. "I will."

I fell asleep and never woke until I heard the voice of the pilot saying that we were fifteen minutes from landing in Singapore. I had slept through the entire flight. I could see the lights of the runway as we approached it and wasn't too pleased to be back, although I knew it was my job. After the plane touched down and parked. We got loaded into the trucks for the billets and some needed rest.

On the suggestion of Rod, we all agreed to meet in the NAAFI for something to eat and a few pints after a little rest.

"Stan," he said as we reached the door. "you can rest assure that if she ever needed my help, I will do so without hesitation."

"Thanks friend," I said and shook his hands.

We joined the boys and everybody became anxious to tell their stories of Nairobi. I heard somebody shouting my name and looked, it was Helen.

"Oh darling," she said excitedly in that same sing song tone of voice. "I wasn't sure when you were coming back, Mark wouldn't say. Only that you were all on a mission somewhere...that's all."

Although I was happy to see her, I only wanted to see my bed. But she had other ideas. She quickly drank her beer and grabbed my arm.

"Lets go now," she said in my ear. "I am very horny and it cannot wait."

I could see the boys laughing at her actions. She was behaving like a wife again.

"Go on superman, see you tomorrow," Bob teased as we departed for her quarters and straight to bed. Helen expressed her loneliness for the week I wasn't there and talked about the love we shared all these years. We made love and slept.

For the next few days we just hung around Singapore doing absolutely nothing. I was sitting alone in the NAAFI having a drink when he walked in. Mark had asked me to meet him there.

"Hey Stan," he said as he sat reverse style on the chair.

I thought he had been watching too many John Wayne movies.

"Tell me about our Lady Catharine," he asked, "Is she still lovely? Did you all have a good time in Nairobi?"

"Yes sir, we did, I replied. "And she looks as lovely as ever, excepting she has now shortened her hair and lost some weight."

He asked and I told him of the places we went and things we did, except for our sexual escapades. There was no reason to tell him because he already knew that we would have had sex, once there.

"Nairobi is a very beautiful city, I enjoyed seeing it and so did Catharine. Thank you," I said.

"I am delighted to hear of the enjoyable times you both had," he said.

I also want to thank you on behalf of all the boys for the holidays there. Everyone enjoyed themselves."

"Oh it's not a problem Corporal," he said proudly. "Whatever I can do to make my men feel relaxed and contented, is mission accomplished."

I felt a compulsion to ask so I did.

"Why don't you want to give up Catharine to me? She would be much happier you know?" I said.

That question seemed to catch him off guard somewhat, because he paused for a long breath and a few puffs on his cigar. He stumbled as he quickly got up from the chair to leave.

"Someday I will," he said, "someday," he stormed out.

It was in the middle of the next week before we were summoned to his office for a briefing. We learnt of our up coming move back to Aden and I expressed my disapproval of the way we were jerked around, last time. He promptly reminded me that I was the one who volunteered for the paras and the Queen's officers don't care where we are sent, as long as the job is completed. I hated Aden and him.

"Mark changed like the wind. One day he could be nice and another....Well, obnoxious. I know it's illegal to kill an officer sitting at his desk, but one day I will kill this fucker and nobody will ever know," I thought.

Within a few days we were on the Aden bound transporter, to the same place in Carter where I was nearly killed on my twenty first birthday. I was shocked when we were told in mid-flight that we would be joining a regiment of paras going to Kuwait to assist in putting down a riot.

"Now that was a shift in plans? Telling your men in mid-air that what we thought was to be, is changed," I thought.

I looked at the faces of my platoon members and saw that they too didn't appreciate it either. That's the second time this method of information had been used on us. Anyway, I wasn't totally shocked, I was beginning to learn the army's way of doing things or maybe just Mark Harrison's. We landed somewhere in the desert in the afternoon, transported and billeted in tents around the sand banks near the city. We were given "special tablets" for the heat and other possible diseases.

"It's for your protection," the medical officer said.

I didn't take them and never did find out what kind of pills they were and their purpose. I remembered Helen telling me some time back, to be very careful of what kind of pills they handed out in the field. Since then I have often questioned the medics on their status and advised the boys to do the same. I never took them.

By the time we were briefed and made familiar with the city areas, I decided to question some of the boys about the people and their politics and wondered why the British were so interested in the Arab's affairs. Then I spoke to Patrick.

"Look man," he said, "this country is a oil producing biggie and the British think they own it. They want to hold on for as long as possible."

"And are willing to have us kill the people to do so?" I asked.

With a sneer on his face he replied,

"What the fuck do you think we were doing in Aden, Cambodia and parts of Northern Malaya? playing tiddly winks?"

He smiled and patted my shoulder as he explained.

"We, my friend, were there protecting the sheiks, Sultans and what have you got, who are loyal to England. The ones who are willing to deprive their people to maintain power and to keeping them entrenched in poverty for the sake of the money, which they call democracy."

"Then why don't they revolt to change the government?" I stupidly asked, although I was serious when I said that.

He looked at me for a moment.

"Then what the hell do you think they are trying to do now?" he asked. "Look around. Look at their weaponry they have and at ours. Theoretically they cannot win, we could annihilate them in quick time, but they are willing to die for the cause."

Patrick spoke at length on this subject and in each notation he compared it to that in Ireland. He was giving me a lesson in practical politics.

"Watch," he said. "When we move to the city, the orders will be to kill anyone that appears to be a leader or what is termed guerrilla. We're their killers. We're here to do their dirty work and to protect the crown's interest. And you can bet that it was them who instigated it."

He was getting excited and began beating his chest with the palm of his hand, something he always did whenever he got into this mode.

"King Eberkaneza ruled with authority. The Pharaoh had his Philistine army and so did Julius Caesar, they all did the same thing to the people and now it's the English turn."

When the conversation was over, I was totally convinced that democracy was just like communism and was implemented strictly to oppress and control the masses and we're like the Philistines army of old, here to conquer and destroy their mentality and control them in any way shape or form, even if we have to convince them that their god didn't exist.

The first time we marched into the city, after cleaning out most of those who were holding a fighting position, which only took a few days to do, we didn't encounter much resistance. Patrick was right, our orders were to shoot anyone who appeared to be the leaders and to arrest any others. Their effort was futile against our might and superior weaponry and our task seemed very easy to accomplish.

With our tanks, three Para regiments, one Ghurkha regiment and our Company they fell apart in short order. I felt sorrowful for the people and their struggle, but I was sent there against my beliefs, to do a job for the crown of England. And if I failed to protect that, I might be imprisoned or dead. And I am a little selfish on the latter.

One night I arrested five young Arabs and had them tied up. Mark came to interrogate them and began speaking to them in Arabic. I didn't understand anything that transpired between them, but I could see one of the prisoners refused to speak to him. He got very upset and began slapping the man's face, several times, with a pistol.

At another time I probably wouldn't care, except this man was already bleeding badly from a shot wound. Mark got crazier, hitting the man several times and asking him the same question over and over again in Arabic. Finally I grabbed him around the shoulders and dragged him to the ground. I didn't realize how strong I was to be able to handle him. He tried to fight me off but I had him in a choke hold with an arm stretch. A hold designed to kill.

When he was subdued enough, I let go of him. He was turning blue in the face by then. He sat on the ground rubbing his neck.

"You realize you could've killed me?" he said.

"Certainly sir," I replied. "When you're not behaving as an officer should, then restraint is an absolute necessary precaution." quoting from the officers hand book. I felt sorry for him, although I hated him for all the things I felt he did wrong to others. We sat on the ground for sometime talking about things, and I asked him many questions. He evaded and lied a lot about his questions to the Arabs
and his attitude towards the platoon. Finally he told me to take my prisoners to Headquarters for further questioning.

As I was taking the prisoners to the HQ one of them spoke to me in plain English. I was surprised of his ability and asked him why he didn't answer the Captain's questions.

"My friend," he said, "this is not just a riot as proclaimed by the sheiks. It's a revolt against them. It's a struggle of the poor to obtain a little more to live on. It doesn't seem like much to ask for, but they don't want the people to have any."

He spoke as though he had known me for many years.

"We the poor ones," he said, pointing to his friends, "know that none of us are capable of carrying out the political requirements to deal with the world's economics, where the oil is concerned. But the people now in power do not want to share any of the profits with the common people. They say that it's theirs and want to horde it in their foreign banks, for their power hungry selves and their families.

As we demand social improvements, they took away our civil rights to strike, so we felt there was a reason to revolt. Indignantly, they brought people as you to shoot us down and here we are."

"Well my good man," I said with authority, "that's the way of democracy, isn't it? And socialism is not any better either."

I was expressing my personal feelings to a person I had never met before, which was strange for me to do, but surprisingly I felt sympathetic towards them.

"The people in power want to stay there and will take yours to make more for themselves," I continued, "and they don't care if you all had food to eat."

I really surprised myself making that speech, especially to a stranger. I smiled inwardly to know that some things Patrick had told me, was now coming to my mind and lips.

I was beginning to rationalize my observations and had confidence in my own opinions, no matter where I was. The man and I spoke at length on the matter of wars and its relation to common human survival. I felt sorry for them, remembering the black people's plight back in England. I took them to the medics to be patched up, then to the temporary holding camp and left. Two days later, I returned to the camp to enquire of them and was told that they tried to escape and were shot in the attempt. I was devastated.

"I wished I had let them go, maybe I would be doing a good deed for them," I thought.

I hurried over to talk to Patrick and told him the story. He reminded me that we were there only to carry out orders the British government requested and I should not allow my personal feelings to over shadow my duties.

"And you did your part," he said, "it's not your fault those others had different ideas."

I trusted my friend's wisdom, because I could've been court martialled for letting them go. For the duration of time spent in Kuwait, I was more cautious with anyone I arrested and took to the camp. I made sure that I drew the officers in charge attention to my interest in the welfare of the people I brought there. I let them know that if anything should happened to any of them, I would personally jump on them. There weren't any more incidents to speak of, well not to my knowledge anyway.

In the weeks that followed, the British military had prevailed and the so-called leaders of the rioters were either killed or captured.

"Law and order had been restored," said Mark.

I watched the sheiks and their entourage back on the streets again, shaking hands and celebrating the triumphant downfall of the "Communist insurrection."

"Those fucking hypocrites," I said out loud.

Then I heard the voice of Patrick beside me.

"Don't be too upset laddie, that's the way of their lives my friend, whenever one oppose their policies, you are automatically branded as a Communist, and in Ireland we're branded as getting assistance from the Red Russians. There is nothing one can do to protest the injustices in their country, without being branded as something derogatory."

We both walked around the city observing the reactions of the people and to see only unspoken sadness in the faces.

"I feel sorry for them too my friend," he said, "but I have a problem of my own to resolve in my country."

Returning to Aden was a sour spot for me, because of the traumatic experience I had there. I was beginning to develop a phobia for the place and getting occasional flashbacks of that day. A sort of "Da ja vous." Which served as a reminder to be careful. It was a place where I couldn't relax at any time and the mere mention of the area Carter, brought chills to my body. It was an evil word. So when the commander informed us that we were required in Cyprus to assist the United Nations peacekeeping forces there, I was more than delighted to go. We were told that the forces there were having a bad time with the two sides involved and some cut throats were required to neutralize the parties. They believed our Company and two other para regiments could do just that. The preparations for that operation took ten days.

I didn't care where I was sent, as long as it was as far away from Aden as possible. That evening my platoon sat together to go over some of our codes with the three new boys and to remind one another of taking unnecessary risks. We discussed the politics that seemed to surround the people of Cyprus, but here Patrick could not explain the hate between the Greeks and Turks, although he compared it to that of Ireland. We all had a field day laughing, to think that the great Patrick O'Reilley was stumped

Mark Harrison also came to check on our weapons and to remind us whom we were representing and what was expected of us. We were told that our only orders would come from him and our business there should only take a couple of weeks; then we would return to Singapore.

"Aaaah Singapore," I thought, "and my good friend Helen Butterworth."

My thoughts wondered to a lovely place, although I would rather go to England so as to be with Catharine, even though I hadn't received any correspondence from her in weeks.

"Any mail for me?" I asked Mark as he dished out to the other boys.

"No, none for you and Rod," he replied.

"That's the fucking army for you," said Rod. "Your business must take second place to theirs."

I wondered a reason why Catharine suddenly stopped writing but couldn't rationalize one.

"Anyway," I thought, "if there were any mail, Mark would have brought them. Or would he?"

Mark spoke at length on the conduct of our men and the strategic application for British military requirements, to ensure that the proper political people maintained power and control.

"It's to prevent any Communist from taking over," he said.

I listened to Mark's words and realized that he was trying desperately to convince us that we would be doing the world a service if we could kill the Archbishop also. I smiled at his suggestion and asked him if he was serious. That patented sardonic grin caressed his square reddish face again, then in a low tone of voice he said,

"That action is not part of the operation," he replied, "not yet anyway. But if it should accidentally happen, the country might see some peace."

He got up and left.

We landed on the island of Cyprus and everything went faster than expected. We hurriedly secured our position then within minutes we were into the action. Our orders were to seek and destroy everything that resisted. The firepower of some were well positioned, so the work was intense and took a while to gain control. There were casualties on both sides, including a young chap who had joined us on patrol that evening. We were in an area that was classified "highly risky." As we walked along a street we were confronted with fire from a house. Ian's voice crackled on the radio.

"Nigs. Red hot fools cabin at sunset snow zero. Nig 14-9-13 under. 1-4-5 sunrise ice. Tchaikovsky plays green oranges. Nig 8-10- 12 sunrise, sunrise ice. behave green."

We quickly took cover to assess the scenario. The impatient young man got a little nervous and ran out into the street. His head was blown completely off, but his body kept on walking. I was very mad and surprised that he did not show any patience as us, but then I realized that he was not properly seasoned and very inexperienced, thus the end result.

Later that evening Williams saw an opportunity to get across the street. He lobbed a couple of grenades through a window, which seemed to do the job, because the rest of the fellows were able to get across and complete the cleanup in the house.

I often wondered about the young man, who's name I was never told and frankly I never enquired of, but his face will always be in my memory.

Although the fighting was intense, I was not as nervous as I was in Aden and in three weeks, things were back to, what they perceived as normal, according to the army. But as far as I was concerned, our activities were abnormal to that of a conventional war book. We went from house to house taking prisoners and killing anyone who resisted. Some of my colleagues found this kind of free movement, was a license to kill and so they did.

At times during the lull in fighting, I would ask Patrick if he ever felt any remorse for his actions. Sometimes he would say that he didn't care and at other times, he would say that he was getting practice for when he returned home to defend his rights in his land. But to watch them carry out these unwarranted acts on an order, amazed me. I often wondered where Mark Harrison were getting his commands from, but never asked. On one occasion I got Patrick so mad that he pointed his SMG towards me and said,

"If you were an enemy, I wouldn't hesitate to pull the trigger. Not because I hated you or your politics or you personally, but because you are on the opposite side."

I reminded him that I could be one of the people sent to Ireland to protect the British rights, when he is there defending his rights. He only laughed.

"I know you," he said, "and you would not go there for any reason.

You're a different kind of person. You have something many don't."

"And what's that?" I asked.

"Loyalty and Integrity my boy," he replied as he walked away from me.

I smiled internally, thinking that he believed I could be conned. Anyway I was sure that he was still my friend and trusted him with my life. So the doubts disappeared instantly.

For the duration of my stay in Cyprus, I was always trying to conclude in my mind the reason these white people were so rigid in their beliefs. They can hate forever. I began to think that God must have made them purposely to destroy the world. I spent most of my waking time thinking about their thoughts on politics and religion and writing this into my book. I wrote about the way they would scheme and connive ways to destroy anyone or anything that opposed them. I was now beginning to learn about their attitude and to find comfort in my little head time, and to write my thoughts.

"This military presence, is an education in itself," I wrote. "I've met so many who have differences in life's scenario and possess the ideology that they have supreme rights above everyone else, obsessed in proving that right, although they knew it could be wrong and easily become fanatics. I am now comprehending fully what it's all about, as time progresses."

I thought about the things I had read about Julius Caesar, Attila the Hun, Napoleon and Adolf Hitler and many more like them before and after Christ, and came to realize that there will always be people as them, immaterial of the changes of time. They all displayed these obsession for power and felt "God." was on their side."

Talking to Patrick and Mark, I could see the vast differences in their life beliefs. I concluded, that neither of them had any compassion for the people involved in the conflict of this small Island of Cyprus. They could kill both the Greek and Turks without any feelings; yet still hate each other. The politics surrounding Cyprus doesn't really matter to neither of them, because neither one had any vested interests, except for their military duties. But then again, it's all in the name of God.

"This Island is policed by the United Nations peacekeepers with limited fire-power," I wrote, " and I am sure it will flare up again and continue long after we leave. This conflict is deep rooted and it will never end.

Chapter Eight

"The South Seas."

On returning to Singapore, we were told that it was agreed by the upper brasses to send the entire Company on a rest period to Australia in a couple of weeks time. I was excited about going there again, although last time I had encountered some of their bigotry. Only this time we will be going to Brisbane and I heard that it was nice and was really looking forward to the rest period. One night, I told Helen of the upcoming trip and she reminded me that her sister Joanna lives near Brisbane and I should go to visit with her. She gave me the address and phone number and reminded me every day thereafter, that I would be killed by her, if I failed to see her.

The two weeks elapsed quickly as though in twenty four hours and the morning of our departure was nigh. It was a long journey and my nervousness showed. I am petrified of seas and ships. I would rather be in the air than on water. But although I was nervous, I felt relaxed with all my friends there and the help of some of the Navy boys. I was teased most of the time by them although they did assist me throughout the trip. I noticed that Patrick was always calm.

"You know something Nig?" he said, "I can't remember a famous black sailor in history, although I am sure there must have been some, because they even reached northern England."

"Are you talking about the Moors in Scotland?" I asked.

"Yes," he replied.

"I'm sure there must have been some but nobody wrote about them in your white history books," I replied.

He thought for a moment then said,

"That could explain it. But there must be something written somewhere about them. Maybe in the bible. I will have to check," he said.

I really didn't care about black sailors, not even the Moors. All my thoughts were focussed on getting off that tin can and on to dry land, far away from the land of killing.

The docking took almost as much time as getting there, but when we did, we were greeted by an army Colonel and transported to a camp near one of their tactical fighter Air Bases. This time we were all billeted together and the accommodations were much improved from the first time.

"Look you ugly bastards," I announced, as soon as we reached the billets, "we're in Aussie land again, so I would appreciate you keeping your sarcasms to your fucking stupid selves. These people hate blacks and I don't want to get into any more fights like we did last time, okay?"

"Yes," said Williams, "but it was fun. I hope this commanding officer isn't as racist as that other one."

"Well, if he is, then we will just have to straighten him out, won't we?" replied Taffy.

Patrick, as if given a podium for his birthday, began to tell us again about the political ideology of this country and reminding us of the last experiences.

"Australia," he began by waving his hand in circles as though he was conducting an orchestra. "Is a very large piece of land in which the Englishman came to and took by fraudulent means from the aboriginals. They did, like was done to the Red Indians in America, they drove the people into the desolate desert areas so as to starve them into extinction and to prevent them from becoming any kind of a political force. They formed a parliament and implanted laws to rob them of their lands and cultural rights."

I was intrigued by his knowledge of the Australian geography and promised myself to study some more on my own, it seemed to be a fascinating country.

"They brought in the undesirable Irish and English criminals from the prisons," said Paddy, " to steal and inhabit the lands here and the King of England deemed it legal."

While Paddy was rambling on about Australia, I was day dreaming of the slave trade and visualizing all those Africans being forcefully transported to the Americas to work in the fields. Then I heard Patrick's voice again saying,

"And they will fuck it up as they had done elsewhere."

I saw the opening and said,

"Like that in Ireland?"

"Exactly, so my friends, the struggle for freedom is on- going," he replied.

"Yes," said Bob, "but remember that a man called Jesus had tried to change things and the result was his physical destruction. They tried him in their courts and crucified him according to their laws."

I was surprised to hear Bob Muldoon repeating some of Paddy's teachings.

"Yes," said Paddy angrily, "I know they can crucify me too at anytime, but I will destroy many of them in the process, prior to my departure. What is needed is a mass uprising of the poor people of the world."

"Like they did in Russia and China?" Rod asked. "Like what Moses did against the Romans? Or that in Poland? My friend, in each case the people were crushed one way or another just like we are doing out there to these people."

"Ah!" Said Bob. "Where is and whatever happen to Helen of Troy? Didn't she also battle to the bitter end against oppression? She also succumbed to the relentless pressures and her people were driven into oblivion."

Paddy didn't reply. He just sat there listening to everybody inserting their thoughts.

"I also red about Attila the Hun and Hanabol, who incidentally, were black men. They had fought fearlessly for the freedom of their people, without success," said Williams." Look at the people in the Southeast Asia. Malaya, Laos, Cambodia, Vietnam; are they not fighting the same battle?"

"Then there's the people of Kuwait, Cyprus, Aden, Kashmir. Isn't it a mass uprising against oppression and injustice?" I asked.

The silence was thick. Patrick thought for a long moment.

"Brothers you are all correct," he replied. "They all had a legit right to fight and we're here to protect the British, French and the American industries that are here to exploit them. But they can't just lay down and be trampled upon. Look I'm here killing people who I don't know and who haven't done a damn thing wrong to me or Ireland, while in Ireland my family is also being mistreated. It saddens me to do it, but the army gave me an order."

Although we all could empathize with his point of view, there was a reality to be faced and we could recognize it.

"Paddy," I said, "every person in this world has a God-given right to exist freely. How they manifest that existence is their own problem. I in turn, would like to pass through this fucking life without any form of a conflict or animosity with anybody. Although I am quite aware that trouble is everywhere and I could be confronted with it at anytime."

He took my hand and shook hard.

"You can sure make a point when you want to," he said.

Rod spoke at length about many aspects of Australia and the British foreign policies, as it applies to others around the world, and we listened.

"There are different laws for those who aren't English and for those who are, just like here in Australia. We the Queen's own soldiers are sent to places like these as the protectors of these policies, at all costs. We are here to do a job and be paid for it, just like the Philistines of a long ago era," he said.

Rod was right. Anyway, all I wanted at this time was to enjoy my rest period and to find Helen's sister.

The next morning, I awoke very early and slipped out of the room to absorb some of the Australian "down under," air. I walked for almost a mile, then returned to the billets to enquire where the breakfast was being served. I was hungry.

"What's for breakfast?" I wondered aloud.

"Maybe stewed Kangaroo balls," said Williams.

Everybody laughed at his corny joke. Then my thoughts of food and my search for Helen's sister resumed. I took the note from my wallet to read the name and address.

"Mrs Joanna Cockrine, 376 Bailor Street, Brisbane," I said. An Air Force Sergeant came around to inform us of the direction to the mess hall, so we left. We all sat together and as always the conversation was about women. They started to take bets on who would be the first to find one. I deliberately kept out of that kind of unfair betting. It would be stupid of me to take the bets, because I have already experienced their racist attitudes on my first visit here. I know that actions would be taken against any black men who are admired by their white women. We saw it last time and from what I see now, the majority of women here is white. I have concluded that what I learnt about the Australian people's thoughts of black people, and seeing that there aren't any black ones in the area, I decided to be very careful and try to control my hormones.

I asked the Sergeant for directions to the address that I had. He told me that I could not get there by bus and advised that I should take a taxi. He also wanted to know who I was visiting there and was very persistent about it. His questioning only came to a stop when Ian told him to mind his fucking business.

The taxi driver never got personal and took me to the address. Along the way he spoke about his father who was born in London, England and had lived in Brisbane until his death about a year ago. He asked me many questions about London. He wanted to know about Putney and Greenwich. I had to describe to him in detail the Tower, Big Ben, the Palace and other places he had read or was told about.

"I would like to go there someday, to visit father's place of birth," said Ralph. "Some day I will accumulate enough money and the courage to go."

By the time we got to my destination, we had become very good friends. He promised to be on call for me at anytime.

I was surprised to find the house in a really nice and clean neighbourhood. I told Ralph to wait and I knocked on the door and she opened it.

Joanna was a tanned, neatly dressed, shapely but slimly built woman of about five-five. Her brunette hair was properly trimmed and styled, unlike that of Helen. Although they both had bluish grey eyes Joanna's features were more Normadic.

"Yes, can I help you?" she asked in a typical southern English tone.

"My name is Stan Martin and I....."

Before I could complete my personal introduction, she threw her arms around my neck and kissed me.

"I was expecting you to call first. Didn't Helen give you the phone number?" she asked excitedly.

"No," I lied, "she only gave me the address."

She waved for Ralph to leave and he returned the wave as we entered the house.

"You have a very nice place here," I said. "Your husband must be a very wealthy man."

She did not reply, only to acknowledge that it's a nice place. I observed from the rear, as she walked into the livingroom ahead of me, that she moved her parts with controlled motions. I could see from her posture, that she was properly trained in the best schools in England, where culture and poise are taught along with education. But then her sister is a medical doctor in the army as was their father in civilian life. Their mother was also into politics, which means her parents had to be rich for them to achieve this standard. And it showed when she sat on the couch and crossed her legs with grace. She made tea and provided some cookies. I again commended her on her wonderful house.

She asked and I talked about Helen and the army for a while. Then we fumbled through some politics unable to find a subject to talk about.

"You know something?" I said casually. "You have a distinct resemblance to Helen," which she did, "except you're younger."

She giggled and shook her shoulder-length brunette hair and stuck out her chest proudly.

"Do you really think so?" she asked. "I'm really one year older than that ugly girl you know," she said proudly.

"I would never have guessed it. You are a very attractive woman," I said.

She giggled again as she shook her body around and pampered her hair.

"Thank you for telling me that I'm attractive. You know just the right thing to say to a woman, don't you? You can have my heart. But then again, Helen told me that you're a charmer," she said.

"Oh? Helen told you all my secrets, eh?" I said.

She hesitated for a moment.

"Yes, but only some. The rest I will have to evaluate for myself. But don't stop the compliments! Keep them coming. My ego needs the boosting."

Joanna and I talked for an hour and she seemed happy to have someone to talk to. I realized that she was a lonely woman, from her conversation about her times with Helen as young girls in England. She talked about her subsequent marriage to a real estate man, having her two children, Miriam who is now fourteen and Charles, nine. She talked about their migration to Aussie-Land and of the farm he had put her to live on, with their two children and some smelly animals in the backyard.

"I got bored with that life style and decided to leave him and move to this area," she said in a slightly dejected tone. "He bought this house for me and the children and he remained on the farm."

I did not comment, except to say that I was sorry that things didn't workout for her.

"Don't get me wrong," she pointed out, "I love Australia, but I cannot spend the rest of my life on a farm, amongst those smelly animals, with nothing much else to do." She paused. "I'm sorry, but they are other things in life to be enjoyed and I have every intention of doing so. Even if it means doing it alone."

She checked her watch, got up and headed for the kitchen.

"Going to make supper for the children now eh?" I asked.

She slightly glanced over her shoulder as she walked.

"We will be dining alone this entire weekend. The children are spending time with their father on the farm," she said.

My mind wondered about the way everything was falling into place. Then I realized that her sister must have called her, with details of my arrival. I assisted her in the kitchen doing whatever she asked. On occasion, we would bump into each other and on one of these bumps, we both hugged and kissed. I almost pulled away but she held on pulling me closer to her. I slowly reached up to cup one of breast and she pressed her body even closer, at the same time telling me that we were alone in the house for the entire weekend.

The dinner was consumed and the dishes washed and put away. We retired to the livingroom where she offered and poured a couple of brandies. It was during the second drink that she motioned for me to sit beside her on the settee. She seemed to be more relaxed when I put my arm around her shoulder and pulled her head towards me. Finally, she just laid on the couch with her head in my lap. I pulled the buttons to her blouse, exposing her bra and cupped her breast. When she realized that I was having a problem unhooking it, she got up and headed for the bedroom. I did not wait for any invitation and followed her in.

Joanna seemed patient and was trying desperately to appear that way. But her need for companionship was quite evident. The anxiety was now coming to the forefront in a rush.

"Oh, this Australian heat," I said.

She reached over and retrieved a towel from the bed side- table to wipe our bodies.

"Making love to you is a thrill," I remarked.

"Thank you. Am I as good as Helen?" she asked.

"Weeeel......!" I replied smiling.

She propped her head on her palms and said,

"You can tell me if I'm not doing it right?" she said. "I would be delighted to keep on trying."

I jokingly promised to evaluate her performance at the end and give her lessons, if necessary.

"Please do," she replied, "because I simply have to be better than Helen."

She became very serious.

"Stan, I've been wanting to do something like this for a long, long time. Ever since we were teenagers, I've often wished to have something positive to be radical about, but the opportunity never came until now."

I realized that Joanna was a woman who needed a sexual encounter of this nature, to bring her back to life. She appeared to be desperate for some kind of male interaction and wondered silently of the reason. I decided not to ask about it because she was enjoying herself thoroughly with me, as I with her. I wondered how the boys had made out but didn't care. I was having a wonderful time with Joanna.

The morning sunlight came in on us. I could feel the days' heat beginning.

"It's a good thing you had these fans going all night," I said, not knowing if she was awake. When I didn't get a response, I got up for the bathroom and my motion awakened her.

"What would you like for breakfast?" she asked. "It would be a pleasure to make some for you."

"Anything," I replied. "Whatever you have in the kitchen."

Within minutes I could hear the clanking in the kitchen. I laid in bed having a smoke, feeling proud that I was able to make love to a woman on my first evening out in Brisbane.

"Breakfast is ready," she shouted from the kitchen.

"Oh hell," I shouted, "I was suppose to be in camp for a commander talk this morning."

"Is it very important?" she asked.

"I'm not too sure," I said, "we're here for some R&R and I can't see what importance this meeting could have."

"Well then, there's the phone," Joanna shouted. "Call and tell them that you were detained by a lady who wouldn't take no for an answer. You'll find the number in the book."

She giggled as she did the evening before.

"And also tell them that you will not be there for another day and night," she added.

I thought about it for a while then placed that call.

The Sergeant didn't apply any pressure for me missing the morning's session, but urged me to be back the following evening.

"Corporal Martin," he said, "you're a guest of our government and we must take all the necessary precautions to ensure your safety, while you're in our care."

"I thank you for your concern Sarge," I replied. "but I'm spending the weekend with a lovely woman and I think that I will be safe enough."

He laughed out loud and said,

"Good luck matey, we'll see you Sunday evening then."

I sat at the table looking at her face. To be honest she was more attractive than Helen, in truth, and do look much younger. She was busy telling me stories of their childhood days in England. Then she spilled it.

"This is the first time I have ever made love to a black man, I have often fantasized about one that was in our neighbourhood when we were young girls, but never had the guts to approach him," she said.

I realized then why Helen risked her commission to make love to me in Bordon.

"She was living out her fantasy and now her, sister also," I thought.

I wasn't sure if I should be angry at their exploitation of my person or happy to be the one that made it a reality for them.

Nevertheless, I felt obligated to stay the weekend with Joanna and try to repeat the performance of the previous night and to compare her sexual appetite to that of her sister. Our conversation swung from her family in England, to the political scene in Australia. I mentioned the racism I had experienced on my first visit and she expressed her disappointment with the people for the same reasons.

"Oh, don't get me wrong," she said. "I love this country immensely, but they are things I would like to see change politically, but as a woman I find it very hard to accomplish. One cannot be herself in this community, everything you do is scrutinized and criticized."

I looked at her puzzlingly, then asked,

"Do you think they, the community, will know that I had spent all this time with you?"

"I guess so," she replied, "but I don't really care what they think. My husband wanted and tried hard to keep me in a state of psychological bondage, he only had sex with me whenever he felt he needed it, and expected me to respond to him whether I wanted to or not."

She sounded very angry as she spoke and I was getting a little concerned for her safety after I left.

"What do you think your neighbours will do to you and the children after?" I asked. "They will see us at clubs and places you know."

"They will call me nigger lover, slut, whore, any name they think will hurt me. But you know something Stan? I will not care..... because, I've enjoyed myself with you immensely this weekend and want to share the rest of your time here in Australia, with you."

"Maybe we could, but your neighbours are my concern, they could do things to you later."

She exhaled a loud laugh as she replied.

"Some white men only hate black men because they think you're more virile and studly. They are the ones who don't know how to satisfy a woman sexually and are jealous of that fact. And that would be their only reason to attack me."

I sat there watching and listening to her, trying to evaluate her degree of eccentricity. But then again, I could be very wrong in my assessment of her, because she might be more normal than many members of the Royal family. I smiled inwardly and promised to write it in my notebook, which I did later.

"To think I was evaluating someone for a degree of madness after what I had become for the army," I thought. "Me, the mild- mannered person of only a few years ago, here killing people. People I have never met and had no animosity towards. Could this be madness unrecognized in myself?"

I promised to analyse myself someday.

On returning to camp on Monday morning, Ralph told me to call him any time I wanted to go back to her house.

"Not any other taxi," he warned. "Some of them don't like coloured people and probably would take you somewhere to do you in."

I found the Sergeant waiting for me at the gates. Although he seemed concerned about my welfare, his main thoughts were of me spending the weekend with a white woman somewhere. I pushed pass him and hurriedly got my things to attend the meeting. All my friends were dumbfounded by my silence of my absence. I discovered that they had brought in some women and had a party for them at the hall on Saturday night.

After the meeting, Mr O'Reilley made it his prerogative to question me on my escapade.

"Now young man," he began, "I don't mind you wondering off on some unknown adventure, but at least you should have told me where you would be. At least give me some idea where."

"I'm so sorry Pop," I replied sarcastically, "but I had met a most lovely lady in Bordon, she gave me her sister's address in this town, who is a very luscious, horny, beaut. She was lonely and wouldn't allow me to leave without a fuck. So I obliged her with my presence. Are you satisfied?"

"Yes, but....remember you're now in small minded town Australia and you should be more careful," he told me.

He sat there looking at me as though his young son had just reported the loss of his virginity.

"Do you realize that you are in a strange country where the people hate blacks and you sleeping in a white woman's bed?"

"Hey, friend!" I said, "you sound like a bigot also."

"No, friend," he replied. "I'm not being a bigot. I just wanted for you to have told one of us where you were going, that's all."

We sat there looking at each other as though we were in a problem state. I felt he was right and was protecting me. We smiled at each other, shook hands then began our meal. We talked about Major Helen Butterworth and her sister and the good time we enjoyed. My interaction with Helen wasn't a secret to him, because we had talked about it in Aldershot and in Singapore. He also knew that I enjoyed female company and would have gone to see Joanna Cockrine sometime, no matter what.

Throughout the rest of our stay in Australia, Patrick had always found something to contradict or confuse our guide with. From their politics to religion. He knew more about their country than the Corporal did. I was always sitting or standing close by to hear their conversation and laughed inwardly listening as Paddy made a mock of everything the man had to offer. On one occasion, while arguing about who were the prisoners brought into the country. I heard the Corporal say.

"And the Irish were the majority," he said. "That should indicate to you that all Irishmen are criminals."

"Yes," agreed Patrick, "only in accordance to your stupid English protestant laws. What they didn't teach you was that the Irish were the most persecuted in all of England. But someday they are going to feel the wrath of a reprisal for all their nasty ways."

He was angry and I could see it in his eyes. The Corporal didn't realize how close he came to be beheaded.

"And it will be a devastation," I mockingly said.

Everybody laughed and that was the end of the conversation.

In the evenings, I would be picked up by either Joanna or Ralph and taken to her house, beach or to some club or restaurant, sometimes with the two children. We spent a lot of time on the beach talking, with me telling them stories about England and playing games. Miriam and

Charles took a liking to me and would sometimes run from the car to greet me with a kiss. Some of the Aussies saw this and asked my boys about it. I heard that Paddy had taken exception to the questions and they all got into a fight.

I decided that once they reached to that point, it was time to straighten things out with the commander. I approached the officer in charge and stated my disgust to him, about their racist attitude. The discussion reached up to the camp commander, who desperately tried to appear impartial and understanding of the matter, but his true colours kept showing up. Anyway, the problem was quietly resolved after Patrick threatened to take it up with our supreme commanding officer, Mark Harrison.

For the rest of the stay in Australia, I became more aware of their bigotry and subtle discrimination. I realized then that although I was an educated and skilled NCO in the British Paratroopers there wasn't any respect from the whites. My colour was a hindrance in their eyes and when it came to their women, it was a devastation to their creed. I also became aware of what Patrick had been drumming into my head all these times about the application of their politics to other people.

"The learning process," I wrote in my book.

I kissed Joanna and the children goodbye as we prepare to leave, and promised her to write as often as I could.

"Stan," she said, "this experience was the best I've ever had, thanks to you for being a part of it. Would you deliver this letter to Helen for me?"

I promised I would as soon as I reached Singapore. Joanna seemed happy and was smiling all the time. She let out a laugh and kissed me again for the others to see.

"What's so funny lady?" I enquired quizzically.

"Darling," she said, "for all my life I have been looking for something to be radical about. I have been searching for something to believe in, something of interest to defend. Now I know a cause to fight for and I have you to thank for it."

"And what might that be?" I asked.

"Racism," she replied. "Racism in Australia."

She seemed happy. I stood there thinking of her words and realized that, maybe I did give her the courage to stand up for a cause.

"I wish you well my dear," I said. "I sincerely hope that we'll meet again in a different place. But if we don't, maybe we will remain friends mentally if not in person."

We kissed again and I was off to the carrier back to hell.

Back in Singapore, the orders were for us to stay there because an assignment was coming up and Viet-Nam was the place. Rumours throughout the base was that we were being sent to Viet- Nam. Everybody in our platoon laughed at that thought, although some were sure it was true. One day I met Mark Harrison returning from Division Headquarters. I saluted him.

"Look Sir," I said, "those boys have been hearing a lot of things, including going to Viet-Nam. Is there any truth to any of this?"

"First thing's first," he replied. "How have you been, did you boys have a good time in Australia?"

He spoke as we walked towards his office. I felt something wasn't right, because Mark appeared too happy and that was his demeanour for bad news.

"I hope everything went well in their camp and you all made some friends because you'll be working with them in Viet-Nam."

"So it's true!" I said. "We were sent to Australia to familiarize ourselves for that purpose?"

"That's right," he said. "Absolutely correct. I hope you did enjoy your stay with Joanna Cockrine also."

I stopped in my tracks with my mouth open.

"Don't look so dumbfounded," he said. "I asked Helen to give you her address in Brisbane," he said grinning.

"Why?" I asked.

"Because I wanted you back here in a good frame of mind, that's why."

We entered the NAAFI and I sat across the table from him. He spun the chair around and sat straddle style like a cowboy would.

"I bet you must have seen that in a John Wayne movie," I commented without a response.

"Listen to this," he said enthusiastically, totally ignoring my statement. "The British military had decided to send two regiments of us to assist the Aussies and Americans in that country. I'm not sure what our duties will be or who will be giving the orders as yet, but as soon as they inform me, I'll brief you all."

I did not respond. He avoided my eyes...but continued,

"Somehow the brasses think we could make some difference there to dislodge the VC's," he said. "We'll be operating along with a Ghurkha regiment and two other para regiments."

He sounded happy even to give the news.

"Ah," I said. "Now I get the picture. Our help is needed on the quiet, to try and dislodge the Congs eh?"

He looked at me very strangely and I could sense a little uneasiness in him.

"You're right in a way," he replied. "Yes, the chinks are giving them a hell of a time and somehow they want us and the Ghurkhas along with the Aussies to go in, to recapture an area and to try to re-establish some kind of hold around some towns and villages."

I didn't really care for neither his or the military's reasoning, and seeing that we had never been told of what was happening in Viet-Nam before, I was rather curious of it now. All I knew, was that they were fighting against Communist aggression, as we were doing in Malaya. I am slowly discovering that the army lies a lot. I hated the idea of going to Viet-Nam although it would be nice to be working with the Ghurkhas and see Sergeant Kito again.

The Briefing on Viet-Nam was not as informative as expected. I realized that we were being sent to a place blindly, not like the other operations and without proper directives or specifications.

"Anyway," I thought. "We're not to reason why, just to do or die,"

I whispered repeating a quote I had heard from someone else.

Within two weeks, I was somewhere in Viet-Nam, north of Saigon. Our orders were to protect an area near where the American, Australian and British engineers were busy expanding the runway, to accommodate the US Air force. The VC's kept coming to disrupt the work and we fought fearlessly to protect it. For the first eight weeks we were there, I never got involved with any of the women because I was too afraid to be caught with my pants down.

The inactive times were spent mostly discussing the political implications of the country and the usual British and American control of other people's country. I found that Patrick was more perturbed here than anywhere else. Then the American forces moved in to take over. They had the best of everything including food and sleeping equipment. This seemed to cause more dissension amongst the forces than anything else and at times fights would break out amongst our allies because of this.

I found that some of the Americans were very boastful and many of them made fatal mistakes in the field and died as a result and some would panic under fire. That, in my opinion was because they were not properly seasoned prior to being sent to the front. I have had many conversations with Mark about this, but he would say that he couldn't figure out why either. At one gathering of our company, Bob took exception to a statement by Mark regarding the Americans.

"How do they perform in the field?" Bob asked. "The same as in New York?"

Mark replied that he didn't know, but assumed that they were well trained men. Many times they were caught by surprise and many of them died just laying around with their weapons carelessly left unattended. On a couple of occasions, we had to return to clean up an area where the VC's had broken through.

I often wondered where the VCs were getting the personnals from but couldn't. I fail to believe they were from China. That thought left me in a daze. The fire fights were frequent and the casualties in our company rose.

One evening while our platoon was on patrol, we came upon an American unit under fire. Quickly we got involved and assisted them, killing some of the attackers.

Ian spotted a Marine who was shot, so we both crawled out to try to get him, but got there just in time to see the VC bringing his machete down on the soldier. We opened fire and shot three of them, but the other two ran off. We waited to make sure they weren't hiding in the bushes, then approached the still convulsing body laying there. I felt sick instantly. There weren't anything we could do for the headless man, so we radioed in and left.

At times, there were brief lulls in the fighting and we would be given some recreational time in Saigon. I became friendly with some of the black American marines and learnt a lot about the segregation within their troops. One told me that most blacks don't have a choice, but to be drafted. I learnt of how some white senior officers treated the blacks with disrespect and contempt. Some of the blacks thought they would get respect on returning to America.

I found that although they were fighting for the same army, their cause and ideas were different and sometimes even killed each other, either accidentally or purposely. A marine told me that some of the young white officers got killed by fracking and the incident is reported as "killed in action." And seemed happy to tell the news. I often questioned them about it, but the explanation was never clear, although I came to the conclusion that American whites behaved the same as the English. They usually considered themselves superior in every respect, until they find out that they also bleed red blood.

Although the South Vietnamese city was free of direct fighting, I could sense the impending disaster. It seemed that the VC's were trying to get the Yanks intoxicated so as to kill them quietly and did in large numbers, by planting explosives in and around their camps. Some died accidentally by triggering the Bamboo, Grenades and other explosive springe, set by the VC's. Mark continuously told us not to divulge any of what we had seen there in the Viet-Nam jungle, "For security reasons," he would say. I sometime pointed this out to my boys, and for them to be very selective in whom they acquaint with and where they go, while there.

On a quiet day, a Sergeant Avery Blakely came to our sector to visit. I could hear his southern drawl as he asked for me.

"Who and where is Corporal Martin?" he asked approaching our area, "Is he around?"

One of the boys pointed in my direction and he followed the finger to my location and flopped himself down beside me.

"Hi, Corporal," he said as though we knew each other a long time. "My name is Avery Blakely of the U.S. Marines. My commander was talking to yours and he suggested that I should talk to you. He said you and your boys might tune me in on something of importance in this "Hell hole."

Although Blakely seemed a little cocky, I observed how relaxed he was within my company. I noticed that he seemed like a professional veteran from the way he checked his surroundings before sitting.

"Hell hole is almost the right word," I replied as I took a drag on my cigarette, "but it's going to get a lot worst as time goes on."

Blakely and I talked for a while then were joined by Patrick a little later.

"You see my friend," said Paddy, "these people have a reason to fight and they're doing it in their own back yard, with any kind of weaponry they can find."

Although he seemed intrigued and willing to learn about some of the tactics employed by the Cong's, I could feel his brains making mental notes of the words.

"Teach your boys not to lean on anything," Paddy said. "Check everything for springe. The VC's are very good with booby traps and whenever they are wounded, they can act dead until you turn your back."

Blakely sat quietly, listening very intently absorbing the lesson. At times looking directly into my eyes then into Patrick's. We spoke for hours and he asked many questions about how we dealt with prisoners and what kind of treatment we gave them.

At times, whenever I mentioned the American attitude, he would remind me that I was only there to help to maintain the airfield.

"You guys are here only for a specific job, so don't lecture me on our attitude," he angrily said.

At this point Paddy got up and left. I in turn advised him that he would see many of his friends die, due to their lack of training for the Viet-Namese jungle. He laughed and told me that they will have things wrapped up in a short while.

Blakely and I met on and off for a couple of weeks after that first meeting. At one time he brought a couple of his NCO's to visit. The conversation was about the American presence in Nam and how soon they plan to clean out the VC's.

"I do have business plans back in the states," said Blakely, "so this thing must be over before I get to leave and my boys here are willing to work overtime to wrap it up."

Before I was able to reply Paddy stepped in.

"Look you fucking Yankee idiots, let me educate you with a little history. This fucking country have fought many wars with the French, who have been raping it for years and who thought they owned Indochina. The French were getting their arse kicked, so your country, the great America made an agreement with England and came to preserve it for their purpose, just like during the other world wars. Yes, the VC's lost a few over the years, but they got better every time and this campaign seemed to be their best effort yet. And don't be overly surprised if you end up fighting the Red Chinese army also."

"How the fuck do you know so much about Viet-Nam?" Blakely asked.

Patrick smiled as he said,

"Common sense my dear boy. Plain common sense," replied Paddy. "Plus I read many books, and after a few months here, it's quite evident what they are up to."

After that day of education, Blakely and his boys rarely came back for any political discussions on Viet-Nam and whenever he did, he came alone and only spoke to Patrick and I.

On the last day that Blakely came, the three of us were sitting at a tree talking, when he asked Patrick about the Irish problem.

"You know what I think Paddy?" Avery began with a smile, "You Irish boys need some good weapons over there. You can't be fighting with old machines like you have. Look at the VC's here, they won't last long, I can assure you."

I was about to contradict him again, when Patrick motioned for me to be silent.

"Who and where could we get some from? Weapons I mean?" Paddy asked.

Blakely responded as though I was not present.

"My boy, you're in luck. I will give you a name in New York and my name in Virginia and whenever you're ready to make your purchase, contact me or this man and you can buy anything your little heart desire. As long as it's cash and is cold hard American money."

Blakely wrote the information on a piece of paper and gave it to Patrick. He left our area with a hand shake and a promise to see us again.

But that meeting never came, because we were dispatched to another sector to carry-out our duties and left it in the hands of the Americans. I spoke to the boys about some of the things Avery Blakely and I spoke about and they weren't overly impressed with him or his army. I remembered Ian telling him that he was dumb for thinking this wasn't a war.

"You're here to spread American terrorism," said Ian, "and it's going to blow up in your face."

To which Sergeant Blakely replied.

"For every life lost or a piece of equipment destroyed here in Nam, somebody back in America is making money. I only have a few months to be here and when I return home, I know the exact business to go into."

I was getting angry, so I left them alone to complete his arms purchasing discussion with Blakely.

By the end of the fifth month I had enough of Viet-Nam and went to confront Mark Harrison, in what I classify as a clash of our personalities.

"And what brought on this line of questioning Corporal? Pray tell," asked Mark mockingly as though I was nuts or just plainly projecting negativity.

"Sir," I said in a serious tone, "this Viet-Nam defence is not our business, it's the Yanks problem and the way I see it, they're an uppity group and I don't feel comfortable working with them."

He sat there looking at me with those weird green eyes.

"I agree with you," he replied. "I don't like it either, but we have to stay here as agreed by the upper brasses, although it's my bet that we'll be out of here in the next couple of weeks."

I didn't reply or question him any further. I was too angry inside to continue and he knew it.

"Look Stan," he said, "I'm in this as you are and would like to go to safer grounds. Them Yanks shoot at nothing and somehow I wished they would coordinate their ship's guns, so as not kill their own people."

We both laughed at that, although I often wondered why.

"I assure you that we'll be getting our travelling orders soon, tell the boys, okay?" he said, knowing that I would have a cheerful thought.

We talked a little about Catharine. But on the question of him giving her up to me, he never answered. I keep getting the feeling that he didn't intend to do so.

"Why can't he be compassionate in this matter as that of the war zones?" I said to Patrick. "He has always evaded the question or ignored me completely."

"Wait until you return to England then you and Catharine can make that decision by yourselves," Patrick told me. "Stan, if that woman loves you as she said, then it will all work out in your favour."

Lately, I noticed that Mark wasn't around us as much as he used to and very seldom mentioned her name. Whenever I asked him about not being near the men, he would also evade that.

"Hey!" I said, "I get the distinct feeling that you've been so busy teaching the yanks how to steal and plant phoney political documents, that you can't find the time for us."

He only stared at me for awhile and I could see in his eyes the concern for my words, then nodded his scruffy looking red head in acknowledgement saying,

"Soldier, fighting against communism is not an easy task. Those people only understand terrorism, and both the British and Americans are expert in this kind of fighting, so we have to teach their people how to do it properly."

Mark spoke these words as if he was describing the Holy Grail.

"Is this why the Vietnamese solders are paid to bring home the heads of their victims?" I asked.

The silence was so thick, it couldn't be sliced with a sharp razor.

"Corporal, it's none of our business what the Americans and the Vietnamese do. We're here only to assist in whatever way we can with their efforts. so don't question their policies," he replied angrily.

I could feel more hate within me for him.

"Yeah! And you will apply the same to the Irish when the time comes, I presume?" I said to antagonize him.

He became even more enraged. As a matter of fact he was fuming and began to shout.

"I bet it's them fucking Irish bastards that's been telling you all this shit," he said.

I didn't wait for him to complete his spiel, I just whirled and marched myself towards my position. I joined Patrick, Rod and Ian in some swampy area and sat.

"You know something boys," I said. "I am going to write that book and I intend on telling how hateful and devious Mark Harrison is."

Patrick laughed loudly as he waved his SMG in the air.

"You mean to say that Mark Harrison and I will be on the same page?"

"Imagine," said Ian, "we will be in good company. Stan my boy, you can't be too nice to people like him. Mark doesn't have a heart, he has a rock in his chest."

Suddenly Patrick became serious.

"I am glad that you are now understanding about their politics my boy, and there is a lot more in store for you," he said.

I listened and wondered what they would do to the blacks in South Africa. Then I remembered a book Patrick had taken from the library entitled "The Rise and Fall of the Roman Empire," the wars exploits of Julius Caesar, and realized that they too will fall, just like Rome and Babylon did.

"Hey Paddy," I said, "tell me more about your thoughts for changes in Irish politics, that you intend to make whenever you reach back home."

I felt a compulsion to question him for my own comfort of mind.

"You see," I continued, "it might be of importance when I begin to write. As you know, a writer must tell about the good side as well as the bad."

He stared at me for some time in deep thought, then he spoke.

"Well," he began, "I would like to get home and join the party and hopefully get nominated as a candidate for the national election. I'm confident that I will be elected. From there I'm going to make sure to maintain contact with my people always, so as to be directly involved with their concerns. It's my intention to work hard to bring about legislation that will enhance the total population of northern Ireland, so that all Irish people can live in harmony. No lies or deceptions. I intend to be as honest with the people as I can."

I felt he was being rather genuine in his words. I could feel the earnestness in him.

"You know something," I said. "I have a feeling that you will accomplish your promised dreams. I wish you luck and I know you'll be the best politician in the whole damn parliament. And that, my friend, is what I will write when I do so."

Again he just stared at me. Then when he felt something, he replied.

"I know you will write that book my friend and have all the confidence in your justification for my life."

We shook hands.

"Friends?" I asked.

"Friends forever," he replied.

One afternoon unexpectedly, our Company got the call to return to Saigon. The trucks were already there to take our equipment and three American choppers were in position to take us. I was delighted to be getting out and watched the happiness on the faces of my platoon. They were happy to leave. My mind was strictly on Singapore and Major-Doctor Helen Butterworth again.

"It will be nice to lay in a soft bed beside her and to feel her touch," I thought.

On reaching Saigon, I decided to seek out the Marines unit and questioned an officer for the whereabout's of Sergeant Avery Blakely. After some long search I was told that he was still up front, but they will try to get word to him for me. I wrote a good luck note to him and left. Patrick also wrote a note. That night as I laid in a real bed, I gave thought to many things in my life in the last few years. I wondered about some of the people around me and tried to evaluate the degree of madness within them, which I wrote in my notebook.

"It's inconceivable to imagine those Yanks and Vietnamese soldiers raiding and killing innocent people in their villages and reporting it as "killing VCs." I spoke out loud to myself. "And bringing their heads back as proof. That, I think, is terrorism."

My suspicions of the Americans and their actions brought my thoughts to Mark Harrison and his personal policy in the other places we had been.

"Maybe he knew of their policies in Viet Nam and the political implications, for the perpetration of mass murder that have been carried out and is hiding it from us. I do believe he was having a vendetta for the accident that disabled him in Hong Kong. Am I mad too for being part of this war? I must remember to ask Patrick what or who is Sinn Fein." I fell asleep still unsure, but the things I saw here, will always be embedded in my mind."

The next two weeks were spent coordinating our gear to go back to Singapore. One day while I was checking the boys as I normally do,

I noticed that Ian wasn't there.

"Hey!" I shouted. "Where is Mulligan? He is missing. Where is Ian?" I asked, looking around and checking everybody else.

"Maybe he went for a shit," somebody responded.

"Come on!" I shouted, "Where the fuck is he?"

Rod began to speak but Mark Harrison approached us at the same time. He told us that Ian had volunteered to stay on in Viet Nam with another regiment and was sent back to the location where we were. He was shot while on patrol with some Americans the very next night and his body was quietly sent home.

"Balls!" I shouted. "Why didn't he tell me or Paddy that he was volunteering then? He would have told me or Patrick or one of the others.

"We didn't want to alarm you about it and you will have to accept my word for it," Mark said in that condescending tone of his.

Rod and I were now pointing our Sterlings at his Mark's mid- riff not taking our eyes off him. I shouted for Patrick to come. When Paddy was next to me, I asked him if he had heard that Ian had volunteered to stay in Nam. Patrick responded negatively.

"Well my friend, he is now dead," I shouted again.

By this time the rest of our platoon had gathered and Rod repeated everything of the conversation to them. Everybody's facial expression changed immediately to a solemn steer at Mark Harrison.

"No my friend," Paddy said in response to my question, "this is the first news to me. Why didn't you tell us before, that he was going alone?" Paddy asked, directing his question to Mark.

Mark stood there without an answer.

"Where's his body?" Bob asked.

"It has been sent home to Ireland to his parents," Mark replied while looking awkwardly at the ground.

"Why was he separated from the rest of us?" Rod asked angrily. "How the fuck do we know that it wasn't you who killed him, eh?"

There was total silence.

"You know something Mark?" I said. "I feel you were the one that killed Ian. You sent him to his death. For all these years you have had a hate for the Chinese people for your presumed accident in Hong Kong. Then you hate me because Catharine loves me and hate these Irish boys for talking about the ills in their country. It seem you wanted us all dead for those reasons. You're a stinking bastard."

I was displaying an anger which even surprised myself, but I felt it was justified. My mind was now working at a speed faster than light.

"Did Ian know or see something?" I thought.

I wanted to know exactly how Ian was killed and Mark was not willing to divulge that kind of information to us. And the less he told us made the hate for him grow. Patrick must have sensed that I was about to pull the trigger, because he quickly reached out and forced the barrel of my gun to the ground. Some shots rang out and into the ground near to Mark's feet.

"Not here Stan," Patrick said. "Let it be another time."

Just then a high ranking American officer came in our direction and Mark seemed relieved. He told the officer a lie that my gun had jammed and accidentally discharged when we tried to cleared it. He then told us that the discussion was at an end, but maybe we could continue it in Singapore and left.

The entire platoon talked about the implications and charges we had labelled against Mark Harrison, the man who had been our Commander from Aldershot.

"Can we really trust him anymore?" I said, still enraged. Everybody was in deep thought, until Bob said,

"My friends, it sure does look suspicious. Every time he sent us on assignment in the past, we were always together. But lately, whenever we are sent to an area like this and even in Cyprus, we were separated. Is it deliberate? Remember on our Hong Kong border operation? Peter Baron died. Then in Borneo, Jack was seriously injured. Charley is shot in the leg and Brownie is dead. And now here in Nam, Ian."

I was getting more convinced that Mark was trying to eliminate us one at a time. Patrick began to make a case with his Sherlock Holmes style deductions.

"Yes fellows," he said, "we should all remember how Jack, Brownie and Green got it in Borneo and never forget about young Powell in Cyprus or Peter in Hong Kong. I don't like the looks of it either. Who will be next?"

My mind was racing and the more I thought about Mark and our suspicions, the more I was hating him and desired to kill him. But like Paddy had said, "Not here," but I know it will come someday. Either him or me.

"Boys," Patrick said, "I think we know too much of their policies and operations here. We must be careful from now on, because we cannot trust him any more."

We all shook hands and promised to watch more closely.

"Friends?" shouted Rod.

"Forever," came the reply.

I was happy to be back in Singapore and Helen Butterworth and the solitude of her love, we had so many things to talk about. I also wanted to find out if Catharine still remembered me with a letter. I made plans to write a million letters, bearing in mind that the army could send me anywhere at any time. But, I intend on having some fun times to make up for the last five and a half months. I went to my room, showered and laid down for a short one hour kip before going to Helen's place. It was the voice of Paddy that awakened me from a beautiful slumber.

"Hey lazy bones, get your arse up!" I could hear the voice but couldn't identify the face.

"Hey Nig, it's almost tea time get up! You've got to eat sometime you know?"

I was getting angry at the voice, but still no face.

"Fuck off," I said, "leave me alone. Don't bother me."

The person came closer to the bed and I rolled over to one side to see the face.

It was that of Paddy and he was smiling as he prompted.

"Boy you were really tired. You slept all of last night and today," he said.

"What time is it?" I growled, as I tried to get up from the bed.

"It's a quarter past five in the evening," he said.

I jumped from my sitting position and dashed over to the closet.

"I have to meet Helen at six o'clock," I said excitedly.

He laughed loudly.

"You horny little boy," he said, "you've already blown it. Your sexcapade was last night and if you don't get up to eat now, you won't have the strength to even come once."

He was still laughing at my uncoordinated behaviour. I felt myself getting more stupid as I tried to get dressed. Maybe it's a good thing nobody was present with a camera to record my actions. Patrick kept laughing as we left for the mess hall. We got our food quickly and sat. I observed that our conversation was about everything else, but that of Vietnam. Neither of us wanted to express our feelings about it or our doubts in Mark's attitude towards us, but I knew that it would have to come up some time.

We ate and I left as the crowd began to arrive. I was getting anxious to see my dearest Helen. Patrick stayed back to see the rest of the boys. I quickly brushed my teeth and rushed over to the hospital to find her, only to hear that she had gone home.

I took a taxi to her place and knocked on the door. She must have seen me from the window, because the door opened almost instantly.

"Get in here you little devil," she said with a broad smile. "I stayed up until three forty five last night waiting for you. And now that you're here, I intend to make you pay for it."

She was dressed only in her panties and a shirt that she had confiscated from me sometime back. I wondered how she could've known when I would be coming back.

"Is it customary for the military commander to tell others of our movements or what?" I asked her.

"No my darling, they don't. But I have ways of getting my information from some officers and I don't have to have sex with them either," she said sarcastically.

"Don't give me that guff, that you never fucked with anyone while I was away," I said trying to aggravate her, but she was not taking me on.

"No I didn't," she said. "As an officer, I am privileged to some detailed troops information, especially yours."

I sensed that there was more to her statement, but I could also see that she was ready to have intercourse.

"Did you already have tea?" she asked as though I was looking hungry.

"Yes," I said, "and I'm ready for some relaxation with you."

"Not tonight dearie," she said as she dashed her body next to mine on the bed. "There won't be any relaxing tonight, until I am completely satisfied."

Helen was anxiously removing my clothing, so it did not take long for us to get romantic. Helen was ready, like I was. For the three and a half years that we have been lovers, I cannot remember an unpleasant time. We went after each other's body as two people who were lost for sex for a hundred years, would.

"Maybe that was our stimuli, and didn't know it," I thought.

The next morning she was still laying in bed.

"Not working today darling?" I stupidly asked.

I should have recognized what her game was.

"Come lay beside me darling," she said giggling, "there is much I want to talk about today. Furthermore, I want to prove that I am better than my sister, sexually."

I became aware that women do tell each other of their sexual conquests of men and then compare the pleasures derived from such adventures. In the first place, she told her sister about me, then the sister returned the favour. I got back in bed.

"Why did you tell Joanna all those things about me?" I asked.

" Because I knew that the girl is very slow when it came to seducing a man. And knowing that you probably wouldn't have tried my sister, I had to psyche her up to it. I am glad that you both had a good time together," she said proudly.

I laid there smiling to know that I had pleased Joanna sexually and helped her to fulfil her fantasy. I was reliving my memory of Joanna here, by pleasing her sister in the same fashion.

"Do you realize that Joanna looks very much younger than you?" I said just to annoy her, but it seemed not to achieve the intended objective.

"Yes, I realize that," she replied. "But does she screw as well as I?" she asked.

I didn't answer.

"Well?" she prompted, still awaiting my answer.

"No, I don't think she is on the same sexual level as you are." I replied. "There are some techniques that you possess that she has only now learnt recently."

She laughed and threw her head back as Joanna had done, very proud of her sexual appetite and expertise.

"Darling," she said, "at forty one years old I am proud to say that I have enjoyed some lovely times with men. But I have enjoyed the last three years with you the most, and during that time I didn't feel that I needed anyone else."

She went to the refrigerator and returned with a beer for me. Her naked body seemed to glow in the light.

"I know that many of my colleagues have questioned my reasons for being with a young black private soldier, but if some of those women had the times with you as I have, they too would understand my desire. Jealousies of the mind my dear, that's what it is. Many of them have the same fantasies as I do, but are afraid to explore it and despise me for doing so. I am not concerned about their thoughts," she said proudly.

I couldn't find anything to contradict her logic, so I reminded her that her sister Joanna might encounter some difficulties in her neighbourhood, due to my visit to her home and our times together on the beaches and restaurants.

"Stan, please don't worry about her," Helen said in a stern voice, "Joanna is a big girl and can defend herself in any matter, and whatever her husband or their bigoted neighbours might put her through, she can handle it."

Helen told me of an argument she had with the General about her charges of misconduct, by other officers.

"Why did you do that?" I asked her.

"Because," she said. "I have found out that many of them are involved in a drug smuggling ring to England."

"Are you sure?" I asked. "I mean positively sure that this is true?"

I wanted to assure my mind that she was aware of the implications.

"Certainly, I am sure," she said. "I have been talking to some of the RASC officers who had been up to Northern Malaya and some of the air force boys here in Singapore. They told me about the shipments. Some even brag about not being caught for their deeds. I have a list of army, navy and air force personnel names and I intend on exposing them."

I gave thought to what she was embarking on and realized that she could be seriously hurt, if her plan failed.

"Helen," I said. "Although you are an officer, you could be treated badly for bringing charges against the officers corps. They could make your life miserable for doing so."

She assured me that she was cognisant of her litigations and the consequences thereof and felt justified in carrying out her charges.

For the next two months nothing special happened militarily. Most of my times were spent with Helen, walking the parks or the shops in the beautifully clean downtown Singapore and some times with my friends. Although the platoon and I had exchanged thoughts on Mark's questionable actions, we agreed to maintain a closer watch on him only and not to discuss it with anybody else. We decided to question only the thing deemed not in the best interest of ourselves. I was keeping notes of all discussions with him and of records we had handed over to him. I refrained from discussing the matter with Helen, for some reason, although she had indicated her concern for some of Mark's attitudes.

She talked about my friends who had been injured and killed and warned me of the dangers of Mark's personal agenda.

"Maybe she was reporting to Mark. How does she know so much

about our movements? And how did he know about her sister in Australia?" I asked Patrick.

I was getting a little suspicious of Helen also.

"That information might be in her records and Mark might have seen it and told you to upset your relationship with her," he said.

"Maybe so," I said. "Yet I still enjoy being with her. Maybe someday I will ask her."

Patrick gave thought to my suggestion.

"Maybe you should," he said, "but think it out carefully first. She might be totally innocent of any wrong doings."

"Here is another thing," I said, "for all these years, Catharine had never asked me anything about any of you Irish boys either, I mean personal things. Yet Mark had told her of our movements also."

Paddy waved for us to walk.

"Maybe so," he said. "I think Mark is trying to discredit you with those ladies. He wants you to get upset and walk away from them. But I am ceratin they both love and respect you and won't deceive you. If I were you, I wouldn't ask of them any embarrassing questions. Stan, as far as I am concerned, none of those women are suspects in deceiving you."

I faced him as I spoke.

"Hey! You might be right, he is trying hard but without success eh?"

I was happy to hear my friend's assurance that these women were not deceiving me. I couldn't understand though why I wasn't getting any letters from Catharine. Mark kept telling me that she had not written to him either. I missed her lovely letters and wondered if mine were getting to her.

The "Pythons or Nig-Nogs," frequently met to discuss the problems surrounding us. We spent an enormous amount of time talking about the scenarios and circumstances that caused the death of our friends. We devised plans to counteract any elimination plan or conspiracy by Mark or other officers and agreed to take it to the top whenever we gathered enough evidence of our suspicions.

At one of my head time evenings I wrote the names of the women I knew and to choose one that I felt I would marry and why.

"Teresa is Irish, very beautiful and my age. She's Patrick's sister. I am certain that she is madly in love with me and I love her too. Our sex life would probably be more than just good and I have the confidence that she would be a fantastic mother, but marrying her would mean living in Ireland and getting involved with their politics.

As a Black man, I don't know how the masses would react to me and vice versa, and if we choose to live in England, which I doubt, we might still encounter the same problems as a mixed couple, and worst if they find out she is Irish. Plus if Patrick and his friends really lived up to their threats, I might become a hindrance to their political movement, so it might be best not to."

"Fiona:- Born January 7th 1942, is a very good looking olive coloured skin and dark haired woman. Fiona is also proportionately built and wore the type of clothes that complimented her body. Because of her mixed heritage, Scottish/Barbadian and is the same age, she and I found comfort in talking to each other about many private things in our lives. I admire her pretty greyish brown eyes. She is lovely sexually and wouldn't care what others think of us. I am confident that she loves me. She is a hard working woman who loves children and would be a great mother. I am sure we could make a good life for ourselves. But I've lost her. I haven't got a clue where to find her now."

"Faye:- Is in England with whomever she wants at this time. She has been in love with me for all my life, although her parents hates me and the fact that she is a flirt. She's a very physically beautiful black woman of my age, likes sex and parties, but I would certainly marry her. These points might be the only factors in our marriage relationship, which might also be filled with anguish, because of her demanding attitude.

Our life together might have some adversities also, because of her parents. They might be our hindrance to a decent life. At this moment, she might even have my child and I don't know it. I haven't received any letters from her over a year now. I cannot be certain of Faye either, but

I must remain optimistic that she still cares for me."

"Helen:- Is older. At forty two, she is twenty two years my senior. Helen is a doctor with a major's commission in the army, who I met in Bordon and have enjoyed a strong companionship with ever since. I still cannot understand why she risked her status to have sex with me. She is a very sexy woman with long brunette hair that matches her pear-shaped face. She also loves me and has been honest in our strange relationship and has very deep concerns for my psychological and physical well-being, in all aspects of my response to military life. She is dedicated to her work and doesn't intend on being married to anyone, anytime. That is a shame, because we could be good for each other.

"I intend to die an old spinster in this army," she told me. So our relationship is purely sexual, until we become tired of each other, although she has been behaving like my wife ever since I got into Singapore."

"Catharine:- Is my first choice. She is a slender, well shaped, sexy woman at thirty eight years old. She has shoulder-length honey- blonde hair. Unlike Helen, she dresses coordinately well always in clothes that brings out her dark pigmentation and highlights her baby blue eyes. Her radiant smile seems to light up my mind whenever her full lips part to expose her perfectly aligned set of teeth. She enjoys mimicking other people's accents, mainly Jamaican.

Her qualities are purely beautiful through and through. She is well educated , a very assertive person in all aspects of her life, and never tried to dictate mine. She comes from a wealthy family and loves to flaunt it. Catharine knows what she wants in life and is not afraid to attack it face on.

I met her on the train to Aldershot and have been in love since. She is married to the commander of my company, who refuses to grant her a divorce. He might be our hindrance for the future. She might also have a child for me and I don't know it as yet. I haven't received any form of correspondence from her lately, which infuriates me to anxiety and at times, depression."

"I have already given up on Yvonne, because she had not replied to any of my letters since Aldershot. So she is off the list. This seemed to be a very depressive period for me. Imagine, it will be my twenty second birthday in two months and I am alone and depressed. Maybe Helen and I could do something special."

I have forgotten to question Patrick about Sinn Fein again, I wonder what it's about? I closed my book and headed for the NAAFI to find my friends. "Maybe a few brews will help to rejuvenate my soul," I said as I entered the door.

I was a little happier when I was sent to Hong Kong to give instructions to some of our men doing border patrol there. A very menial type of assignment, I thought. They were to seek out and prevent all drug smugglers and illegal aliens from China, entering Hong Kong. There was a "shoot to kill" order in place and the last time we were there, Dave Powell got killed. I didn't want the job, although they said it was a very important assignment. According to Mark. "They must be stopped." It struck my mind that Mark was deliberately breaking up our unit, for whatever reason. Patrick, Skinny and I spoke about this assignment.

"This will be the first time I have ever been sent to another place without any of you all," I said to them.

"Some of us will probably have to do the same sometime too," Williams said. "You watch yourself and all the others very carefully, especially now that we are certain that Ian was sent to his death."

We shook hands and promised to maintain contact, immaterial of where we might be sent.

In Hong Kong, since I didn't have to be on patrol at all times, I was given the freedom to go into town whenever I pleased, which I did often. This city is one of the most interesting I have ever been to. Although small in land area, it contains some of the most aggressive pedlars I have ever encountered. Everybody has something to sell. There were many new constructions going on, they seemed to be a high rise building at every open space available. After about two weeks there, I met a Chinese girl named Yan Sue, who attracted me. We began meeting and having dinners together. She taught me how to use chopsticks. My visits into town became more frequent for the purpose. But although Yan Sue and I enjoyed some good sex together, I was never quite comfortable or relaxed with her. She had even taken me to her parents home for dinner on Christmas day, even though it wasn't a holiday for them.

At times, I would walk around town alone aimlessly, absorbing the atmosphere, looking at some of the new high-rise that were being constructed, thinking and making notes. One evening as I was in town walking alone, I saw her. It was Fiona McDougall. I rushed up beside her and in stride.

"Well hello, you sexy little lassie," I said, mimicking a Scottish accent. She was elated and surprised to see me. She threw her arms around my neck and kissed my face nonstop. We decided to find a restaurant or something for a private quiet drink. That was a task in itself, because "quiet," doesn't exist in this hustle-bustle city of Hong Kong.

"Fancy seeing you in Hong Kong," she said. "It's a very beautiful bustling city, isn't it? Millions of people doing whatever."

We sat at an out-door cafe.

"Yes it is," I replied, "and it's more beautiful when there are beautiful people as you in it."

Fiona held on to my hand so hard, I thought my blood would stop circulating.

"Stan, seeing you here is unbelievable," she said, "I was told that you had been killed in Aden."

The tears began to run down her face.

"No sweetheart," I said, "they can't kill me. As you can see, I'm still here and very much alive. Touch my hand, see?"

"Well darling," she replied, "the good lord has brought you back to me."

She then explained the details of the incidents that took place.

"When I returned to Bordon and heard that you were posted and they wouldn't give me the postal address, I was devastated," she said.

She paused to take a drink, wipe the tears from her eyes and touched my hand again. She was making certain that it wasn't a dream. I in turn held hers tightly.

"I thought it was the end of our lives," she continued. "The army wouldn't tell me anything about you, except for the letter a few months ago, telling me that you got killed in Aden."

"I too was disappointed," I replied, "when I wrote to you in Scotland and did not receive any reply."

I leaned over the table to kiss her. She was very receptive to my touch. Fiona and I walked and talked for at least a couple of hours not realizing where we were.

She told me that she was on a seventy two hour pass.

"Stan, I'm delighted to see you again and I'm going to show you today that I really did miss you," she said.

I looked up. We were standing in front of a hotel.

"Should we go in here?" I asked.

"Most definitely," she said, "I haven't had a good screw for a long time and this seems to be that time."

I wondered about that.

"Have you really been waiting for three and a half years for a screw?" I asked doubtfully.

"No," she replied. "I have screwed with someone else in that time, but I said a "good screw," and only you can do that for me."

I was happy she wanted me, but then again women will lie about things of this nature, if it's advantageous at the time. I had no intention of disputing her. We entered the hotel and booked in. The clerk looked at us curiously and seeing that both us were in uniforms, he pretended not to care. Fiona was already naked by the time we reached the room. Her skin was the smooth pinkish brown as I knew it. She waited long enough for me to feast my eyes on her firm round breasts, then she pounced on me. We both hit the bed with me on the bottom with her tongue busy in between my lips.

"She might be telling me the truth," I thought as we sank into a very heated passionate grip of each other's body and made love immediately.

Fiona was always a very enjoyable screw and we've had some good ones in the past. Today seemed to be a beautiful reunion of that first meeting in Bordon, on the park bench. It was about two thirty in the morning when we stopped talking and fell asleep. I was awakened at about six thirty the next morning, when I felt her kissing my face again. It was a nice feeling to awaken to. I never thought I would see her again after all these years.

"I love you and I missed you," she said, "please make love to me again."

This time she kissed me hard and we made love.

"Happy belated birthday darling," she said.

"And a happy birthday to you too darling," I replied.

We both laughed, because yesterday was mine and today the seventh of January, is hers.

"I want to see you as much as possible while we are here in Hong Kong," she said. "I want you to promise me."

"I promise," I said holding up my fingers in a scout salute.

"And from here on," she continued. "I want to know where you are at all times, so that we can get together more often."

"Yes," I agreed, "but darling you know the army, nothing stands still. We could be anywhere at anytime."

"Yes, I know the army too well," she replied, "but it's for us to find a way to keep in touch and not let them stop our relationship."

We were happy to see each other and to have spent this time together. We got dressed and I headed back to the camp and she to the hospital.

Throughout the rest of my stay in Hong Kong, Fiona and I had many evenings of splendour and we talked about many things, even marriage and children. She answered my question on who told her about my demise in Aden.

"That was a very weird thing," she said. "I got this letter from an officer whose name I didn't recognize. A Captain Cameron? Not from the usual War Department, explaining that you were shot and died. Now that I think about it, the letter did not have the usual government style of presentation. Why is that so Stan?"

"Well my dear," I said, "someone wished I had died there. Unfortunately for them, I'm still here. Would you believe it happened on my twenty first birthday? That's why I hate Aden."

She hugged and kissed me again saying,

"Well darling, thank God that it didn't happen and we did spend our twenty second together."

That also got my mind working. But I could not decipher the reason somebody would send a letter of my demise to her. I decided to follow up on it later. Fiona told me that she would be posted to West Germany in about six months time, so we must maintain our communications at all cost if we ever intended on carrying out our promises. I agreed and told myself that I wouldn't loose her this time. I was again very happy to be with her and to talk of life as we used to.

"We will spend every free moment together, while here in Hong Kong my love," I promised her.

And so we did, until suddenly eight weeks later, I got my orders. I was on my way back to Singapore. The night before leaving, we sneaked off down town to the hotel which became our regular love nest and had a very nice parting party for two. Fiona cried almost all the time and wanted to screw all night.

"Stan, I don't want to loose you again, so please keep writing, I beg you," she begged.

"I will my dear," I said. "This time will be different."

On reaching Singapore again, I discovered that what was left of the platoon, was sent to Vietnam again. I rushed over to Mark's office to enquire the reason and he explained that the General felt that our unit had to be dismantled for reasons known only to himself.

"Mark," I said angrily, "I know that you're lying to me. You are the one who did put us together and it's you who is killing us off," I said angrily. "Maybe we were getting to understand your plots and gamesmanship too well. Is that it? We know too much? So you decided to kill us off, eh?" I shouted.

He sat there staring at me without saying a word. I could see the redness coming in on his fat face. When he finally reached the point of anger, he sprung out of his chair. I thought he was going to attack me, so I slipped my razor into my hand and in a flash it was under his neck. He stopped in his tracks in a hurry with a changed thought.

"Stan," he said in a sorrowful tone, "I'm not hiding anything from you and I am not trying to kill you or any of the rest of those Irish bastards. I'm only obeying and carrying out orders."

"Then why can't you tell me what's the plot. What's their game?" I said.

He stared and I could sense that he would have liked to beat me to a pulp, but for the razor under his neck. I decided to take my leave of him and as I walked towards the door I spoke over my shoulder.

"When I return to England, I'd better find Catharine in good health. If not, I will hunt you down and kill you and that is a promise."

I left his office to seek solitude and comfort in sweet horny Helen, but she wasn't in her office. I left the camp and took a solo walk down town. She found me sitting on a park bench in the down town area and sat beside me.

"Oh there you are," she said. "I came back to the hospital and was told that you came and left. What's the matter love?" she asked in that cheery sing song tone of voice.

"Well Sweetheart," I replied, "it's a long story, but... I think that someone somewhere is trying to kill off the members of my platoon, systematically."

She was shocked to hear this and seeing that I was visibly upset, she placed her arm around my shoulder.

"Come, come now," she said, "why do you say that?"

"All of my friends have been sent to places with new people and every time that happens, somebody gets hurt," I said. "And I don't think they were acts of war either."

"That's understandable," she said. "You all have been together since Aldershot, is it not?" she asked.

"Yes, as a matter of fact," I replied.

She was in deep thought as she said,

"I wonder if Mark Harrison has anything to do with it? He has been very protective and secretive about all of you, ever since you all got here."

"I don't know," I said, "he told me that he has nothing to do with it, but I still have my doubts about him."

She was thinking and I did not want to disrupt her train of thought, so I kept silent. Finally she spoke.

"Sometimes during the officers monthly meetings, he would be questioned about you lot and he would get angry at the person, stating that the Company was not up for questioning by anybody and that he was responsible only to the General. And whomever didn't like it, must see the General for their answers."

She paused again.

"Maybe someday I will question him," she said. "Whenever I gather enough evidence."

"Well isn't that dangerous? What if you can't prove your charges?" I asked.

"Then I will be penalized according to the rules," she replied.

"Tell me Helen, did you ever tell Mark about your sister in Brisbane?" I asked.

"No, not that I can recall," she replied. "Why?"

"Well, he knew about her," I said. "He told me that he had asked you to set me up with her, to keep me from mingling with the natives there."

"That bastard!" she exclaimed. "He must have listened in on my phone call to her. I'm going to report him to the General first thing tomorrow morning," she said angrily.

Helen and I went home still discussing Marks attitude as an officer and a person.

"Stan," she said, "if that man is proven to have neglected his commitments to his men, I will personally make a report to the officers corps at Sandhurst about him," she said.

"Thank you my love," I said, "but no you won't. I don't think you should jeopardize yourself for my cause. Remember he is a Military Intelligence Officer and they will protect him over you."

She nodded her head in acknowledgement, but I could see the cogs working in her head.

"So he is my love," she replied, "but there's always different angles to attack from, understand? And as an officer, I am aware of the rules of bringing charges against another officer too."

"No my darling, don't be hasty. Get the facts first then bring your charges, okay?" I said.

"Okay, I will," she replied.

Although she agreed, I could feel the insistence in her. I was now comfortable in her arms and making love, which erased most of the disturbing thoughts, for a while.

"Thank you Helen, for being here for me," I whispered in my mind.

I wasn't surprised, when I got orders to join up with another regiment a few weeks later, for an operational jump in North Borneo. I found it very strange that the instructions in the briefing were so vague. I was not given the specifications like we were used to and no particular job. I decided only to protect myself on this mission.

The morning prior to the operation, I saw Patrick coming towards me.

"Hey arse hole!" I greeted him.

He had a sad look in his eyes as we shook hands.

"How the hell are you? Where are the boys?" I asked.

"My friend," he began, "it's nice to see you again. Taffy is dead, stepped on a mine in Nam. Both Tom and Rod got injured from that blast also, although not bad,. I was told Derrick was badly wounded in Aden also."

"Oh my God!" I exclaimed. "What's happening to us?"

We found a quiet area to talk and we spoke of many things, from the first day we met in Aldershot to the last dead friend sent back to England.

"Can you remember the days when there were thirteen of us and we protected each other?" he said.

I replied to him with a nod and he continued.

"There were a loving kinship amongst us then. It's not there anymore. We are fragmented as a unit at this point in time."

"Paddy my boy," I said, "I'm glad that you will be on this mission also. You and I are the only two from the old army, who will be there."

"Mmmmm," he replied. "I was surprised when they informed me that I was returning to Singapore to join up with another regiment. And seeing you is a bonus. We better watch out for each other on this operation."

"We certainly will have to," I said, "there is no one else here."

I felt a little depressed at this displacement of our friends. I sat listening to Patrick talked about going back to Ireland to begin his work with the IRA. I felt this might be the ideal time to ask, so I said.

"You know something Paddy?" I said. "When you all were getting those tattoos, I should have got mine done too."

He smiled for the first time.

"No my friend," he said. "I wouldn't want to see you be subjected to any unwarranted pressures due to it. And secondly it's an Irish problem. People of your calibre would be totally destroyed without proper justification."

I felt relieved to know that my friend had the same confidence and respect for me as always. We shook hands in our usual manner and promised to watch out for each other on this upcoming operation, in Borneo. We parted company so as to get prepared.

I walked towards the stores to begin gathering my equipment, my mind surveyed all the things that had been going on in my life. The words of Sergeant-Major Wickham rang in my head. "Protect yourself at all cost my boy, don't let anyone take advantage of you. Protect your arse."

"Sure I will Sir," I replied silently. "Not even Mark Harrison will be able to penetrate my armour." I smiled at the thought and continued on my way. I got out my note book and wrote:-

"This business of killing people in the name of democracy is now getting to me, especially people who have not offended me. I am deeply concerned for myself and what my behaviour will be back in civilian life. But according to them we will live a normal existence once we leave this. I will wait to see. I am glad Patrick will be there too."

I put it back into my pocket and continued to collect my equipment.

Chapter Nine

" MY INJURY."

When I woke up, I found myself hanging in space, dangling by the straps of my chute in a tree. I looked down to see I was only about ten feet from the ground. We were taught ways to avoid these kinds of dilemma and how to counteract if it ever happened. Firstly, I released my kit allowing it to fall, then I cut through my harness and fell to the ground. Only to find that I was having difficulty in standing. I could feel a numb tingling pain in my leg and knee area.

"Something had happened," I thought.

I quickly cut through my trousers to inspect the magnitude of the injury. It was badly swollen and discoloured. Fearing that it was broken, I took my scarf and tied it very tightly around the knee. I found a branch and modified it into a crutch, then I set-out to find my new company.

"I'm a lost sheep," I said, "tweet, tweet. Nig 13 Green loose."

I kept repeating the phrase so that others would recognize and don't shoot me accidentally. I must have taken the right direction for the company, because within a half hours walk, or should I say hobble, I came face to face with Patrick. He realized that I was missing and came out to find me, as we have done in the past. He rushed to my assistance.

"What happened nig?" He enquired anxiously.

"It's the knee old man, I think it's broken or something," I said."

Although I was laughing, he knew I was in pain, so he opened my pack and gave me a pain killer pill.

"My friend, it hurts like a bastard," I said. "Find me a medic please."

He helped me to sit down and I leaned back against a tree. Quickly he took out three magazines along with a bandolier of ammo and three grenades and placed them beside me.

"You keep alive now," he said. "I don't want to lose you now, we have already lost nine friends, okay?" He was playing nurse maid. "You stay right here and shoot anything that moves, unless you hear my signal."

He rushed off in a direction, which according to my compass was due north.

I laid or sat for some long time in pain, then I heard a rustling sound in the bushes. Immediately I cocked my SMG and laid flat to the ground. I saw the eyes looking in my direction from within the bushes. A few moments went by then it came towards me. I fired a bust and saw the body fall. I waited and listened for other sounds but nothing came. An hour or two went by, although I could not tell how long I waited, then the sound of Patrick's voice came, it was a welcoming sound.

"It's a good thing we have these codes," he said to one of the medics, pointing to the body of the baboon laying there. "See he shoots everything."

They did not hesitate to get me on the stretcher and we were on our way to the camp area. As soon as we arrived in the area, the Doctor went to work. First he gave me an injection in my arm, then cut off the entire leg of my trousers. He cleaned the knee with something then an injection in it. I can honestly say I did not feel any pain after. I was numb and dazed, but conscious enough to see him cut through my flesh.

I watched the blood and fluid gushing from my body part but didn't care as long as the pain went away. I watched him take some of my inner flesh with tools I have never seen before. I remembered the stories of count Dracula who loved blood.

"Or is he a Frankenstein type?" I thought.

I think it must have taken a couple of hours for that knee operation in the open field, but I was in no shape to question him.

During all of this, Patrick was sitting beside my shoulder quiet as a lamb. I could see them wrapping the bandages on it, then I fell to sleep. I heard sounds as I slowly regained consciousness. I opened my eyes to see the face of my friend Doctor-Major Helen Butterworth looking down on me.

"Come on sleepy head wakey, wakey; it's time for work," she said jokingly.

"Go away," I said. "I need to sleep some more."

My mind shouted without moving my lips. I started to search around the room for my weapon as the focus of my eyes returned. Then I realized that I was in the hospital. I scanned the surrounding for any recognizable objects and found my leg hanging from the ceiling in a cast.

"What happened? What did they do to me?" I asked.

"It's your brains and knee," she joked, "the rest of your body is fine darling."

"How did I....?" I began, but she interrupted by saying,

"It will be fine in a few weeks time," she patted the cast. "Just relax and no sex, okay? I'll be back to see you later this evening." She winked at me teasingly then at almost a run, she left the room.

I laid there for what seemed like a half hour, then from the corner of my eyes I saw him. He was sitting on the floor in the lotus. Patrick's face looked sad and drawn. I sensed that he was angry about something.

"Hey you Irish git," I said, "why didn't you make some sound, so that I would know that you're there?"

He got up and came over to the bed.

"I only wanted to prove that I could stay in someone's room quietly, without them knowing that I'm there," he replied.

"Bull shit," I said, "you were afraid that I might die and you wouldn't have anybody to talk to. Well not on your Nelly friend, I plan to be around for a long time to come. I have some unfinished business to attend to."

He sat closer to me on the bed and whispered,

"On that jump, Lieutenant Weyburton checked your pack, didn't he? Well I think he must have done something to it, because your chute didn't look right going down."

He paused took out two cigarettes and lit them, he placed one in my mouth. I took a drag and it tasted awful.

"It's the medication," I thought, as he continued to speak.

"I'm very curious to find out who checked the packs of Jack and Tom and how Ian got it in Nam. I also heard that Bob is seriously injured in that second visit to Viet-Nam also."

I was quiet in thought.

"Stan," he said, "we are slowly losing the entire platoon, one at a time, and they all look like accidents. Yet somehow I keep thinking that, that man is responsible."

By the time he was through analysing Marks apparent involvement in our friends mishaps, I was convinced that I was supposed to be the next victim. We talked for about an hour, then a nurse came and told him to leave as she was there to gave me a bed bath and some medication.

He reluctantly obeyed her. He took my upper arm in a tight grip and promised to be back the next day. I fell asleep shortly after the bath.

The attention I received from everyone in that hospital for the first ten days, was unquestionably the best. I think Helen made sure that all the nurses knew who I was, and her interest in me. I got the best of everything and she came every day to do the personal body rubs. She was protecting and caring for her property. But every time I tried to discuss my suspicions of Mark with her, she would put her finger over my lips for silence.

The cast was taken off after the ten days, to begin five weeks of therapy. At first I wished the doctors had amputated the damn thing when they had the chance. I had never felt so much pain in all my life. It was hell. When the cast was on, it wasn't so bad, but without that support, it was agony. I could feel the pain throughout my entire body.

That first day I had Patrick on one side and Helen on the other, holding me under my arm pits trying to guide me around the room.

"Come on darling," she said, "you have to try to walk, otherwise you will have a stiff leg forever." She kept on prompting and encouraging me to walk.

"Oh my God," I mourned, "please get me back to the fucking bed," I shouted repeatedly. But I might as well be talking to the wall, because neither of them obeyed.

After about fifteen minutes of that torture, I was laid back on the bed.

"Ooooh," I groaned.

"Will you stop the blasted groaning!" said the Irishman. "You sound like a fucking old woman. Be glad that you're alive, and I will be back every day for the exercise," he promised.

"Oh my god Helen," I begged. "Do I have to have him here?" I asked.

"Yes you do and he will also tell me if you start touching any of the nurses too, right Patrick?" she replied unsympathetically.

She bent to kiss me and left the room.

About the fourth week, Mark came to see me for the first time and he was being regimental and official.

"Corporal Martin," he said. "I have arranged a posting for you to Germany after your recovery. You have a choice of going to Dortmund or Wuppertal."

He never once looked me directly in my eyes or to enquire of my injury.

"You are a cold hearted bastard," I said through clinched teeth. "It's not surprising that Catharine had to find someone else to fuck with." I was now getting very angry. "And you have the audacity to come into my room to tell me this shit? You don't give a hoot how I feel. Your only interest is to have me out of here and that's fine by me."

I think the anger was coming out good from the look on his face.

"Look sir," I continued. "One of these lovely days I am going to kill you and I will make it very painful for you. And that is a promise."

I knew he understood that I meant it. He had trained us in the art of killing and helped to develop the madness within me, so I am positive that he knew I would do it. He did not reply. He got up from the chair patted my head and left the room.

"Whatever happened to Catharine and the baby?" I shouted after him. There was no reply only a wave and he was gone. I laid there with my eyes closed wishing to be well again soon to carry-out my threat on Mark Harrison, or maybe going to England to find Catharine.

My moment of solitude was interrupted when I felt a hand on my face. I opened my eyes to see Helen standing over me. She knew I was crying.

"I say old chap," she mimicked,"I think you need something to cheer you up, what you need is a good back rub."

She turned and locked the door and told me to remove all my clothing, although there weren't much. I obeyed her orders and she began to massage my entire body.

"You know something Stan?" she said, "in Bordon I never thought I would feel this way for you, as I do now. It's times like this, that I give thought of spending the rest of my life with you," she stated.

"Then why don't you?" I asked.

"No darling, I don't ever want to be married. It might defeat my purpose on earth," she said. "And furthermore, we might not have the same feeling for each other in later years. Please believe me, our pleasant memories will be most valuable to us later in life."

She was telling me something of her inner feelings, although we had discussed this same topic on many occasions. The feel of her soft hand on my body caused a stir in my mind. I rolled over on my back to see Helen in only her panties. She didn't need any coaxing to get into the bed with me. We made love there for the first time since my injury.

"Helen," I said. "I think you are afraid to have someone care for you."

She looked at me for a while.

"I thought you of all persons would understand my reason for not wanting to," she said as she retrieved her panty, "you could do much better with Catharine, she really loves and needs you."

"How did you know about Catharine?" I asked.

She smiled as she brushed my hair.

"You must always be your best, and look good sweetheart," she replied avoiding my question.

"Forget about my hair," I shouted pushing away her hand. "How did you know about her?"

"Mark told me," she said, "and also about the baby boy she had. He also told me about Fiona. We met you know?"

She stopped talking instantly. I could see the formation of a tear in her eyes.

"That's all? What else did he say?" I demanded.

"Nothing," she replied. "Nothing bad anyway. He was trying to get me to do something and when he was unsuccessful, he decided to tell me about you and the other women, in hope of turning me off you. But as you can see it did not work."

I became more curious.

"What did he want?" I prompted her.

"Corporal there are some things an officer will never tell against another officer, even if you know that he is breaking military law. But I will deal with him through the proper channels, okay?"

I realized that Helen wasn't about to talk any more and I felt she had shown me her inner most feelings. We got cleaned up and were sitting on the bed talking, when the knock on the door reminded us that it was still locked. Patrick came in and told her that he was taking me down to tea. He knew what was going on, but he knew that as soon as I could walk, she would want sex.

"Hello Helen," he said, "I'm here to take this bloke down for tea. Is that alright?"

"Sure it is Patrick old boy," she replied. "He will need the exercise."

"Come on Nig," he said, "you're going to walk down for tea and some talk."

The two of them guided me down the stairs, then she left us alone. At tea, I felt I should talk about Catharine.

"Paddy," I said, "if anything should happen to me, please find Catharine and help her for me, okay?"

"I already told you that I would," he replied.

I spoke at length and even gave him her parent's address and a detailed drawing of the house underground passage. He put it into his pocket and promised to do my wishes if need be. Then we talked about Mark.

"Nig, I want you to understand something. If I should survive this period out here, I intend on returning to my homeland for the purpose of liberating it from the British Protestants. It's my duty to assist in the political changes that are required there."

I decided to remain silent, so that he would continue to talk, and so he did.

"I'm going home to ensure that the IRA will escalate its actions against the mainland of England, with proper military equipment and strategy. I will employ ex- Irish service men who are willing to die for the cause, both in Ireland and England. I know that you and some of the rest would be willing to help us, but it's an Irish problem and only the Irish can resolve it. It wouldn't be the same, if some of my friends got involved."

"So, are you saying that our friendship will be dissolved after service is ended?" I asked in a sombre tone.

He thought for a moment, then with a trickle of tears in his eyes replied.

"My friend, it would be much safer for you not to have any knowledge of my activity at that time. The British government would persecute you unfairly and I couldn't bear to see you in that position."

I understood quite well what he was indicating and felt delighted that my friend was protecting me.

"Paddy old boy," I said, "I completely understand and wish you all the luck in every way. I would have liked for our friendship to be forever, but...se la vie old chap."

We shook hands.

"Friends?" I asked.

"Forever," he replied.

The sex between Helen and I got better as the weeks rolled by and I became stronger and more independent of the hospital and the drugs. Every day Patrick came to either get me walking or for tea or some times bringing books to read. I could see he was getting happier as I improved. Helen was the only person he would allow to be alone with me. We talked about him and Greta Paisley and his promise to marry her.

At times he would read her letters to me. Greta always wrote jokes to cheer him up. I, on the other hand was not getting any kind of correspondence from anyone.

Twelve weeks had gone by and the knee had improved. I was much better now although I was still hobbling along. One afternoon I went to Mark's office to confront him about my posting to Germany, Catharine and my mail. But before I could open my mouth, he told me that a phone call was in the works in five minutes. I waited and sure enough it was Catharine on the line. Our conversation was rather short because the reception was bad, but I was happy to have spoken to her.

He sat there with that smirk on his face, happy that he had arranged it, there was no reason for an argument after that, so I left his office.

"There are still some questions that I need answers to, to be asked but they can wait," I said silently.

Another four weeks went by then I got my travel papers to Germany. That evening I went to show them to Helen. She cried all night, even throughout our love making time.

"Darling," she said, "I will try to get a posting there to be with you," she promised and we talked about love ending.

The next morning I was almost late for the plane because of her. Patrick met me at the airport and again we promised to keep corresponding.

"If you ever visit Ireland again," he said smiling, "go to see my parents, okay?" I knew what he meant, so we hugged each other.

"Friends?" he asked.

"Friends forever," I replied and strolled off to the plane.

I looked from the window to see he had his arms around Helen as we taxied away. I sat there with my eyes closed and felt the plane pick up speed and we were airborne. My thoughts ran back to the last four years and thirteen days in the Far East. I reached into my bag for my notebook. On the cover was the number four. I opened it and wrote:-
Jack O'Leary:-Dead. Cecil Brown:-Dead. Taffy Llewellyn:-Dead. Peter Baron:-Dead. Dave Powell:-Dead. Charley Green:-Injured. Ian Mulligan:-Dead; Rod Langley:-Injured. Tom Matterson:-Injured. Bob Muldoon:-Injured. Anthony Williams:-Disappeared. Patrick O'Reiley:-Healthy; Stan Martin:-Injured.

"I will miss you all my friends. Add Helen to book when writing. This is going to be a long flight, so I will try to get some sleep," I whispered.

It was late night when we reached Gibraltar. I don't know how long was the flight and I didn't care, my focus was now on a different life in Germany. I promised myself to return to England soon to find Catharine and to see the baby. I wanted to see my friends George, Ruddux, Alpine, Faye and my cousins Lorna, Barbie and Cherry again. It's been four years since they last saw me. I already knew that my brother Frank had left for Canada.

The Captain in Gibraltar told me that I would be riding the train, rather than flying to Germany, which meant a few days of good European scenery and one does meet people on the trains too. I could feel myself starting to relax a little. From what I saw in the previous little time in Germany, I was looking forward to it again. The first time I was in Wuppertal for two weeks and Dortmund for three. But this time I was going to Dortmund permanently. I loved that city and had been to the Westfallen Halle for a concert and toured the Bochum brewery. I had met some nice people there last time and hoped to do so again. The army promised that I would be getting some holidays in England as soon as it could be arranged and that delighted me.

"What a great thought," I replied to the officer, "a train to Dortmund."

At any rate, I did not care about anything else, I was on my way home, slowly. The train ride was very interesting and scenic, because it had to pass through Spain and the city of Madrid. The mountain ranges in that country were very beautiful and so was that of southern France.

On reaching Paris, I decided to alight and spend a few hours there, then catch the next Europa to Dortmund. As I got off the train, I realized that I was breaking another military law, but what did I care now.

"When I got there it would be time enough," I thought. "Anyway, soon I'll be a civilian again and for them imprisoning me would not be in their best interest at that time."

I walked the streets of Paris aimlessly for two whole days refreshing my mind and met some interesting people along the way. I wondered along the Champs Elysees and tried to speak to almost everyone I met with the few phrases of French I learnt in school. Many of them just laughed at me and some replied in languages I didn't understand. But I was having fun clearing my mind.

I was offered sex by a couple of nice looking women on different occasions, but for some reason I had no interest.

"You're getting old my friend," I said to myself, "you refusing pussy?"

I walked and talked to myself and even laughed at my own jokes. I am sure some of the people passing probably thought I was crazy, but to me it was therapy. I sat at the foot of the Eiffel tower to eat my lunch, like many others were doing.

"I think I will save it for one of the ladies in England," I thought.

I had a lot of time to think, and to refresh my mind and to evaluate the things that Patrick and I had talked about. I stayed awake doing nothing for two whole days in beautiful Paris and enjoyed every minute of the solitude it offered. So leaving was a little sorrowful, but my life still belonged to the army, for now.

The train sped along quite nicely until it reached near Luxembourg. I was laying back with my eyes closed when I felt a hand on my forehead. I looked up to see the lovely lassie Fiona standing over me.

"Hello sweetheart!" I exclaimed. "What are you doing here?" I was shocked to see her.

She stood there with her hand still on my head without saying anything.

"What the hell are you doing in France?" I asked again. "I see you did get the posting to Germany, eventually."

Fiona sat down beside me then took a military letter from her bag, opened it and read out loud.

"Corporal McDougall, Fiona T. This is to inform you that your boyfriend and or associate Corporal Martin, W.L. Was killed during an operation in North Borneo and his body has been returned to England.

This notice is by his request that you be notified of his death."

It was signed by my only commanding officer, Mark Harrison.

"So when I received this letter," she said, "I immediately requested the posting to Germany and two months ago I arrived at B.M.H. Iserlohn. I was given a seven day pass to France and are now returning today. But when I saw the person looking like you getting on this train, I decided to search for you to be certain and here you are, what luck."

She began to cry and I again had to comfort her.

"This is the second time I have been told of your death," she said between sobs. "I get the distinct feeling that someone is definitely trying to keep us apart."

"Or is trying to create a scenario so that whenever my death is nigh, it will be viewed without any suspicion." I said in a positive tone, to ensure her that I knew somebody is really trying to do me in. But in my mind I told myself that I would have to defend myself at all cost.

Fiona and I rode the train to Germany talking about the boys and I had to tell her about each of their accidents.

It was getting late in the afternoon and tiredness was now setting in. We both laid on the seats and slept until we reached Essen. The two other passengers, who had joined us in the same car in Koln, had left the train while we were asleep. She told me that she will not get another pass for sometime to come, so we should make love there on the train, which we did all the way to Dortmund. It was great. I remembered the time with Catharine on the train to Aldershot, only now I am with Fiona.

I felt happy that I didn't accept the offers of those French girls as we both got off the train in Dortmund. She was picked up by a driver for the Iserlohn military hospital and I to the Twenty First Company RASC camp.

The driver, was a fellow I had met in Bordon, Aldershot and Yeovil, Somerset. We spoke about many things and he enlightened me on everything in that camp and the do's and don'ts of the Sergeant-Major. I went to the billets, had a shower and to the NAAFI for a few beers. As I was crossing the parade square, as a short cut to the NAFFI centre, I heard a voice behind me shouted.

"Soldier, halt!"

I obeyed the command and stopped short in my tracks. The person came in front of me and shouted in my eyes.

"This is a parade square and you are treading on holy grounds and....."

His eyes popped wide open, then he exclaimed.

"Oh my god! Corporal Martin you are here? I heard that you were coming to my camp for a while, but I was expecting you next week!" Wickham shouted ecstatically as he grabbed my hand and almost pumped it out of joint. I stood there smiling just happy to see him. Then I said in a soft tone of voice.

"Sergeant-Major Wickham, you old goat. I am delighted to be in your camp again and I intend on causing you a lot of problems while I'm here."

"I bet you will," he replied. "I bet you will. Go have some nosh and see me in the morning at eight thirty sharp."

He walked away, paused a little while, then shouted back at me.

"No, make that ten thirty sharp. You need some sleep and don't walk across my parade square again, the boys will think I've gone soft."

He shook my hand again then about turned and was gone in a flash.

The next day was very interesting, because Tashie had me in the office talking for two and a half hours. He told me his story since Aldershot to Dortmund and I gave him mine throughout the Far and Middle East. We went for dinner and talked some more.

"Whatever happened to the boys? Patrick O'Reilley, Jack O'Leary, Ian Mulligan and Thomas Matterson?" he asked.

"Well Sir," I began. Ian was killed in Viet-Nam, Jack got seriously injured in North Borneo and later died, Tom was slightly injured in Nam and Patrick was doing well when I saw him in Singapore a few days ago."

Tashie had a very solemn look in his eyes.

"And the others?" he asked.

"Cecil Brown was killed in Borneo, you didn't know him; at the same time Jack and Charley Green got injured. Rod Langley and Bob Muldoon were slightly injured in Nam also. I don't know where they are posted now. The others who had joined us in Yorkshire. Dave Powell got it in Cyprus, Peter Baron in Hong Kong and Bill Llewellyn killed in Viet-Nam....."

"And now you in Borneo?" he asked.

"Yes sir," I replied.

He sat looking at me sadly. I could see the tears in his eyes.

"Tashie, some of these accidents weren't accidents," I said. "I believe they were plotted by Mark Harrison. In my opinion we knew too much and I felt he wanted to silence us."

Tashie sat there looking very intently into my eyes.

"What could he derive from killing or injuring you all? He asked. "You boys were his pride and joy and all trained by him for specific duties, whatever that was," he said.

"I don't really know why either, but I think we must have seen or handled some documents of importance during that time and he became afraid that we might divulge their contents, or something. But all the evidence points to him."

I could see the shock on Tashie's face. His mouth was now hanging open.

"We were loyal in our duties, nobody ever hid or botched up any assignments that we were on. But I'm convinced that there is something Mark thought we knew about and he became nervous and wanted to hurt us for it. This might even involve some of the other personnal."

We completed dinner and walked back to his office and talked some more.

"Martin," he said, "there had been some accusation lodged by an officer named Helen Butterworth, requesting a military investigation into army personnel moving drugs coming out of China, through Hong Kong, to England. Maybe he is mixed up with that," Tashie said in a contemplative tone.

"Sir," I replied. "I don't have any knowledge of that, but you could be right. I hope someday I will get even with that bastard for some of the things he has done to me."

Tashie, for some reason, decided to change the subject and we spoke about his family instead. That afternoon I was taken to Colonel Bailey's office. Bailey and I had met in Yorkshire during training. I noticed that three other officers were sitting there as Bailey introduced me with some respect in his voice.

"Gentlemen," he said. "This is Corporal Martin of the 106 para regiment. He's here awaiting demobilisation. I am hoping that he will accept my offer to conduct the special instructional training sessions of those selected personnal of our regiment. I don't want anyone or anything to disrupt his stay in our camp. All matters relating to his movement must be kept quiet. Please let this be a warning to each and everyone. Don't get into a fight with him, you'll get the opportunity to understand why later. There will be more as soon as he is rested and ready."

It was the first time I ever heard that I was attached to the 106 para regiment. They all got up and shook hands with me, then left the room. Bailey closed the door behind them and returned to his desk once again.

"Welcome, Corporal Martin," he repeated. "It's so nice to see you again. I have heard so many good things about you from Mark Harrison. He had you sent here to assist with some special training of our troops, before you return to England. Sergeant-Major Wickham, will see that you get everything you desire to carry out this special programme and for you to have a comfortable time here with us."

I asked Wickham to explain what he wished to implement for his men and he told me that some of the techniques that we used in the Far East, is what he really needed.

"Because," he said, "whenever some of the well-trained men as yourself, who have served in the areas as you did, leave the army, the practical first hand knowledge leaves with them. So I would like to utilize you to hand over some before that time comes."

Although I was delighted and proud to be chosen and to be near Tashie again, I wasn't particularly interested to do that kind of training.

"But sir," I said, "you could always send them to Farnham or better yet get Mark Harrison to come here. He's the one with the knowledge," I emphasized.

"Yes, I know that too," said Tashie, "but you're available and free." He laughed and continued. "And furthermore, it will give me the chance to see and interact with you again. Remember how we use to box in Aldershot?"

We laughed like old friends do.

I wasn't suspicious of Tashie, because he has always been a gentleman to me. As a matter of fact, I have only him to thank for turning my life around. But Bailey? I have never trusted him.

"I will have to deal with him differently," I thought.

"Sir," I said, "what about some holidays in England?" I asked.

"I will leave that up to you and Sergeant-Major Wickham to arrange," said Bailey. "Right Sergeant-Major?"

"Yes sir," replied Tashie, "as soon as he's ready."

We all exchanged some more pleasantries and we left Bailey's office to Tahsie's again.

As I walked to the billets, I gave thought to the fact that Mark

Harrison was still involved in my life and wondered if he was still trying to kill me. I wondered if Patrick was right about him.

"Maybe he is still mad with me for fucking his wife, even though she didn't want to be with him.

"Maybe I will go to England to see her," I said.

I realized that I was talking aloud and looked around to see if anybody was hearing me, fortunately there weren't. I took my jacket off and laid on the bed, but my solitude was interrupted almost at once by Desmond Walton.

"Hey Corporal Martin," he said, "what would you like to do this evening? I have a staff car at my disposal."

I laid there without answering. I really didn't want any visitors at this time, but if I could reach Iserlohn, I might be able to see Fiona. Before I could agree to his proposal, another bloke whom I had met in Aldershot, walked in.

"Hello Freddie," I said, sitting up in bed.

Fred Parks is a Jamaican who grew up in Manchester and we had many things to talk about.

"What the hell are you doing in this place?" I asked him.

"Stan my boy," he replied, "there's not a better place to be."

The three of us sat and talked for a long time about everything we did in Bordon and Aldershot except the Far East. They never asked and I didn't say. It was late when they left and I went to sleep.

For the next few days I was busy setting up the course with assistance from a lot of people. Wickham and Bailey did everything to make me feel at home. I was beginning to like the camp and the people and things progressed rapidly. And then the first day got on the way. There were fifty or more squadies in the programme. Major Bailey and his entourage of officers was present, including Tashie Wickham. The four officers who were in the programme, were told explicitly that my orders were to be obeyed and unquestioned. I felt good. I put them through a short rugged first day, I could see that many weren't up to par physically, so at the end, I announced that a physical training extension will be added to bring some up to standard.

"I know that some of you might be asking why I am here ordering you around," I said in a firm tone of voice. "Well the answer is I am damn good at this. The first fiver is at six thirty tomorrow morning. Thank you and have a very good evening. Dismiss."

I watched as they all came to attention then ran off to their respective quarters.

Sergeant-Major Wickham stood there waiting for me.

"Mr Martin," he said in that rolling Scottish twang of his. "I wish I was younger and my heart could take it. I would love to be in this programme with you."

I smiled to remember the times we boxed and ran together in Aldershot. We both walked and talked like we used to do back then.

"Stan, I don't want to pry," he said, "but is there some bad blood between Mark and the rest of you fellows? I mean those Irish boys?"

He was serious and I knew he meant good.

"Yes sir," I replied. "Some of them believed that Mark was setting them up for a kill. We were sent into areas that we could've been killed, but maybe we were too well trained to let it happen."

He was quiet for some time. I could hear the marbles rattling around in his head.

"Remember to get me a good PT. NCO by tomorrow," I said.

"Okay," he replied nonchalantly. " I would like for you to come to my house for tea this evening. I have a request that I want my family to hear." He paused as we reached his car. "Have Parks drive you over, okay? The children are anxious to see you."

I nodded my head and left.

The evening with Tashie's family was nice. Mary and the girls showed me how much they missed me in those few years. We laughed and talked throughout tea until we retired to the livingroom for a drink. Tashie became serious and asked all present to sit.

"I asked Stan to come here tonight because there's something I have to tell you all."

He spoke in his familiar Scottish accent, which he always reverted to whenever he wanted your most undivided attention.

"Last week I went to see the Doctor, and he informed me that I have a bad heart and has recommended to the CO. for me to return to England," he began.

I could see the tears begin to manifest itself in his eyes. Mary and the girls began to cry also. I moved between them to console them. Mary sat beside him.

"I don't know how long or what's in store for me. So I've decided that if anything happens to me, I'm asking you Stan to assist my family to obtain the proper burial for me and to make sure that the letters of my will are adhered to."

He looked at me with those piercing steel-grey eyes that I knew so well.

"Will you do that for me Stan?" he asked. "Mary doesn't have a clue how to deal with the army and I want a very stern positive person to take care of things for me."

I thought about his words for a moment.

"Tashie," I said, "ever since we met in Aldershot, I felt very confident that you're a friend and it's a friend's duty to carry out a friend's request," I said.

"Like the Irish Pact you agreed to with O'Reilley? Oh don't look so shocked, I knew about that many years ago and I think it is quite admirable."

I nodded my head in agreement.

"You know something," I said, "I really learnt a lot from him. Patrick is a good friend and yes.. there's a pact to inform each other's relations personally, in case of any one's death."

He smiled again.

"That secret will be going to the grave with me and also the fact that he is an IRA personnel."

I sat there looking at him, wondering how he knew all of this.

"Look man," he said smiling, "I'm an intelligent person and I knew his thoughts from the first day he walked into my camp in

Aldershot, so don't be too surprised."

I felt obligated to explain, but it did not seem necessary then.

"I will have a letter typed up, giving you the authority over my will tomorrow, okay?" he said.

I agreed and he changed the subject to my life and women. I told him that I will need a pass to Iserlohn to see Fiona. I also told him that she was Scottish. He laughed.

"I knew that," he said smiling. "Mother Superior in Bordon Hospital told me, and I also know about the Major. By the way how is Mrs Harrison?"

He sat there grinning like a Cheshire Cat.

"I don't really know at this moment, but I would like a pass to England to see her. Tell me something Tashie? Is there any part of my life that you don't know about?"

"Yes my son," he said, "your future. But I am confident that you will secure that in your own time."

I also told him that after the six weeks with his men, I will need three to four weeks holiday in England. He agreed to all of this, telling me that major Bailey had already signed for them. I thanked him and we talked some more then Parks came and I left.

For the next six weeks I really put them through the grinder. I taught them at least thirty ways to kill. The same as taught to me by Mark Harrison. Some of them felt sick to hear the sordid stories of Malaya, Cambodia and Viet-Nam and to see the demonstrations on the dummies. Some of them were ecstatic to be a part of the classes and seemed to enjoy them.

With Sergeant Clayton doing the PT., we had them in shape in no time at all and even took thirty five of them to a secret base in Bietefeld to do their para jump, with the full assistance of two training officers from Farnham, one of whom was an old friend of Mark Harrison. Everything went well and I was given full credit for the training, also an offer for promotion to Sergeant and a permanent posting in Farnham. The only draw-back to that offer was, I would have to sign on for more years. I told them I would consider it, after I returned from England. Wickham was very proud and was not reserved in his expression of that fact. He made absolutely sure that they recognized me in every respect.

Also during those weeks Parks, Desmond and I spent some nights in down town bars of Dortmund. Mostly in the Nordpole. And whenever Fiona came, we would go to restaurants and bars with their girlfriends also.

Gatwick airport looked different to me on my arrival. They seemed to have made some changes for the necessary improvements to enhance the public's requirements and comfort.

"Very good," I thought.

Returning to the soil of England seemed to re-energize me somewhat. I thought out my plans as I would do them.

"First I will go to visit my cousins and friends, I whispered to myself as I retrieved my bags from the conveyor. "Then I shall go to Ireland for a week to see my friends there. Then I will spend the next two weeks with Catharine. Yes, that's what I'll do."

The Customs officer didn't even ask my name, he just waved me through.

"Maybe it's my uniform," I thought. "The red beret seemed to have an influence on them."

I took the train to Waterloo station, and decided to spent some time looking at its splendour. Then a taxi for home. I asked the driver to go by way of Piccadilly Circus. "For sentimental reasons," I told him. Then on to Penge and home.

My family was delighted to see me home and stated their appreciation for the gifts I brought them from Germany. We spent the next two days talking about love and my life in the army and my intentions hence forth.

Cousin Shirley requested my presence to meet a nurse girlfriend of hers, who would be coming to visit that evening. Although I wasn't interested in any other woman, I decided to stay to meet her. I had Catharine on my mind, although I had not received any communication from her, except the phone call in Singapore and I wanted to know why. I was told that Faye got married to an American serviceman and left for the United States to live.

Shirley's nurse friend was a very attractive Jamaican woman and we hit it off immediately. Sylvia had never seen London prior to this day, so for three days, I showed it to her. We talked about her life as a nurse up in Yorkshire and mine in the army and promised to write as often as possible and parted company.

I caught the ten fifteen flight to Belfast the next day, because I wanted an early start at the many things I wanted to do and quickly. I was anxious to hear about Patrick. I had been writing letters to him, without response.

"Maybe the family will have words from him," I thought.

The military had given me a special pass to fly or ride the train to anywhere in the British Isles and I intended on using it up. The cabby took twenty minutes to the house from the airport. It was a delight to see those streets once more. I knocked on the door and Teresa screamed loudly when she saw my face. She became excited and pounced on me, hugging, kissing and crying all at the same time. I picked her up and gently squeezed her.

"Oh my god!" she exclaimed, "You're supposed to be dead. That's what the army had said in the letter."

I remembered what Fiona told me on the train to Germany about the letter she had received. Teresa was very comfortable in my arms, as many of the neighbours gathered to shake my hand and to ask questions of my health. Some only waved from their windows as they recognized me.

I felt like Sir Gallahad returning home after a long crusade, although they treated me more like the Prodigal son. Everybody followed us into the O'Reilley's house. Ella hugged and kissed me and pounded on my chest crying and talking at the same time.

"Stan," Ella cried, "I am delighted to see you again. I knew they were lying about your death. How is Patrick? Tell me about him please.

Is he all right?"

"Well, for one I am alive and well and when I left Singapore Patrick was a healthy man. Didn't he tell you all? I know that he wrote letters every chance he got and so did I," I said.

"No," Ella replied. "We haven't heard from either of you in over a year."

I told them the stories of our visit to Australia and NewZeland, Hong Kong, Cyprus and Aden. I made the stories good, deliberately omitting the military operations and confidential parts. While I talked, Ella was busy in the kitchen making the dinner. Some of the neighbours asked questions about the people and the politics. I was in my heaven talking my head off.

I assured Ella and Teresa that Patrick had written to them and would hear from him soon, but lied that mail in the army takes a long time to get to its destination. Although in my mind, I knew that Mark was deliberately confiscating his letters, as he did mine. I got the addresses of Ian and Tom's parents and asked Teresa to accompany me, after tea, to visit with them, she agreed.

I felt depressed to be telling them of their son's death.

Although they had already heard from the military and had received monies from the army's insurance for their funeral, my explanation was the most valid to them. They knew we had made a pact to see the families personally. We visited with each family for about two hours and in each case, I talked about the boys and the things we did out there. They wanted to hear about things concerning their son's death over and over again. I did, but left out the restricted information as usual. I told them that I would come to see them for tea another evening before I returned home. It was around five in the afternoon, when we left their house.

"It's a beautiful summer's evening," I told her as we began our walk back to her house.

She didn't mind as long as we were together.

We got to about a hundred yards from the house, when a car pulled along side us with two fellows inside. One of them greeted us with a polite good evening and asked us to come with them because someone wanted to talk to me. I didn't feel threatened and neither did Teresa. We got into the back seat of their car and relaxed. They drove out into the country and along a very scenic dirt road then stopped the car. The same fellow told us that we will have to be blindfolded for security reasons. We offered no resistance.

"If they are going to kill me, then I would be the fool," I thought.

After the blindfold was affixed, they drove for what seemed like an hour then stopped again. I could have easily peaked under the blindfold because my hands weren't tied. But for some reason, I didn't. I was asked to come with them and for Teresa to stay seated in the car with the blindfold in place. She agreed to follow those instructions I was guided through a door and down what seemed like a long passage way. I heard a door open and I was in a large room. The blindfold was then removed and I quickly looked around the room to notice about ten men and women dressed in military like fatigues, sitting or standing. Each carried a machine gun. None of them paid much attention to my presence, they were more occupied with some kind of map on the table.

I felt no fear nor intimidation. Somehow I felt I was amongst friends. I heard a voice at the right side of me.

"Welcome Corporal Martin," the voice said.

I looked to see Shaun O'Reilley standing beside me. My face must have shown the shock as I gasped.

"Yes, my friend," he said. "I knew that you would be surprised to see me. I was supposed to be dead, right? That's what you were told, right? Well not even my family knows that I am alive as yet; hence the reason Teresa's in the car."

He was smiling and talking as though I was his son. He placed his arm around my shoulder and guided me to a chair at a long table.

"Stan my boy," he began, "nobody, no none Irish has ever entered my headquarters and it's not a normal thing for anyone to be brought here either. They would never get near this place. Sorry for the blindfold but security you know."

I smiled when I saw the tattoo on his arm.

"I was not afraid Shaun," I replied. "I felt your men weren't taking me for a kill, and if that was so, they could have done it any time."

We talked about the family and Teresa's lost pregnancy and the death of Ian and Jack. Nothing was ever mentioned about the British military involvement in his country or his IRA activities. There seemed to be a mutual respect between us, because our personal feelings weren't questioned.

"You know something?" I said, "I have a feeling that Patrick will soon be home and I know you will reek havoc on the British. My only hope is for you to resolve the problems amicably without the guns."

He shrugged his shoulder.

"Maybe my lad, maybe," he replied.

I was about to leave when he spoke again.

"Thank you for coming Stan. We might never see each other again my friend. Maybe not in this life anyway and remember this meeting never took place, right?" he said.

"Where? When? Who?" I said, as we both laughed, hugged and shook hands again. Then I was blindfolded and led to the car.

The drive took us around in circles, probably to confuse my mind of the time and area, but I did not care. When he stopped and the blindfold was removed, I quickly checked my watch to see it took thirty five minutes to this point and concluded that it was much closer than I initially thought. They let us out near the bus stop in town and waved goodbye as friends.

On the way home, Teresa kept asking questions about who the people were, but I evaded her totally.

"You know something?" I said, "I am going to write a book someday about the people I have come to know."

She laughed at that. It was her first laugh all day.

"Will I be included also?" she asked, while flashing her eyes at me.

"Sure," I replied, "along with Patrick and the many others I've met."

"Do you think anybody would buy it? They mightn't believe your story you know," she said.

"The sale is not the ultimate reason although important," I replied. "It's seeing it in print. But if it happened to sell, then some people will understand the reason some people's lives are what they become."

Teresa became quiet and after a long pause she said,

"Can we go home now? I would like to make love again."

I decided that I wouldn't concern my mind too much about their struggle. I felt very confident in their ability to resolve it, one way or another. I felt certain that Patrick and all the others had their reasons for opposing the policies of the ruling parties. I also felt that some of the men I had trained in Dortmund, would possibly be sent there to enforce the British rule. I shuddered to think of the killings that were going to take place in Ireland and promised myself not to come back here while this was going on.

"It might be best for me to leave the army for good," I thought. "I could not fight against my friends, even though I do believe in my oath to the crown. Furthermore, they do have a rightful reason to fight and they will be doing so in their back yard. A blood bath?" I whispered.

I stayed in Belfast for two days then Teresa and I decided to take the train to Galway Bay for a look again. We totally enjoyed our selves and talked about our uncertain future life. She also told me of the lost pregnancy and that she would like to try again.

Although she realized that we both could never be together, as long as the political atmosphere remained the same in England and Ireland.

"You know Stan?" she said sadly, "I have always dreamt of a man that I was madly in love with, one whom I intend on spending my entire life with, and here you are and it's impossible to be together."

"Are you angry?" I asked.

She paused for a breath then replied.

"Yes I am," she replied. "I'm angry at the damn politicians for depriving me of my happiness. Somehow I feel God has failed me," she said with tears in her eyes.

"Come now Teresa," I said, comforting her. "Don't speak like that, put some faith in God. One can never know what the future will bring. I agree that it's impossible at this time, but you'll never know."

She cried and cuddled up in my arms.

Teresa and I were able to talk about us and to realize it was things beyond our control, that will keep us apart. We made promises to keep in contact for as long as time will allow. I felt sad to be leaving another woman in tears.

"Why is life so complicated?" I asked myself.

The seven days in Ireland were relaxing. I was satisfied to have spoken to the families of Tom and Ian in Belfast and to Jack's father in Dublin. They too were happy that I had come as his friend.

On reaching London, I only took enough time to have my clothes cleaned and re-packed and left for Somerset to find Catharine.

"I sincerely hope to find her in good health. I love her very much and I know she loves me too. I must find out if she did have the child and get to know it also," I said to myself in thoughts.

I told my cousins to expect me in a week's time and left. I sat in the train car as I did the morning I was to be in Aldershot, only this time I will be going to Somerset and in my uniform. I was mentally planning all my approaches and strategy to get through anybody who might confront me.

"I am going to see her one way or another," I said out loud.
Then I noticed the other people sitting in the car. An elderly lady, who seemed to think what I just said was funny, replied.

"That's the spirit lad," she said in her cockney accent. "Find her and let her know that you love her."

I thanked her for the comment and took out my note book and began to write.

Maybe an hour had elapsed when the elderly lady touched the gentleman beside her and said,

"You see this Irish thing?" She pointed to the newspaper headlines that stated in bold print, IRISH TERRORIST KILLS.

"They are going to make it worse before making it better."

Immediately my thoughts reflected on Patrick and Ireland. I began to recall our actions in the Far and Middle East for the army. I wrote in my book:-

"It seems that the Irish policies are no different from the British and American policies as applied in the Far and Middle Eastern people, which I was a part of. They are willing to perpetrate and promote terrorism freely within their beautiful country."

I heard the woman's voice as she continued.

"I'll bet you any money that them politicians will escalate it before making it right."

"I agree with you," the man replied, "but it's my belief the IRA won't be able to withstand the onslaught of our army."

I looked up to contradict him, then thought better of my action. I kept quiet and listened to their conversation for a long time, and for most part they made sense. But all along I realized that they wanted a comment from me. Finally the man remarked,

"I see that you're a Paratrooper. Are you going back to Aldershot or what?"

"No sir, I am here on a rest period," I replied. "I was stationed in the Far East and it's been nearly five years since I've been home." I said obliging them with an explanation, as I patted the three ribbons on my chest proudly.

Quickly the woman came beside me to have a closer look at the ribbons.

"Hey look!" she shouted. "They are real! We have a real war hero in our midst. Where and where have you been and did you get shot?" she asked, seemingly excited to be able to touch me. Just then the train pulled into a station and in a short while the people were aboard and we left again. A nice looking woman came into our car and sat to the right of me. I detected some sort of sadness within her, but elected to stay mum.

"Go on then, tell us," The elderly woman prompted in her real Putney accent.

"I served in Singapore, Malaya, Borneo, Hong Kong, Aden, Kuwait, Cyprus and a little bit in Vietnam," I said. "And because of an injury, I am now in Germany."

I was proud of my little public relations.

The man sprung to his feet when I mentioned Germany and began to tell of his world war two stint in that country. But the old girl shut him up in a hurry.

"I only want to hear from this young man," she said, "not you, you old goat."

Everybody laughed and I resumed my stories of the places, without the gory details. I had them laughing at silly things. I felt I was becoming an entertainer of sorts. By the time they reached their station, we had become friends. The old girl kissed my cheek on leaving and the old man shook my hand.

"Good luck on your expedition soldier," the man said.

"I hope you'll find her," said the woman. "Ta, ta love."

The young woman and I were the only two left in the car.

"And where are you going, may I ask?" I said in a firm but controlled tone.

She looked directly at me with her large greenish eyes, then kicked her shoes off and laid back with her head on the arm rest. Her motion caused her dress to ride above her smooth thighs. I could almost see her crotch.

"To Somerset," she said after she was comfortable. "Do you know that place?"

"Yes I do, matter of fact," I replied. "I was once stationed in Yeovil and I have a few acquaintances there," I said proudly.

She didn't seem interested to hear about my friends there, but surprised me by saying,

"Imagine, I went all the way to London for a job interview and to see a boyfriend, whom I was hoping to marry. But I didn't get the job and then found out that the man has another woman."

She sounded really dejected.

"I am sorry to hear of your misfortune," I said in hope of cheering her up. "Life certainly has a lot if disappointments, but we must go on, don't you think?"

"I'm not sorry about going on," she said as she placed her feet in my lap giving me full view of her crotch again. She seemed quite comfortable, "but there are other things in life that needs fulfilment also," she said.

"Like what?" I asked.

She didn't reply. There was silence for a moment, then she said,

"I see you're in the army and have heard you telling the old couple the stories. My name is Dorothy Scott and I live in Yeovil, for all my life. What's yours and why are you going to that god forsaken place?" she asked without moving.

"Stan Martin and I'm going there to find a friend whom I've not seen for over two years. But she promised to be in Somerville when I returned and here I am," I said.

"Frustrating isn't it?" she said. "It's very frustrating when somebody promise you something and when the time comes they cannot deliver."

"It seemed you've encountered some disappointments in your life before too," I said, hoping to prolong the conversation.

"I'm glad that you're going my way, I'm desperately in need of a screw, after all that disappointment in London. Imagine, I had saved myself for him. Six months! I went without sex, just for him and then, wham! He has another woman, leaving me high and dry," she said angrily.

She stretched out her hand and beckoned for me to lay beside her. I realize that was my invitation to screw with her recalling another experience sometime before, I got up and latched the door and pulled down the blinds, then laid beside her.

Of all the women I have had sex with, Dorothy was the most vocal. She shouted instructions throughout our intercourse. I am sure that people in the next car could have heard her. I smiled within remembering a simular train ride to Aldershot with Catharine some years ago, and decided not to mention her to Dorothy Scott just in case they were related.

"And your friend in Somerville, is she nice?" Dorothy asked.

"Yes," I replied. "She's a lovely woman."

"Have you known her long? And does she love you?" Dorothy asked.

"Yes," I said. "I met her almost five years ago and I am hoping that she loved me enough to wait."

"Mmmmmmm," Dorothy mumbled and began to tear at me again. "Well don't tell her that you had a bunkup on the train with a stranger. Let it be our little secret."

I agreed with her as we screwed again before reaching the station. She gave me her address and made me promise to meet her that evening, if I didn't find the person I was going to see. We parted company with a light kiss.

I got into the taxi and gave him Catharine's parents address. He looked at me sidelong and I suspected that he was curious why a black man was going to those very wealthy people's home. I circumvented his intended question by saying,

"I have a personal military message to deliver."

He bowed his head in an understanding acknowledgement and sped to the destination. I got out of the cab and looked around the estate remembering my previous visit there. The architecture of this house really held an attraction to my mind. Now like then, I felt fascinated by the splendour of it's magnificence. I knocked on the door and the butler enquired of my reason for wanting to see Mrs. Catharine Harrison. I told him that I had a message from her husband and must see her. He showed me in and left me in the foyer. He strode to another room then returned to beckon me into the room he had emerged from.

"This way please," he said gesturing.

I stood there looking at Mrs Gwendolyn Compton and saw where Catharine had obtained her good looks from. The lady was a beauty, like a Rembrandt painting. I was in awe to see her in front of me, and my face must have shown it. I was looking at an older version of Catharine. She was a rather petite astutely well dressed lady of about five foot five, with pale baby-blue eyes like Catharine. Her medium length blonde hair was pulled tightly, wrapped in a bundle on her head. She offered, and I kissed her hand and felt the softness of her skin, which probably had never touched the ground in it's entire existence. I sat on the settee as directed by her and scanned the room, remembering my first visit there. All the furnishing seemed to be in the same places as then. She quietly instructed the butler to get some tea and other things.

"And how is Mark?" she asked in a matter of fact tone, as though she did not really care for a reply.

"He's fine and representing the country well out there," I told her. "He's doing good things for the army."

The butler returned with the tea and left again.

"Mrs Compton," I said after the butler left, "I lied about a message from Mark. I really came to see Catharine and...."

"Aaah, Stan Martin I presume?" she stated before I could complete my personal introduction.

She stood up and began to pace a little. The smile on her face was matching to her poise and by her use of my first name, I realized that Catharine had told her about me.

"Catharine told me all about you, and now that we've met, I am delighted to see that you are as charming as she had described," Gwendolyn said smiling. "Mr. Martin I know my daughter well, and when she told us of her love for a black man, I had a feeling that he had to be a handsome one as you are."

"Thank you, ma'am," I replied. "but flattery seemed to run in all the family."

From her fidgety actions, I felt something else was coming. She spoke in circles about many things related to their family, from their paintings and horses to their businesses in all of England. Then when she thought I was getting restless and she was running out of stalling tactics, the words came in a flurry.

"Catharine had informed me that someday you might show up

here and the story I'm about to tell you might not be too pleasing to your ears. I had rehearsed it for months, but it seemed very hard to articulate now that we have met."

She paused and began the story of Catharine as a child, through to her ultimate unhappy marriage to Mark Harrison.

"It was a bad marriage from the start," Gwendolyn said. "Her father, God rest the dead, and his father knew each other since boyhood school days, insisted on it. So her marriage to Mark became a business merger, which Catharine and I had objected to in the first place."

I listened to her story, not knowing what else she was about to say. She silently contemplated her words before speaking again.

"So a few months after she came back from Nairobi, she announced her pregnancy to father and I and told us about you. Then she locked herself away in that apartment in London where only her sister Doreen was allowed to see her. It's the first time in years I have seen Catharine so happy and realized that she was in love."

Again Gwendolyn procrastinated.

"Catharine had the baby, and since Mark had refused to give her the divorce and even threatened to kill her if she told you about it, she decided to leave the country for somewhere unknown to us. All I can tell you is, one evening two men came and took her and the baby in a car. That is all I can tell you."

Somehow I believed her and told her so. Because Gwendolyn seemed honest of her knowledge of Catharine's whereabouts.

"I had a feeling that things might go this way for sometime now," I said, "but failed to think it would."

Gwendolyn Compton stood there, looking down at me pitifully with those pretty baby-blue eyes. I could tell that she wasn't telling me the whole truth, but I did not want to pressure her. Then when she thought I had exhausted my wave of thoughts, she assured me that the rest of the family would have welcomed me to their midst, with open arms.

"Sure they would!" I said silently.

I didn't want to tell her that I had met Doreen and John Hetherington and their family. I thanked her for the tea and left. I was about to walk out the door when she shouted after me.

"Mr Martin!" she said. "If you do find her and I know you will, please give her my love, will you?"

I nodded my head.

"Thank you Mrs Compton," I said . "It was nice to have met you. I do love Catharine and will make all effort to finding her and the baby. But if ever she makes contact with you, tell her to see my cousins in London."

"Does she know their address?" she asked.

"Yes she does," I replied and exit the mansion.

I walked down the driveway. I turned to absorb the house architecture again knowing that I mightn't see it ever again and to remember my birthday weekend that Catherine and I had enjoyed in that house. I wondered if she had told her mother of that event too. When I was totally satisfied with the picture, I walked for about a mile, then I gave thought to taking a cab. But I wanted to get some Somerset air to clear my head.

"So she had the baby," I said aloud. "A black and white baby at that. I could imagine the pressures the family must have applied to her, for the disgrace she have brought to their family name."

I knew that there weren't anyone around to hear me talking to myself. I smiled to think that maybe it was some of Patrick's associates who had taken them some place.

"I sincerely hope it was them," I said.

I looked around again completely aware that nobody could hear me except for the few animals in the field and they wouldn't give a hoot for my problems. I took out my note book and wrote the days events.

I got back into Yeovil about six forty five and entered a pub for a couple of solo beers. The hate for Mark Harrison was at the forefront of my mind again and realized that the longer I stayed alone the worst it would get. So before I reached that point, I decided to take on Dorothy Scott's offer.

"If you don't find your friend, please come to see me," she had said.

She answered the door dressed in only her panty and a gown.

"Hello general sir," she said smiling, pleased to see me. "Come on in. I see you didn't find your party. Did they leave town?" she asked.

I entered the open door and threw my jacket on a chair in the livingroom and sat.

"Yes they did," I replied. "So what can you do for me, seeing that I'm a broken hearted lonely man in need?"

She stood there with her arms folded across her chest compressing those lovely large breasts.

"You know what?" she said. "I would like to see a picture, then have a couple drinks, then come back here for a good bunkup."

"In that order?" I asked.

"Not really," she said, "but I must have a drink. So let's go."

She quickly pulled on her dress and we were gone in a few minutes. She drove fast to the same pub I was at earlier and we had the two drinks. Which only took twenty minutes to be consumed.

"What about the movie," I asked, "are we going?"

"I don't think we should," she said. "It will only take away from the bunkup time."

She laughed and slowly rubbed her hand on my crotch.

"Come on love, let's go home. I'm really randy now," she said.

We dashed out of the pub with the same speed as getting there and drove back to her apartment. Dorothy didn't spare any time to undress and was anxiously plucking at my clothes. Dorothy was so different a woman sexually, anxious to have intercourse and very vocal during the process, giving instruction and screaming loudly on her orgasms. This went on almost all night. Unlike Catharine, Fiona or Helen, Dorothy never deviated.

"Only the missionary position for this lady," she told me.

And that's the way it was for the three days we spent together. I left Dorothy Scott promising to write from Germany and took a bus to see the camp. The place looked the same as when I left it. So I wandered about aimlessly, remembering some of the things we did there, and since I was in uniform, nobody bothered me. Some probably wondered why a REME Paratrooper was there, but nobody asked.

It was dinner time, so I headed for the mess hall. I got in line about the third spot and got served. I was about to sit when I heard a thundering Guyanese voice behind me.

"Hey Martin! What in hell are you doing here?" Big Mac shouted. He never seemed to change.

"Hey Johnnie Scrumpy, you old dog," I replied. "I thought you were dead. What are you still doing here?" I barked back at him.

"Look man!" He said looking about the room, making sure that no one could hear him.

"This place is an easy skive. When they offered me this posting, I couldn't refuse it. The WRAC camp is still across the street with fresh ones coming every day and Yeovil pubs are down the road there. What more could I have asked for?" he said grinning.

We ate and talked for almost two hours about almost everything. He asked about the boys and the action in the Far East and I told him as much as I could. I told him of those who got killed and those who got injured, where and when, omitting some of the details of the specific operations.

MacIntosh was happy to see me and so was I of him. Later that evening he took me to meet some of his girlfriends at a pub. One of the girls knew Patrick and Greta well, so we talked about them for a long while. I told them stories about Patrick in the Far East and how he will be back in his home country of Ireland to run for parliament.

"Knowing Paddy," said Beth, "he probably will be a good politician for his people and if Greta had not latched on to him, I would."

I was happy to hear that somebody cared for my friend and agreed with her.

"You're so right girl," I said. "I hope all of you Irish girls will support him in his efforts."

Beth seemed genuine as she spoke again.

"I'll be writing to all my relations back home to tell them to vote for him. Will you be seeing him again?" she asked.

"That depends on what the army does between now and then," I replied.

The four of us talked and drank for a good portion of the night and I got a little intoxicated. We went back to camp and I crashed out in Mac's room and slept in one of the spare beds.

The next morning the Sergeant came in to awaken the men. He must have seen my uniform hanging on the chair.

"Soldier!" he shouted, "What the hell are you doing in my camp?"

I slowly opened my eyes and told him that I was on a special assignment to kill noisy Sergeants. He did not like my comment, but then he saw the stripes, the medal ribbons and the Para wings and quickly changed his mind.

"Okay, you get some kip," he said, "but as soon as possible you get your arse over to the Sergeant-Major's office, he would like to hear your story."

"Yes sir, most definitely sir," I said sarcastically. He spun and disappeared out the door. All the men laughed, then someone yelled.

"It's the first fucking time anybody ever put Monroe straight. Who is this man any way?" the voice asked.

With all the commotion going on I couldn't sleep anymore. Big Mac loaned me a towel, so I got up and washed for breakfast. In the meanwhile I could hear Mac's big mouth busy telling them who I was.

"That man has just returned from the Far East and he's a real killer," said Mac.

Some body questioned his statement and he pointed to the medals.

"See those boys? He got them for killing people in dangerous situations. He's not an idiot."

Mac was very proud and as a black man and an old friend, I was his hero. Mac and I sat alone at breakfast talking, until the Sergeant-Major came to our table and sat down.

"Hello sir," he said in a sarcastic tone. "Anyone who comes into my camp must first have clearance from me. You understand?" he shouted in my face.

"Well Sergeant-Major sir," I replied and at the same time removing my ID card from my wallet. "I'm in total agreement with you. My name is Martin, I'm home on holidays for a few weeks in England, so I came down here to see some old friends,"I said pointing to Mac.

"Well then that's fine," he said, "as long as I know about your presence in my camp."

I acknowledged that his point was well taken and if he didn't mind I would like to have breakfast, then I would come to his office to see him. He agreed to that and left.

"These people act as if they had not seen a soldier for a hundred years," I said to Mac and we both laughed.

"Not like you old boys," he said. "It seems that the army doesn't allow you active service fellows back here because you all are trouble, especially for the newer ones."

"Oh, I see!" I said in a bewildered tone.

After breakfast I left to see Sergeant-Major Conley. His office was small, clean, door-less and at the very far end of the corridor.

"Well sir," I began as I walked into his office, "I came into Yeovil to visit some friends but they were away, so I came to revisit this camp. You see, I was stationed here sometime ago for REME training and I thought that some old friends might still be here. I got drunk last night, so I slept instead of going back to London."

Through-out my speech, he sat there listening with a smirk on his face. But all his attention was on the medal ribbons.

"Is it true about active service, that it's a cushy number?" he asked.

"Yes sir, it's truly easy," I said. "That is why we send the bodies home in sealed caskets," I replied sarcastically.

He didn't find my last statement funny, but was afraid to scold me. Instead he welcomed me and gave his permission for me to stay as long as I wanted. I thanked him for the gesture, but told him I would be leaving that evening. He said he would've liked to talk with me some more, but gave me leave with a hand shake.

I got on the train to London, after making a phone call to Dorothy

Scott, wishing her a good life and a promise to write her whenever I reached back to Germany. I took an empty car so that I would be able to stretch-out and think for a while. There were a few things on my mind that I wanted to mull over. My thoughts of Catharine kept me occupied for almost two hours.

"Catharine has disappeared to some place on planet earth and I don't have a clue where. I haven't heard from Helen either. Fiona is in Germany but I am not too sure what to do about her as yet."

I was delighted that no other passenger came into the car to interrupt my thoughts. I gave thoughts to Patrick and wondered about his movements. I envisioned their actions and felt a shudder at the thought of the blood which would be spilt in that country.

"I hope they will be able to resolve the problem through dialogue," I said aloud.

I took the underground train immediately to Hammersmith to find Doreen. The neighbour next door told me that they had moved to Somerset and the old RAF man had died.

I left England for Germany, after assuring everybody that I would write. The BEA flight into Dusseldorf arrived early in the day and the four hour train to Dortmund seemed relaxing. I estimated to be there at about four thirty that evening. I relaxed as best I could and when some of the Deutsches spoke to me, I was happy to try out my few phrases of German. There were a couple of teenage school children in the car and they took the task of teaching me the language. One of them spoke almost perfect English, so by the time we reached Dortmund I was speaking fairly well to them. I promised to continue learning and to visit them in Ansburg, some day.

On reaching the camp, I learnt that the regiment were all out on an exercise and would not be coming back for a week. I conned the Provo sergeant into lending me one of the staff cars to go to Iserlohn. He knew what I was about, but did not object. I got showered and changed in a hurry and was on my way to Iserlohn. I reached the hospital and ran directly to the nurses quarters and just burst into the door.

"Hey Corporal! This is not a barn," the orderly nurse shouted at me. "Please close the door behind you, and whom do you wish to see?" she asked.

"Fiona McDougall, please," I said slightly gasping for breath.

She hesitated for a minute then she looked around me and said,

"She's right behind you."

I turned around just in time to catch her as she leapt into my arms. We almost fell. We kissed and she dragged me up the stairs happily saying how she was glad to see me. I could see the puzzled look on the orderly's face, wondering who I was. Fiona explained that she was planning on coming to Dortmund to visit me, but now that I was there, she was extremely happy. Fiona locked the door behind us, which indicated her intentions.

After we had enjoyed our short lovemaking interlude, she said,

"Tell me about England and all the women you have been screwing over there."

I lit a cigarette and gave thought to her question.

"Well darling," I replied, "firstly, I went to find Catharine and found out she had left to an unknown country, then I spent a couple of relaxing days with a girl I had met on the train to Yeovil and two with another one in London. I also went to Ireland to see Ian, Tom, Jack and Patrick's family. All in all it was a great holiday."

She was happy to hear that I did have a good time and for the rest of the night, we talked, screwed and then slept.

The next morning we went to the mess hall for breakfast and was joined by one of her friends.

"Do you remember me?" she asked. "I was Patrick's girl in Aldershot. I am Greta Paisley. What happened to him? He stopped writing to me over a year now. Can you tell me something about him?"

I thought for a moment then I said,

"It's a strange thing. Ever since I met that man I have always had to tell people about him. Just a couple of weeks ago I met a girl named Beth in Yeovil and had to tell her about him. But aside from that he was in good health when I last saw him in Singapore."

"You spoke to Beth?" she said excitedly. " Oh my god! I miss that girl. I want her address too if you have it, as Patrick's. I am happy to hear that he was okay," she said.

"Well you know Patrick," I said, "he always rises to the occasion."

"But does he have other girls? Why didn't he write to me since we were in Nairobi, Kenya?" asked Greta. "Now that was a very wonderful time and it would be nice to do again."

I didn't acknowledge her comment, but told her that Paddy was doing alright and gave her the address to write him in Ireland. She was happy to get some news of him and to express her feelings for him.

"I really loved that man," she continued, "but I must also face the fact that he has changed."

After breakfast, we bid Greta good day and started back to her room.

"Aren't you working today?" I asked her.

"Not today," she replied. "I am a Sergeant now you know? And I'm allowed these little privileges."

On reaching the billets, the little desk orderly with her glasses sitting crooked on her face, told me there was a phone call for me and I should take it at her desk. I took the call and it was the Provo Sergeant calling to advise me to return to camp by the next evening. I assured him that I would and hung up. Fiona and I continued to her room as I explained the phone call.

"So tell me about Nairobi," she asked. "It was with Catharine wasn't it?" she enquired.

"Yes," I replied.

I wondered what her reaction would be, but she made no bones about making love to me. She was almost completely undressed by the time we reached inside.

"I want to have as much now," she said. "because I'm not sure when I will see you again, and every time we drift apart, you go to her."

Fiona and I made love and then slept until that evening. We left for a restaurant in town for tea and a private conversation.

"There's something I want to tell you in total privacy," she said, producing the letter again. She read it aloud.

"Stan, do you know why Mark wrote this letter to me?" she asked.

I shook my head negatively.

"It's because he wanted me to believe that you were dead, so I could go on to somebody else and to forget you. This, I think, was done deliberately to discourage any recurrence of our love. I can assure you that the same will hold true with Helen and Catharine too," she said and paused for breath.

"You see darling," she continued, "sometime ago back in Aldershot, Mark Harrison asked me to keep in close touch with you, so that I could tell him of any kind of plots you Patrick and the others might have in mind."

I sat there wondering about Mark's reasons and realized that it was his way of killing me. She was telling me the truth and I knew it.

"You can believe me, because he also had Catharine and Helen Butterworth doing the same thing to you. But what he didn't realize is that all three of us would have fallen in love with you. When my father died and I went back to Scotland, I wrote a letter to the matron that I wanted to quit. Somehow it got to Mark and he came there to persuade me to stay in."

Again she paused.

"I agreed, after he promised a posting where ever I wanted and a promotion, thus the posting to Hong Kong. He also told me about your affair with his wife and that he had caught both of you in his bed many times and...."

"Not in his bed love," I interrupted. "Maybe that's what he wanted people to believe and that would be the appearance, but in fact it was in a car. What he didn't tell you is that he was impotent and couldn't satisfy her sexually."

"Well he told me it was public news in Farnham, and I would be a fool to think that you loved me," she said and continued. "He introduced Catharine and me in England. She and I talked about you. Then he also brought Helen and me together in Hong Kong with the same intention. What he didn't know was that we agreed to protect you. Matter of fact, Helen's job was to prevent you from associating with any local women in Singapore."

"I see," I replied. "That's why she was always behaving like a wife most of the time and didn't allow me any breathing room. She knew everything about you and Catharine."

"Right!" she said.

"So now I know," I replied wonderingly.

"How did you meet Catharine anyway?" she asked.

"We met on a train to Aldershot for my induction and thought our meeting had ended there. Then I met you and Helen in Bordon and began enjoying our times together. Then after you had disappeared to Scotland and Helen got posted to Singapore Catharine and I met again at the post office in Aldershot, and the sexual fires got relit. The dilemma I faced was, I couldn't choose one of you. You all meant something special to me."

"I really didn't mind sharing you with Helen because she was a very fine Doctor and a friend to me eventually," said Fiona. "But Catharine was a married officer's wife. Did you know about her marriage then?" she asked.

"Yes," I said, "but she had explained that she was forced to marry him to satisfy her father's business wishes. You know, one of those family merge thing. She told me that he could not satisfy her sexually and requested her interacting with some of his friends, for the purpose of having a child. I never expected her to fall in love with me under the circumstances and vice versa."

Fiona listened in silence to my story, then she replied.

"Well anyway, he wanted me to spy on all of you," she said. "I was supposed to question you about Patrick and Jack's home life and of their family. So he got me the Hong Kong posting and brought Helen to meet me. He told Helen, in my presence to confirm his story that you were fucking all three of us."

"Did he?" I asked.

"Yes, but Helen and I talked a lot about you and realized that Catharine was your first choice of us all, we agreed to protect you.

Although Helen had no desire to be married, she wanted to spend her time with you too. We discovered that Mark was trying to use us to spy on you, so we both agreed to keep you occupied when- ever we could."

I sat there listening to Fiona, as she spoke in a low and mild tone of voice while holding my hand tightly and realized that she was not angry, and to know she really was loyal to me.

"If you don't believe me, please ask the other ladies. We are very much in love with you, although I am sure that Catharine is your favourite."

We sat there discussing Mark and what the army meant to us in the future. Fiona talked about a businessman whom she had met on holidays in Scotland and her intentions to leave the army and get married and settle down.

"Maybe with a couple of children," she said, "but I would very much like to maintain a friendship with you, even if you were to get married to Catharine.

"I will have to evaluate that proposition at that time darling Fiona," I said, "but if that doesn't happen, then we shall have this memory for the rest of our lives, won't we?"

We laughed and chatted for a long time, then I took her home.

"Stan!" she said in a serious tone. "Go and find Catharine, she really has sacrificed a lot for you and I know that you've endured a lot under Mark's command. Risking your life daily to satisfy his political desires. I've come to realize that his aspirations were high and he would go to any length to achieve them. But if you're unsuccessful in finding her, please come back to me, I would be a happy woman."

I promised to do just that, kissed her goodbye and drove back to my camp in Dortmund.

I reported my presence to the Sergeant. He expressed his happiness that I had returned with his car in one piece and saved him from the wrath of the commander. I smiled inwardly to think he was afraid of someone human. I decided to catch up on some letter writing and did not fall asleep until late after completion of my endeavour. I had no estimate of the length of my sleep time, but had many dreams of people who had been on my mind of late. Some were very pleasant, whilst others were like nightmares.

I woke during one of these flashbacks and found myself sweating and shaking. This has been happening of late without explanation or understanding and I was beginning to be concerned about my mental health and promised to speak to the Sergeant-Major about it soon.

They returned to camp and my training sessions began again. I was lecturing and demonstrating the art of killing in every form and becoming a real expert at these lectures. The course became an every day event as they were implemented at different camps with different personnel. My only relief was whenever I got some time off to see Fiona when she could come to Dortmund or I go to Iserlohn. It continued for about two months, then I decided to question Major Bailey on the length of time I was required to do this training.

"Corporal Martin," he said, "there are some things in this man's army that have to be maintained. The service you are providing, is an essential one. These men you are training, would have to be sent back to England, but with you here it's not necessary to do so. In other words, cheaper."

I listened very intently to Bailey's speech without questions or comments. I knew I was being used again. I also knew that some of them would be going to Ireland when they were ready. When he was through talking, I seized the opportunity to inform him of my up- coming spring wedding in England and will be needing a few weeks holidays with my wife. He agreed to my request and informed me to make the request official through the Sergeant-Major. I thanked him, saluted his rank and we parted company.

January in Germany is very beautiful, because the winter snow is much drier than in England. I was happy when lovely Fiona phoned to asked me to spend our birthday together in Denmark.

"Darling let's enjoy this one like we did in Hong Kong for our twenty second, remember?" she said.

"Yes I do remember and it was lovely," I quickly agreed.

I was happy and talked Tashie into giving me a four day pass. I loaded my gear into the car I had borrowed from a friend, eager to test it on the autobahn. I picked her up at the hospital and was on our way to Copenhagen, Denmark. All the way we talked about how nice we could be to each other and our reason for marrying somebody else.

"You know something Stan?" he said. "We do make wonderful sex partners, but...." she paused, and the silence was almost deafening.

"So?" I asked.

"Oh, I was talking to one of those gypsies, who told me that although we can be very good sex partners, and we've proved that, and although we Capricorn's might love each other immensely, it's not recommended for us to get married," she said.

I glanced at her. She sat there smiling.

" Now what the hell are you talking about?" I asked in a bewildered tone. If people love each other it doesn't matter what's their signs," I said.

She opened her bag to retrieve an astrological book and asked for the interior lights to be switched on.

"Look," she said. "See they show the various signs and the persons they are most compatible with and why. They even showed and explain the positive and negative traits of the male and female of each sign and the political and social aspirations of each one. You can read about it when we get there."

I thought about her reason for bringing this book on our birthday trip.

We reached Kiel late and decided to stay in that city for that night and to catch the ferry in the morning. We got a room and got comfortable into bed. As usual Fiona was horny, so we made love right away.

"Did you know that the army has made astrological files on you all? Yes sir, Mark told me that they do along with a psychological profile of the ones they think might be a problem."

I shook my head negatively.

"No, I can't believe the army would do this kind of thing to fighting men," I said.

I was rather shocked to hear that Mark had told her this and probably a lot more.

"Can you imagine what Patrick's files look like when they completed his? He would resemble both Adolf Hitler and Josef Stalin rolled into one. My god! What else?!" I asked in a shocked tone.

She laid there smiling.

"What's so funny?" I asked.

"Everything," she replied. "The book, the army, you and I. After all I'm still in love with you and know that I would do anything for you, and you've proven that you would do the same for me. I still cannot comprehend why I'm confused about us. Anyway, we are here to celebrate our birthdays, so let's begin okay?"

"Yes, my lovely little Scottish lass," I responded, "although we're not compatible in life, we can still enjoy our fucking, right?" I said.

"Especially for our birthdays," she replied.

And so the four day weekend was totally enjoyed making love and seeing the beauty of northern Germany and Denmark.

Chapter Ten

" THE ARMY ENDS "

Being married in the army and living off camp was fine to an extent, but it was hard to maintain a silence of my service, unable to tell my wife anything that I was doing for the army, and the recurring nightmares I was experiencing made my life very frustrating at times. I had gone back to England to marry the lovely Jamaican girl whom my cousin Shirley had introduced me to the year before. I discovered that some young wives don't have the patience to understand the reason their husbands leave them alone for days, and some times weeks, without explanations.

I learnt later in Hastings hospital that the nightmares that haunted my life so badly. were called "Flashbacks." I would wake up sweating or even screamed out orders to my platoon in my sleep or even fight. She didn't know anything about these flashbacks and my explanations were not explicit enough to satisfy her curiosity. At times we got into quarrels due this.

She was given a job as an officer's secretary in one of the other camps as a distraction, and whenever I was away, she would be told that I was on an exercise with another regiment or that I was on a special assignment in another city. They tested her regularly to find out if I talked.

Fiona, in the meantime, had left the army and gone back to

Scotland and married the man she had told me about, in April. I couldn't attend the wedding, but I did send a gift and wished them well. She was to be stationed in Yorkshire near Ripon until her discharge. When it was time for my wedding in June, she and her husband came to London to see me. She tried to explain to my wife that we had served in the same regiment for a couple of years, but it didn't help to reduce Sylvia's thoughts of my "suspicious movements" which she interpreted as philandering. She gave me, and I kept the astrology book she had in Denmark as a reminder of our trip and birthday celebration.

In the meantime, the training programme had intensified and expanded with many more officers and men from the BAOR, who were sent on special assignments wherever the army requested.

I, sometimes was also sent on special assignments elsewhere with them and doing the things I was trained to do and what I had become proficient at. But it would be kept a secret and sometime when I returned, I would have to stay on camp or at the medical room for a few days, without my wife knowing that I was home. But it was my job.

On one occasion, I was requested for Cyprus with another regiment of Paras for a highly secret drop. I refused to do it and Bailey promptly had me charged and demoted to a private, even- though Tashie had argued with the Brigadier on my behalf. It seemed that I was made some kind of a scape-goat, for reason known only to Bailey and the Brigadier.

They had been badgering me for months about signing on again and I wouldn't comply. I realized that the problem in Ireland had escalated and wanted no part of it and they wouldn't accept my objection.

"Maybe it was the doings of Mark Harrison," I said to Tashie the day he was leaving for England, due to his illness. "Maybe I was supposed to be killed in Cyprus."

"Maybe so my son," he replied seriously, "the army has certainly changed in the last few years. It seemed there is no more compassion and a person's feelings are not important anymore.

Goodbye Stan, enjoy the rest of your time and hope the future will be better."

Mary and the children cried while kissing me, and begged for me to maintain contact with them. I was sad to see them go, but it was necessary for his health. And furthermore, I had made a promise to attend to his request in case something fatal happened to him.

"I definitely will see you in England, sir," I promised them.

Whenever I visited another camp I would enquire about my friends, but without any luck. It seemed they had all disappeared from the face of planet earth. None of them seemed to exist even though I was given BAOR addresses for them.

Since Tashie was gone, my source of information had also gone. I noticed that although I was reduced to a private, my pay had not changed and I had no intention of bringing it to their attention.

My first child Stephaney, was born in Germany the following June and I became a changed person. I requested that my assignments be reduced and gave up the training responsibilities. For the remaining eight months, I did menial jobs mostly in the physical training areas and organizing the sports events. Finally I was sent back to England and a discharge.

At the Hastings hospital, which I call "The Head Shrinking Regiment," every young white student of psychiatry was there, to use the ex service personnel as their guinea pigs. I observed their line of questioning and their suggestions and decided to become a very difficult subject. I never ate their food. Most times I would ask people out side to purchase things from the confectionary for me. The toilet swallowed all the pills I was supposed to take, and never slept at nights. About the third week, I met a young man whom I had met in Aldershot named John Inde. He had requested a transfer and luckily got back into school to study Psychology. Johnnie and I talked at length about the army and everything my friends and I did in active service. I discussed the sleepless nights and the nightmare I had been experiencing, with him.

He directed and assisted me in a method of relaxation, which included blanking my mind. But he never indulged in any questions relating to my association with the Irish boys and their possible link to the IRA, like the others did.

When they realized that I was not going to comply with their programming, I was virtually left alone. Then one day I received a phone call that my good friend Tashie Wickham had died in Chelsea, London. I quickly requested and got a pass to attend his funeral, and to carry-out the promise I made to probate his will. Everything went smoothly and in five days I had completed the task. Mary and the children were happy that I had spent some time with them and to see my family. I stayed another couple days in London with my family and returned to Hastings for more "debriefing."

About two weeks later, I was told that my attitude was rotten because I had refused to adhere to, or comply with their methods of psychological manipulation, and was released to a civilian life. That's because they could not penetrate my mind, not without drugs and I refused to be subjected to any such test. I was afraid to eat or sleep there for fear; just in case they decided to poison my food or inject me with some unfamiliar medication. Johnnie helped a lot too, by telling them that I was not typical to the army personnel profile of men who were about to be discharged. He told them that all I wanted was my family. And he was right. I was written up as uncooperative and was released under surveillance.

During all this time, my wife Sylvia never suspected or questioned anything of my military movement, even though at times I wanted to tell her, but refrained. I did believe in maintaining my oath to the crown and Loyalty and Integrity to the people I had served with. They knew that I would never divulge anything to anyone, not even to my wife. She was always made to believe that I was screwing other women somewhere and no matter how many times we quarrelled over this, I maintained the secret for the army. I would lie to her, explanaing that due to the drugs I was given in the army,

It was my desire to screw with other women. I knew she didn't believe me, but it reduced our quarrels somewhat, although she had her own opinion.

Although I was now a civilian again, from time to time I would be summoned by a Colonel, whom I was told to refer to as "Davis," for meetings in the most remote areas around London. He always met me in civilian clothes, never in uniform. The conversation was always on the same topic. "Ireland and my friends." I realized he was from Military Intelligence and I was being watched for whatever reason. I assumed it was because of my position in our unit and the area of my service, but concluded it was because of the Irish boys. I really didn't mind them following me around, because I had no intention of doing anything beyond looking after my family. I sometimes took it as fun to deceive and dodge them with my movements, then watch their reactions.

Many times, I gave thought to the reasons I was being harrassed and periodically pulled in and interrogated, and smiled silently to know that I had no intention of talking about the people they wanted to know about.

Then one night it happened. I had, had enough of their bull shit and gave Colonel Davis, or whatever his real name was, the shock of his life. We met at the Clapham Common park and was having the regular discussion about the Far East, when he asked the question.

"Tell me Corporal," said Davis," did you and those Irish boys ever indulge in homosexuality?"

I felt something snap inside of me. I sprung from the bench and in a second my razor was under his throat. I must have pushed it a little too hard, because he was bleeding slightly from the little nick. My mind flashed to Mark Harrison immediately.

"Sir," I said angrily, "you are asking to die and don't think for one minute that I would care if you bleed empty in this fucking park. Those men were my friends and that's all. You're a dirty bastard just like Mark Harrison is, so fuck you forever. The only reason you're alive now is my young family."

I turned and walked towards the underground station for the Bakerloo line home. Within my heart I was deeply angry about his statement, but happy that I did not kill the bastard. Later I realized that Davis only said that, in hope of aggravating me enough to talk. But instead, I damn nearly killed him, which surprised him totally.

"This might be the last I will ever have to meet or talk to him again," I said in thought.

All the way home I was smiling silently as my mind began to relax.

"That fucker is finally off my back," I whispered, "tonight if my wife accuses me of screwing another woman, I can laugh knowing that I'm free of Mr. Davis and the army, and Davis can tell that to Mark Harrison, then they both can go to hell."

I sat on that train thinking of all the things I had done during my time in service. I had made friends with some white Anglo Saxons and received an education on the subject of brotherhood, that I would not have obtained ordinarily. My sexual expertise had been broadened because of the women I had met. I was taught a lot and retained it all. I didn't care if I ever had intercourse with another woman again, I have had enough to last me a lifetime.

I had not seen Catharine for over three years. She had gone to wherever with our child. Fiona got married and is living somewhere in Scotland and Helen don't need me anymore. She probably was now getting it from some other young soldier, somewhere. I smiled thinking that it has been a very interesting six years of my life and this evening's event had concluded a very uncomfortable period for me. I slowly walked along Sudbourne Road, towards my house and my family.

About a month went by, then I received a letter from Hastings. The notice said.

"Your presence is required urgently." A train ticket had also accompanied the notice. I told my then pregnant wife, that I had to go there for two weeks.

"It's only for them to check my head again dear," I told her. "I won't be too long."

After what had happened with Davis in Clapham Common park, I felt he had made a report of the episode and they decided to lay charges against me now. But on reaching Hastings I found-out that he never did tell them of the incident and there weren't any charges pending. The stay was rather uneventful and the questioning was basic and without threats. As a matter of fact, I was more suspicious of their actions than before, but decided not to ruffle anyone's feathers. Everything went fine and I was released with their promise not to follow me around anymore.

When I came back to London, my cousin greeted me with the news that my second daughter Sonia Fay, was born the night before. I rushed to the Waterloo hospital to see them and promised to forget all about the army and some of the people who had been occupying my mind of late. I realized that my children meant much more to me than Mark Harrison, Colonel Davis and Patrick O'Reilley. I was more determined now to achieve for my family than anyone else.

"Davis should consider himself a lucky man," I thought. "But I'm also lucky to have a family now, Stephaney and Sonia Fay, to distract my mind from the other problems."

The news of the escalating conflict in Ireland kept my mind puzzled. I could not get any words of Patrick or the others no matter whom I asked. I gave thoughts of going there but Davis had strongly suggested for me not to. Maybe it was a good thing they didn't contact me either, because a letter from Ireland might have landed me in prison or more harassment from the intelligence people. My job became very important in maintaining a family and I worked hard at it to provide for them. Being a good father was my only desire.

Then on a beautiful May day, I received a letter from the Canadian Consulate in London, clearing my request for migration to their beautiful country. I was surprised to see that my most important military clearance documents, were signed by Colonel Davis.

Right away, things became rather hectic with all the preparation and things. I was very anxious to leave London and the depression of constantly hearing the bad news about Ireland's problems. But the urge of seeing my friends kept a hold on my mind, so I decided to make a run there for the purpose, for a the last time.

I chose the first Thursday in June, telling my wife that I was attending a reunion of some of my old regiment in Ripon Yorkshire, and I would be gone for about four days. She agreed and I began my plot to evade the military people who had been watching me, even though Davis promised they wouldn't, since I left Hastings.

For all the time they were there, I am sure they were certain I would never try to dodge them although I had done so before unaware to them. But this time I intended on making it a good one. I borrowed a female wig from one of my cousins and some old clothes from another friend's retired father. I spent a few days thinking out my plans. The plot was becoming very intriguing and a test of my ability in army style deception. The Wednesday afternoon I went to see my foreman pretending to have the flu. He bought my story and told me that if I did not feel well the next day, I should stay home. I was delighted with his generous offer and left.

That evening I got dressed, and left the house with the borrowed clothing in a bag and drove very carefully not to loose them, to a friend's house in north London. I told my friend and wife not to ask for an explanation and luckily they didn't. I used their basement to get changed into the grubby clothes, then requested his father stayed home for a couple of days. When I was through with the disguise, I took my other clothes in a bag and with the help of a walking cane, I left the house.

I walked directly pass the car that had followed me there, just testing their eyes of course. I walked to the Plastow underground station and took the train. Periodically checking to be sure that I was not trailed. I had safely deceived them and boarded the train up north. I reached Belfast early the next morning. I went to the washroom in the ferry station to change my clothes, and at all times, making sure that nobody followed or was watching me. I took a locker in the station and left my bag of disguise clothes and began to walk to the bus stop. I got off the bus at the corner and slowly walked to the house and knocked on the door. I could see the surprise in Ella's face as she literally ran to open the door for me.

"Stan my son!" she screamed. "I'm so glad to see you, come in," she exclaimed with happiness.

She hugged and kissed my face all over then began to cry.

"I hope you are not here to join the Brits," she said.

"No my love," I replied. "I'm here to see you, Patrick and the rest of the family for the last time, because I will be going to Canada in a couple of weeks and might never see you all again," I said proudly.

She sprung out of her chair and began rustling in the kitchen to make something for me to eat.

"I am happy for you my boy, I heard that you got married and you're a father," she said.

"Yes, Two, matter of fact." I replied. "We just had our second a few weeks ago."

"Oh? Just wait until Teresa hears this, she will flip," said Ella. "I'm sorry that it couldn't have been you and her, but that's also understandable. She will be home soon. She's now a nurse and works at the hospital at nights and I will make arrangements for someone to take you to Shaun, okay?"

She was talking and running around as though I was the long lost son returning home. Teresa came into the house and went crazy with excitement seeing me. The hugging and kissing started all over again.

"Stan Martin," Teresa said in a stern tone of voice, "you are not leaving this house today, and I don't care if you are married one hundred times over, we are going to make love all day, you and me, see?"

Ella rushed around to make tea for us and talking perpetually during this self imposed moment of anxiety. We ate and talked for a while, until Teresa demanded we go to bed.

"This time," she said, "I intend on having this baby and neither you nor anyone else, will be able to talk me out of it, see?" she was very stern about her decision.

"But Teresa..." I began, then thought better and shut up.

We had intercourse almost all that day and didn't sleep very much.

She had to work that night.

That evening after Teresa left for work, Ella and I went to the pub for a couple of pints and she introduced me to a man whom she said would be taking me to Shaun the next day. We spoke of the procedure and agreed for me to meet him at the corner of a street near the bus station.

"To protect the both of us," he said, "we cannot be too obvious."

The next morning I got up to a beautiful late breakfast, then took the bus back to the station and changed my clothes, resuming my disguise. I walked to the corner as previously arranged and entered the back seat of the car. He looked at me through the rear view mirror and began to drive.

"Sir," he said grinning, "if I didn't know that you were coming to my car at this point, I wouldn't have recognized you. I heard that you are a Brit. Are you?" he asked.

"Yes, you are absolutely correct in your assessment of me to a degree," I said, "but this disguise is to protect you and myself. You understand don't you?"

He was satisfied and drove without talking until we came to the dirt road. He stopped the car and put the blindfold on me.

"I won't be tying your hands," he said. "You won't peek will you?"

I assured him that I wouldn't and it was done. I quickly checked my watch before he did so and rechecked it when we reached the house, after he removed the blindfold.

I entered the door and there was Shaun standing there.

"Stan Martin you dog," he said. "I was told that you were coming to see me, but I wasn't expecting to see an old man."

He laughed heartily and hugged and kissed my cheeks.

"I knew that you're a bit of an Irish," he said. "Only an Irish rogue would think up a disguise like this. Nobody would take a second look at an old black man in the streets."

"Thank you," I said with a grin. "I didn't want them to know where I was going and right now they are sitting in front of my friend's house waiting for me to come out. But for now, I just wanted to talk to my friend, maybe for the last time."

I paused.

"You see Shaun," I continued. "I will be going to Canada in a couple of weeks time and I might not get this opportunity again, so here I am. Where's Patrick?"

"Your friend is now in Australia doing some business," Shaun replied without hesitation.

"I assume the business is buying arms?" I asked.

"Stan, you know I can't tell you that?" Shaun said. "Let's just say he's on an assignment."

"Okay, okay," I said. "I apologise for the inquisition. I didn't mean for it to sound like an interrogation, but I would love to see him in person again."

He guided me to a back room for a drink and some food and a lot of talk. We talked about Teresa and the loss of her pregnancy, my marriage and the two children and my life as a civilian. I told him that I will be leaving for London the evening after next, so we hugged and shook hands and he wished me well for a good life in Canada.

"I came here to see my friend and he is away somewhere," I said.

Shaun told me that Patrick would be around, but could not elaborate on when.

"But I am sure he would be happy to hear that you came and he would also wish you the very best. So on behalf of Patrick....." He hugged me again, "Goodbye my friend, and good luck in your new Country."

The driver dropped me off at the same corner near the bus station and I preceded to reverse the dress.

I stopped at a little park near their home and wrote in my notebook.

"I will be leaving Ireland disappointed not seeing my friend for the last time. There are a lot of problems facing this country and the future doesn't look too bright for them."

I left the park and was so engrossed in my thoughts that I almost passed the house.

"I'm so glad you came," said Ella, "because I might never see you again."

She began to cry again. I took her into my arms to comfort her, then I noticed Teresa and another man sitting on the couch. He was very serious. He wore an English hunting hat and a pipe in the corner of his mouth. I turned to face him fully.

"And whom might you be?" I queried as though I was the man of the house. He got up from the couch and introduced himself as a "Major nine." whatever that means. I acknowledge as though I knew him.

"Mi lad," he said, "times in this country are getting worse and it will deteriorate even more as time goes on," he paused. "But somehow we intend on getting the message across to the Brits, one way or another. They forget that we are in our backyard."

I smiled at that statement because I had once used that same phrase to another person in Viet-Nam.

"Patrick! You son of a gun," I whispered in my mind.

I almost smiled but didn't. I listened to him explaining their political position and the need to fight to attain it. Without changing expression, he spoke for almost twenty minutes until Teresa butted in to inform him that I had a date line in London and she also had a date line with me. He quickly apologised for delaying me. We shook hands and he left. Teresa expressed her unending love for me and I promised to continue writing to them. All the way back to London, my mind reflected on the people in Ireland.

"What is their destiny? Will it be a success for them?" I asked in thought.

I was talking to myself again and at the same time feeling a little angry for not being able to express my emotions to Patrick. I realized he was in disguise to protect his family as well. I got the train for London and had a good sleep for most of the way home. I gave a little chuckle as I passed the parked car still in the same spot in front of my friend's house. They had been there for the four days.

"My disguise worked," I thought. "I wondered what they will report to the Governor.

"The subject stayed at his friend's house all weekend, unobserved by us," I said and laughed at the thought.

My friends and I talked about my family moving to Canada and how much we were going to miss each other. They didn't ask where I had been or any suggestion of what I did. We agreed to keep in touch as often as possible. I felt sad to know that I had to be leaving them again too, but it would take a lot of explanation to justify my decision. I walked to my car and drove the same way home, making sure not to lose them.

My wife was waiting for me, so I had to think up a story about the great reunion for her satisfaction. When I got relaxed, I looked out of the window to see them still sitting there, watching my house. The next morning, I walked pass the car deliberately and smiled at them, when they realized that I had recognized them, they drove away quickly. I smiled, happy to know that Patrick was home and alive.

"I can now go to Canada with the feeling of knowing he's alive," I said out loud. Then for some reason I began to pray for Ireland.

"Dear God, I began,"let there be peace in that land and guide the hands and mouths of the people. Give them the wisdom to understand when there is a necessary compromise. Dear god save my friend's."

That also surprised me, because I had not prayed openly for many years. But I was still hoping that God would somehow hear my plea anyway.

Chapter Eleven

"Welcome To Canada."

The plane landed at Toronto airport about ten thirty on a very bright and beautiful moonlit night in June. I was told that the flight to Winnipeg would be the next day. All of the in-transit passengers were billeted in the lovely Constellation hotel across from the airport.

As is normal for me, I left my bags in the hotel room and took a bus to the down town area of the city and walked along Yonge Street and around the city hall area for most of the night. I took a taxi back to get my bags and to the airport in time for the flight to Winnipeg. The flight there was not too bad, although it was an old DC nine that shook, rattled and rolled all the way.

The immigration officer, a gentleman of Ukrainian heritage, welcomed me to Canada with a hearty hand shake and gave me a brief synopsis of his parent's plight on their arrival in Canada. He also gave me, what seemed like a thousand pieces of information about western Canada, and wished me a successful life there. I was happy to be in this new environment of a new country and starting my life over again, although my mind still wondered back to my Irish friends periodically.

The flight into Saskatoon was bumpy on that old DC six but I didn't care. I was happy that my brother Frank, his wife Betsy and son Esmond, were there waiting for me. We greeted each other and left for home where we talked almost all night. They wanted to hear about all the friends and relatives back in England, and I was happy to tell them about all of it.

In the months that followed, I was so preoccupied with the new job and finding a place for my family to live when they arrived in October. Especially after that very disappointing job thing with Hawker Sydley in Vancouver. I was very fond of living in Saskatoon, because it's such a clean and well laid out city. I was fascinated with the friendliness of the very courteous people and to see the south Saskatchewan river that actually runs north. I quickly found many acquaintances and delightfully settled in.

By October my family came and we got settled in for the winter months. That Christmas was the first Frank and I had shared in years, and our respective families seemed to enjoy it also. I wrote many letters to all my friends back in England telling them of my new life and of the new people I had met. By the time spring rolled around, I was a member in a local cricket club and a musical band with my brother Frank, Ken Northy, Cecil Allyne, Harry Van Der Hoof, Jerry and other friends.

"The Caribbean's," as we were known, played many of the local clubs, bars, weddings and parties in and around Saskatoon and Regina. During the summer, I played a lot of cricket and didn't have any time for boredom. My thoughts of Patrick and the IRA was diminishing slowly, because I had not receive any correspondence from them since I came, although at times I still got upset reading about their actions in that country.

On many occasions, I would read my notebook about the boys and promise to begin writing the stories, then just as quickly would decide to leave it for another day.

My feelings changed whenever I came across something that reminded me of the bad times in the army. Although periodically, I remembered them fondly, it was difficult to write it on paper. I found that my mind could not maintain a consistent concentration level to do so, and the bad memories would prevail. And then there were the times I would get angry, whenever I read in the newspaper about bombs exploding in Ireland or in England. That disturbed me. I could not condone it and would get angry at them for doing it. I felt sad to know that my friends were involved in any way in such destructions.

"Killing innocent people, just like in Malaya," I thought.

The periods of flashbacks and sleepless nights was enough aggravation within itself, although it was diminishing slowly and to get agitated over Ireland's problems was depressing me even more. But mostly, I was concerned that they never replied to any of my letters and the question of their friendship cast a thought of doubt, which began to manifest itself in my mind slowly.

I was getting quite comfortable and relaxed and my wife was also comfortable and relaxed, seeing that I was not out chasing women, according to her. Although I was socializing quite a bit more, I refrained from talking about my military experiences to anybody. Sometimes my brother would tell his friends that I had been in the military and they wanted to hear about it. I would only tell them about the good parts of the countries I had been, but never mentioning anything about the conflicts.

Except for Remembrance Day of 1968. During the minute of silence a W.W.2 veteran, who was also a work mate, saw the tears on my face and asked me where I had lost my friends. I told him about my service and found by so doing, I made a friend in him. He was an understanding person to whom I could relate. From then on I wasn't afraid to discuss things that were troublesome to me, which assisted me in forming a sort of self-psychological relaxation therapeutical programme. Harold and I talked many times thereafter, on coping with the reality of Prairie life.

It was in August of 1968, when my cricket team travelled to Winnipeg to play it's annual long weekend game against a team from that city. My wife had gone back to Jamaica to give birth to our third child, Suzanne. We reached Winnipeg late on the Friday evening. After checking into a Motel, we decided to go down town for a drink and found a bar near Portage and Main streets. While having our beers, I noticed a man sitting across from us. His appearance seemed familiar, although he wore western cowboy clothes, had a beard and long black hair, his characteristics was that of a person I knew.

I became intrigued. His facial expressions and his gesticulations were that of a person I knew as Patrick Monaghan O'Reilley. I sat there studying the person for a long a time, that even my cricket companions were remarking at my preoccupation.

Finally I got up from my chair and walked over to him. I placed my hand on his shoulder.

"Hello Mr O'Reilley," I said in a strong but low tone of voice, "how are you sir?"

There was a long moment of silence. Then the man slightly turned his head to look directly into my eyes as he very deliberately removed my hand from his shoulder.

"I am not Mr O'Reilley," he replied, "and I don't like nig- nogs putting their hands on my person."

I stood there for a long moment.

"I am sorry sir," I said, "please accept my humblest apology. I mistook you for a friend of mine."

I gave him a very wide grin, whilst bowing to his two lady friends and retreating to my table and to some very curious cricket club friends. A half hour later, I went to the washroom prior to leaving and as I was relieving my kidneys he came in to join me at the urinals.

"Hello sir," he said without looking at me. "Did you think you knew me from somewhere?"

"Yes, but I was clearly mistaken," I replied.

"I was born in Lethbridge Alberta. Have you ever been there?" he asked.

"No sir," I said, "but your resemblance is almost as that of a friend of mine. But seeing that I had not seen him in such a long time, I mistook you for him. I apologise."

He finished his piss and washed his hands. I began to leave when he said,

"Oh! Do you live in this city sir?" he asked to prolong the conversation.

"No, I live in Saskatoon, Saskatchewan," I replied.

"I too have an acquaintance in Saskatoon, Ivan Leyland is his name, do you know him?" he asked.

"No, the name dose not ring a bell," I said.

"Well," he said, "when you return to that fair city, please find him in the phone book and tell him you have been talking to Charley Leyland from Lethbridge."

He whirled and disappeared through the door.

"Goodbye Paddy," I smiled and whispered to myself then I flushed the toilet.

Our cricket game was enjoyable although we lost.

Back in Saskatoon I made the check to find the man Ivan Leyland. I found his address and went to his house, I knocked on the door and introduced myself. He was surprised when I told him of my meeting Charley Leyland from Lethbridge Alberta. He told me that his brother had joined the American forces and had served a period of time in Viet-Nam. We went to a little restaurant/ bar named the Mari-gold for a drink and talked for about two hours. He told me about his younger brother's life in Lethbridge where they went to school.

"I haven't seen Charley since school and he went to join the American army. The last report was that he was missing in action over there," Ivan said.

I told him that his brother was in Winnipeg and said he would contact him some day.

"Mother never got over his action," Ivan said. "She used to wait up all night thinking Charley was coming home. Charley and I aren't real blood brothers, we were both adopted by the Leyland's separately."

Throughout the entire conversation he never once mentioned anything about the Irish problem, so I realize that Patrick had somehow managed to get this man's identity and is now operating in Canada. Ivan told me about a phone call from Charley a few weeks earlier.

"He promised to come to see me, but he didn't," Ivan said dejectedly.

"Maybe he's afraid to face you and the rest of the family," I told him.

Ivan expressed that he understood quite well but hoped Charley would put their differences aside and come home.

After that day, Ivan and I never met again, although I lived in that city for another year. We only spoke on the phone a few times and promised to keep in touch after I moved. I decided to move to Ontario due to the work shortage in Saskatchewan.

I made so many attempts to start writing, but I found that I could look back on my notes about Mr Patrick Monaghan O'Reilley and his family and could not find words to describe them and discarded the scripts every time.

Our move to Hamilton was good for the family. I found a good job, joined a cricket club, a band and worked as a volunteer in the black community. Hamilton had become a home to me and my young family. We could go to Toronto to see long lost friends and to New York to our relatives. It was a full life and my thoughts of ever seeing Patrick again had diminished.

I was shocked nearly out of my skin to see him again. It was on a Friday night in 1973 in Burlington's Tree Top bar on the Lake- shore Boulevard, when I made my usual stop with some work mates for a couple of beers. We had become regulars there.

He was sitting at a table with two very sexy looking ladies, like the ones I had seen with him in Winnipeg. I got up from my table and walked past him. But as I did, I deliberately kicked his chair.

"Oh, I am so sorry sir," I said, "please accept my humblest apology."

I said this to assure him that I had seen him and wanted for him to follow me to the bathroom. Within minutes he was standing alongside me at the urinals. He looked around the room to ensure that we were alone then said,

"Do you know that it's a long way to Tipperary from here?" he asked.

"Yes, I believe so," I replied. "And a hundred miles walk to Nijmegen if you are Irish."

He never said anything else, he pulled up his zippier and left and I followed suite.

I drank a couple more beers, then I made a phoney excuse about promising my wife to be home early and left. I walked across the street to my car, opened the door and started the engine. I heard the knock on the opposite window, but I refused to acknowledge his knock. He ran around to my side of the car with a kind of a happy smile on his face.

"Hello number 13," he said grinning, "the number one nig- nog in my book."

I looked at him for a long moment.

"Fuck you, you Irish twat," I said angrily. "You never replied to any of my letters. Then you refused to talk to me in Winnipeg and now you want something. So fuck you, arse hole."

He stood there listening to me venting my displeasure of him for a moment, then he said in a very serious tone.

"Number 13, please let me in. It's very important," he said and continued. "I have some good and bad for you. Firstly I have an address for Catharine and secondly I am in a lot of trouble and need your help."

With that he ran around to the passenger door again. I reached over to open it for him. I began to drive as soon as he got into the car. We stayed quiet until I reached a location on the beach strip and parked near the lake.

"My friend, life has taken some turns since service. Some of it is good and some very bad. I'm not going to explain in detail, because if you are ever asked, then you really don't know anything. I deliberately did not reply to any of your letters for the same reason. You see my friend I wanted you to have a decent life with your family in your new country, and I know that they would be watching you for any evidence of me contacting you. If the authorities could have made any connection to me and you, you and your family would have endless amount of problems. They would've hounded you endlessly. But now I do need your assistance for one thing only and it won't be anything illegal. All you have to do is deposit some cash in a bank account for me. You will have the number and name," he said.

I sat there dumbfounded, thinking of the possible dangers to me and my family and could not find any logical reason at this time, to deny his request. I turned on the light just to look at his face.

"Turn the fucking light off arse hole," he bellowed at me.

I slowly carried out his request.

"They did a good job with the plastic on your face, but I was able to know you just the same," I said laughing.

He looked slightly puzzled.

"Yes it seems so," he said, "but I doubt very much if anyone else could've recognize me in the same fashion as you did. And never, if I don't want them to. But I made an exception in your case," he stated.

I didn't want to continue the senseless conversation so I got directly to the point

"Where is Catharine?" I said. "let me have the address."

Paddy reached into his pocket and gave me a piece of paper. I didn't open it, I just placed it into mine.

"So it was your people that got her out of England, right? I asked, "and Mark is also here in Canada too right?"

He nodded his head.

"What!" I exclaimed loudly. "What is he doing here? Is he with Catharine?"

"No, my friend," said Paddy, "he doesn't know that she is here either. He still believe she's in Australia. But he's the Military Intelligence Officer that is looking for me and I have stood beside him many times, at different places and he didn't recognize me."

"So now he might know that you've seen me," I said. "How did YOU know where to find me?" I asked.

"Well," he said smiling. "I phoned Ivan in Saskatoon and he told me that you had moved to Ontario. I searched the phone books in Toronto and London before coming to Hamilton. I found your address and followed you to work a few times and saw that you came to that bar to drink. And the rest was easy."

"So you were following me?" I said. "That means Mark is doing the same thing too."

"Yes he is," said Paddy. "He has already gone to Rod's place in Niagara Falls and caused a disturbance with his wife."

"Have you been to see Rod also?" I asked him.

"Yeees," he replied, "although I haven't approached him as yet. Mark's people have been watching his house too closely."

I thought about it for a minute.

"So I can expect some problems then?" I asked.

"I don't think so," he said.

He let out a loud laugh, slapped his thigh and pointed towards the lake.

"Stan," he said. "I'm to Mark like that lake is to some. Mark never did get to know me at all. But then, I deliberately took evasive actions to keep myself private from him." Patrick became serious at this point. "But I can feel the Mounties know something about me. They are closing in. Although I'm still free to carry out my job here in Canada, I'm sure it's only a matter of time before there is a confrontation."

I stared at him for a long time thinking of why he was here in my new country with his fucking war.

"Do you realize that I could turn you in to the police? I am a citizen you know?" I said very proudly. "And furthermore I don't like you white people coming here to make trouble for the rest of us blacks. The fight is between you and Mark, not me. Give me a good reason for me to help you?" I asked.

He sat there staring out into the lake for some long time, then he spoke.

"Brother, I'm not here to involve you into my troubles. My sincere reason is to see you. Which might be the last time we might talk, because they are closing in on me very quickly. I cannot predict the ending, but I am almost sure I will be killed and an explanation of my IRA involvement will be given to the newspaper and nobody will care to know the truth."

He paused to fish a cigarette from my pocket and lit it.

"Whatever happened to you running for the parliament?" I asked. "I thought you were going to be in the political arm of your movement?"

"Yes," he replied, "that's what was supposed to happen, but there was a need for my expertise in other areas of the movement, so I decided to do this job instead. And believe me I'm damn good at it."

I realized that he was not afraid of dying or being caught, but the question in my mind is. Has he become callous to the welfare of others in his own country?"

"Tell me something friend," I said, "do you feel any remorse for some of your acts on your oppositions, in Ireland and England?"

"Not at all my friend," he said. "This is open war like it was out there. Only this time I'm fighting for my country with their tactics and believe me I intend on seeing it to the end."

Paddy was really looking old and worried, but I could see his determination to carry out his assignments for his beliefs. I could see a kind of sad expression on his face. I was beginning to feel sorry for him too and could almost envision his inner feelings.

"Look," I said. "I will do the bank thing for you, but that's all. Just tell me when and where."

He sat there without words for almost ten minutes. Then he pulled the zipper on his pants and lowered his draws to remove the piece of paper taped to his thigh.

"Here's the account number and the bank is in Oakville. We will have to go to a friend's apartment first to pick up the money, then tomorrow you can do the business, okay?" he said.

I silently agreed.

"Then that's settled?" he asked.

I nodded my head.

"By the way, do you still plan on writing that fucking book?" he questioned.

I again nodded my head in acknowledgement.

"Good," he said, "but remember, you spell my fucking name right or else."

"Yes I will," I said, "but I'm worried that you two gubshite has brought your personal war to my back door. Why couldn't you have kept it in England?"

"Because our problem also involves Canada too; but that's irrelevant and won't affect your family life in anyway."

It seemed he had everything planned out properly. I surprised myself by taking the piece of paper from his hand and started the car for the drive to Oakville.

"You know something number 5? My wife is going to think I was fucking some woman somewhere tonight," I said. "I am going to have some serious trouble with her for staying out all night."

He seemed not to care about what I was saying. He kept on talking about not involving me into their affairs, and of things Mark had done to kill him throughout the rest of his time in the army. I listened quietly, knowing that I too had a vendetta with that man.

"What about Catharine?" I asked. "Does she know that Mark is here?"

"No, she doesn't," he replied, "he will not find her. You see it was some of our people who helped her to this country and changed her name. They gave her a new identity."

He was looking at me from the corner of his eyes, watching my reaction very carefully.

"Oh, I'm delighted to know that," I said. "Is she married now?" I asked.

"Yes, and have two other children," he replied. "So be very careful not to disrupt her life, when you see her."

I waited for him to continue but he had completed his speech.

"Hey!" I said. "What about Teresa and the family?"

He kind of glanced sidelong at me then he said,

"You're the father of a very handsome black Irish boy named Stanley, who, incidentally, is even more handsome than his father. His mother spends most of her time telling him of his great father who died in the Far East to save the world."

"Oh good, and what do you tell him about me?" I asked.

"Nothing, I'm dead remember? My family doesn't even know the truth about me," he replied.

We both laughed at that. Suddenly he became serious and his words came out in a flurry.

"Mark and Sandhurst has fucked up Helen Butterworth real good and proper. You see, she had presented her case to the military college against him and other officers, for their conduct involving drugs and their men. Anyway she lost her commission and was drummed out and is living back in Exeter in Southern England, near her birth home, as a recluse."

"My God!" I exclaimed. "Didn't she realize that the military intelligence corps would've protected him to the end?"

I felt very sorry to hear of Helen's demise, but she went like everyone else who opposed Mark Harrison and his policy. Then Paddy sprung another surprise on me.

"My friend," he said. "allow me to tell you also that Mark and whomever else responsible, have destroyed all evidence of us, the Company and it's men. We have been erased, obliterated. We never existed. All records of us and our operations out there have been wiped out."

"What!?" I asked in a disbelieving tone.

"Yes my friend, there is no evidence of that Company's existence and whomever served in it. My record shows that I was stationed in Germany for all my time and so will yours," he said.

"How did you know this?" I asked.

"A girlfriend who works at the record office got them for me to scrutinize. I've also seen Jack's, Ian's, Rod's and Bob's. I never asked to see yours, but I'm sure that it will read the same."

"That son of a bitch," I said, "he did successfully kill us off, eventually then?"

"Yes sir, he did. We are totally obliterated from the Far East military records," he replied.

I wanted to laugh, but for some reason I couldn't. It did not feel right, although I was confident that Patrick was telling me the truth.

"Where are the boys now?" I asked. "Have you seen any of them?"

"Yes," he began. "Bob is married to a Jamaican girl and have two nippers and lives in Tooting Bec. They own a large confectionary store there. Skinny Williams has a dry cleaning shop in Brixton. Charley married a German girl and is now living in Germany and working at Bochum Steel. Rod lives here in Niagara falls, as you know."

"What about Tommy? Where is he?" I asked.

"He's...." he paused. "He's in England."

I thought about it for a while and realized it wasn't worth knowing what he was doing in Canada. I thought about the problems Rod might be experiencing with his wife due to them.

We drove to Oakville and stopped at a gas station for him to make a call. The person acknowledged him and we parked the car and began to walk in silence. Finally I said,

"You know something Paddy? This reminds me of some of those long evening walks in Aldershot."

"Yes," he said, "and like some in the jungle of Borneo too."

"Hey!" I said. "What about the two girls in the night club? Who are they?"

"Don't worry about them. They're Canadian agents. Police my boy. They are trying to get some information from me about somebody they think is a friend of mine. So I keep them close for my own purposes. The police are trying to use me to find O'Reilley, so it's convenient, even for my sexual needs."

We both laughed at that.

It must have been four blocks or so to the person's apartment. It was a kind of roach infested type building that had no lights in the hallway. He knocked and it was opened. She stood in the doorway dressed only in a negligee. The light from the room shone through the thin garment exposing her body. I could see her long slender legs all the way to her crotch. We entered the apartment and I noticed that the colour of the negligee matched her deep blue eyes, and her blond hair did not show any black roots either. She was very beautiful.

He introduced us.

"Stan? Anne. Anne? Stan," he said and entered the room.

I stood there gawking at this lovely woman, wondering where Paddy finds these beauties.

"It's a pleasure to meet you Anne, but the pleasure would have been much nicer under different circumstances," I said.

He pretended not to hear my pass at his girlfriend. He was too busy getting a briefcase from somewhere in another room.

"This is it," he said, showing me the briefcase, "and you will have to stay here tonight. So make yourself comfortable and she's not my woman, so feel free to fuck her if you want to."

I sat on the sofa. Anne left to the kitchen to make us some tea while Patrick and I counted out the money. All thirty seven thousand of it. I have never handled this much money at any one time.

"I will not ask any questions, I said, " I don't want to know."

Then Anne spoke for the first time.

"You mean you don't know what we are doing here? And for what reason?" she asked.

But before I could answer, Patrick shouted at her.

"He's a brother and that is all you need to know. You have a job to attend to, so do it."

After we had completed the count, we got relaxed to watch some television.

"Anne is one of us," he said. "She's a very good soldier, but she is young and always asking questions when she shouldn't, and I am getting tired of telling her."

There was no need for me to enquire anymore. I fell asleep on the couch. The morning came in a hurry. I awoke to the smell of bacon being fried in the kitchen and felt hungry immediately.

"The tall beauty was also a good cook," I thought.

"Hey Anne!" I shouted to the kitchen door, "make enough for me too, okay?"

"I hope you have medical coverage," she shouted back. "It's considered, by some, dangerous to eat my food."

"He was a good soldier and had taken a lot of risks in his life time, so I am not surprised to hear he intended on trying your food, right Nig? But it's your life."

I was surprised to hear Patrick's voice in a cheerful tone. For the first time since we reached the apartment, he sounded relaxed.

"Hey Stan!" he shouted again. "Remember to see our friend, but remember what I asked you not to do, okay?"

I almost forgotten that he had given me Catharine's address. I fished out the piece of paper from my pocket and read it to be sure that I had it.

"Maybe I will do that some time next week," I said. "It might be an experience."

I could hear him chuckle in the bathroom.

"Hey Charley," I said, "you were going to tell me about Mark."

I barely got the name off my tongue when he appeared at the door.

"Yes my friend," he replied in a whisper, "he's the bastard they send to find and destroy me but I have news for him. I will kill him before he gets me."

I had no doubt that he would do it. I had no comment. I almost forgot that Anne was still in the kitchen. Only when she responded.

"Come on you two, let's eat. And who the hell is Mark?" she asked.

We both looked at each other then sat at the table not knowing that the woman was still awaiting an answer.

"Who is Mark?" She asked again.

"He was a friend of ours during our Far East service," I offered sort of casually, "and as you have heard, we do love him immensely. I am just hoping that I will have the opportunity to do the honours to his throat."

We all laughed and ate breakfast in silence.

When the time came near for me to leave for the bank, I asked Anne to loan me one of her wigs and some make up. She was surprised to see me do a make-up job on myself. I used a scissors to trim the wig and some black polished to colour it. I turned my coat inside out and rearranged my hat. I felt it was a good disguise. I took the briefcase and left for the bank. I stopped at a variety store and bought a cheap pair of dark glasses.

Doing the business at the bank was easy. It took all of fifteen minutes to complete. It seemed the manager and his assistant's only interest was the money, they did not even look at me. The money was more attractive than I. I took the receipt and headed back to the apartment, smiling to think I had done my friend a favour. I knocked on the door for almost five minutes without an answer. They had left. But to be sure, I got the superintendent to open the door to check. There weren't any sign of them or their things.

"The bastards," I whispered angrily.

The super was also shocked of their departure, but he was already paid so he did not care. I thanked him and left.

I drove home. My wife wasn't pleased that I had stayed out all night and most of the morning.

"Where have you been? You left work yesterday evening and is now coming home?" she asked fuming.

"It was an emergency," I said. "I had to do a friend a favour."

"Where, what friend? What kind of favour? Was that friend a female?" she asked insisting on an answer.

"No, it wasn't a woman," I said, "and I am not going to tell you about it, not now anyway."

I heard her voice for the rest of the day, asking the same questions over and over again. I fell asleep on the chesterfield to shutout the sound. Nevertheless she kept up her bombardment seeking answers to her suspicions. I was deliberately evading her and down right blatantly refused to answer her. I know that it will be the topic for the next couple of weeks.

All I will hear about is, my "night with a woman," somewhere. I really never knew Anne and didn't really care to. Only that she was beautiful. But I could not offer my wife any logical explanation without telling her things I didn't want to. The thought of Patrick and his lady friend's disappearance, embedded itself into my mind.

"Why would they just leave after asking me to do them a favour?" I thought. "I really didn't appreciate that of my friend. But if that's the way he wanted it, so be it."

I felt sad that we didn't share enough time together.

About a month had elapsed before I decided to check for the Lady Catharine. I searched my wallet for the piece of paper with her address and decided to find her. I told my wife I was attending a union meeting in Toronto, which was legit, just in case she decided to check. I drove to the Toronto's meeting then left early. I found the address in Mississauga and parked across the street from her house. I contemplated going to the door to ask for her but decided against it. I waited unsuccessfully for about an hour to see if she would come out, but to no avail. I returned to Hamilton a little dejected and disappointed at not seeing her.

All that night I gave thought to her. Wondering what she would look like at this time. I was counting the years trying to calculate her age and what her thoughts would be of me. My wife recognized that I could not sleep and asked me what was the matter. I told her that I was concerned about a bill I owed and where to get the money to pay it. I knew that she did not believe me, but she did not pursue the conversation beyond my statement.

The next morning my wife cornered me in a discussion on my philandering. We argued for a good hour, wherein she expressed that the children would start asking questions about my absence, if it continued. I was surprised to hear my wife saying that although she did not like me going to other women, it would be fine as long as I come home after and at a reasonable time. That amused me immensely, but I refrain from comment or laughing out, because the person she thought I was with, was totally wrong.

Two weeks elapsed before I decided to make another attempt to see Catharine again. This time I got my disguise clothing together and took a day off work. I drove to her house again and waited out front for about half an hour, then I decided to do it. I drove to a near- by service station men's room to make my change. As I left the washroom a young-man who was standing outside, mumbled something obnoxious about "Fucking old nigger's." I laughed and told him that I didn't have the time then, but I would love to discuss the matter with him at another time. I drove back to the house and parked a little way down the road and walked the rest of the way. I rang the bell and waited. She came to the door.

"Yes?" She asked. "What can I do for you?"

She was as beautiful as the day I had met her on the train to Aldershot, although there were some signs of age in her face. I took a quick glance at her body and saw that although she had put on some weight, she was still shapely. Her baby blue-eyes was still as bright and dancing as I knew them.

"I'm sorry to disturb you ma'am," I replied hoping that she wouldn't get suspicious and closed the door in my face, "but I'm a poor old man passing through your fair city and is in need of something to eat. Could you please spare something?"

She hesitated for a moment then she said,

"Wait here, I might find some money."

She disappeared, then she returned and handed me five dollars. I looked down on the money and smiled.

"What's the matter, is it not enough?" she asked in a sympathetic but angry tone.

"Oh yes ma'am," I said, "but I would rather a sandwich and a cup of tea, if you don't mind."

She folded her arms across her chest as she opened her mouth to say something, then decided against it and asked me in. I entered the doorway and told her how lovely the house was. She walked towards the kitchen, beckoning for me to follow. I could see she still had a very nice looking rear end and with the same swing.

"I don't normally allow any strangers into my home," she said, "but I will make an exception in this case. For some reason I feel very comfortable to do so with you."

She turned around and starried into my eyes very piercingly. I began to feel that she was about to recognize me any minute and go crazy on me. She made the tea and got a tin of salmon from the cupboard and some bread. She sat there watching me eat as we talked.

"I guess you do this sort of thing to a lot of people, eh?" she asked. "Freeload. and I'm probably your tenth sucker today, right?"

I did not reply, because I was busy thinking whether I should blow my cover or not.

"I might not get this opportunity again," I thought. So I said, "To some people it might seem like freeloading, but don't you think that an old soldier need some kind of sustenance at times? Especially if they are old friends?"

Catharine sprang out of her chair. Her eyes popped open wide as she screamed.

"Stan Martin!" she exclaimed. "It's you! You're alive! Oh my god, I was told that you were killed in North Borneo. How did you find me? Oh my god."

She almost jumped over the table to me.

She sat on my lap half crying and laughing in a happy way. She kissed and hugged me as she rubbed her hands all over my head and face to assure herself that I was not a ghost.

"Yes, my Darling," I said. "I'm real and very much alive."

I held her tight in my arms as I whispered into her ears.

"I tried desperately to find you in England. I went to Somerset and spoke to your mother and she didn't know where you disappeared to either. I only recently got your address from Patrick. It's a delight to hold you in my arms again darling."

We stayed in that position and talked for a long while. She even confirmed that her mother didn't know where she went. We both cried.

Then I broke the bad news to her that Mark was also here.

"Is he in this city too!? Here in Toronto!?" she exclaimed nervously.

"Yes," I said nodding my head.

"Oh my god," she said.

She seemed very perturbed by this news.

"What will I do now?" she asked.

I began to feel the old hate for Mark creeping into me again.

"Look Catharine," I said, "he doesn't know where you are and nobody will tell him. He's here on assignment to capture Patrick and others, then he will go back to England. After this visit you might never see or hear from me again, so there's no fear of him following me to your home."

I paused to see her eyes, then I said to assure her.

"Furthermore, if I do come back to see you, I will be in disguise like I am now, okay? And I will not come when your family is at home either."

"Okay," she said and stopped crying. She looked at my old clothing and wig and began to laugh.

"Okay sir," she said giggling. "I will be seeing you again then. For a moment, I thought I was going to lose you again, forever."

She had that happy look in her eyes again.

"I have so many things I want to talk to you about, also there's someone I really want to introduce to you."

With that she looked at her watch and I got the hint and left. The goodbye was a short kiss and a squeeze of the hands. I walked up the road without once looking back. I could feel her eyes in my back. Catharine was as lovely as ever and showed very little evidence of her sixty years. Every time I looked at her, I had to conclude that I was still in love with her.

I phoned her at home regularly, but was always careful not to disrupt the household. She would call me also, according the same respect for my family. We met several times after our first encounter in

Mississauga and whenever we did, it was always in a public place and with me in disguise. I took precautions not to be followed.

Sex wasn't a part of our agenda, although we talked about it regularly. We would talk lengthily about each others family and joked a lot about the past. She talked about her husband Peter Lousby being a very nice man who treated her, and our son, excellently, together with their other two kids.

"They are such beautiful children, only that sometimes they would question me about why Lloyd is black and where is his father," she said.

"And what do you tell them?" I asked.

"I usually tell them that his father died in action in either Viet-Nam or Borneo; anywhere I could think of at the time. You know something? I should have suspected that the letter of your death was not genuine."

"And why so?" I asked.

"Because it was signed and delivered to me by a friend of Mark, in England." She paused for a moment then in a kind of angry tone, said, "I was thoroughly beaten once to tell him things he suspected of Patrick and you. Things, he thought, you might have told me."

"Darling," I said. "I am sorry to hear of the horrible ordeal that you suffered for me. But someday Mark will get his own back."

"Stan, he brought Fiona McDougall to me in his attempt to try and get me to hate you. She and I talked and realized what Mark was doing to both of us and agreed not to succumb to him. Did you know that Fiona loved you too?"

I nodded my head that I was aware of the fact.

Catharine told me of how she got in touch with Greta Paisley after her beating. They met in Somerset and Greta gave her Patrick's parents address in Ireland and so she went there to find him.

"His mother gave me the name and address of a friend in London. I told him about you and what Mark had done to me. At the time I wasn't getting any correspondence from you or anybody to either confirm or deny your death. Your cousins didn't know how to find out either. I did the next best thing by contacting Patrick's friends.

Pauline Townsend was a good friend of my mother who lived here in Toronto. She was on vacation in England, where she suddenly took ill and died. Somehow, those people were able to rig it so I could travel with her papers, and two weeks later Lloyd and I were here in Canada."

She paused long enough for me to digest her monologue.

"They also arranged for me to meet and eventually married to Peter Lousby."

"I am delighted that my friend was able to assist you and the child," I said. "Do you have a picture of him?" I asked.

She hurriedly took it from her bag and handed it to me.

"Isn't he handsome?" she asked proudly.

"You bet he is," I responded feeling proud to have fathered the person in the picture. "Maybe someday we could meet to talk. But I will not tell him who I am. I don't want to disrupt his life now."

Catharine agreed for our meeting, but added,

"You could always say that you were missing in action but was recently found, couldn't you?" She asked.

"Maybe, but..." I stopped and refrained from any further comments.

Everything in her present life was fine. She, like myself, was having a wonderful life in Canada with our families. I was very happy for her and made no attempt to seduce her eventhough it had crossed my mind. She was enjoying every minute of our meetings.

We met at the Science Centre in Toronto as agreed along with the children, who were then all teenagers. I found them very easily and approached cautiously. I waited until he was standing alone at the Space Exhibit to approach. I was dressed in my old clothes and pretending to be a retired teacher.

"Hello sir," I said approaching him. "I am impressed to find a young person as you, interested in this futuristic exhibit."

"I am very much interested to know what lays ahead," he replied.

Being an old man, I was able to enquire from Lloyd his interest in the mechanical discipline.

"I am now attending McMaster University in Hamilton," he said proudly. "Engineering you know."

"Excellent," I replied. "McMaster University is one of the best in the world for engineering and wish you all the success in your studies."

He was very receptive, so we talked for about twenty minutes.

"Might I enquire your name sir?" I asked him.

"My name is Lloyd Compton which is my Grandfather's name," he said as he reached for my hand, "although my mother has remarried as Lousby."

"Oh? Whatever happened to your real father?" I asked.

"My real father died in Borneo or Viet-Nam before I was born," he answered without hesitation. "I am now twenty two years old."

"That sir," I said, "is a very respectable name for a very handsome gentleman as you, and I am delighted to know of your educational interest. My name is Stan Martin; I am a retired teacher of sorts."

We shook hands again.

Just then Catharine came to join us.

"Mother," said Lloyd. "I would like for you to meet a friend of mine. Mister Martin this is my mother Catharine Lousy."

I offered my hand and she took it and squeezed it.

"I'm delighted to meet you Mrs Lousy," I said.

"Lloyd," she said without taking her eyes off mine, "are you ready for lunch? And will Mr Martin be joining us?"

"Oh yes mother," he replied. "Won't you Mr Martin?"

"Certainly, I will." I happily replied. "And it's my treat. As a retired teacher I don't often get the opportunity to spend my money amongst good friends."

"Good, then let's go to McDonald's. We passed one on that road over there," he said pointing in the direction of Don Mills road.

We left the science centre and for lunch. Catharine introduced me to her other two children, George and Simone. The lunch was nice as we talked for a long time. I impressed the children with some jokes of my mechanical knowledge and that of my geographical savvy, especially Lloyd. He was most impressed with my imitation of a Cockney accent and some times Kentish tone.

"It's not often I hear a black man speaking proper English you know," he said in an inquisitive tone as his eyes pierced into mine, "Where were you schooled Mr Martin?"

"Well," I said. "I was educated partly in Jamaica and England, so it is quite natural a language to articulate. And whenever I meet a man of your stature, it brings out the best in me. Now that I am a retired respectable old man, I feel I must exercise this and other skills more often in public."

I was showing off and they all laughed.

After lunch, the children went to the bathroom to wash their hands. Catharine told me how happy she was for our meeting.

"I wanted for you both to meet and to be friends. I will tell him later that you're an old army friend of his father and hoped to tell him the entire truth someday," she said.

I thanked her for the gesture as the children returned and got ready to leave. Lloyd promptly asked for my phone number.

"Could I call you sometimes Mr Martin?" he asked.

I quickly wrote my name and phone number and told him that I was delighted to have met him and would enjoy a call from him. We shook hands and I watched them leave. They waved goodbye and I reciprocated. I whispered silently to maintain contact with him, as they drove away. I got into my car and entered the FEW for the drive back to Hamilton.

Lloyd never hesitated in calling me, and being at McMaster, the phone calls were at least once per week. We even met at a restaurant for dinner a few times. Sometimes I would be invited to their house to talk. Mostly about religion and global politics. Peter never objected to my presence and never questioned her for any reason although I never let my guard down, I was always in disguise and very careful not to mention any part of my military activity. Although I would always explain that I read a lot about the Far and Middle East countries. Both George and Simone were happy and very friendly to me, as was Catharine.

During all these times, I often wondered of the whereabouts of

Patrick and his girls. They had literally disappeared from sight, not even at the club. Although I was also glad that they had chosen to stay away from me. I read in the newspaper a lot about the IRA's activities in England and was not overly concerned. It had been over a year since Catharine and I had met, and were doing so secretly periodically. We had worked out a code to use, whenever we called each others home, without arousing our respective spouses suspicion. Although we weren't involved sexually, we agreed neither one of us should change our behaviour pattern and so meetings were easy. On every occasion, we would talk about Mark and Patrick and what they represent in society today and how it affected us. In all of the scenarios we mentioned, we concluded that we would not allow ourselves to be drawn into their scheme of business. But from the time I had banked the money for him, I never saw or heard anything of them again. I constantly checked the news for any mention of their names, but it never appeared.

One Thursday evening I got home a little later than usual. My wife informed me that a nameless friend in Mississauga, asked for me to call her, urgently. I was shocked because Catharine didn't normally do this. I told my wife that I would explain later and quickly drove to Mississauga. I made a phone call from a call box at a gas station. She answered on the first ring.

"Hello?" she answered anxiously.

"This is Stan," I replied. "What's the matter love?" I asked.

"Oh Stan, I'm glad you called. Where are you now?" she said sounding very anxious.

"I'm at the gas station down the road," I replied.

"Please come over now," she said. "I need to talk to you."

"Okay," I said. "Where's your husband?" I asked.

"He's in Boston darling, thank god," she said. "Come on over quickly please, I have got to talk to you now. It's very important."

I drove to the house, conscious that I was not in my disguise and parked in the drive way. I rang the bell and she opened the door almost instantly. She grabbed and hugged me and was crying all at once.

"Stan," she said, "I must go to England tomorrow because my mother died last night, and I have to take care of things. She hasn't been well for about a year and I...."

"Calm is required my dear," I said interrupting her.

I looked around the room and realized that the children were not home either.

"Where are the children?" I enquired.

"They're over at a friend's house until I return," she replied gesturing in a mindless wave.

She was shaking from crying so hard, so I comforted her as I have done a lot of times before.

"Darling, I am afraid to go there. What if Mark sends someone to kill me or to do something to me?" She said nervously as we sat at the kitchen table over a pot of tea.

"Nothing will happen," I assured her. "Mark is right here in Toronto and is so preoccupied with Patrick's Irish problem, he won't even know that you're there."

We talked for almost an hour. Finally she got up from the table to visit the bathroom. I was surprised when she called for me to come to her bedroom.

"Stan," she said seriously, "please make love to me and don't remind me of it's immorality. I feel this trip might be the last for me and I want to remember my last act."

I was really shocked, but knowing Catharine, I knew she was serious in her request and there is no point in arguing with her. She was already naked. I removed my clothes and laid beside her on the bed. The taste of her nipples brought back some enjoyable memories. We made love like we did in Aldershot and stayed like that for most of the night. Then about three in the morning, I decided to leave, hoping that none of her neighbours had seen me. I did not want this to break up her marriage, although I was happy to have made love to her. I also felt sad that I had violated her husband's space, but my feelings on that subject changed in accordance with my thoughts, as I drove home. I began to think of something to explain my all night absence, to my already suspicious and will be angry, wife. I reached home to find her waiting for me.

"So what was the urgent problem that you had to run off to?" she asked in a perturbed tone. I could sense the old woman's scornful attitude in her voice.

"It's a long story," I said, "but I will tell you in a condensed form, okay?"

She didn't reply only sat there awaiting my story to judge whether it's believable or not.

"Now," I said to begin the story, "please visualize a time as a young man, when I first joined the military in Aldershot. I had met a lot of people then."

There were no response except for the look in her eyes telling me not to lie or else. I told her the story of meeting Catharine, the wife of my company commander on the train, without the explicit details of our relationship. I told her about the feud between Mark and Patrick without mentioning the military operations, which I kept secret. She seemed intrigued with my story but never asked for more details. I spoke for about two hours non-stop. When I was through she got up and said,

"In England, I always thought and believed something was definitely strange about your military activities. The way you would leave the house without any explanation. I had often questioned it, but as I was told in Germany that, it wasn't wise for a wife to question a military husband about his movements."

I realized that she did believe some of my story, even the part about the death of Catharine's mother, and that I had to comfort her.

"She needed my advice on some financial matters for the funeral," I told her.

Sylvia chose not to argue the issue.

About seven weeks had elapsed since Catharine had left for England and returned.

We spoke only on the phone, but had not seen each other. She sounded very happy on the phone to have accomplished the task to comply with her mother's request. She told me of many happenings with the family businesses in England and that she might have to move back there to oversee the management. She also told me that she had visited

Helen at her home in Exeter, Devon.

"Stan," Catharine said, "Helen is a very broken woman since the stroke, please write to her; your letter might help to bring her back to normality," she pleaded.

"I will soon," I promised, "she was a special person in my life especially out there in Singapore. And I know that Mark was the person who placed her in that position."

Two weeks later we met for lunch and Catharine resumed telling me about Helen's dilemma. Sat there looking into space without touching her food.

"Her health is fading," said Catharine. " She doesn't practice medicine anymore and doesn't go places, not even into her garden. But I....." she cut the statement short.

I waited for the resumption, but nothing. Patrick had told me about Helen's unjust demise with Mark and the military, and now Catharine confirmed its effects on the lady. I raked my mind for some kind of answers to assist her in her times of need, but realized that my efforts were limited. Although I had written a letter to her a week ago, I thought another wouldn't hurt.

"She seemed absent to the rest of the world and only when I mentioned your name, she would respond," Catharine said. "She was able to partially recollect things whenever the name Stan Martin was mentioned, so please write to her."

"Yes I will," I said. "It's a damn shame, things like this should never happen to nice people like Helen."

"I know, and that's why I'm going to give her some financial assistance when I return home," she vowed.

I last saw Catharine the night prior to her leaving for England. She called me that afternoon to say goodbye and to tell me of her controlling share in the family's business. During the conversation she asked about my wife and I told her that she and the children went to New York city to visit her sisters. Catharine insisted we meet at a motel in Burlington for some loving.

"It might very well be our last chance darling," she said. "We might as well enjoy it."

And so we did, with her getting home at daybreak.

Catharine and I had relinquished seeing each other publicly due to my accidental meeting with Mark in Hamilton, which I believed was wilfully planned by him. I was in a depressive state because of it and had to keep a distance from her for their safety. So when she called to inform me of her decision to go home and to meet her at the motel, I felt good. I believed her decision to go home was the correct one, because she would have the protection of her family and their business and she would be living in the style she was accustomed to and Mark couldn't get to her there. Lloyd, Simone and George would be sent to a good college there and have all the things they wanted.

"England could be good for them," I thought.

I wished her luck and we promised to write and or call each other often.

Chapter Twelve

“ THE LAST DAYS.”

It was a nice clear summer’s evening and I was making my way from the Churchill Park cricket field, to the Paddy Green Pub for a few beers with the boys, to celebrate the club’s win over the Toronto team. At the corner of Longwood and Main, I stopped to allow the oncoming traffic to pass, then WHAM. Some idiot hit my car from behind.

“Shit! My new car,” I shouted as I got out to assess the damage. I became angry as I approached the other car and the driver, who just sat there smiling. I could imagine the look on my face as I recognized the man in that car.

“You son of a bitch,” my mouth shouted over and over again as he sat there grinning.

“Hello Corporal Martin,” he said. “It’s so nice to see you again.”

“Sure you are, you arse hole,” I replied. “You’ve smashed up my car and tells me it’s nice to see me?”

“I’m sorry about the damage to your car, but I had to get your attention some how,” he replied.

“The hell you’re sorry,” I replied angrily, “and don’t give me that guff about glad to see me again. You’ve had people watching me ever since I left the army, so don’t give me that shit.”

He sort of hesitated then pointed to the Paddy Green across the street.

"Over there for a beer? We're blocking the street," he said.

I returned to my car and drove to the parking lot and he parked beside me.

Captain Mark Harrison didn't looked the same. He had large patches of grey in his reddish hair now and a very ugly scar above his right eye brow, which extended down his cheek. He was showing his age.

"Now what was the extent of the damage to your car?" he asked as we sat at a table.

I didn't answer, but from what I saw, it was not much, although it was a new car.

"Come on man!" he insisted. "How much will it cost to repair the damage?"

I still didn't answer. My only thought was to take out my knife and cut his fucking throat. But before I could do anything stupid, Mark sprung another surprise on me. He removed a big roll of money from his jacket pocket and peeled off ten one hundred bills and dropped them on the table in front of me. I did not take my eyes off him, so he repeated the motion again and drop another five hundred on the pile.

"What do you want from me?" I finally asked.

He kept an unblinking stare into my eyes.

"Patrick O'Reilley," he whispered.

I didn't respond, and I am sure he knew what my thoughts were so he continued.

"Stan," he said. "I know that you know where and who he is. We know that he is in Toronto, doing the bad things for his people in Ireland and I want him."

"Then go get him," I responded. "Why ask me?"

"Because you can identify him positively," he said.

"Well Sir," I said, "you two have been fighting your personal war since our time in Aldershot, and for all those years you have been trying to get me into it. But I am not getting involved. So take your money and fuck-off, leave me alone and don't come back. Do you understand me?"

We sat there in silence, drinking beer after beer. Finally I said.

"Look Mark, I should be thinking of killing you for all the evil things you have perpetrated against me and the others in that platoon. I should be taking revenge for what you did to Catharine, Fiona and Helen. Do you realize how much damage you've done to people's lives?"

He did not show any sign of nervousness. Then he dropped another on me.

"Do you think that the authorities have not been watching you for years? When we suspected Patrick of doing business in Canada, I passed on information that he might contact you or some of the others for help."

He paused to light up one of his large cigars. He took a large suck on it, then blew the smoke into the air.

"Yes," he continued, "I gave information to the Canadians that you were a good friend of his and if he needed some help, he might contact you or Rod. By the way Rod lives in Niagara Falls, you know? I could give you his address."

I didn't respond. I pretended that it was all news to me.

"Yes he is," he continued, "and we were also watching Big MacIntosh, who is in Vancouver. So I am asking you. Has he made contact with you and if so, where can I find him?"

I started a little chuckle and he automatically realized that I was not going to say anything. He decided to take leave of me. He pushed the chair back and got up.

"If you see or hear anything of him," he said, "call me at this number."

He dropped the piece of paper with his number in front of me, spun and headed for the door.

I sat for almost fifteen minutes in thought. Then I got up to leave. A real diabolical thought hit my mind and I began to smile. I turned back, looked at the money on the table and decided that I could use it.

"I'm gonna spend this in his fucking name, thank you," I whispered to myself and scooped up the fifteen hundred dollars.

"I'm going to give Mark Harrison something to think about," I thought as I reached my car.

Monday evening I left work and started my drive for home and noticed the car behind me. It had being following me for almost four blocks. I realized that it had to be some one for Mark but I didn't care. I drove home and parked in the usual way. I gave thoughts to the reason these men were tailing me.

"They think I know where Patrick is? Shit, they wouldn't like to know how wrong they are. But I am going to lay a red herring for them," I thought.

I was talking to myself again, but I felt good about starting my form of fun with them. I was beginning to plot out my deceptions of them.

"I will lead them on a wild goose chase they will never forget," I said, " and I'm going to the Tree Top this evening for a drink with my friends and let the fun begin.

I showered, got dressed and left home heading to the club in Burlington as usual. I parked and entered the club not caring if they had followed me. My work mates and I sat and talked until about ten thirty, I decided to leave. I was almost through the door when I saw her. She was as pretty as when I first saw her in Oakville with Patrick. Only now Anne's hair was brunette and not blonde. I started to walk over to her, then I saw two huge white-men join her. I stopped in my tracks and decided against the idea and left the club, with my face intact. I snapped my fingers thinking that I had my chance in Oakville.

For the next couple of weeks my tail became more frequent. To and from work everyday and to everywhere. Even when the family went shopping. Sometimes I gave them a good exercise, walking throughout the stores, but I could never get a good look at their faces.

That Saturday morning, Catharine called to say that she had cancelled her family flight because her husband had to go back to Boston to clear up some work problems and asked me to come to her.

We arranged a designated spot to meet and I got my disguise together and a plan. Firstly I told my wife that I had to work that day and left the house as normal. I got into work then left by the back door with my bag of clothes in hand. I knew they would never come into the garage to find out if I was still there or not. I was very careful not to be seen leaving the garage. I kind of walked and ran up the road, until I was certain I was out of their sight, then I found a gas station to do my quick change routine. I walked to the closest on ramp to the QEW and hitched a ride to Mississauga and met her at our designated spot on Southdown road.

I told her all that had happened with Mark in Hamilton. She sat without asking any questions until I was through.

"Darling," she said, "I am afraid for what could happen if Mark finds me. What if he decided to come to my home?" she asked nervously.

"Don't worry," I promised her, "he'll never find you. I will lead him away from you."

We talked for a while, then I reversed the process going back to the garage.

I left work, making sure that my tail was right behind me. I promised myself to see them close up that night. I deliberately parked my car in the back of our apartment, so that they would have to do the same. Some children were out kicking a soccer ball around so I joined then and took a shot in the wrong direction that deliberately hit their car. I ran over to retrieve it and to apologise for the accident. I took a good look at their faces, pretending not to know them.

"Now I know you, you bastards," I whispered in my mind as I rejoined the kids and did it a couple more times to make sure.

They stayed parked there until about midnight. Then I went to bed.

Anne was sitting at a table in the Tree Top club like a regular. She wore a very tight low cut green dress that revealed almost every curve of her body. I ignored her presence and sat alone at the bar, with a scotch, but kept a watch on her from the corner of my eye. It wasn't long before the two men from the car came in. One went directly to to speak to her, while the other spoke to some people at another table. Later in the evening, she came over to me and introduced herself and remind me of our meeting in Oakville. I pretended that I was happy to see her again.

"I haven't seen you since the morning in Oakville," she said. "I didn't know he had intended to leave in such a hurry. Mr Leyland is such a peculiar man."

I waited for a continuation, but she offered none.

"Have you got time for a drink?" I asked as I motioned for her to sit.

"Well yes!" she said in a matter of fact tone.

We found a table and sat. She sat to the left of me rather than across and made sure that her dress was high enough for me to get a good view of her crotch.

"I was hoping that you would have attempted to seduce me that night in Oakville," she said leaning forward closer, so that I could get a good whiff of her perfume.

"You did!?" I asked. "I felt you weren't interested in me and I didn't want to push the issue. And you know something? I came back from the bank hoping that you would be there, but you were all gone by then. Is it too late now?" I said indicating my interest in her.

She looked kind of pleased that she did not have to do the amount of work in getting me to talk. She spoke as she placed her right hand on my thigh.

"Have you seen or heard from him lately?" she asked. "Mr Leyland is such a hard person to know."

"No," I replied. "I haven't seen or heard from him since."

"In Oakville," she began, "he told me that you would know what to do, if I ever needed help. If I have to do another transaction that is."

"Oh?" I said, "so you have to do another transaction?"

"Yes I do, and I need your help," she begged.

"I'm sorry," I said, "but I had destroyed the paper with the number the same day."

"Well I don't know what I am going to do with the money now, and I can't find him."

"Good old Charley," I said. "He never tells anyone what he was doing next. I'll bet you any money he's in Lethbridge spending time at his mother's house," I suggested.

Without hesitation she said,

"No, we have already checked and she has not seen or heard from him either."

I began to smile as I realized that my red herring was now beginning to bait the hook. So I offered,

"What!? He's always in contact with her," I said. "Are you sure you spoke to the right mother? Remember he was adopted by the Leyland's and his rightful mother Claudel still lives in the that city and he sometimes goes to her house for weeks on end. Although only when he is depressed or broke."

She seemed surprised to hear that, but tried desperately to hide it.

"I know Claudel," she said anxiously, "but I never thought of checking with her for him. Maybe I will give her a call tonight or tomorrow."

I realized that she did not know anything about Patrick or his real name.

"Oh well," I said, "maybe you should have the police find him for you. File a missing person's report and they will find him," I suggested.

Anne seemed more at ease then.

"Look man," she said, "tonight I want to spend sometime with you and not talk about Charley or anybody else, okay?"

I felt that I had accomplished the deception I wanted to, so I suggested we go to her apartment for the rest of the evening. That evening with Anne was delightful. She put all her effort into trying to please me. To show her complete understanding for my wife's feelings about me coming home too late, she decided to complete our act quickly. I could see she was well briefed on my home life. But in every conversation, she would come back to Patrick, or Charley to her. She found that I wasn't responding to her satisfaction, and quickly hustled me out of the apartment.

"I am going to ask you to leave now," she said, "I have been having this headache and I am very tired. I need to get some sleep. Could we do this next Friday night? I will meet you at the club."

"Very well," I said. "I will meet you there and maybe Charley might show up also.

I left the apartment smiling all the way home.

All that week I kept myself good, I never left the house for anything other than work. Then on Friday night I dressed and left the house, driving slowly deliberately not to lose the tail. I did not go to the club as normal because on Wednesday Anne had called me at work asking for me to come directly to her place.

"I will be making dinner just for two Friday-night," she told me.

I reached her apartment about seven thirty and made sure to park in the front lot so that everybody could see the car. After I had entered the apartment, she made all effort to complete dinner in a hurry, which tickled my curiosity. She hurriedly washed the dishes and was now relaxing in the living-room, when the action began.

"Darling," she said. "I'm going to slip into something more comfortable. Have a drink in the meanwhile."

She planted a little ëwait here for me kiss,' on my lips and left. I made a scotch on the rocks, removed my jacket and tie then laid on the couch awaiting her return. Within ten minutes and another scotch, she came back into the room wearing a negligee without anything underneath.

"What took so long?" I asked her. "And what did you say? More comfortable or more accessible?" I queried laughing.

Anne modelled herself in the doorway for a minute, then slowly came over to me on the couch and began to remove my clothing. I allowed her to do whatever she wanted, until I was in my drawers only. She kissed my lips then my neck and slowly got down to my stomach. She pulled my drawers off. It seemed she couldn't wait for some reason. Last week when we screwed, she was more subtle in the beginning but this time she's in a hurry. She quickly had her orgasm, then when she realized that I had not had mine, she got up and hurriedly dragged me to the bedroom, where she continued in the same anxious fashion. We screwed until damn near eleven o'clock, which seemed to anger her even more.

Then all hell broke loose. They bust into the bedroom and the tall fellow began to get upset, accusing me of screwing his wife. They dragged me from the bed and started to lay a good beating on me.

When they stopped and left the apartment, I rolled over to look at her. Although I was conscious, my ribs and jaws hurts like hell. As a matter of fact, everywhere on my body hurts. I scrambled into my clothes and literally crawled to the door and held onto the knob and lifted myself to my feet. I looked at her standing in the middle of the room pretending to be crying. I noticed that dear Anne was untouched and did not do anything to help me.

"You bitch," I squeaked out. "You lousy stinking bitch, you set me up. You went inside to call them, didn't you? Yours will come on another day sweetheart, I swear. You stood there and watched them beat the living shit out of me," I said through swollen lips.

I left Anne's place and scrambled down the steps and out to my car. The drive home was very unpleasant, but I made it. I was smiling to know that she showed me who she really was and they still didn't get the information they wanted. I entered my house and went directly to the bathroom for a hot shower.

"They really beat me up," I keep repeating to myself. "They beat my arse good and proper."

"Who did?" My wife asked. Her voice brought me back to reality.

Quickly I had to think of something. I told her a story about a little car accident in the club's parking lot with two guys and when I tried to settle with them, the fight started. She stood there laughing.

"I told you!" She said. "One of these night something was going to happen at that club? Come let me rub you down with some oil and get you some aspirins."

I fell asleep almost instantly.

The next morning was very painful. Every bone in my body ached. I got out of bed to look at the clock, it was one twenty five p.m.

"First I must call into work, then get something to eat, then I must take another couple aspirins," I assured my mind.

I was no good for anything else except sleep. Which I did all that day. It wasn't until my wife and children returned from shopping, that I realized it was Saturday. I had to repeat the same story to her again, in between sleep and aspirins.

Monday morning felt better, so I started out for work as usual. They were awaiting me at the lift bridge on the beach strip. An OPP car pulled alongside me and waved me to stop. I did and was told to park in the gas station and get into the police car. I was taken to the office on the Lakeshore road. And there all hell broke loose again. I was taken to a room, which seemed sound proof and the interrogation began. Firstly I was tied to a chair hand and foot as one of the officers began threatening me with more beating, and talked about the destruction to my family, which came frequently while prodding me with the rubber hose.

"So where's the sparking electrical wires?" I angrily asked from between clinched teeth. "The interrogation cannot be completed without the wires you know!"

I sat there tied to the chair thinking that I must give only my name, rank and serial number. I was getting back the mental state of Viet-Nam and North Borneo. The hate feeling was coming back to my mind. I could hear Mark's voice in another room saying that I was only to be questioned not interrogated.

"That man in there was trained by me," he said, "so I know that he will not talk. You would have to kill him first."

"So? It's just another nigger," said another voice.

Mark's voice grew louder.

"This man is not just another nigger," he shouted. "He was a member of my command and you could be asking for more trouble with your actions."

I tried desperately to turn to see in back of me, but the damn chair would not oblige. Finally he came into the room. He seemed very perturbed about things. His greying reddish scraggly hair was even worst looking now than ever. I hated him, but was happy to see him at this time.

"Look Martin," he said as he pulled a chair and sat straddle cowboy style.

"I know that you know very little about O'Reilley's activities here, but there are things that only you knew of his characteristics, things that would help us identify him," he said.

He paused to stare into my eyes, although mine never left his.

"The man is a menace to society," he said angrily. "He's an IRA shopper and has been purchasing deadly things in America, bringing them here to Canada and shipping them back home, and the British Government wants him stopped. My job is to find and take him in for trial."

There was a feeling of gratification within my soul, realizing that they did not have total ID of him. Even though I knew it was wrong.

"Give them hell Paddy," I kept saying in my mind. Over and over again.

"Mark," I said, "for all these years, I have been waiting for an opportunity to do you in for sending some of the boys to their death out there. I knew all along the inner hate you had for us. I stood by and watched as they died one at a time and myself almost got it twice."

I looked around the room to ensure that everybody was listening.

"You could not stand the knowledge that your wife had fallen in love with a black man, and you hated those boys for their choice of religion and political beliefs. So being our Commander you did everything possible to kill us off by sending us on many dangerous missions. What was it? Did we know too much? You can tell me now that it's over. But we were too well trained to let it happen, right?"

I paused to allow the others to grasp my words.

"Was it something we saw or did? Or maybe something you did and think we saw? Something you didn't want the government to know about? Do you want me to reveal all the intricate details of our operations out there? I could you know."

I could see that I had struck a nerve with something I had said, so without delay I continued.

"Both you and the army turned us into thieves and murderers for your personal revenge on those people out there. You taught us the criminal ways of life. How to be deceptive, then you expected us to maintain normality back in civilian life. You and the army brass are a bunch of arseholes if you thought it could be done. Some of us were successful in dealing with ourselves and even started new lives. But some couldn't, and after all these years, still can't."

He had his head hanging low, but I knew that he was only thinking. Nothing anyone could say hurt Mark Harrison, he is a man without heart. He sort of waved his hand and somebody loosened the bonds off my hands and feet. I stood up and headed straight for him, but the two bulls grabbed me from behind. I knew that they could have killed me, but I would accomplish my task and he knew this.

I began to walk out the door, but again the two goons blocked my advance. This time my hands and feet got loose and Moose was laying on his back and I was holding the other one's gun in my hand.

"You see gentlemen," I said, "I was trained very well, and I know how to use this thing."

I walked over to Mark, spun the gun around and handed it to him, butt first.

"Please advise them dear commander, that the man they are after is not as mild mannered as I am. He might kill first, then ask questions later," I said sarcastically.

I looked down at Moose on the floor still asleep.

"And maybe you should get him to a doctor, because that punch behind the ears was designed to break some blood vessels. Ask Captain Harrison, if you don't believe me."

He turned to face me, with that grim sick look on his face.

"Stan," he said, "I want O'Reilley one way or another, and I am not going back to England without him."

"Sure you do and you can have him. But the fight is between you both. Leave me out of it, I am not Irish. But when you start fucking with the black people, then I will be delighted to be involved," I said.

He stood up and came closer to me.

"Because of some of the purchases O'Reilley has made, there are many people, women and children included, in England and Ireland walking around with parts of their fucking bodies missing. He is a very dangerous individual."

He was now pleading with me.

"Sure I know that," I said, "and I sympathise with them. But it was you who trained him to do these same sort of thing in the Far East against the Chinese people, and you must also understand that he has a cause in his own country. If the British government do not want to change things in accordance with the so-called democratic process, then one can always expect violence from people such as Patrick. And there are many more like him just waiting their turn to take his place," I said as though I was lecturing him.

"Yes," he said, "I know the government is adamant and is very reluctant to succumb to the Catholics demands, and...and for me it's a job. I don't care about the politics, I just want him."

"Oh yes, I know you do," I replied. "Good luck old chap. But remember, for every one Patrick O'Reilley you kill, another six is born. Can I leave now?"

He waved his hand and I left. I walked all the way back to the beach strip for my car and drove home. I tried to evaluate the events of the last few days.

"First Mark Harrison came to see me in a phoney accident, thinking that I knew where to find Patrick, which I don't. Then he put the RCMP on to following me, who hooked me up with dear wicked Anne to pick my brains. When that did not work, the huge cops beat the living shit out of me. That also did not work. So I was arrested, or as they put it, detained for questioning and would have been beaten again if he Mark, did not intervene. He is searching for the illusive Irishman and it's driving him insane."

I got home and took a shower, had a scotch and some sleep.

The next evening during my television relaxation time, I answered the phone.

"Hello," I said.

"Hello Stan, it's me Mark," he said.

"Okay! What do you want now?" I asked him. "Haven't you disrupted my fucking life enough in such a short time?" I said angrily, although I was curious.

Mark was direct to the point.

"We know the person that we are looking for and have him under raps. But I want to know if he's Patrick O'Reilley in real flesh. I need a positive ID."

I didn't reply for a long moment.

"Mark," I said, "I've already told you. The man and I have not been in contact since Singapore, and if you have already captured the person who has committed the crimes, what more do you want from me?" I shouted at him.

"I want to be absolutely sure that it's him, please meet me in Toronto tomorrow evening at seven thirty. At club LaCoc Dor on Yonge street. Don't be late. It's very important."

With that, he hung up. I sat there holding the phone thinking of what's next.

"He want to be sure that he gets Patrick. Not just the man who is doing the buying and selling of arms. It's a personal vendetta," I concluded in my mind.

I remember Johnnie telling me in Hastings that some people become obsessed with their jobs for many different reasons, and those two are prime examples.

"Imagine these two individuals have been at loggerheads for all these years and only death is going to stop it. And even if they both died, there will still be others who will be willing to continue the war, indefinitely," I thought.

Driving to Toronto on a Tuesday evening seemed strange to me, usually it was always on a weekend. Anyway I was relaxed, feeling assured that nothing was going to happen. I swung the car off the Gardener on to Yonge street and found a parking around the corner on Gerrard street, then walked towards the club. I stopped dead in my tracks, when I saw the scuffle across the street. I stood there just looking when I heard the shots and a piece of the concrete fell on my head. I retreated slightly and took cover, as another shot came in my direction. The thoughts of being set up for a kill by the one and only Mark Harrison, crossed my mind.

"That son of a bitch!" I said as I began to withdraw slowly.

I spotted Mark at the club door. He was just standing there, as though mindlessly detached from the action across the street. I stayed low while I sneaked around until I was behind him. Then in the military fashion, as I was trained, I sprung to my feet and placed my razor at his neck.

"It would be a pleasure," I said. "All you have to do is sneeze."

Immediately he knew it was me, so he stood very still. We both stood there watching the scene across from us. Finally he pointed to the gathering of people the police had brought out of the building.

"See anyone you know?" he whispered.

"No sir," I replied and folded my razor and put it away. "Was there to be someone for me to recognize?" I asked.

"Yes," he said, "that fucking Irish git was supposed to be there also. I tell you Stan, I'm sure he's the one I am looking for. All the MOs are identical to some we had used in the Far East. I know it's him and I'm going to get him."

I did not reply nor change my expression.

"Look old man," I said, "both you and Patrick are having a private war since Aldershot. I don't really care to be involved. For years I have been living here in Canada without a problem, until you two cunts came here and I don't like the idea of it at all."

He turned to look deeply into my eyes. Then in a slow, but deliberate tone of voice he said,

"I'm a very sick man. I'm dying of cancer and this will be my last job for the government and I want to go out in glory. I know it seems selfish to think this way, but I want Patrick's head to take back with me. You know, just like they did in Viet-Nam? Physical evidence."

I didn't respond. But within me I felt a kind of pity for him, because he really did look sad and a sick case at sixty plus years old.

"No, I don't see anybody here that I know. Whenever I do, I will let you know," I replied.

I left Mark standing there and headed for my car.

"Paddy was a political activist, a soldier fighting for a cause. He was not a terrorist. That was the only undignified label they could pin on him," I thought. "They trained him and then drove him to this point."

I was again talking to myself, but this time I was conscious of doing it. I realized that they did not have a clue about the man they were pursuing. My mind was very busy trying to sum up the man, as I drove back to Hamilton.

"What's the difference between the two?" I asked myself. "Activist/Terrorist."

I promised to look in my dictionary for the definition and at the same time I will get started on the book I said I would write. I was talking out loud, mimicking the different voices of the characters involved and describing the scene as that of a James Bond movie.

"Here's a man! One man alone! Causing the Governments of two countries a lot of problems," I laughed to myself.

Driving back to Hamilton seemed relaxing as my thoughts on the last few days events, swung to and fro. The car seemed to know where it was going by itself. I was just breezing along until I got to Southdown road. I saw the police car with flashing lights behind me. Then it over took and signalled for me to pull over. The officer parked behind me. I wondered what could be the reason I was stopped. I couldn't think of one so I waited for him to come alongside my car then I asked the question.

"What the hell is the problem officer?" I shouted.

He did not seem too anxious to argue or explain.

"Sir," he said, "I was told to stop you and escort you back to Toronto, on the request of a Mark Harrison."

Immediately I became very irate at the idea of going back to Toronto and that lousy bastard.

"What the hell does he want now? He came into my life and fucked up things for me. Now every fucking policeman will be stopping my car for no reason."

The officer did not respond, he just stood there listening to my spurt of anger. I finally agreed and motioned for him to lead the way.

He turned on to Southdown road and made an illegal turn across a medium and picked up the QEW to Toronto. I followed him as close as I could at speeds in excess of the limit, to our destination.

I parked my car in the middle of the street as directed by the officer and ran up the stairs two at a time. I was very upset with Mark for dragging me back to Toronto for his bull shit pursuit of a man I think has disappeared.

"This time I'm going to punch his lights out," I mumbled to myself, in between the puffing.

By the time I reached the top steps, I was almost out of breath. Then I got the surprise of my life. I entered the dimly lit room to see the body laying there. I looked at the faces of Inspector Webster and that of Jack and Melvin the RCMP officers. I felt a sadness for Mark who seemed like a broken man. He did not appear jubilant for his accomplishment in his capture of this so called terrorist. There seemed to be a degree of uncertainty in his voice as he escorted me through the door.

"I am satisfied that you have identified the dead person, and I will report that back to my superiors in England. I hope you realize that he had also shot and killed two undercover police officers? One of them is the girl you had met in Oakville name Anne."

He paused to see my reaction, but I had not changed my expression.

"That man," he continued, "and many more like him, has killed a lot of people in Ireland and England and ridding the world of his kind, is a pleasure."

I could feel the hate started to creep back into my heart again, but I felt there wasn't any need now.

"Look Mark," I said. "The only reason you are standing beside me at this time is because you are a dying man and it's not right to kill a defenceless reprobate like you. So please, let's say goodbye and leave it as is, okay? Charley Leyland is dead."

He quickly removed his arm from around my waist and smiled for the first time. He stopped, as I kept on walking without looking back. Then, as an after thought, he shouted after me.

"Stop for a minute will you!" he shouted. "I am still curious about something."

I stopped, but continued to face my direction as he lumbered up alongside me.

"What is it now?" I asked, as if I did not know.

"Tell me," he said. "Are you saying that the body in there is not Patrick O'Reilley's? Was there really a Charley Leyland?" he asked anxiously.

"I suppose so," I replied. "Maybe you should ask his brother, the one who lives in Saskatoon, or his mother in Lethbridge, they would know."

Mark stood there with his mouth hanging open.

"He was the person I'd met in Burlington wasn't it?" I said, rubbing in the salt, "Your spies should have told you that."

"Yes they did, but I thought...." he began. "But how were you able to identify his body positively from the distance you were?" he asked.

I smiled back at him in a sense of satisfaction that he is still in suspense. That he's still in doubt of the person lay dead on the bed.

"Don't worry your little pointy head," I said. "I would know Paddy anywhere. But that is Charley Leyland in there."

Then without any further adieu I continued walking to my car.

"Hey," he shouted again, "whatever happened to O'Reilley then? Where is he? You've got to tell me where to find him," he shouted.

Mark was now acting like a mad person, half crying and half laughing.

"Stan, come back here!" he hollered. "You've got to tell me where he is. Was that O'Reilley?"

I too was feeling like an insane person to be enjoying this torture of his mind.

"Make your choice," I shouted back to him. "Was it Patrick O'Reilley or was it Charley Leyland?" I said.

He once again lumbered to my side repeating the questions. I felt I was now in command of him for the first time.

"Mark," I said, turning to face him. "You have destroyed a lot of good people in your time. People like Catharine, Helen, Fiona, Ian, Jack, Charley, Bob, Powell, Patrick and many others including myself.

There were many Malayans, Chinese and Arabs who suffered under your destructive mind. You have perpetrated a lot of crimes in your time against people who didn't deserve it. Maybe now GOD is smiting you for those deeds."

I was now feeling good to be taking my non-physical revenge on him for destroying most of my life. And just as I was getting over the lousy past, he had to come back to do more damage to it. I was in my glory, getting my own back without being physical.

"Did you know that due to your visits to Rod's home, his wife divorced him?"

He stood there; still with his mouth open.

"Well yes, she did." I said. "And now the dear boy's life has been ruined, by you, and for selfish reasons."

I felt good rubbing the salt in his wound.

"Go my friend," I said. "go home to your quiet death. If Patrick wants to kill you, he will find you in his own time. And don't think for one moment that you have solved the Irish problem with your action here. There are many more like him growing up. Things won't change until people decide to respect other people's rights. As for me, I'm going to continue living quietly in this unjust world a little longer. As far as I am concerned, you don't exist any more so Good-bye commander, forever goodbye."

I turned away from him and got into my car. I slowly drove back to Hamilton, using the Lakeshore Road deliberately so as to think out this little episode. I was somewhat happy to know that Mark had driven himself insane, trying to destroy someone he couldn't see. That very elusive person that he hates.

" Just like Don Quixote and the windmills," I thought. That someone whom he had spent so much time building, he now wanted to destroy. In essence he was trying to kill himself and not know it. I was also happy to know that neither Catharine nor me would ever have to be concerned of his existence any more.

I was happy that in conclusion, I was able to get my revenge on him by not assuring him of his conquest of the individual he sought.

"Mark will go to his grave uncertain," I thought as I drove.

I laughed all the way home. I parked the car, had a shower, poured myself a double scotch and sat in my favourite chair to relax.

"I should begin writing that book," I thought.

Chapter Thirteen

" To Tell The Story."

The next morning I slept late. My wife realizing that I was sound asleep, did not awaken me. Instead she phoned into my place of work telling my boss that I was out all night helping a friend. So I was allowed to sleep until about noon. I got out of bed, had a shower and some brunch. I went to the basement to get out her old typewriter, which she had bought a couple of years earlier and put a sheet of paper into it and wrote:-

"In the Beginning, there was a friend named Patrick Monaghan O'Reilley."

The tears begin to rush from my eyes as I two-finger typed.

"To me he was not a terrorist. He was a political activist seeking justice for his people, from a cruel and unjust society. He was isolated and discriminated against from birth and became disillusioned when he found out that the system does not allow him the so-called freedom, that democracy said he could have. He had studied every piece of literature he could find on the truth of democracy, and the policies and ideology of all the politicians throughout history. He came to recognise that, many leaders, past and present, only adopted the principles whenever it was advantageous to their selfish quest of that so-called true society, only for themselves and the rich people that surrounded them. He also realized that the peasants were always the ones used to attain this end. He learnt of nation after nation that have been annihilated, conquered or created through wars and political manipulations, strictly for power and control over the people This perplexed his mind even further.

He was also disillusioned to find out that, due to his choice of a religious belief, he was deprived from obtaining a decent certified education. And that act of discrimination would prevent him later from actively participating in the political scenario, with the society required credentials. Subsequently it deprived him of a decent life. A life that he desired to assist in the development of his people in peace, in the country of his birth. During these studies he also discovered that socialism was identical to capitalism, with some small changes to satisfy the people's minds. Where the dictatorial powers are in the hands of a few people in one, and the industrialist in the other. In every respect, it's strictly for profit. Although communism seemed to allow some of the common souls a little latitude in their decision making process, their ideology also included discrimination and persecution, as was preached by Christ on earth before he was arrested, tried and duly crucified according to their laws.

That in itself, was a confusing and complicated deduction for a young mind to decipher, although it was a decisive conclusion for him. He was not an ordinary or easily confused person, he was rather a very meticulous and calculating individual, who was determined to be of help to his people and country in any capacity deemed necessary. He was absorbed by the same government, who trained him in the art of killing. They took the time to develop his ability to preform in a totally different manner, than he was born to, then he was sent to areas that they wanted to control, conquer or destroyed to perform those taught acts of terrorism on people he had no grievance with.

He cried tears of resentments within, realizing the illegitimacy of the actions he was perpetrating for the same society that had deprived him since youth. Yet there was no confusion as to where he intended to apply this newly learnt knowledge of democracy, which was evident in his actions.

After he had performed in the areas they wanted him to, he was then expected to return to a normal existence back in his troubled homeland, which was full of hate, persecution of some, discrimination and under privileged existence, without question.

I feel very sad, to know that the same society that had educated him in this fashion, to kill and destroy; is so blind as not to see the harm they are condoning by refusing to negotiate in good faith. It seemed that as long as he was perpetrating this act against others, he was classified as a good soldier. But when he demanded and was denied his civil rights in his homeland, he was hunted down and destroyed like an unwanted animal, by that same society.

Good luck Patrick Monaghan O'Reilley. May you get to the palace of God and be explained to, the reason for your thoughts and actions. May your efforts be not totally in vain, as someday the governing bodies will recognise that it takes people like you, to make changes in our society for the betterment of all mankind of the future.

You might be dead, but your name will always be with those that love you. My FRIEND forever, goodbye."

THE END.